# SWEEP
*Super Edition*

# Night's Child

## Cate Tiernan

**speak**
An Imprint of Penguin Group (USA) Inc.

*With much appreciation to all the*
*generous and dedicated fans of* Sweep

Night's Child

Puffin Books
Published by Penguin Group
Penguin Group (USA) Inc.,
345 Hudson Street, New York, New York 10014, U.S.A.
Penguin Books Ltd, 80 Strand, London WC2R 0RL, England
Penguin Books Australia Ltd, 250 Camberwell Road, Camberwell, Victoria 3124, Australia
Penguin Books Canada Ltd, 10 Alcorn Avenue, Toronto, Ontario, Canada M4V 3B2
Penguin Books (N.Z.) Ltd, 182-190 Wairau Road, Auckland 10, New Zealand

Published by Speak, an imprint of Penguin Group (USA) Inc., 2003

3  5  7  9  10  8  6  4  2

Cover photography (primary image) copyright © 2003 Kauko Helavuo/The Image Bank
Cover photography (left image) copyright © 2003 RubberBall/Alamy
Cover photography (right image) copyright © 2003 John Churchman/SolusImages
Photo-illustration by Jennifer Blanc
Series Design by Russell Gordon

Produced by 17th Street Productions,
an Alloy company
151 West 26th Street
New York, NY 10001

17th Street Productions and associated logos
are trademarks and/or registered trademarks of Alloy, Inc.

ISBN 0-14-250119-0

Printed in the United States of America

# Prologue

Three minutes to five. In three minutes it will all begin, Morgan Rowlands thought, wrapping her hands around her heavy mug of steaming tea. She swallowed hard, refusing to start crying until later, when she knew she wouldn't be able to help it. "Cool the fire," she whispered, circling her left hand widdershins, counterclockwise, over her tea. She took an experimental sip, trying to wash down the lump in her throat.

She gazed out the plate-glass window of the small tea shop in Aberystwyth, Wales, where she and Hunter Niall had agreed to meet. It was darkening outside, though it was barely five o'clock. After living in Ireland for three years, Morgan was used to the early darkness from heavy clouds, but she sometimes missed the stark cold and thick, glittering snow of upstate New York, where she had grown up.

Heavy raindrops began to smack against the window. Morgan took a deep breath, the weather outside reflecting her emotions inside. Usually she welcomed the rain as the main reason that Ireland and Wales both were so incredibly lush and green. Tonight it seemed dreary, dismal, depressing because of what she was about to do—break up with the person she loved most in the world, her mùirn beatha dàn. Her soul mate.

Her stomach was tight, her hands tense on the table. Hunter. *Oh, Goddess, Hunter.* It had been almost four months since they'd been able to meet in the airport in Toronto—for only six hours. And three months before that, in Germany. They'd had two whole days together then.

Morgan shook her head, consciously releasing her breath in a long, controlled sigh. *Relax. If I relax and let thoughts go, the Goddess shows me where to go. If I relax and let things be, all of life is clear to see.*

She closed her eyes and deliberately uncoiled every muscle, from her head on down to her icy toes in her damp boots. Soon a soothing sense of warmth expanded inside her, and she felt some of the tension leave her body.

The brass bell over the shop door jangled and was followed almost instantly by a blast of frigid air. Morgan opened her eyes in time to have her light blocked by a tall, heartbreakingly familiar figure. Despite everything, her heart expanded with joy and a smile rose to her face. She stood as he came closer, his angular face lighting up when he saw her. He smiled, and the sight of his open, welcoming expression sliced right through her.

"Hey, Morgan. Sorry I'm late," Hunter said, his English accent blunted by fatigue.

She took him in her arms, holding him tightly, not caring that his long tweed overcoat was soaked with icy rain. Hunter leaned down, Morgan went on tiptoe, and their mouths met perfectly in the middle, the way they always did.

When they separated, Morgan stroked a finger down his cheek. "Long time no see," she said, her voice catching. Hunter's eyes instantly narrowed—even aside from his powers of sensing emotion as a blood witch, he knew Morgan more intimately than anyone. Morgan cleared her throat and sat down. Still watching her, Hunter sat also, his coat sprinkling raindrops onto the linoleum floor around his chair. He swept his old-fashioned tweed cap off his head and ran a hand through his fine, white-blond hair.

Morgan drank in his appearance, her gaze roaming over every detail. His face was pale with winter, his eyes as icy green as the Irish Sea not three blocks away. His hair was longer than Morgan had ever seen it and looked choppy, uneven.

"It's good to see you," Hunter said, smiling at the obvious understatement. Under the table he edged his knee over until it rested against hers.

"You too," Morgan said. Did her anguish already show on her face? She felt as if the pain of her decision must surround her like an aura, visible to anyone who knew her. "I got tea for two—want some?"

"Please," he said, and Morgan poured the spare mug full of tea.

Hunter stood up and dropped his wet coat over the back of his chair. He took a sip of tea, stretched, and rolled his shoulders. Morgan knew he had just come in from Norway.

What to say? How to say it? She had rehearsed this scene for the last two weeks, but now that she was here, going through with it felt like revolting against her very being. And in a sense, it was true. To end a relationship with her mùirn beatha dàn *was* fighting destiny.

It had been four years since she had first met Hunter, Morgan mused. She absently turned her silver claddagh ring, on the ring finger of her right hand. Hunter had given her this ring when she was seventeen, he nineteen. Now he was twenty-three and a man, tall and broad shouldered—no longer a lanky teenager, the "boy genius" witch hired as the youngest Seeker for the International Council of Witches.

And she was no longer the naive, love-struck high schooler who had just discovered her legacy as a blood witch and was struggling to learn to control her incredible powers. She'd come a long way in the few years since the summer after her junior year of high school, when she'd first learned there were actually a few surviving members of her mother's coven, Belwicket. She'd been spending the summer studying in Scotland when they came to her, finally able to reveal themselves after the dark wave was defeated and— more importantly—Ciaran MacEwan was stripped of his powers. They'd told her how they'd survived the destruction of their coven by escaping to Scotland, where they'd been hiding for decades. When they'd heard of Morgan's existence, they'd come to enlist her help in rebuilding the coven that had shaped their families for hundreds of years. And she'd been doing just that since moving to Ireland a year after her graduation from high school, and loving every moment—except for the fact that being in Cobh meant being apart from Hunter.

Hunter reached across the table and took her hand. Morgan felt desperate, torn, yet she knew what she had to do, what had to happen. She had gone over this a thousand times. It was the only decision that made sense.

"What's the matter?" he asked gently. "What's wrong?"

Morgan looked at him, this person who was both intimately familiar and oddly mysterious. There had been a time when she'd seen him every single day, when she'd been close enough to know if he'd cut himself shaving or had a sleepless night. Now he had the thin pink line of a healed wound on the curve of his jaw, and Morgan had no idea where or when or how he had gotten it.

She shook her head, knowing she couldn't be a coward, knowing that in the end, with the way things were, they had to pursue their separate destinies. In a minute she would tell him. As soon as she could talk without crying.

As if making a conscious decision to let it go for a moment, Hunter ran his hand through his hair again and looked into Morgan's eyes. "So I spoke to Alwyn about her engagement," he said, refilling his mug from the pot on the table.

"Yes, she seems happy," Morgan said. "But you—"

"I told her about my concerns," Hunter jumped in. "She's barely nineteen. I talked to her about waiting, but what do I know? I'm only her brother." He gave the wry smile that Morgan knew so well.

"He's a Wyndenkell, at least," Morgan said with a straight face. "We can all thank the Goddess for that."

Hunter grinned. "Uncle Beck is so pleased." Hunter's uncle, Beck Eventide, had raised Hunter, his younger brother, Linden, and Alwyn after their parents had disappeared when Hunter was eight. Hunter was sure that Uncle Beck had always blamed Hunter's father, a Woodbane, for his troubles.

"Anything but a Woodbane," Morgan managed to tease. She herself was a full-blood Woodbane and knew firsthand the kind of prejudice most Wiccans had against her ancestral clan.

"Right," said Hunter, his eyes still on her.

They were silent for a moment, each lost in their own thoughts. Then Hunter finally said, "Please tell me what's wrong. You feel weird."

He knows me too well, Morgan thought. Hunter was feeling her uneasiness, her sadness, her regret.

"Are you ill?"

Morgan shook her head and tucked a few bangs behind one ear. "No—I'm okay. It's just—I needed to see you. To talk to you."

"It's always too long between times," Hunter said. "Sometimes I go crazy with it."

Morgan looked into his eyes, saw the flare of passion and longing that made her throat close and her stomach flutter.

"Me too," Morgan said, seizing the opening. "But even though it's making us crazy, we seem to be able to see each other less and less."

"Too true," Hunter said, rubbing his hand over his chin and the days' worth of stubble there. "This has not been a good year for us."

"Well, it's been good for us separately," Morgan said. "You're practically running the New Charter yourself, setting up offices all over the world, working with the others on guidelines. What you're doing is incredibly important. It's going to change how witches interact with each other, with their communities. . . ." She shook her head. The old council was now barely more than a symbolic tradition. Too many witches had objected to its increasingly autonomous and even secretive programs to search out witches who were misusing magickal power. In response to that, Hunter and a handful of other witches had created the New Charter. It was less a policing organization than a support system to rehabilitate errant witches without having their powers stripped. It now included improving witches' standings in their communities, education, public relations, help with historical research. Wicca was being pulled into the twenty-first century, thanks in large part to Hunter.

"There's no way you could stop now," Morgan said. "And me . . . Belwicket is becoming more and more important to me. I really see my future as being there. It supports the work I want to do with healing, and maybe someday I could become high priestess—a Riordan leading Belwicket again."

Morgan's birth mother, Maeve Riordan, had died when Morgan was a baby. If she had lived, she would have been high priestess of her clan's ancestral coven, Belwicket, just as her mother, Mackenna, had, and her mother before her.

"Is that what you'll be happy doing?" Hunter asked.

"It seems to be my destiny," Morgan responded, her fingers absently rubbing the cuff of his sweater. Just as you are, she thought. What did it mean to face two destinies that led in opposite directions? "And yes, it makes me happy. It's incredibly fulfilling, being part of the coven that my birth mother would have led. Even though we're now on the other side of Ireland from the original one, the whole experience is full of my family's history, my relatives, people I never had a chance to know. But it means I stay there, commit myself to staying in Cobh, commit myself to making my life there for the foreseeable future."

"Uh-huh," Hunter said, a wariness coming into his eyes.

Now that she had gotten this far, Morgan forced herself to press on. "So I'm there. And you're . . . everywhere. All over. Meanwhile we're seeing each other every four months for six hours. In an airport." She looked around. "Or a tea shop."

"You're leading up to something," Hunter said dryly.

Over the last four years she and Hunter had talked about the distance between them many times. Each conversation had been horrible and heartbreaking, but they had never managed to resolve anything. They were soul mates; they were meant to love each other. But how could they do that when they were usually a continent apart? And how could that change when each of them was dedicated, and rightfully so, to their life's work?

Morgan didn't see any way to make it work. Not without one of them giving up their chosen path. She *could* give up Belwicket and follow Hunter around the world while he worked for the New Charter. But she feared that the joy of being with him would be tempered by her frustration of not pursuing her own dream and her guilt that she was letting down her coven—and even her birth mother, whom she'd never known. And then what good would she be to Hunter? She didn't want to make his life miserable. And if she asked him to give up the New Charter and stay with her in Ireland, he would be in the same position—thrilled to be with her, torn that he couldn't be true to a meaningful calling of his own. She couldn't ask him to do that.

Breaking up—for good—seemed like the fairest thing for

both of them. She wanted Hunter to be happy above all else. If she set him free, he would have the best chance of that. Even though the idea of never holding him, kissing him, laughing with him, even just sitting and looking at him again seemed almost like a living death, still, Morgan believed it was for the best, ultimately. There seemed to be no way for them to be together; they had to do the best they could on their own.

Back at home Colm Byrne, a member of Belwicket, had confessed he was in love with her. She liked him and he was a great guy, but he wasn't her mùirn beatha dàn. There was no way he would ever touch what she felt for Hunter, and she wasn't breaking up with Hunter to be with Colm or anyone else, for that matter. This wasn't about that. This was about freeing herself and Hunter to give all of themselves to their work and freeing them from the pain of constantly longing for these achingly brief reunions.

"Hunter—I just can't go on like this. We can't go on like this." Her throat tightened and she released his hand. "We need to—just end it. Us."

Hunter blinked. "I don't understand," he said. "We can't end us. *Us* is a fact of life."

"But not for the lives we're living now." Morgan couldn't even look at him.

"Morgan, breaking up isn't the answer. We love each other too much. You're my mùirn beatha dàn—we're *soul mates*."

That did it. A single tear escaped Morgan's eye and rolled down her cheek. She sniffled.

"I know," she said in frustration. "But trying to be together isn't working either. We never see each other, our lives are going in two different directions—how can we have a future? Trying to pretend there *is* one is bogging us both down. If we really, really say this is it, then we'll both be free to do what we want, without even pretending that we have to take the other one into consideration."

Hunter was silent, looking first at Morgan, then around at the little tea shop, then out the black window with the rain streaking down.

"Is that what you want?" he asked slowly. "For us to go our own separate ways without even pretending we have to think of each other?"

"It's what we're already doing," Morgan said, feeling as if she was going to break apart from grief. "I'm not saying we don't love each other. We do—we always will. I just can't take hoping or wishing for something different. It's not *going* to be different." That was when her voice broke. She leaned her head against her hand and took some deep breaths.

Hunter's finger absently traced a pattern on the tabletop, and after a moment Morgan recognized it as a rune. The rune for strength. "So we'll make lives without each other, we'll commit to other people, we won't ever be lovers again."

His quiet, deliberate words felt like nails piercing her heart, her mind. Goddess, just get me through this. Get me through this, she thought. Morgan nodded, blinking in an unsuccessful attempt to keep more tears from coming to her eyes.

"That's what you want." His voice was very neutral, and Morgan, knowing him so well, knew that meant huge emotions were battling inside him.

"That's what we have already," she whispered. "This is not being lovers. I don't know what this is."

"All right," Hunter said. "All right. So you want me to settle down, is that it? In Cobh? Make a garden with you? Get a cat?" His voice didn't sound harsh—more despairing, as if he were truly trying to understand.

"That's not what I'm saying," Morgan said, barely audibly. "I want you to do what you want to do, what you *need* to do. I want you to be happy, to be fulfilled. I'm saying that I *know* that won't be with me in Cobh, with a garden and a cat." She brushed the sleeve of her sweater over her eyes.

Hunter was quiet. Morgan pulled the long ends of her sweater sleeves over her hands and leaned her face against them. Once this was over, she would breathe again. She would go back to the bed-and-breakfast, get in the shower, and cry.

"What if . . . things were different?" Hunter said at last.

Morgan drew a pained breath. "But things *aren't* different."

"*Things* are up to you and me," Hunter said. "You act like this is beyond our control. But we can make choices. We can change our priorities."

"What are you talking about?" Morgan wiped her eyes, then forced herself to take a sip of tea. It was thin and bitter.

Quickly Hunter reached across the table and took her hands in his, his grip like stone. "I think we need to change our priorities. Both of us."

"To what?" How could he manage to always keep her so off-kilter, even after four years?

"To each other," Hunter said.

Morgan stared at him, speechless.

"Morgan," Hunter went on, lowering his voice and leaning closer to her, "I've been doing a lot of thinking, too. I love what I'm doing with the New Charter, but I've realized it just doesn't mean much without you there to share it with me. I know we're two very different people. We have different dreams, different goals. Our backgrounds are very different, our families . . . But you *know* we belong together. *I* know we belong together—I always have. You're my soul mate—my mùirn beatha dàn."

Morgan started crying silently. Oh, Goddess, she loved him so much.

"I knew when I met you that you were the one for me," Hunter said, his voice reaching only her ears. "I knew it when I disliked you, when I didn't trust you, when I feared your power and your inability to control it. I knew it when you learned Ciaran MacEwan was your father. I knew it when you were in love with my bastard half brother, Cal. I've always known it: you are the one for me."

"I don't understand. What are you saying?" It was frightening, how much she still wanted to hope they could be together. It was such a painful hope. She felt his hands holding hers like a vise—as strong as the hold he had on her heart.

"You came here to break up with me forever," Hunter answered. "I won't stop you, if that's what you want. I want you to be happy. But if there's any way you think you can be happy *with* me, as opposed to without me, then I'm asking you to try."

"But how? We've been over this." Morgan said, completely confused.

"No, not *this*," said Hunter. "*This* definitely needs to change. But I can change. I can change whatever I need to if it means that you'll be with me."

Morgan could do nothing but stare. "With you in what way?"

Hunter turned her hand over and traced the carvings of her claddagh ring. "In every way. As my partner, the mother of my children. Every way there is. I need you. You're my life, wherever you are, whatever you're doing."

Morgan quit breathing.

"Look, the one constant in our lives is our love," he said. "It seems like we're squandering our most precious gift—having a soul mate. If we let that slip away, nothing else will make sense." Morgan gaped at him, a splinter of sunlight seeming to enter her heart. *Oh, Goddess, please. Please.*

He went on. "I can phase out the field work I'm doing for the New Charter. There's any number of things I can do based out of Cobh. We could live together, make a life together, wake up with each other more often than *not* with each other. I want to see you grow old, I want us to grow old together. I want to have a family with you. There can be cats involved, if you like."

Could this possibly be true? Could this really be happening? After her despair of the last two weeks the sudden, overwhelming joy Morgan felt seemed almost scary.

"I still have Dagda," was all that Morgan could think of to say. Her once-tiny gray kitten was now a hulking sixteen-pounder who had developed a distinct fondness for Irish mice. "But—can you do this? Do you really mean it?"

Hunter grinned. It was the most beautiful thing that Morgan had ever seen. He moved his chair till they were close, side by side. His arm went around her waist, and she leaned against his warmth, his comfort, his promise. The faded half life she had resigned herself to had just burst into brilliant colors. It was almost too much. It was everything.

"Do you want to be with me, Morgan?" he said softly. "You're my heart's love, my heart's ease. Will you join me in handfasting—will you be my wife?"

"Oh, yes. Yes," Morgan whispered, then rested her head against his shoulder.

Dawn. Dawn is the most magickal time of day, followed of course by sunset, Morgan thought dreamily. She stretched her feet toward Hunter's warmth and let sheer happiness, hopefulness, and contentment wash over her like a wave of comfort. From her bed Morgan could see a small rectangle of sky, pale gray, streaked with pink. It was the dawn of a whole new life, Morgan exulted. The life where she and Hunter would always be together. They would have a handfasting, she thought with a shiver of mixed awe and delight. They might have children. Goddess, Goddess, had anyone ever been so happy? Her eyes drifted closed, a smile still on her face.

"Sweet," Hunter whispered, kissing her ear. Morgan reluctantly opened her eyes, then frowned as she realized Hunter was out of bed and already dressed.

"What are you doing?" she demanded sleepily. "Come back here." Hunter laughed and kissed a line of warmth beneath her ear.

"My last New Charter meeting, over in Wexford," he explained. "I'm taking the eight-oh-five ferry. I'll do my meeting, tell them to get a replacement, and be back by dinnertime at the latest. We can go get some of that fried stuff you love, all right?"

"All right," Morgan said, stretching luxuriously.

She saw a familiar roguish gleam in his eyes as he

watched her stretch, then curl up again under the covers. He looked at his watch, and she laughed. "You don't have time," she told him.

"Love you," he said, grinning, opening the door.

"Love you, too," Morgan replied. "Forever."

Morgan felt as if she'd closed her eyes for only a moment when she was awoken by a loud banging. Frowning, she looked at her watch. Eight-twenty. So Hunter had been gone only half an hour. What was all that noise? She sat up. The lash of rain made her look over at the window. It was pouring outside, thundering and lightning. So odd after the clear dawn.

Downstairs, people were shouting and running, and doors were banging. What could possibly be the matter? A fire? There was no alarm. Had the roof sprung a leak? That wouldn't cause this much commotion.

In a minute Morgan had pulled on her jeans and sweater and shoved her feet into her boots. She put her head out the doorway and sniffed. No smell of fire. She cast her senses, sending her consciousness out around her. She picked up only choppy, confused feelings—panic, fear. She grabbed her coat and trotted downstairs.

"Help!" someone was shouting. "Help! If you've got a boat, we need it! Every able-bodied seaman! Get to the harbor!"

A man in a burly coat brushed past Morgan and ran out the door, following the man who had shouted the alarm.

"What's going on?" Morgan asked the desk clerk. The woman's lined face was drawn taut with worry, her black hair making her face look even paler. "What's happened?"

Outside the front door two more men ran past, their hats pulled low against the driving rain. Morgan heard one shout, "Get to the harbor!"

"The ferry," said the woman, starting to tie a scarf around her head. "The ferry's gone down in the storm."

The icy rain felt like needles pelting her face as Morgan tore down the cobbled road toward the harbor. The three blocks seemed to take half an hour to run, and with every second an endless stream of thoughts raced through Morgan's head. *Please let Hunter have been late, for once in his life. Please let it be a different ferry. Please let no one be hurt. Please let Hunter be late. He's missed the ferry, he's missed the ferry, he's missed the ferry. . . .*

Down at the harbor the driving rain obscured vision, and at first Morgan could see only people running around and men starting the engines in their fishing boats. Then the local fire truck screamed up, looking ridiculously small and inadequate for this disaster. Morgan grabbed an older man's arm, hard, and hung on. "What happened?" she shouted, the wind tearing her voice away.

"The ferry went down!" he shouted back, trying to tug his arm free so he could go help.

"Which ferry?" An icy hand was slowly closing around Morgan's heart. She forced herself to have hope.

The man stared at her. "The only ferry! The eight-oh-five to Wexford!" Then he yanked his arm free, and Morgan watched numbly as he ran down a pier and jumped onto a fishing boat that was just pulling out into the choppy, white-capped waves.

*This isn't happening. I'm going to wake up any minute. I know I'll wake up soon.* Slowly Morgan turned in a circle, the rough wet stones beneath her feet making her feel off balance. Silently she begged for Hunter to come running toward her, a bag in his hand, having missed the ferry because he'd stopped to get a muffin, or tea, or anything. She cast out her senses. Nothing. She sent a witch message. *Hunter, Hunter, come to me, come to me, I'm here, waiting.* Nothing.

Rain soaked her hair, and the harsh wind whipped strands of it across her face. Morgan stood at the edge of the concrete pier, a heavy, rusty chain making a bone-chilling scraping sound as the wind pushed it to and fro. She closed her eyes and let her hands fall open at her sides. With experience born of years of practice, she sank quickly into a meditative state, going beneath the now, the outside, time itself, going deep to where time and thought and energy and magick blended to become one.

*Giomanach.* Her whole being focused on Hunter's name, his eyes, his scent, the feel of his skin, his smile, his laugh, his anger, his passion. In seconds she relived years of memories with him— Hunter fighting Cal, herself throwing an athame at Hunter's neck, him toppling over the cliff to the cold river below. Hunter placing sigils of protection around her parents' house, his fair hair glinting in the moonlight. Hunter holding her, wrapping his coat around her after she had shape-shifted. She had lain weeping in his arms, feeling as if her bones had snapped their joints, her muscles ripped in half. His voice, murmuring soothing spells to take away her pain and fear. She and Hunter, making love for the first time, the wonder of it, the beauty, the shock of pain and discomfort as they joined their bodies and their hearts. His eyes, wide and green above her. Other snatches of memories flew past, image after image; a remembered laugh, an emotion; a scent; the phase of the moon; circles of magick; witches wearing robes; Hunter's glowing aura; Hunter arguing, angry; Hunter crying silently as Morgan broke down.

"An nall nathrac," Morgan whispered into the rain. "An di allaigh, nall nithben, holleigh rac bier. . . ." And on the spell went, the strongest spell she could weave with no preparation. She called on the wind and the rain and the clouds. She opened her hands and the clouds lightened and began to part. She threw up her hands and the rain lessened, backing off as if chastised. Morgan didn't care if anyone was watching or not. Everything in her wrought a spell that would snatch Hunter back from the very brink of his grave.

When she opened her eyes, the rain had slowed to a repentant drizzle; the seas had begun to calm. Morgan felt weak, nauseated, from working such powerful magick. Slowly she forced her legs to take her to the crowd of people huddling on the dock. Voices floated to her over the sounds of sobbing, like chunks of debris on water.

"Never seen nothing like it."

"Unnatural, that's what it was."

"Wave reached up and pulled them down."

"And then like that, the storm stopped."

Morgan froze when she saw the line of sheet-covered bodies on the ground. Men and women were crying, arguing, denying what had happened. Some ferry passengers had been saved, and they sat huddled, looking shocked and afraid.

Hunter wasn't among them. Nor among the dead, lying on the ground.

Morgan gathered every ounce of strength and power within her and sent it out in the world. *If Hunter is alive, I will feel it. If any part of his spirit is there, I will feel it. I will know.* She stayed perfectly still, eyes closed, hands out. Her chest expanded and was aching with her effort. Never had she cast her senses, her powers with so much strength before. Never had everything in her striven to sense someone. She almost cried out with the strain of it, feeling as if she would fly apart. *Hunter, are you alive? Where are you?*

Suddenly Morgan dropped to her knees on the sharp cobblestones, feeling as if she'd been knocked to the ground. She saw the dock, the rain, the covered bodies, but the scene seemed muted, all sounds muffled, all objects leached of color. It was like the whole world had lost something, some element that made it clear and rich and full. And then she understood.

*Oh my God. Oh my God. He's really gone. Hunter's gone.*

She stared unseeingly at the churning, gray-green water. How could the sea dare to take the one she loved, her soul mate, her mùirn beatha dàn? Anguish poured out of her, and she howled, *"Give him back!"* She flung her arms wide, and then, to her astonishment, her silver claddagh ring—Hunter's ring—flew off her rain-slick finger and sailed through the air. Unbelieving, Morgan watched the silver shine dully in the thin gray sunlight, then drop into the sea without a sound. It disappeared in an instant, sinking quickly and silently into the opaque water.

Her ring, Hunter's ring. It, too, was now gone forever. *No, no.*

Her world collapsed around her in a furious whirl of gray despair. Hands out, Morgan fell forward onto her face, not caring if she ever got up again.

# 1.
# Moira

"So I said, 'Oh, Mum, don't get your knickers in a twist,'" Moira Byrne said, licking the steamed milk of her latte off the spoon. She smiled angelically at her friends and took a big, slurping sip. Finally the long "regular" school day was over, and she, Tess, and Vita had headed to Margath's Faire, on the outskirts of Cobh. The first floor was an occult book and supplies shop; the second floor was a café, where they sometimes had readings or music; and the third floor was for various Wiccan classes or study groups. The three girls had grabbed a table in the café, in the back corner.

"Away with ya," said Tess Summerall, laughing in disbelief.

"Right, I can see you being cheeky to Morgan of Belwicket, mum or no," Vita O'Shaunessy agreed, grinning. "Are you grounded, then?"

Moira took another sip and shook her head. Her light, reddish-gold hair, with its three green streaks on the left side, swung over her shoulders. "Amazingly, no," she admitted. "I turned on the famous Moira Byrne charm and convinced her it was for my spellcraft class."

Tess's blue eyes widened. "I can't believe your charm works on your own *mum*, and you know, spelling your initials with *ladybugs* on the garden wall was *not* what Keady meant for spellcraft class."

Moira laughed, remembering again how astonished she had been when her spell had worked. It had been the most complicated one she had ever tried, and watching the tiny, red-winged ladybugs slowly spell out *MB* had been incredibly satisfying. Until her mother had come home and caught her. "It was brilliant," she said. "I really should get top marks for it."

Vita rolled her eyes. "You probably will. Especially if you use the *famous* Moira Byrne charm."

Moira giggled. Keady Dove, their spellcraft teacher, was as traditional as her own mother. Admitting that she had toyed with the wills of ladybugs just for a lark would not go over well.

Standing, Tess asked, "Anyone want anything? I'm getting another espresso." At her full height, Tess was five-foot two, six inches shorter than Moira and with all the fine-boned daintiness Moira felt she lacked. Tess's naturally black hair was cut short and spiky, with magenta-dyed tips. Much more daring than Moira's three green stripes, which were supposed to have been wash-out dye for St. Patrick's Day but had turned out to be permanent. She'd asked her mum to take them out with magick, and her mum had refused. Her dad had just laughed and hugged her. "It's not so bad, Daisy. It'll probably only take six or seven years to grow out."

Moira had moaned, allowing herself to be held by her

dad, even though she was fifteen—too old to be cuddled or called Daisy, the pet name her father had always used.

"Think of it as character-building," her mum had suggested, and her dad had laughed again. Her dad and mum had met eyes and smiled at each other, and Moira had known it was a lost cause. She'd called Tess and complained about the permanent dye being the "worst thing" to happen to her.

That had been seven months ago. One month later her dad had been killed in a car wreck in London, where he'd gone on business. Now she wished more than anything that the green streaks could really have been her worst problem—and that Colm Byrne was still waiting at home to back up her mum in a lecture about the latest trouble Moira had gotten into.

"Moira?" Tess asked, waiting for an answer.

"Oh, no thanks. I'm fine." Moira forced a thin smile.

"All right, then?" Vita asked once Tess had left. Her round face looked concerned.

"Oh, you know," Moira said vaguely. Vita nodded sympathetically and patted Moira's hand in an old-fashioned gesture Moira found touching.

"I know. I'm here, whenever you want to talk."

Moira nodded. "I'd rather be distracted, really," she said.

"Well, good," Vita said. "Because I was wondering if you could help me study for herbology. I got all the nightshades mixed up on the last test, and Christa was *very disappointed*." Vita lowered her voice to sound like Christa Ryan, one of their initiation-class teachers.

"Sure," Moira said. "Come over tonight or tomorrow and we'll go over everything. I'll share all the Moira Byrne wisdom with you."

Vita threw a paper napkin at her, and Moira laughed.

"You mean the Moira Byrne wisdom that had you spelling your initials with bugs?" Vita asked dryly.

"Right! That wisdom!"

Tess came back and sat down, curling one leg neatly beneath her.

"You're so dainty," Moira said with a sigh, wishing the same could be said about her. Then she froze in her seat, her hazel eyes wide. One hand reached out to grab Tess's arm. "Goddess—I think he's here, downstairs," she whispered. She hadn't deliberately been casting her senses, but her neck had prickled, and when she concentrated, she thought she felt Ian's vibrations.

Vita fluttered her eyelids. "Oh, no—I don't think I can take the excitement of seeing Ian Delaney. Someone help me. Fetch a cold cloth." She swayed in her chair while Tess broke up with laughter. Moira looked at her.

"I'll fetch you a cold cloth," she said, "for your *mouth.*"

Vita and Tess laughed harder, and Moira narrowed her eyes. "Could we have more sympathy, please?" she asked. "How often do I fancy a lad?"

"Not often," Tess agreed, sobering. "Everyone, be casual."

This made Vita laugh again. Moira turned her attention to her latte as though it were all-absorbing. *Come up here,* she thought. *Come upstairs. You're thirsty.*

She wasn't putting a spell on Ian or sending him a witch message. She was just wishing hard. Ian Delaney had transferred to her regular school two years ago, and Moira had immediately developed a crush on him. He was gorgeous in a rough-cut kind of way, with thick brown hair that never looked quite tidy enough, deep blue eyes, and one dimple in his right cheek when he smiled. He'd been such a refreshing change from some of the more upper-class snobs that went to Moira's school—outspoken, funny in a cheeky way, and completely unable to be intimidated, either by teachers or students.

Best of all, he was a witch.

Unfortunately, all last year Moira had been invisible to him—not that she had even tried to get his attention. But this year . . . he had sat next to her in study hall. Lent her some graph paper in maths class. Borrowed a quid from her—*and* paid her back. And just in the last month Moira had started trying to actually flirt with him, in a lame, inexperienced way, she admitted. But he seemed to be responding.

"I can't feel him," said Vita. "Is he coming up?"

"Not yet," said Moira. "He's still downstairs."

Tess grinned. "Shall I fetch him up here? I'll stand at the top of the stairs and yell, 'Oy! You there, boy. Up here!'"

Moira's chest tightened. "If you do . . . ," she breathed in warning, shaking her head. Tess was so much more confident about lads. It wasn't that Moira didn't have confidence—she knew that she was good at magick and that she had an ability to learn anything if she put her mind to it. She never questioned how much her family loved her. But where she did fall apart was with the whole world of boys, dating, and flirting.

*Come upstairs, Ian. You're thirsty. Or hungry. Or you're looking for me.*

"Does your mum know about Ian?" Tess asked.

Moira shook her head. "No. We're not dating—it's not like I've had him home to tea."

Two pairs of blue eyes looked at her. Tess's were expectant, shrewd. Vita's were politely disbelieving.

"So you've not mentioned your unquenchable love for Ian Delaney, son of Lilith Delaney, high priestess of Ealltuinn," Vita stated. "Ealltuinn, who's been getting members of Belwicket up in arms because they don't seem to know the boundary of when it's not right to use magick?"

"It's not unquenchable love, and no, I've not mentioned it," Moira said pointedly. "Am I supposed to only date Belwicket lads, then? There's precious few. Or should I try a nonwitch?"

Half smiling, Tess held up her hands as if to say she gave up.

"Just wanted to ask," Vita murmured, shrugging. "I mean, everything aside, Ian's deadly hot. No one says he isn't."

Moira paused. "Wait—he's coming up!" She bent over her latte, face carefully expressionless. Out of the corner of her eye she saw Ian the second he passed the top step into the café. She looked anywhere but at him, shooting subtle but threatening looks at Tess and Vita, each of whom was trying to smother a smile.

"So," said Tess brightly. "You want to take in a film this weekend, then?"

Moira nodded as if it were a serious question. "Yeah, maybe so." Her eyes widened as she realized Ian was coming straight at their table, a mug in his hand.

"Moira!" he said.

She looked up with an Oscarworthy expression of surprise. "Oh, hey there, Ian."

He smiled down at her, and she felt her heart give a little flip. That smile . . .

"'Lo, Ian," said Tess, and Vita smiled at him.

"Hi," he said, and Moira loved the fact that his gaze didn't linger on either of her (she thought) prettier or more feminine friends. Instead he looked right at her, his chestnut brown hair flecked with mist, his eyes dark blue and smiling. "I don't want to interrupt—I was just downstairs and fancied a drink. It's wet outside."

"Do you want to sit down?" Moira asked, mentally patting herself on the back for her boldness.

"Aye, sure," he said, pleased. He asked a neighboring table if he could take a chair, then pulled it over and wedged it right next to Moira's. She could hardly keep herself from wiggling with happiness. Cool. I'm very cool, she thought, feeling almost glad about her green-streaked hair.

"Oh! Look at the time!" Tess said in a non-Oscarworthy performance, complete with wide eyes and O-shaped mouth. "I have to be getting off. Mum'll slay me if I'm late again." She stood and pulled on her suede jacket.

"I didn't mean to interrupt anything," Ian said again, concerned.

"Not at all," Tess assured him. "Pure coincidence. Come on, then, Vi."

"Why?" Vita frowned. "Your mum won't slay *me* if *I'm* late."

Tess just stared at her, and then Vita got it.

"Right. I'm late, too." She stood up and pulled on her plaid trench coat. "Later on, Moira. Nice seeing you, Ian."

"You too," he said.

Then they were gone, and Moira and Ian were sharing a table alone for the first time. Moira felt all quivery inside, happy and anxious at once. Her latte was ice-cold, and she quickly circled her hand over it, deasil, and murmured, "Heat within." Ian sipped his mug of tea. Just as Moira was starting to feel alarmed by the lingering silence, Ian said, "I was looking at books downstairs."

"Oh?" *Yes, that was witty. You go, Moira.* "I've always liked the illustrated books—the ones with old-fashioned pictures of witches. Or the really pretty flower ones." *Do I really sound this stupid?*

Ian didn't seem to think so. He only said, "Yeah. I love the plant ones. I'm still taking private herbology lessons."

"But you got initiated last year, right?"

"Yeah, they usually do it at fourteen in my coven," he replied. "You're not initiated yet?"

"No. I'm aiming for next Beltane. Me and Tess and Vita."

"Well, you've got some time, then."

Moira nodded. "We're all taking classes—spellcraft, herbology, astrology, animal work. The usuals."

"What's your favorite?"

*He's interested in me!* "I like spellcraft." She couldn't help smiling, remembering her ladybug triumph. "Last weekend I wrote a new spell by myself. I spelled ladybugs to form my initials on my garden wall."

Ian laughed. "Did it work? Or did you just get a bunch of confused, ready-to-hibernate ladybugs? Or maybe bees?"

Grinning, Moira knocked her side against him, then was thrilled at the warm contact. "Yes, it worked." The truth was, she'd been pretty amazed herself—but she didn't want Ian to know that.

"Yeah? Ladybugs spelled out your initials? That's very cool," said Ian, looking impressed. "And you're not even initiated yet. But I guess you've got your mother's power, then."

Self-consciously Moira shrugged, although by now she was used to having a mother who was famous in Wiccan circles. All of Moira's life, she'd heard people speaking respectfully about Morgan Byrne of Belwicket—her powers, her incredibly strong healing gifts, the promise of her craft. Moira was proud of her mum, but at the same time it was hard, always wondering if she would ever measure up.

"With your powers, why weren't you initiated earlier?" Ian asked. "It seems like you would be amazing by now."

"You don't think I'm amazing?" Moira said teasingly, feeling incredibly daring. She had a moment of anxiety when Ian quit smiling and just looked at her thoughtfully. *I went too far, I went too far—*

"No," he said quietly. "I do think you're amazing."

Her face lit up, and she forgot to be cool. "I think you're amazing, too."

"Oh, yes, me," Ian said. "I can move forks. Look."

As Moira watched, Tess's leftover fork slid slowly toward her, about an inch. Moira grinned and raised her eyebrows at him, and he looked pleased.

"Pretty good," she said, an idea popping into her mind. Hopefully she could pull it off. "Watch this," she said boldly. "Look at everyone in the room who's reading"—which was three-quarters of the people there. Most tables seemed to have an open book or magazine or paper on them. Moira closed her eyes and pictured what she wanted to do, tamping down the mote of conscience that warned her it was probably not a good idea. *Right, then, I hope this works.*

*All the pages move as one, as if the story's just begun. I flip the pages lightly so, and my will tells them where to go.*

Then, seeing it in her mind, Moira turned one page in each paper, book, or magazine throughout the café at Margath's Faire. In perfect unison, every piece of reading material in the room had one page turned.

Most people noticed, and the witches in the room instantly looked up to see who had done it. Hearing that it had worked, Moira opened her eyes and carefully looked at no one besides Ian. She finished the last bit of her latte and gave Ian a private smile, thrilled that she'd really done it.

"That was bloody beautiful," Ian breathed, looking at her in a way that made her feel shivery. "So delicate and simple, yet so awesome." He took her hand, and Moira loved the feel of his warmth, their fingers intertwining. His hand was larger than hers, which made her feel better, because in fact Ian was only the same height she was.

*I'm holding hands with Ian Delaney,* Moira thought, letting happiness wash over her.

"I'm impressed, Moira of Belwicket," he said quietly, looking at her. "You are your mother's daughter."

# 2.
# Morgan

"Thank you for coming." A man with a weathered face and brown hair gone mostly gray stepped forward and took one of Morgan's hands in his.

"Hello," she said quietly, giving him a smile. Automatically Morgan sent out waves of reassurance and calm, trying to soothe nerves stretched taut by fear and worry. Since she'd lost her husband, Colm, six months ago, it had been a struggle to continue her work without her emotions interfering. But she needed the salary from the New Charter to support herself and her daughter, and also, she needed the relief from her own sadness that came from helping others. Luckily Morgan had been honing her skills as a healer for years now, and the routine of easing someone's concern was second nature.

"You must be Andrew Moffitt," she said. She was in the county hospital in Youghal, a town not far from where she lived, right outside of Cobh, Ireland. The Moffitts' daughter was in the last bed in a long, old-fashioned ward that housed eight patients.

"Aye," he said with a quick bob of his head. "And this is my missus, Irene."

A small woman wearing an inexpensive calico dress nodded nervously. Her large green eyes were etched with sadness, the lines around her mouth deep and tight. Her hair was pulled back into a simple braid, practical for a farmer's wife.

"Hello, Irene," Morgan said. She reached out and took one of Irene's hands, sending her a quick bit of strength and peace. Irene gave her a questioning glance, then shot an anxious look at her husband. "Irene, you seem unsure." Morgan's voice was gentle and compassionate.

Irene's eyes darted around the room, pausing to linger on the pale, thin girl lying in the hospital bed. The hushed whoosh, whoosh of machines filled the small room, with a steady beeping of the heart monitor keeping time.

"I don't hold with this," Irene said in a low voice. "We're Catholics, we are. I don't want to lose my Amy, but maybe it's the Lord's will." Her face crumpled slightly.

Morgan put down her large canvas carryall and deliberately sent out more general calming waves. "I understand," she said. "As much as you desperately love your daughter and pray for her recovery, you might not want it if it means endangering her soul. Or yours."

"Yes," Irene said, sounding relieved and surprised that Morgan understood. Of course Irene couldn't know that Morgan had been raised by devout Catholics, Sean and Mary Grace Rowlands, and knew better than many the fears Catholics had about witchcraft. "Yes, that's it exactly. I mean, she's my baby, but . . ." Again, withheld sobs choked her. "It's just—Eileen Crannach, from church—she told us what you'd done for her nephew, Davy. Said it was a miracle, it was. And we're so desperate—the doctors can't do much for her."

"I understand," Morgan said again. "Here, sit down." She led Irene to one of the two nearby plastic visitor chairs and sat down in the other one. Looking up, she beckoned Andrew to come closer. In a low voice she said, "I can promise you that anything I do would never have evil intent. I seem to have a gift for healing. My using that gift feels, to me, what you would describe as the Lord's will. Here's another way of looking at it: maybe it was the Lord's will that brought me to you. Maybe your Lord wants to do his work through me."

Irene gaped. "But you're not Catholic," she whispered. "You're a . . . witch!" The word itself seemed to frighten her, and she looked around to make sure no one else had heard.

Morgan smiled, thinking of her adoptive mother. "Even so. He works in mysterious ways."

An unspoken consultation passed between Andrew and Irene, looking into each other's eyes. Morgan sat quietly, using the time to cast her senses toward Amy. Amy was in a coma. From what Andrew Moffitt had gruffly told Morgan on the phone, Amy's brother had been practicing fancy skateboard moves, and in one of them he'd shot the board out from under his feet. Amy had been playing nearby, and the edge of the board caught her right in the neck, cracking her spine. But they hadn't realized the extent of her injuries, and over the next several days the swelling and injury had been worsened by her everyday activities. They hadn't even known anything was wrong until Amy had collapsed on the school playground.

She'd had surgery six days ago and hadn't come out of it.

"Do what you can for Amy," Andrew said, calling Morgan back to the present.

"All right," said Morgan, and that was all.

Because she was in a county hospital, with people coming and going constantly, Morgan couldn't use any of her more obvious tools, like candles and incense and her four silver cups. However, she did slip a large, uncut garnet beneath Amy's pillow to help her in her healing rite.

"If you could just try to keep anyone from touching me or talking to me," she whispered, and wide-eyed, the Moffitts nodded.

Morgan stood at Amy's bedside, opening her senses and picking up as much as she could. Right now Amy was on a respirator, but her heart was beating on its own and everything else seemed to be working. There was an incision on her neck with a thin plastic drain running out of it. That was where she could start.

First things first. Morgan rolled her shoulders and tilted her head back and forth, releasing any tension or stiffness. She breathed in and out, deep cleansing breaths that helped relax and center her. Then, closing her eyes, she silently and without moving her lips began her power chant, the one that reached out into the world and drew magick to her, the one that helped raise her own powers within her. It came to her, floating toward her like colored ribbons on the mildest of spring breezes. Feeling the magick bloom inside her, Morgan felt a fierce love and joy flood her. She was ready.

As lightly as a feather, Morgan placed two fingers on Amy's incision. At once she picked up the drug-dulled sensations of pain, the swollen sponginess of inflamed cells, the cascading dominoes of injuries that had escalated, unchecked, until Amy lost consciousness. Slowly Morgan traced the injuries until she reached the last and mildest one. Then, following them like a thread, she did what she could to heal them. Clots dissolved with a steady barrage of spells. Muscles soothed, tendons eased, veins gently reopened. Morgan's mind traced new pathways, delicate, fernlike branches of energy, and soon felt the rapid fire of neuron impulses racing across them. Love, she thought. Love and hope, joy and life. The blessing of being able to give. How blessed I am. These feelings she let flow into Amy's consciousness.

The injury itself was complicated, but Morgan broke it down into tiny steps, like the different layers of a spell, the different steps one had to learn, all throughout Wicca. As with anything else, it was the tiny steps that added up to create a wondrous whole. Morgan banished the excess fluid at the site, dispersing it through now-open paths. She calmed swollen muscles and helped the skin heal more rapidly. The final step of this first stage was the actual crack in the spinal column, where a minute shift of bone had compressed the nerves. The bone was edged back into place, and Morgan felt the instantaneous rightness and perfect fit of it. She encouraged the bone to start knitting together. The crushed nerves were slowly, painstakingly restored, with new routes being created where necessary. Then she waited and listened to the overall response of Amy's body. It was sluggish, but functioning. With every beat of Amy's heart it got stronger, worked better, flowed more smoothly. It would take longer to heal completely, Morgan knew. Maybe months. But this was a great start.

Her own strength was flagging. Healing took so much energy and concentration that Morgan always felt completely drained afterward. This was the most difficult case she'd had in months, and it would leave Morgan herself weak for several days.

But it wasn't over. Amy's body was functioning. Now she had to find Amy. Ignoring her fatigue, Morgan concentrated even deeper, silently using spells that would link Amy's consciousness with hers in a tàth meànma, a joining of their minds. Amy wasn't a blood witch, so it wouldn't feel good for either one of them, and Amy's ability to either receive or send energy was going to be very limited. Amy's spirit was sleeping. It had shut down and withdrawn to escape the horror of paralysis, the pain of the injury and the surgery, and the flood of nerve-shattering emotions that everyone around Amy was releasing.

*Amy? Are you there?*

*Who—who are you?*

*I'm here to help. It's time to come back now.* Morgan was firm and kind.

*No. It's too yucky.*

*It's not so yucky anymore. It's time to come back. Come back and see your mum and dad. They're waiting for you.*

*They're still here?*

*They would never leave you. Come back now.*

*Will it hurt?* Her voice was young and afraid.

*A little bit. You have to be strong and brave. But it won't be as bad as it was before, I promise.*

Very slowly and gently Morgan eased her consciousness back, then swayed on her feet as a wave of exhaustion washed over her. But she backtracked quickly to herself, sent a last, strong healing spell, and opened her eyes. She blinked several times and swallowed, feeling as if she were about to fall over. Slowly she took her hand away from Amy's neck.

With difficulty, she turned to Andrew and Irene and smiled weakly. Then, knowing Amy could breathe on her own, she carefully disconnected the mouthpiece from the respirator.

"No!" Amy's mother cried, lunging forward to stop her. Her husband grabbed her, and in the next moment Amy coughed and gagged, then drew a deep, whistling breath around the tube that was still in her throat.

Her parents stared.

"You need to get a nurse to take out the tube," Morgan said softly, still feeling only half there. She swallowed again and glanced at the clock. It was three in the afternoon. She'd arrived at nine that morning. Time hadn't made an impression on her during the healing.

Then Andrew seemed to notice her, and his heavy eyebrows drew together in concern. "Here, miss. Let me get you some tea." Awkwardly Morgan moved to a chair and dropped into it. Andrew pressed a hot Styrofoam cup into her hand and appeared not to notice her quickly circling her hand over her tea. She drank down half of it at once. It helped.

Irene's anxious calls had alerted a nurse, who, faced with the undeniable fact that Amy was breathing on her own, removed the respirator tube. She watched in shock as Amy gagged again and took several convulsive breaths. Andrew and Irene gripped each other's hands tightly as they stared down at their daughter. Then Irene tentatively reached out and took her daughter's hand.

"Amy, darling. Amy, it's Mum. I'm right here, love, and so is Da. We're right here, lass."

Morgan sipped her tea. There was nothing more she

could do. Amy had to choose to come back.

In the hospital bed the pale, still figure seemed small and fragile. She was breathing more regularly now, with only the occasional cough. Suddenly her eyelids fluttered open for a moment, revealing a pair of green eyes just like her mum's. Her parents gasped and leaned closer.

"Amy!" Irene cried as a doctor strode quickly toward them. "Amy! Love!"

Amy licked her lips slightly, and her eyes fluttered again. Her mouth seemed to form the word *Mum*, and her pinkie finger on her left hand raised slightly.

"Good Lord," the doctor breathed.

Irene was crying now, kissing Amy's hand, and Andrew was sniffing, his worn face crinkled into a leathery smile. Morgan finished her tea and got to her feet. Very quietly she picked up her canvas bag. It seemed to weigh three times as much as it had that morning. And she still had an hour's drive to Wicklow. She was suffused with the happiness that always came from healing, an intense feeling of accomplishment and satisfaction. But the happiness was tinged bittersweet, as it had been every time she'd healed someone since Colm's death—because when her husband had needed her most, she hadn't been there to heal *him*.

She was almost out the door when Irene noticed she was leaving. "Wait!" she cried, and hurried over to Morgan. Her face was wet with tears, her smile seeming like a rainbow. "I don't know what you did," she said in barely more than a whisper. "I told the nurses you were praying for her. But it's a miracle you've done here, and as long as I live, I'll never be able to thank you enough."

Morgan gave her a brief hug. "Amy getting better is all the thanks I need."

"You're working too hard, lass," Katrina Byrne said as Morgan came up the front walk.

Morgan shifted her heavy tote to her other shoulder. It was almost five o'clock. Luckily she'd had the foresight to ask her mother-in-law to be here this afternoon in case she didn't get back before dinner.

"Hi. What are you doing? Pulling up the carrots? Is Moira home?"

"No, she's not back yet," said Katrina, sitting back stiffly on her little stool. "I would have expected her by now. How was your day?"

"Hard. But in the end, good. The girl opened her eyes, and she recognized her mum."

"Good." Katrina's brown eyes looked her up and down. The older woman was heavyset, more so now than when Morgan had met her, so long ago. Katrina and her husband, Pawel, and her sister, Susan Best, had been among the handful of survivors of the original Belwicket, on the western coast of Ireland. Morgan had known her first as the temporary leader of Belwicket, then as her mother-in-law, and the two women had an understated closeness—especially now that they were both widows.

"You're all in, Morgan," Katrina said.

"I'm beat," Morgan agreed. "I need a hot bath and a sit-down."

"Sit down for just a moment here." Katrina pointed with her dirt-crusted trowel at the low stone wall that bordered Morgan's front yard. Morgan lowered her bag to the damp grass and rested on the cool stones. The afternoon light was rapidly fading, but the last pale rays of sunlight shone on Katrina's gray hair, twisted up into a bun in back. She wore brown cords and a brown sweater she'd knit herself, before her arthritis had gotten too bad.

"Where's Moira, then?" Morgan asked, looking up the narrow country road as if she expected to see her daughter running down it.

"Don't know," Katrina said, picking up a three-pronged hand rake and scraping it among the carrots. "With her gang."

Morgan smiled to herself: Moira's "gang" consisted of her friends Tess and Vita. She let out a deep breath, hoping she would have the energy to get back up when she needed to. Lately it seemed she'd been working harder than ever. She was often gone, leaving Katrina to come look after Moira, though Moira had started protesting that she could stay by herself. Last week Katrina had accused her of running away from grief, and Morgan hadn't denied it. It was just too painful to be here sometimes—to see the woodwork that Colm had painted, the garden he'd helped her create. She felt his loss a thousand times a day here. In a hotel in some unknown city, with work to distract her, it was easier to bear. Now she waited for her outspoken mother-in-law— her friend—to get something off her chest.

"When were you thinking of accepting the role of high priestess?" Katrina asked bluntly. Her trowel moved slowly through the rich black soil. She looked focused on her gardening, but Morgan knew better.

She let out a deep breath. "I was thinking maybe next spring. Imbolc. Moira's to be initiated on Beltane, and it would be lovely for me to lead it."

"Aye," agreed Katrina. "So maybe you need to cut back on your traveling and start preparing more to be high priestess." She looked up at Morgan shrewdly. "Meaning you'll have to be home more."

Morgan pressed her lips together. It was pointless to pretend not to know what Katrina was talking about. She scraped the toe of her shoe against a clump of grass. "It's hard being here."

"Hard things have to be faced, Morgan. You've a daughter here who needs you. You've missed two of the last five circles. And not least, your garden's going to hell." Katrina pulled up a group of late carrots, and Morgan was startled to see that below their lush green tops, their roots were gnarled, twisted, and half rotted away.

"What . . . ?"

Katrina clawed her hand rake through the dirt: The whole row of carrots was rotten. Morgan and Katrina's eyes met.

"You did all the usual spells, of course," Katrina said.

"Of course. I've never had anything like this." Morgan knelt down and took the small rake from Katrina. She dug through the soil, pulling up the ruined carrots, then went deeper. In a minute she had found it: a small pouch of sodden, dirt-stained leather, tied at the top with string. Morgan scratched runes of protection quickly around her, then untied the string. A piece of slate fell out, covered with sigils—magickal symbols that worked spells. Some of them Morgan didn't know, but she recognized a few, for general destruction (plants), for the attraction of darkness (also for plants), and for the halting of growth (modified to pertain to plants).

"Oh my God," she breathed, sitting back on her heels. It had been so long since anyone had wished her harm—a lifetime ago. To find this in her own garden . . . it was unbelievable.

"What are you thinking?" Katrina asked.

Morgan paused, considering. "I really can't imagine who would do this," she said. "No one in our coven works magick to harm. . . ." She trailed off as something occurred to her. "Of course, there is another coven whose members don't share our respect for what's right."

"Ealltuinn," Katrina said.

Morgan nodded. "I never would have thought they'd do something like this," she murmured, almost to herself. It wasn't unusual for more than one coven to be in a certain area; sometimes they coexisted peacefully, sometimes less so. Belwicket had been in the town of Wicklow, right outside Cobh, for over twenty years now; they were a Woodbane coven who had renounced dark magick. Ealltuinn, a mixed coven, had started in Hewick, a small town slightly to the north, about eight years ago. There hadn't been any problems until about two years ago, when Lilith Delaney had become high priestess of Ealltuinn.

Morgan had never liked Lilith—she was one of those witches who always pushed things a little too far and didn't understand why it was a problem. But it was more that she'd work minor spells out of self-interest, nothing dangerous, so Morgan hadn't been too concerned. She'd spoken with Lilith several times, warned her that she didn't agree with the direction Lilith was taking her coven in, and Lilith hadn't been too pleased with that. But would she really have shown her anger like this? By ruining Morgan's garden? The spell was minor, petty, but it was working harm against some-one—which was always wrong.

Morgan looked around her yard, distressed. This home had always been a haven for her. Suddenly she felt isolated and vul-nerable in a way she hadn't for decades. A ruined garden wasn't the worst thing that had ever happened to Morgan, but that someone was working to actively harm her . . . She didn't believe Lilith would want to hurt her—but who else could it be?

"When was the last time you saw Lilith Delaney?" Katrina asked, as if sensing Morgan's thoughts.

Morgan thought back. "Two weeks ago, in Margath's Faire. Hartwell Moss and I were there, having a cup after shopping. Lilith was sitting with another member of Ealltuinn, and they looked deep into something together."

"Do they know where the power leys are?" Katrina asked, her eyes narrowing.

Morgan felt a flash of fear. Why was Katrina asking that—was she worried that Ealltuinn was more of a threat than Morgan had thought? "Not that I know of," Morgan replied, her throat feeling tight. "Now that I think of it, though, every once in a while I see someone from Ealltuinn out on the head-lands, crisscrossing them, like they're looking for something."

The two women looked at each other. In fact, Morgan's very house was built on an ancient power ley, or line, as was Katrina's house and the old grocery store that she and Pawel had run in the early days of their marriage. The building was now empty, and Belwicket held many of their circles there. But Ealltuinn must have heard the legends of the power leys, the unseen and often unfelt ancient lines of energy and mag-ick that crisscrossed the earth, like rubber bands wrapped around a tennis ball. Those who worked magick on or around a power ley saw their powers increased. The town where Morgan had grown up in America, Widow's Vale, had had a power ley also, in an old Methodist cemetery.

Morgan dropped the rotten carrots in disgust and retied the little pouch. She would have to dismantle it, purify the pieces of it with salt, and bury it down by the sea, where the sand and salt water would further dissolve its negative energy.

"Morgan, I'm concerned about Ealltuinn," Katrina said seriously. "With Lilith Delaney at their head, what if they become bolder in their darkness? I'll be honest with you, lass: I wish I were strong enough to take them on. I've got some righteous anger to show them. But I'm not. I'm fine, but I'm not you."

"I don't know," Morgan said. "It's been a long time. . . . I'm different now."

"Morgan, you could still pull the moon from the sky. In you is the combined strength of Maeve Riordan and Ciaran MacEwan, Goddess have mercy on them both. You alone are powerful enough to stop Lilith in her tracks, to keep Belwicket safe. Twenty years ago you saved your town from a dark wave—you stopped a dark wave when no one dreamed it was possible."

"It was Daniel Niall and another witch," Morgan corrected her. "I just helped. And besides, this is hardly another dark wave."

Katrina gave her a maternal look, then brushed her hands off on her corduroy pants. "It's getting late," she said. "I'd best be getting back. You know, sometimes I still expect Pawel to come home to tea, and he's been gone six years."

"I know what you mean," Morgan said, her eyes shadowed.

"Think on what I said, lass," Katrina said, getting stiffly to her feet. She gave Morgan a quick kiss, then let herself out the garden gate and headed back up the narrow road to her own cottage, less than a quarter mile away.

For another minute Morgan sat in her garden, looking down at the row of spoiled carrots. She was torn between feeling that Katrina had to be overreacting and her own instinct to believe the worst after everything she had experienced in Widow's Vale. But that was all far in her past, and she hadn't seen anyone practice true dark magick in ages. Of course, she also hadn't seen anyone use magick for harm at all, even on such a small scale as hurting some vegetables. But Lilith was a small-minded person who obviously couldn't handle having someone tell her she was wrong.

Morgan looked up at the sky, realizing that it was getting dark and Moira wasn't home yet. It wasn't that unusual for her to be late, though usually she called. Maybe Morgan was being foolish, but this little pouch had really spooked her, and she wanted her daughter home *now*.

Six twenty-two. Exactly two minutes since the last time she'd looked.

Six twenty-two! Moira was two and half hours late and no doubt off with her friends somewhere. Morgan was sure no harm had come to her daughter. After all, Wicklow wasn't exactly Los Angeles or New York. Everybody tended to know everybody—it was hard to get away with wrongdoing or mischief.

Trying not to look at the clock, Morgan moved methodically around the small living room, kicking the rug back into place, straightening the afghan draped over Colm's leather chair. Her fingers lingered on the cool leather and she swallowed, hit once again with the pain of missing him. Sometimes Morgan would get through part of a day with moments of amusement or joy, and she would grow hopeful about starting to heal. Then, with no warning, something would remind her of Colm's laugh, his voice, his warm, reassuring presence, and it was like a physical blow, leaving Morgan gasping with loss.

Even Moira being so late would have seemed okay if Colm were here with her. He would have been calm and matter-of-fact, and when Moira came home, he would have known exactly what to say. He and Moira were so much alike, both outgoing and cheerful, friendly and affectionate. Morgan had always been on the shyer side, a bit more insecure, needing to have the t's crossed and the i's dotted. Since Colm had died, it seemed that Morgan had developed a gift for saying the wrong thing to Moira, for flying off the handle, for botching what should have been the time for mother and daughter to grow closer. If she were home enough for them to grow closer, she thought with a pang of guilt. She had to quit running. Hard things had to be faced, as Katrina said. Still, how many hard things was she going to have to face in this life? Too many, so far.

Morgan glanced around the already tidy room and caught sight of her reflection in the windowpane, the dark night outside turning the glass into a mirror. Was that her? The window Morgan looked sad and alone, young and slightly worried. Her hair was still brown and straight, parted in the middle and worn a few inches below her shoulders. It had been much longer in high school.

Morgan gazed solemnly at the window Morgan, then froze when a second face suddenly appeared beside hers. She startled and whirled to look behind her, but she was alone. Eyes wide, heart already thumping with the first rush of adrenaline, Morgan looked closer at the window—was the person outside? She looked around—her dog, Finnegan, was sleeping by the fireplace. Casting her senses told her she was alone, inside the house and out. But next to her own reflection was a thin, ghostly face, with hollow cheeks and haunted eyes, but so pale and blurry that she had no clue who it could be. She stared for another ten seconds, trying to make out the person, but as she looked, the image became even less distinct and then faded completely.

Goddess, Morgan thought, sitting abruptly at the table. She realized her hands were shaking and her heart beating erratically. Goddess. What had that been? Visions were strong magick. Where had that come from? What did it mean? Had it been just a glamour, thrown on the window by . . . who? Or something darker, more serious? Feeling prickly anxiety creeping up her back, Morgan took a few breaths and tried to calm down. This, on top of the hex she'd found in the garden. What if Katrina was right? What if Lilith and Ealltuinn were up to something? Morgan hadn't experienced anything like these things in so long.

Standing up, Morgan walked back and forth in the living room, casting her senses strongly. She felt nothing except the sleeping aura of Finnegan, the deeply sleeping aura of Bixby, her cat, and silence. Outside she felt nothing except the occasional bird or bat or field mouse, vole, or rabbit, skittering here and there. She felt completely rattled, shaken, and afraid in a way she hadn't felt in years. Was this part of missing Colm? Feeling afraid and alone? But the pouch and the image in the window—they were real and definitely involved magick. Dark magick. Morgan shivered. *And where is Moira?*

Morgan looked at Moira's cold, untouched dinner on the worn wooden table and felt a sudden surge of anxiety. Even though moments ago she'd been certain Moira was fine, now she needed her daughter home, needed to see her face, to know she was all right. She even felt an impulse to scry for her but knew that it wasn't right to abuse Moira's trust and use magick to spy on her daughter. Still, if much more time passed, she might have to push that boundary.

*Try to calm down.* Worrying never helped anything, that was what Colm always said. *If you can change things, change them, but don't waste time worrying about things you can't change.* Tomorrow she would talk to Katrina, tell her about the face in the window. For now, there wasn't much she could do. Sighing, Morgan began to stack dishes in the sink. She couldn't help turning around every few seconds to glance at the windows. Conveniently, she could see the whole downstairs from the small kitchen tucked into one corner. A dark blue curtain covered the doorway to the pantry. Off the fireplace was a small, tacked-on room for Wicca work. Upstairs were three tiny bedrooms and one antiquated bathroom. When Colm was alive, Morgan had chafed at the smallness of their cottage— he'd seemed to fill the place with his breadth and his laugh and his steady presence. Along with Moira, two dogs (though Seamus was buried in the north field now), two cats (Dagda was now also buried in the north field), and Morgan, the cottage had almost seemed to split at the seams.

Now there were days when Moira was at school and the cottage felt overwhelmingly large, empty, and quiet. On those days Morgan threw open the shutters to let in more light, swept the floor vigorously both to clean and to stir up energy, and sang loudly as she went about the day's chores. But when her voice was silent, so was the cottage, and so was her heart. That was when she looked for an opportunity to go somewhere, work someplace else, for just a while.

What a horrible irony. Morgan traveled constantly on business—her work as a healer had grown steadily in the last ten years, and she was away at least every month. Colm had been a midlevel chemical researcher for a lab in Cork and never needed to travel or work late or miss vacations. The one time his company had decided to send him on a business trip to London, he'd been killed in a car accident on his second day there. Morgan, the powerful witch, the healer, had not been able to heal or help or be with her husband when he died. Now she wondered if anything would ever feel normal again, if the gaping hole left in her life could possibly be filled.

She had to be strong for Moira—and for the rest of the coven, too. But there were times, sitting crying on the floor in her shower, when she wished with all her heart that she was a teenager again, home in Widow's Vale, and that she could come out of the shower and see her adoptive mother and have everything be all right.

Her adoptive parents, Sean and Mary Grace Rowlands, still lived in Widow's Vale. They'd been crushed when she'd moved to Ireland—especially since it had been clear she was going to fulfill her heritage as a blood witch of Belwicket, her birth mother's ancestral clan. But now they were getting older. How much longer would she have them? She hadn't been to America in ten months. Morgan's younger sister,

Mary K., had married two years ago and was now expecting twins at the age of thirty-four. Morgan would have loved to have been closer to her during this exciting time, to be more involved in her family's lives. But they were there, and she was here. This was the life she'd made for herself.

Her senses prickled and Morgan stood still, focusing. Moira was coming up the front walk. Quickly Morgan dried her hands on a dish towel and went to the front door. She opened it just as Moira reached the house and ushered her in fast, shutting and locking the door after her. Suddenly everything outside seemed unknown and scary, unpredictable.

"Where were you?" she said, holding Moira's shoulders, making sure she was fine. "I've been so worried. Why didn't you call?"

Moira's long, strawberry blond hair was tangled by the night wind, there were roses in her cheeks, and she was rubbing her hands together and blowing on them.

"I'm sorry, Mum," Moira said. "I completely forgot. But I was just down in Cobh. Caught the bus back." Her hazel eyes were lit with excitement, and Morgan could feel a mixture of emotions coming from her. Moira eased out of Morgan's grip and dumped her book bag onto the rocking chair. "I went out to tea after school, and I guess I lost track of time."

"It took you three hours to have tea?" Morgan asked.

"No," Moira said, her face losing some of its happy glow. "I was just at Margath's Faire." She casually flipped through the day's mail, pushing aside a few seed catalogs and not finding anything of interest.

Morgan began to do a slow burn, her fear turning to irritation. "Moira, look at me." Moira did, her face stiff and impatient. "I don't want to be your jail keeper," Morgan said, trying to keep her voice soft. "But I get very worried if you're not here when I expect you to be. I know we don't live in a dangerous town, but I can't help imagining all sorts of awful things happening." She tried to smile. "It's what a mother does. I need you to call me if you're going to be late. Unless you want me to start scrying to find you. Or send a witch message."

Moira's eyes narrowed. Clearly she didn't like the idea. Taking a different tack, Morgan thought back to her own parents being upset with her and then tried to do something different. "I need to know where you are and who you're with," she said calmly. "I need you to contact me if you're going to be late so I don't worry. I need to know when to expect you home."

What would Colm have done? How would he have handled this? "Were you with Tess or Vita?" Morgan asked, trying to sound less accusing and more interested. "Their folks don't mind if they're late?"

"No, I wasn't with them," Moira admitted, starting to pick at the upholstery of the rocking chair cushion. "At least, I was at first, but then they went."

After a moment of silence Morgan was forced to ask, "So who were you with?"

Moira tilted her head and looked up at the small window over the sink. Her face was angular where Colm's had been rounder, but Morgan expected Moira to fill out as she got older. As it was, she'd been surprised when Moira had reached her own height last year, when she was only fourteen. Now her daughter was actually taller than she was. At least she had Colm's straight, small nose instead of hers.

"A guy from my class."

Light began to dawn. Despite her natural prettiness, boys

seemed to find Moira intimidating. Morgan knew that Moira's friends had been dating for at least a year already. So now a boy had finally asked Moira out, and she'd gone, not wanting to blow her first chance. Morgan remembered only too well how it had felt to be a girl without a boyfriend after everyone else in class had paired up. It made one feel almost desperate, willing to listen to the first person who paid attention to her . . . like Cal.

"Oh. A boy," Morgan said, careful not to make too big a show of it. "So a boy asks you to tea, and you forget the call-your-mom rule?" As an American, Morgan still said Mom, though Moira had always copied Colm and called her Mum, or Mummy, when she was little.

"Yeah. We were just talking and hanging out, and I got so caught up. . . ." Moira sounded less combative. "Is it really almost seven?"

"Yes. Do you have a lot of homework?"

Moira rolled her eyes and nodded.

"Well, sit down and get to it," said Morgan. "I'll make you some tea." She stood up and put the kettle on, lighting the burner with a match. Crossing her arms over her chest, she said, "So who's the lucky guy? Do I know him?" She tried to picture some of the boys from Moira's class.

"Yeah, I think you do," Moira said offhandedly, pulling notebooks out of her book bag. "It was Ian Delaney, from Hewick, one town over."

*Delaney.* Morgan was speechless, her mind kicking into gear. Every alarm inside her began clanging. "Ian Delaney?" she finally got out. "From Ealltuinn?"

Moira shrugged.

Behind her, the teakettle whistled piercingly. Morgan jumped, then turned off the fire and moved the kettle.

"What are you *thinking*?" she asked Moira slowly, facing her daughter. In her mind she could picture Ian, a good-looking boy Moira's age, with clear, dark blue eyes and brown hair shot through with russet. Lilith Delaney, who was maybe ten years older than Morgan, had the same brown hair, streaked with gray, and the same dark blue eyes.

"You know the problems Belwicket's had with Ealltuinn," Morgan said. "They abuse their powers—they don't respect magick. And Ian is their leader's son." Their leader, who very possibly left that pouch in my garden, she added inwardly. She didn't want to tell Moira that part, though, without being sure.

Moira shrugged again, not looking at her. "I thought no one's sure about Ealltuinn," she said. "I mean, I've never seen anything about Ian that makes me think he's into dark magick or anything."

Morgan's breath came more shallowly. When she'd been barely older than Moira, she had fallen for Cal Blaire, the good-looking son of Selene Belltower, a witch who worked dark magick. Morgan would do anything to protect Moira from making the same mistake. Lilith was no Selene, but still, if that pouch *had* come from her . . .

"Moira, when a coven celebrates power rather than life, when they strive to hold others down instead of uplifting themselves, when they don't live within the rhythm of the seasons but instead bend the seasons to their will, we call that 'dark,'" said Morgan. "Ealltuinn does all that and more since Lilith became their high priestess."

Moira looked uneasy, but then Colm's expression of

stubbornness settled over her face, and Morgan braced herself for a long haul.

"But Ian seems different," Moira said, sounding reasonable. "He never mentions any of that stuff. He's been in my school for two years. People like him—he's never done anything mean to anyone. I've seen him be nice to the shop cat at Margath's Faire when no one's even looking." She stopped, a faint blush coming to her cheeks. "He doesn't talk badly about anyone, and especially not about Belwicket. I've talked to him a few times, and it seems like if he was working dark magick, it would come out somehow. I would sense it. Don't you think?"

Morgan had to bite her lips. Moira was so naive. She'd grown up in a content coven with members who all worked hard to live in harmony with each other and the world. She had never seen the things Morgan had seen, had never had to face true dark magick, had never had to fight for her life or the lives of people she loved. Morgan had—and it had all started when Cal had promised he loved her. He had really loved her power, her potential. Moira showed the same power and potential, and Ian could very well be pursuing her at his mother's command.

But Morgan would never allow Moira to be used the way Cal and Selene had wanted to use her. Moira was her only child, Colm's daughter, all she had left of the husband she had loved.

"Moira, I know you don't want to hear this, and you might not totally understand it right now, but I forbid you to see Ian Delaney again," Morgan said. She almost never came down hard on her daughter, but in this case she would do anything to prevent disaster. "I don't care if he has a halo glowing around his head. He's Lilith's son, and it's just too risky right now."

Moira looked dismayed, then angry. "What?" she cried. "You can't just tell me who I can or can't see!"

*"Au contraire,"* Morgan said firmly. "That's exactly what I'm doing." Then her face softened a bit. "Moira—I know what it's like when you like someone or you really want someone to like you. But it's so easy to get hurt. It's so easy not to see the big picture because all you're doing is looking into someone's eyes. But looking only into someone's eyes can blind you."

"Mum, I can't live in a—a—a *snow globe*," Moira said. "You can't just decide everything I'm going to do without even knowing Ian or totally knowing Ealltuinn. Some things I have to decide for myself. I'm fifteen, not a little kid. I'm not being stupid about Ian—if he was evil, I'd drop him. But you have to let me find out for myself. You might be really powerful and a great healer, but you don't know *everything*. Do you?"

Moira was a much better arguer than Morgan had been at that age, Morgan realized.

"Do you, Mum? Do you know Ian? Have you talked to him or done a tàth meànma? Can you *definitely* say that Ian works dark magick and I should never speak to him again?"

Morgan raised her eyebrows, choppy images from the past careening across her consciousness. Cal, seducing Morgan with his love, his kisses, his touch. How desperately she had wanted to believe him. The sincere joy of learning magick from him. Then—Cal locking Morgan into his seòmar, his secret room, and setting it on fire.

"No," Morgan admitted. "I can't say that definitely. But I *can* say that life experience has shown me that it's very hard for children not to be like their parents." With sickening quickness she remembered that she was the daughter of

Ciaran MacEwan. But that was different. "I think that Ealltuinn might be dark, and I think that Ian probably won't be able to help being part of it. And I don't want you to be hurt because of it. Do you understand? Can you see where I'm coming from? Do you think it's wrong for me to try to protect you? I'm not saying I want you to be alone and unhappy. I'm just saying that choosing the son of the evil leader of a rival coven is a mistake that you can avoid. Choose someone else."

"Like who?" Moira cried. "They have to like me, too, you know."

"Someone else will like you," Morgan promised. "Just leave Ian to Ealltuinn."

"I don't want someone else," Moira said. "I want Ian. He makes me laugh. He's really smart, he thinks I'm smart. He thinks I'm *amazing*. It's just—real. How we feel about each other is real."

"How can you know?" Morgan responded. "How would you know if anything he told you was real?"

Moira's face set. She picked up her mug of tea and her book bag and walked stiffly over to the stairs. "I just do."

Morgan watched her daughter walk upstairs, feeling as if she had lost another battle but not sure how it could have gone differently. Goddess, Ian Delaney! Anyone but Ian Delaney. Slowly Morgan lowered her head onto her arms, crossed on the tabletop. Breathe, breathe, she reminded herself. *Colm, I could really use your help right now.*

It was just eerie, the similarity between what was happening now to Moira with Ian and what had happened to her so long ago with Cal. She had never told Moira about Cal and Selene—only briefly skimmed over finding out she was a witch, then studying in Scotland for a summer, then how Katrina had asked her to come to Ireland. Moira had read Colin's Books of Shadows, and some of Morgan's, but none from that tumultuous period in Morgan's life. Cal and Selene were still Morgan's secret. As was Hunter. As was the fact that Morgan was Ciaran MacEwan's daughter. She'd never actually lied to Moira—but when Moira had assumed that Angus Bramson was her natural grandfather, Morgan had let her. It was so much better than telling her that her grandfather was one of the most evil witches in generations and that he had locked Morgan's birth mother, Maeve, in a barn and burned her to death.

Likewise with Hunter. What would be the good of telling Moira that Colm wasn't the only man Morgan had loved and lost? After Hunter had drowned in the ferry accident, Morgan hardly remembered what happened—losing Hunter had snapped her soul in half. She remembered being in a hospital. Her parents had come over from America, with Mary K. They'd wanted to take her home to New York, but Katrina and Pawel had convinced them that her best healing would be done in Ireland and that it would be dangerous to move her. There followed a time when she lived in Katrina and Pawel's house, and the coven had performed one healing rite after another.

Then Colm had asked her to marry him. Morgan had hardly been able to think, but she cared for Colm and in desperation saw it as a fresh start. Two months later she was expecting a baby and was just starting to come out of the fog.

It had almost been a shock when it had finally sunk in that she married Colm, but the awful thing had been how grateful she'd felt for his comfort. She was terrified of being alone, afraid of what might happen while she was asleep, and with Colm she'd thought she would never be alone again. She'd struggled for years with the twin feelings of searing guilt and humbling gratitude, but as time passed and Moira grew, Morgan began to accept that this had been her life's destiny all along. She'd never been madly in love with Colm, and she felt that in some way he'd known it. But she'd always cared for him as a friend, and over the years her caring had deepened into a true and sincere love. She'd tried hard to be a good wife, and she hoped she'd made Colm happy. She hoped that before he'd died, he'd known that he had made her happy, too, in a calm, joyful way.

She'd also found fulfillment in the rest of her life. Gifted teachers had worked with her to increase her natural healing abilities, and as Moira had gotten older and needed less attention, Morgan had begun traveling all over the world teaching others and performing healing rites. When she was home, life was peaceful and contented. Time was marked by Sabbats and celebrations, the turning of the seasons, the waxing and waning of the moon. It wasn't the flash fire of passion that she'd felt with Hunter, the desperate, bone-deep joining of soul and body that they'd shared, but instead it was like the gentle crackle of a fireplace, a place to soothe and comfort. Which was fine, good, better than she could have hoped.

And until this moment she'd never thought of her life in any other way. She loved her husband, adored her daughter, enjoyed her work. She felt embraced by her community and had made several good friends. In fact, the last sixteen years, at least until Colm's death, had been a kind of victory for Morgan. In the first year of discovering her heritage she'd undergone more pain—both physical and emotional—felt more freezing fear, had higher highs and lower lows than she could have possibly imagined a human being experiencing. She'd had her heart broken ruthlessly, had made murderous enemies, had been forced to make soul-destroying choices, choosing the greater good over the individual's life—even when that individual was her own father. And all before she was eighteen.

So to have had sixteen years of study and practice, of having no one try to kill her and not being forced to kill anyone else, well, that had seemed like a victory, a triumph of good over evil.

Until today, when she'd found a hex pouch in her garden and seen a vision in her window. Now she couldn't shake the feeling that not only was she at risk, but so was her daughter.

Morgan sighed. Was she overreacting because of her past? Getting up, Morgan made sure Bixby was in and that the front door was locked—an old habit from living in America. In Wicklow many people rarely bothered to lock their doors. Then she turned off the downstairs lights and cast her senses strongly all around her house. Nothing out of the ordinary. Later, writing in her Book of Shadows in bed, she heard Moira in the bathroom. Long after the house was quiet, after Morgan sensed that Moira was sleeping and that Bixby and Finnegan had passed into cat and dog versions of dreaming, Morgan lay dry-eyed in the night, staring up at the ceiling.

# 3.
# Moira

"Tell us all," Tess commanded the instant Moira walked up. Vita was eating a bag of crisps, but she nodded eagerly.

Moira grinned. Finally she had a lad of her own for *them* to ask about! After the last six months it was so great to have this huge, fun thing to be happy about. "Well," she said dramatically as the three of them started to walk down High Street. "What do you want to know?"

"Everything," Vita said. "What was said. What was done. Who kissed who."

Feeling her face flush, Moira laughed self-consciously. Tess had called that morning to arrange to meet early, before spellcraft class, so Moira could give them a rundown of her time with Ian. Today was unusually sunny and warm, with only fat, puffy clouds in the sky. It was hard to believe it would be Samhain in a few weeks.

"Well, we were there until almost six-thirty," Moira said. "I got home brutally late and Mum had forty fits."

"Enough about Mum," said Tess. "More about Ian. Six-thirty? All at Margath's Faire?"

They turned down Merchant Street, staying on the sunny side.

"Yeah," said Moira. "We just sat there and talked and talked. I looked up and almost two hours had gone by."

"Holding hands?" Vita pressed.

"After a while," Moira said, feeling pleased and embarrassed at the same time. "He took my hand and told me I was amazing."

Tess and Vita gave each other wide-eyed looks.

*"Amazing,"* Tess said approvingly. "Very good word. One point for Ian. What else?"

Wrinkling her nose, Moira thought back. She remembered a lot of staring into each other's eyes. "Um, we talked about music—he's learning the bodhran. Initiation classes—he was initiated last year but is still studying herbology. Books. Movies—he said maybe we could go see a film next week."

"Yes!" said Vita. "Well done."

They turned into a narrow side street called Printer's Alley. Only a bare strip of sunlight lit the very center of the slanted cobbled road. Buildings on either side rose three stories in the air, their gray stucco chipped in places and exposing stones and bricks. A few tiny shops, barely more than closets with open doors, dotted the street like colorful flowers growing out of concrete.

"It was just really brilliant," Moira said. "He's so great—so funny. We looked around the café and made up life stories about everyone who sat there. I thought I was going to fall out of my chair." She didn't mention the magick they had done. It seemed private, a secret between her and Ian.

Vita laughed. "Sounds like a good time was had by all. Do you think he could be your—" She paused, exchanging a glance with Tess. "Your *mùirn beatha dàn?*"

Moira's cheeks flushed. The truth was, she'd been wondering the same thing for a while now and especially after yesterday. Ever since she'd first learned what a mùirn beatha dàn was, she'd been dreaming of what it would feel like to meet hers. A true soul mate—it was just incredible. And what if Ian really was her MBD? It would be so amazing if she'd already found him. "I don't know," she admitted. "But . . . maybe."

"So did you talk about your covens at all?" Tess asked. "What's his take on Belwicket?"

"We only talked about it a little bit," said Moira. "Like about being initiated. And how he was a high priestess's son, and what that meant, and how my mum would probably be high priestess someday. It's something we have in common, trying to live up to powerful parents."

"I don't know, Moira," said Vita. "Your powers are wicked. The ladybug thing . . ."

Moira laughed, enjoying the remembered triumph. "Anyway," she said, "enough about me. Are you going to circle tonight, then?"

"Sure," said Vita. They were almost at the home of their spellcraft teacher, and unconsciously the three girls slowed down, reluctant to spend a rare sunny day inside studying.

Tess heaved a long-suffering breath. "Yeah, kicking and screaming," she said. "It's bad enough I have to spend part of my Saturday day at initiation class when I don't care about being initiated, but to give up Saturday night, too . . . It's just brutal."

"You still don't want to get initiated?" Vita asked her, brushing her feathery blond hair out of her face. "Ten years from now you'll be the only adult who still can't work the harder spells."

"I don't care." Tess scuffed her black suede boots against the uneven cobbles of the street. "It just isn't for me. It's so old-fashioned. The other day I had a splitting headache, and Mum was like, let me brew some herbs. I just wanted to go to the chemist's and get some proper drugs." She frowned and played with the magenta tips of her dark hair.

Moira gave her a sympathetic look, then realized they were at their teacher's stoop, a single concrete block in front of a red-painted door.

Tess sighed in resignation, and then the door opened and Keady Dove smiled out at them. "Hello, ladies," she said. "Come in. What a beautiful day, nae? I won't keep you too long."

Inside the small house the three girls went automatically to the back room that overlooked the garden. The sun overhead shone on the neat rows of herbs and flowers; there was a tiny patch for vegetables in the southern corner. Everything was tidy, the roses deadheaded, the cosmos tied up, the parsley trimmed. Moira thought it looked soothing and restful, like a good witch's garden should. She saw Tess looking at it also, an expression of disinterest on her face. Moira was torn—she admired Tess's outspokenness and could sympathize with her not wanting to automatically continue on a path she herself hadn't chosen. Still, to Moira, Wicca seemed as natural and omnipresent as the sea.

"Right," said Keady, rolling up her sleeves. She sat down at the tall table, and the three girls sat on the tall stools across from her. "Let me see what you've done since Monday. You were suppose to craft one spell using a phase of the moon and one that would affect some kind of insect."

Moira handed hers over. She'd gone ahead and written up the ladybug spell, planning to emphasize its excellent spellcraft and skim over the fact that it was frivolous and purposeless. She waited silently while Keady looked at it, keeping her face expressionless when her teacher frowned slightly and looked at her. Keady closed Moira's book and slid it back across the table.

"I remember how proud your dad was when you took first place in junior spellcraft," Keady said, her casual mention of Colm making Moira press her lips together. "Your dad didn't make spells often, but when he did, they were lovely, clean, well crafted. As yours are. However, his had more use and were less self-centered. Have you looked at his old Books of Shadows?"

Moira nodded, embarrassed. "A bit. He didn't do many spells."

"No," Keady agreed. "How about your mother, then? She's been crafting rites and spells along with your gran for years. Have you looked at her books?"

"A few. Some of the recent ones."

"It would also be interesting to look at the ones she started keeping right at the beginning, even before she was initiated." Keady looked at her pupils. "That's how we learn, from the past, from the witches who went before us. The books of our families are always particularly helpful because different forms and patterns of spells often run in families and clans. Sometimes that's due to tradition, sometimes to little quirks in our heritage that make one type of spell more effective for us. My mum always crafted terrific spells with gems, rocks, and crystals." Keady grinned, her smooth tan face creasing with humor. "However, we ran like hell when she tried to get us to sample her herbal concoctions."

Moira and Vita laughed, and even Tess cracked a smile.

The class turned to business as their teacher critiqued their homework in more detail and assigned them work for next Wednesday. Then she led them to her circle room for practice.

Quickly and accurately, Keady drew an open circle on the smooth wooden floor. Its once-dark boards were irrevocably stained white from years of making chalk circles. Keady actually made her own chalk sticks, and they were part of her rituals. There were natural chalk pits not far from Cobh, and for a fee one could go and hack bits out of a wall. Keady did this, then carefully carved the hard white chalk into shapes, wands, figures of people or animals, short staffs topped with runes or sigils. She kept Margath's Faire stocked with special chalks and made some extra money this way.

"Everyone in," she directed. The three girls walked through the opening of the circle and sat down, one at each of the corners of the compass, with Keady to the east. "We're going to practice transferring energy," Keady said. "Each of us will meditate alone for five minutes, drawing energy to us, using the spell I taught you. At the end of five minutes, after you've opened yourself to receive energy from the universe, we'll join hands. Going deasil, we'll pass energy to each other through our hands. If we do it right," she said with a grin, "you should be able to feel something."

*What a waste of time.*

Moira jerked her head toward Tess, shocked that her friend would actually say this out loud, in front of their teacher. Tess sat cross-legged, her eyes closed, her hands in a loose, upward pinch on her knees. Her face was blank. Quickly Moira looked at Keady, then at Vita, and weirdly, neither of them seemed to have had any reaction. *Oh, wow, I picked up on it. Cool.* Witches of a certain power could send or receive witch messages—Moira, Tess, and Vita had been practicing for the past year, with varying degrees of success. Moira and her mum could definitely send messages to each other. But to pick up on someone's strong thoughts without their meaning to send them was something else. Moira smiled to herself, pleased at this demonstration that her own powers were slowly increasing.

Moira closed her eyes and straightened her spine, resting her hands lightly on her knees as the others were doing. *Right. Concentrate.* Her trousers were itching her, right in back where the tag was. She wondered if she looked like a scarecrow in them. Vita had soft, feminine curves, with actual hips and boobs. When a dip at school had tried to tell her she was fat, Vita had just laughed. "I think I look good," she had said. "And so does *your* boyfriend." Moira smiled at the memory. Vita was really comfortable with herself, her body. Unlike Moira, who was so tall and thin. Not slender, not petite, not in shape, just thin. Mum kept telling her she would fill out, but—

*Moira's all over the place.*

Moira's eyes snapped open at Keady's voice, ready to deny it. But again, everyone's eyes were closed, and her teacher gave no indication that she had spoken. Moira felt a jolt of excitement. Wow—this was amazing. She was definitely getting stronger. *Now concentrate, concentrate. Focus. Breathe.*

For as far back as Moira could remember, her mother had said those words. In the small room tacked onto the living room, where the family worked their magick, Moira had witnessed her parents, and especially her mother, meditating, focusing, breathing. She had allowed Moira to join her when Moira was three. Moira thought sadly on those days, when she had felt so close to her mum. She'd always felt really close to her until just last year, when suddenly Dad had seemed more understanding. It was when she had begun to prepare for her initiation, she realized. The whole thing seemed to make Mum tense, anxious that Moira do well.

*Breathe. Focus. Quit thinking.* Moira imagined a candle in front of her, a white pillar on the floor, glowing with a single flame. She focused on its flickering, on the ebb and flow of the flame growing and dying, one second at a time. In a few moments she became the flame, inhaling its heat and light and releasing its energy with her breath. *I am the flame. I am burning. I am white-hot. I am made of fire.*

"Right," said Keady's quiet voice, floating gently through the air. "Slowly, slowly, open your eyes, as if they were fine linen being lifted by a breeze."

Moira opened her eyes, and it seemed that the room had changed somehow. Maybe the sun had shifted. Something felt different. Looked different. Moira blinked. Things looked a little hazy. No, wait—it was just around their heads. There was a bright glow around Tess's, Vita's, and Keady's heads.

"Now," Keady said, "let's hold out our hands. When I tell you to, join hands. One person will send, one will receive. Repeat after me: A force of life I draw to me. It fills me with its light. I use this light to help me see. And in my spells I use its might."

Moira repeated the words, and they seemed to sink deep within her, as if they were smooth stones dropping gently through water to land silently on a bed of silt.

"Tess, receive my energy," said Keady, holding out her hand. Tess reached out and clasped her hand, then gave a small but visible jump. Her eyes opened a bit wider, and she lost her bored demeanor for a second.

"Now, Tess, give your energy to me and to Vita."

Tess clasped hands with both Vita and Keady, and though Vita seemed expectant, her expression didn't change. "I don't feel much of anything," she whispered.

"That's all right," Keady said. "Now, Vita, give your energy to Moira and Tess."

Moira held out her hand and took hold of Vita's smooth, soft palm. Vita's hand was smaller than hers and much less muscular. Moira let her eyes close halfway and focused on what she was receiving from Vita. Was that a faint tingling sensation? Yes, she thought it was. So Vita was actually sending her energy? Cool. She opened her eyes and nodded at Vita, who grinned and looked pleased.

"Good, Vita," Keady said encouragingly. "I can see your extra practicing has paid off. Right, then, now Moira. Give your energy to me and Vita."

Moira closed her eyes. *Focus. Breathe.* Silently she repeated the words: *A force of life I draw to me. It fills me with its light. I use this light to help me see. And in my spells I use its might.*

She breathed in, and with that breath she seemed to draw the whole room in with her. Holding her breath, she felt energy rise within her—something she'd never felt so strongly before. It was a bit scary, actually, but Keady was here and would keep her safe. Power and energy and magick and joy seemed about to explode inside her. Slowly she held out her hands, unsure if she was doing anything correctly or if she had gotten it all wrong.

*Energy, I send you out.* Moira imagined herself as a glowing flame, pouring energy out through her hands like sunbeams.

Keady took her hand first, and Moira felt an electrifying contact, like pure heat was pouring through her hand. Suddenly Moira knew a kind of exhilaration she'd never imagined existed. In the next second Vita took her other hand, and Moira felt it all again, but only for a second. Vita gasped and dropped her hand quickly, and Moira's eyes snapped open.

Vita looked startled and a little afraid. She stared first at Moira and then at her own hand. Moira quickly glanced at Keady and saw that the older woman was gripping her hand firmly, easily taking the sent energy and measuring it. As soon as Moira's concentration broke, everything shut down, and within a minute she felt almost totally normal. Almost.

Self-conscious, and a mite dizzy, Moira drew her hands back and folded them in her lap.

"What did you do?" asked Vita.

"What happened?" Tess asked, having seen nothing except Vita dropping Moira's hand.

"Very good, Moira," said Keady quietly, looking at Moira's face. "Have you been practicing?"

"A little. Not a whole lot," Moira admitted. "But I remembered seeing my mum call energy. She talked about how it can increase the power of spells and so on." Moira shrugged and began to trace a random pattern on her knee.

"I see," said Keady. She got to her feet and opened the circle, murmuring words to dispel magick and restore calm to the room's own energy. "I think that's enough for today. You have your assignments for next Wednesday. Go home and work on your spells and your Books of Shadows, and I'll see you at the circle tonight."

Moira started to pull on her jacket, but Keady put out a hand to detain her. Tess and Vita left without her, looking back with raised brows. Moira shrugged a silent "I don't know" and pantomimed calling them later.

Keady put the kettle on for tea, glancing thoughtfully at Moira.

"That was both unexpected and expected," she said, putting out their cups. "It was unexpected because I haven't seen that level of power from you before, and we've been working together for eight months now. It was also expected because you're Morgan Byrne's daughter. I couldn't help wondering if you had inherited her power."

Moira looked into Keady's clear eyes, the color of fog. "I feel like my powers are growing, getting stronger," she said. "But I don't know if it's like my mum's power—I don't even know what her power's *like*. I mean, I know she's a strong healer. People call her from all over the world for help. The spells she works look effortless, smooth and perfect. And I know everyone speaks of her power and her magick. But I don't think *I've* seen her work too much really big magick."

For a minute her teacher was quiet. She swirled the loose tea leaves in the steamy water. The sweet smell of tea filled Moira's nose, and she inhaled.

"If you have the power of a huge, rushing river, sometimes it's most effective to harness it and dole it out, as with a dam," her teacher said finally. "Sometimes if you let the river run free, it can destroy more than it can build."

Moira looked at her. It seemed a quality of witches to never answer questions directly. "It's just strange—I *know* she's powerful, she's Morgan of Belwicket. But that kind of big 'rushing river' stuff doesn't come up in the day-to-day." She laughed a little, and Keady smiled.

"How much do you know about your mum's life before she came here and helped revive Belwicket?"

Moira frowned. "Well, she's American. She was adopted. She found out she was a blood witch when she was sixteen. After high school she went to Scotland for a summer to study with the Gray Witches. When Gran found out Maeve Riordan's daughter was alive, she tracked Mum down and asked her to move here and help re-form the original Belwicket. Then Mum married Dad, and I was born. Now she's become an important healer, and she travels a lot." Moira let out a breath, releasing the tension she felt about how much her mum worked. "Now Mum's getting ready to become high priestess of Belwicket."

"It isn't my place to tell you any more about your own mother," said Keady. "But I can tell you that the fact that you've not witnessed anything that would strike fear into your soul is a good thing." She smiled dryly when Moira frowned. "The true strength of a witch can be measured by how much she or he does *not* resort to big magick, how much they can give themselves over to study, reflection, peace. The fact that someone can work big magick is an accomplishment. The fact that someone can work big magick but chooses not to unless strictly necessary is a greater accomplishment. Do you see?"

This was a picture of her mother that Moira was having trouble imagining. "Are you saying that Mum could strike fear into someone's soul?" she asked.

"I'm saying that yes, your mother is a witch of unusual, and even fearsome, powers," Keady said solemnly. The words gave Moira a slight chill. "There have been very few witches within recorded history who could equal Morgan," her teacher went on. "A power that great is a beautiful and also a frightening thing. And Moira? There are very few happy uses for a power such as that, do you understand? It isn't your mother's place to bring springtime or end war, or make everyone fall in love, or keep a whole village healthy. And your mother would never use her magick for dark purposes, we know. Can you think of a purpose that is left, that is both true and on the side of right, yet would allow the expression of an almost inconceivably great power?"

Moira frowned at Keady, realizing what she was getting at.

"It would be for defense," Keady said, her voice very quiet and deliberate. "To fight evil. It would be used in a battle of good against evil on a scale that's difficult for you to comprehend. And it's difficult for you to comprehend because . . . your mother, and your father, too, worked very hard their whole lives to make sure that you, their daughter, lived in a world where the most appropriate expression of power . . . is to heal people."

Moira felt as if she had stepped out of her normal Saturday spellcraft lesson and into a comic book about superheroes.

"To be fifteen years old, the daughter of Morgan Byrne, and to have no idea of such matters—it's a blessing, a gift. One that you will be thankful for, again and again, in the future." Keady looked at Moira steadily, then seemed to think she had said enough.

In silence Moira finished her tea, mumbled good-bye, took her things, and left.

"Keady says it would be helpful to read your and Dad's Books of Shadows," Moira said that afternoon.

"I think I gave them to you," her mother said, stirring the pot on the stove. She sniffed its scent and then looked at her watch.

"You gave me most of them, but I think it would be good to read your very first ones, even before you were initiated, when you were first learning about spells," said Moira. An odd expression crossed her mum's face for just a moment and then passed.

"Gosh, that was so long ago," her mother murmured. "I'm not sure where they are."

"Didn't Dad say once that all of both of your old stuff was in those crates down in the cellar?" Moira persisted.

Her mother looked thoughtful. "I'm not sure."

"Well, I could really use them," Moira said. "It would help me for my initiation. Can I try to find them?"

Her mum looked distinctly uncomfortable, but Moira wasn't going to back down, not after the things Keady had said.

"I guess," was her mum's unenthusiastic reply. "But I'll get them for you when I have a minute."

"Brilliant," said Moira, standing up and putting her dishes in the sink. As she was heading upstairs, her mom said, "Don't forget—circle in an hour."

"Right," Moira called back.

"I miss having circles outside, like in summer," Moira said. She and her mum were walking briskly down the road toward Katrina's. The sun had set, and with no streetlights the night was a solid velvety black. With magesight, kind of like a witch's night vision, Moira stepped surely on the rutted, uneven road.

"Yes," said her mother. "Being outside is always good. But it's nice to have a place to be warm and dry as well."

Soon they had almost caught up to Brett and Lacey Hawkstone and their daughter, Lizzie, who was fourteen and would start her initiation classes at Yule. Ahead of them Michelle Moore walked with her partner, Fillipa Gregg.

"Today at class I sent some energy to Keady," Moira said.

"Really?" Her mother smiled at her and seemed glad but neither surprised nor ecstatic. "Good for you. I'm sure Keady was pleased. Oh, look, Fillipa needs help carrying that bag. Let's hurry."

As the group approached the store, Moira's gran appeared in the doorway of her cottage. "Hello! Come in," said Gran, smiling. She closed the front door to her house and met them by the store's entrance. Her house was a small, thick-walled cottage, and the old store was attached directly to it. It had been a tiny country store, just one large room. Five years ago the coven had joined together and whitewashed the inside, sanded the floor, and painted good luck charms and symbols all around the room's perimeter. There were four small windows, high up on the thick walls, and a double-wide front door. The only other door led into Gran's back pantry in her house.

"Hi, Gran," said Moira, kissing her. She sniffed, then wiggled her eyebrows expectantly.

"Yes, those are gingersnaps you smell," Katrina told her with a laugh. "I felt like baking this afternoon. We'll have them after circle."

"Morgan," said Hartwell Moss, coming over to hug Moira's mum. "How are you? Rough week?"

"Not too bad," said Moira's mum, but something in her voice made Moira look at her more closely. Were those lines of tension around her eyes? Was her mouth tight? Moira tried casting her senses and picked up on a lot of anxiety. Was it just because Moira had been late last night, or was something else going on?

"Hello!" Gran called, opening her arms wide. "Hello, every-one, and good evening to you. Welcome. Is everyone here, then?" Though she was heavyset and walked slowly because of arthritis, Moira thought her grandmother still made a wonderful high priestess for their coven. Her gray hair was pulled back with silver combs and her long, dove-gray linen robe was imprinted in black with simple images of the sea.

"Hello, good evening," people answered in various forms. Moira counted: twenty-one people here tonight, a good num-ber. In the winter it often drifted down to eight or nine, when the weather made some of the higher roads risky; in spring the number could swell to over twenty. Even their coven obeyed the law of wax and wane, the turn of the wheel.

Standing at the head of the room, Katrina clasped her hands and smiled. "The sun has gone down, and we are embraced by the harvest moon, nae? There's a crispness in the air that tells us leaves will soon fall, days will grow shorter, and we'll be staying more by our firesides. What a joyful time is autumn! We gather in our harvest, collecting Mother Earth's bounty, her gifts to us. We till the soil, and the soil feeds us. Or, for some of us, we think fondly of our soil but buy our veggies from the market!"

People laughed. Moira felt proud of her grandmother.

"Lammas is behind us: we look ahead to Mabon," Katrina went on. "We're planning a special Mabon feast, of course, so please talk to Susan if you'd like to contribute food, drink, candles, decorations, or just your time. Thank you very much. Now, I've already drawn our circle here, you can see, but if you'll forgive me, I'd like to ask Morgan to lead us tonight. Maybe I've overdone things a little lately."

Moira glanced at her mother, who was looking at Katrina with affection. Morgan nodded slightly, and, looking relieved, Katrina moved to the side.

"Can you all please come into the circle?" asked Morgan, and the coven members filed in through the opening that Gran had left. Quickly Morgan went around the circle and sketched the rune Eolh at the east, Tyr at the north, Thorn at the west, and Ur at the south. Moira silently recited their meanings: protection, victory in battle, overcoming adversity, and strength. Powerful runes, runes of protection. As if the coven were under siege. Moira remembered what Keady had said about Morgan's power being used for defense and wondered what was this was about.

Next Morgan lit a stick of incense and placed it behind the rune Tyr. She set a silver cup of water next to Thorn and a silver cup of smooth pebbles at Ur. Next to Eolh she lit a tall orange candle. Finally Morgan took her place in the circle, between Katrina and Lacey Hawkstone. Everyone clasped hands and raised them overhead. Moira had moved till she was between Vita and Tess, who had also edged away from their parents. Tess squeezed her hand—Moira knew she'd rather be home watching television. Across the room Keady Dove smiled at her.

"I welcome the Goddess and the God to tonight's circle,

and I hope they find favor with our gathering," Morgan began. "I dedicate this circle to our coming harvest, to our safe passage into winter, and to our spirit of community. We're a chain, all of us connected and entwined. We help each other, we support each other. Our links form a strong fence, and within it we can protect our own."

Moira saw that a few people were glancing at each other. They were probably wondering what was going on, with the runes of protection and Morgan talking about being a fence. Moira hoped she wouldn't start talking about Ealltuinn. Maybe Ealltuinn wasn't as particular about following the Wiccan Rede as Belwicket was. There were lots of covens who weren't. But that didn't make them evil.

"Since we're in the middle of our harvest season," Morgan said, "let's give thanks now for things that we have drawn to us, for our times of fruitfulness, for the gifts of the land. Life has given us each incomparable riches."

"I'm thankful for my new pony," said Lizzie Hawkstone. "He's beautiful and smart."

"I'm thankful my mum recovered from her illness," said Michelle.

"I bless the Goddess for my garden's bounty," said Christa Ryan, who was Moira's herbology teacher.

"I'm thankful for the wonderful gift of my daughter-in-law and for my beautiful granddaughter," said Katrina. She smiled at Moira, and Moira smiled back.

"I'm grateful for family and friends," Moira said, falling back on an old standard.

"Thanks to the Goddess for the rains and the wind, for they've kept me cozy inside," said Fillipa. "Thanks also to the library in town—they just got in a shipment of new books."

"I thank the Goddess for my daughter," Morgan said quietly. "I thank time for passing, however slowly. I thank the wheel for turning and for helping grief to ease someday."

That was about Moira's dad, and she felt people glancing at her in sympathy. She nodded, looking at her feet, acknowledging her mother's words.

The circle went around, each person contributing something or not as they wished. Then Morgan lifted her left foot and leaned to the left, and the group began a sort of half-walking, half-skipping circle, where it felt like dancing. Moira felt her heart lifting, her blood circulating, and knew that her mum had chosen this to increase the positive, lighthearted energy.

Morgan started singing, one of the ancient songs with words that had lost their definitions but not their meanings. Her rich alto wove a melody around the circle, and Katrina took it up, singing different words but layering her melody above and beneath Morgan's. Soon Will Fereston joined in, and Keady, and then most of the coven members were singing. Some were singing songs they'd learned as children or been taught recently. Some were simply making sounds that blended with the others. Moira was trying to copy Morgan, singing the same notes at the same time. She'd never learned this song formally but had heard her mother sing it often—she called it one of her "power-draw" chants.

People were smiling, the circle was moving more quickly, and Moira could feel a joy, a lightness, enter the room. Even Katrina's arthritis didn't seem to be bothering her. People who had looked tired or stressed when they came in soon lost those expressions. Instead, faces were alight with the pleasure of sharing, with the gift of dancing. Moira laughed, holding tightly to Vita and Tess, hoping she wouldn't trip.

Then slowly Moira started to see a haze in the room—like everyone around her had grown fuzzy. This wasn't like the energy she'd seen with Keady, Tess, and Vita. She squinted, confused, as the haze grew heavier, darker, blurring her vision.

Just then Will, Michelle, and Susan started coughing. Then Moira coughed, not quite gagging, and an oily, bitter scent filled the air. Now a thick black smoke was creeping beneath the doors and around the shut windows, slipping in like tendrils of poison. One tendril began to coil around Katrina's foot.

Katrina flinched and started barking out ward-evil spells. Her sister, Susan, tried to help her but was coughing too much. The circle was broken; several people were on their knees, on the floor. Lizzie was trying not to cry, and old Hamish Murphy looked confused and frightened. Moira felt the panic grow.

"Mum!" Moira cried, dropping Tess's and Vita's hands. Morgan was standing stiffly, turning slowly to see every single thing that was happening in the room. Her face was white, her eyes wide. She looked both frightened and appalled, staring almost in disbelief at the smoke. Moira saw her lips start moving but couldn't hear her words.

"Mum!" Moira said again, reaching Morgan and taking her arm. Her mother gently shook her off, freeing herself without speaking.

While Moira watched, coughing, Morgan closed her eyes and held out her arms. Slowly she raised them in the air, and now Moira could hear her mother's words, low and intense and frightening. They were harsh words in a language that

Moira didn't recognize, and they sounded dark, spiky—words without forgiveness or explanation.

Michelle had reached the door, but it wouldn't open, and people began to panic as they realized they were trapped. Vita was huddled with her parents and younger brother, and Tess was standing by her folks. Keady and Christa were trying to help others, but they were coughing and red faced across the room. Aunt Susan looked as if she were about to faint. Moira stood alone, next to her mother. Once, Morgan opened her eyes and stared straight through Moira, and Moira almost cried out—her mother's normally brown eyes were glowing red, as if reflecting fire, and her face was changed, stronger. Moira could hardly recognize her, and that was perhaps even scarier than the smoke.

Closing her eyes again, Morgan began to draw runes and sigils in the air around her. Moira recognized more runes of protection but soon lost the shapes of the other, more complicated sigils. It was as if her mother were writing a story in the air, line after line. And still she muttered whatever chant had come to her.

Moira felt fear take over her body. The roiling smoke was choking everyone. She'd never seen her mother work magick like this, never seen her so consumed and practically glowing with power. Moira's eyes were stinging, her lungs burning. Coughing, she sank to her knees on the floor and suddenly thought of how she had sent energy to Keady. Could she do it again? Could it help somehow? She closed her eyes and automatically drew the symbol Eolh in the air in front of her. There was no time to draw circles of protection, overlain with different runes.

"An de allaigh," Moira began chanting under her breath, coughing at each word. She knew this power-draw chant well and closed her eyes while she chanted it as best she could. *Focus. Focus and concentrate.*

I open myself to the Goddess's power, Moira thought, trying to ignore the foul stench, the gagging smoke. She shut out the sounds of the room. *I open myself to the power of the universe.* She remembered Morgan's orange candle, set in the east. The smoke had snuffed it a minute ago, but Moira recalled its flame and pictured it in her mind.

Fire, fire, burning bright, she thought, everything else fading away. *I call power to me. I am power. I'm made of fire.* She felt it rise within her, as if a flower were blooming inside her chest. She inhaled through her nose, the acrid smell making her shudder. Holding her arms out at her sides, Moira felt power coming to her as if she were a lightning rod, being struck again and again with tiny, pinlike bolts of lightning.

The room was silent. Moira opened her eyes. People were moving, crying, shouting, trying to break a window. Her mother was standing in front of her, her arms coiled over her chest, her face contorted with effort. Her cheeks were flushed, and her brown hair was sticking to her forehead. Her fists were clenched.

Moira felt as if she were moving through gelatin, slowly and without sound, making ripples of movement all around her. She stood and leaned close to her mother, seeing power radiating from Morgan in a kind of unearthly glow.

*I send my power to you.* Moira reached out and covered Morgan's fists with her own. *I give my power to you.* And she truly did feel it leave her, a slipcase of white light sliding from her, through her hands, and draping lightly over the hands of her mother. Slowly, slowly, Morgan's hands opened, and Moira's cupped them, a two-layered flower of flesh, bones, and a pure, glorious, glowing light.

Then Morgan threw her arms up and open, her head snapped back, and a final shout tore from her throat. She sounded wolflike, Moira thought, startled, as strong as a wild animal, and at that instant a window exploded in a shower of glass.

Instantly the black smoke was sucked out of the room, as if the room had depressurized at a high altitude. Shiny shards of broken glass rained down like crystals, like ice. Moira's hands still touched Morgan's arms, below the elbows, and suddenly cool, damp air washed over her, fresh and clean and smelling of night. She could breathe now and heard sounds of choking and gasps of relief. Around her she felt the warm release of the most desperate fear, the worst of the tension.

Moira inhaled deeply, feeling that nothing had ever smelled so wonderful, so life-giving, as the wet-dirt smell of autumn night air. Her mother opened her eyes, and Moira was relieved to see that they were the mixed shades of brown, green, and gold that she knew. Maybe she had just imagined the glowy redness.

Morgan's arms lowered, and she took Moira's hands. She looked solemn but also brightly curious. "You gave me power," she said very softly, her voice hoarse.

Moira nodded, wide-eyed. "Like I did Keady," she whispered back.

"You helped save us," said her mother, and hugged her, and Moira hugged her back.

"Where did it come from?" Moira asked as they walked home along the country road. The moon was shining brightly, lighting their way. After the smoke had left, people had sat for an hour, recovering. Wine and water had washed the taste from their mouths, but no one had been able to eat anything. Finally, when her mum had been sure they were safe, the coven had disbanded.

"I'm not positive, but I think it was from Ealltuinn," answered her mother. She sighed. Moira waited for her to say something about Ian, but she didn't.

"That smoke—I was so scared," Moira said in a rush. "I was glad you had so much power. And at the same time, it was scary—I've never seen you like that."

Her mother licked her lips and brushed her bangs off her forehead. "Magick transforms everyone," she said.

Moira followed her mother home through the darkness, not sure what to say.

# 4.
# Morgan

Morgan looked up as Keady Dove let herself in through the green wooden gate that bordered Morgan's front yard.

" 'Lo," she said, brushing some hair out of her eyes. This morning, after Moira had left for her animal-work class in town, Morgan had paced the house restlessly. Last night it had taken all of her will to not show Moira how shocked and disturbed she had been by the black smoke. They had walked home in the darkness, with Morgan casting her senses, silently repeating ward-evil spells, trying to sound normal as her daughter asked her difficult questions to which she had no answers. She'd been awake all night thinking about what had happened and trying to make sense of everything. She was almost positive the smoke had come from Ealltuinn—she just couldn't think of any other possibility. And very likely it was connected to the pouch and to the vision. She had underestimated Lilith Delaney. Lilith was practicing dark magick against Belwicket, and Morgan had to find out why—and soon.

Thankfully at least Moira had been able to sleep last night

and hadn't been awoken by nightmares. Part of Morgan had wanted to keep Moira home with her today, not let her go to class. But Tess and Vita had met her at the bus stop, and it was broad daylight. . . .

Morgan smiled as Keady sat cross-legged on the sun-warmed bricks of the front path. She and Keady had been friends at least ten years, and in the six months since Colm's death Keady had been popping in to tutor Moira more regularly. Morgan was glad Moira had such a gifted teacher.

"I'm interrupting," said Keady, watching as Morgan pulled some small weeds from around her mums. They were starting to bloom; she would have some perfect orange, yellow, and rust-colored blooms by Samhain.

"Not at all. I wanted to talk to you after last night."

"Yes. Your garden's looking lovely, by the way."

"Thank you," said Morgan. She paused and sat back on her heels, knowing Keady hadn't come to discuss her garden. "Moira gave me energy last night."

"I saw, just barely," said Keady. "I was helping Will, who was really in a bad way. But I thought I saw her. She's showing quite a lot of promise."

Morgan nodded, quietly proud, then turned back to business. "I couldn't trace the spell last night. It had to have been Ealltuinn, though." She shook her head. "It's been so peaceful here for twenty years. Now to have an enemy who would go this far—" She couldn't express how furious she was at having her quiet life, her innocent daughter, her coven attacked in this way. Hadn't she already been through all that? Why was this happening again? She looked up at Keady. "How bad do you think it was?"

"It was bad," Keady said bluntly. "Another minute or two and Will, maybe Susan, maybe Lizzie Hawkstone, wouldn't have recovered. That stuff was foul, poisonous."

"It was terrible," Morgan agreed. "Thank the Goddess I was able to fight it." She met Keady's even gaze. "Is this about Belwicket or about me?"

Keady knew what Morgan meant. "You're a big stumbling block," she pointed out calmly. "Lilith's been pushing Ealltuinn, trying to become more and more powerful. She can't have a bunch of goody-goody Woodbanes getting in the way."

"I'm not the high priestess," Morgan pointed out, standing up and brushing off her knees.

"No, but it's common knowledge that the coven leaders want you to be. And you're Morgan Byrne! Everyone knows yours is the power to reckon with."

Morgan shook her head, about to howl with frustration. "Why can't power be a good thing? Long ago my power made me a target. Now it seems to be happening again. I can't bear it." Her fist clenched her trowel at her side, small clumps of earth dropping onto her shoe.

"What has a front has a back," said Keady. "And the bigger the front, the bigger the back. Everything must be balanced, good and evil, light and dark. Even if we don't want it to be."

Morgan looked at the sky, clear blue and sunny. So normal looking. This same sun was shining on someone who even now might be planning how best to defeat her, destroy her coven. A weight settled on her shoulders, the dread of what might be in store for her already taking its toll. She turned to Keady. "By that logic, if I turned dark and started doing terrible things, the world would be a better place because of the good that would erupt to balance it."

Keady gave a wry smile. "Let's not test that theory."

"No. Let's decide what we're going to do," Morgan said. "We need a plan. If the coven is under siege, we need to know how to protect it. Come on in and have some tea." She started walking toward the back, and Keady followed. "You know, on Friday, Katrina and I found a hex pouch in the garden."

"Really? Goddess. Had it harmed anything?"

"All the car—" Morgan stopped dead, staring at what lay smack in the middle of the path. Her mouth went dry in an instant.

"Oops, sorry," Keady said, bumping into her. "Problem?"

Morgan felt her friend leaning around to see. She didn't know what to think, what to do. "Uh . . ."

"What's that, then? Is that a chunk of quartz?"

"It's, uh . . ." It was like drowning, drowning in a sea of emotions.

Frowning slightly, Keady moved around Morgan and bent to pick it up.

"Wait!" Morgan put out a hand to stop Keady. Slowly she knelt and reached out to the stone. It was the size of a small apple, pale pink, translucent, clouded, and shot through with flaws. "It's morganite," she said, her voice sounding strangled.

Reluctantly, as if trying not to be burned, Morgan turned the stone this way and that until she found a flat side. Then she felt faint as her world swam and shifted sideways. The morganite had an image on it. *Oh, Goddess, oh, Goddess.* Morgan squinted, but the image was unrecognizable, just as that face in the window had been the other night. It was a person, maybe even a man. But who, dammit? She studied the face, her heart pounding, trying to make out the features, but they were too indistinct. She rubbed her finger over the image as if to clear away dirt, but it made no difference.

"Who is that?" Keady asked quietly.

"You see it, too?"

"Not clearly—oh, wait—it's gone."

It was true. As Morgan watched, the image faded from the stone, leaving Morgan holding an empty piece of quartz. Morganite quartz. One of the first gifts Hunter had ever given her had been a beautiful piece of morganite, and inside it Hunter had spelled a picture of his heart's desire: a picture of Morgan. That was how he had told her he loved her. Now here she was, sixteen years after his death, finding morganite on her garden path. And not just morganite—*spelled* morganite. Horrified, Morgan felt a sob rise in her throat, but she held it back. Her hands were shaking, and she felt every nerve in her body come alive. What was happening to her? Who was taunting her? Was it really Lilith? Why would she go to such lengths just because Morgan had disagreed with her publicly about a few spells?

"Morgan?" Keady touched the back of her hand gently, and when Morgan didn't respond, Keady took the piece of morganite out of her hand.

"It's morganite," Morgan said again, her voice cracking. "A kind of quartz. Not native to Ireland. A long time ago a different piece of morganite had a lot of significance for me. Someone put this here, on my path. Someone who knows me well. Someone who knows my past." She felt a spurt of fear and anger rise in her. She'd thought that her days of battle were over, that she was safe and free to live a peaceful life. Over the last three days that illusion had been stripped from her, and it was devastating.

Keady took Morgan's elbow and led her into the backyard. "Let's get that tea."

"The garden tools," Morgan said in a near whisper. She gestured to the shed, and Keady obediently detoured there. Morgan opened the shed door and mechanically hung up her few gardening tools. Something felt different. Her extra-sensitive senses picked up on something, alerting her consciousness, and Morgan looked around. Now wasn't the time to ignore signals like this. What was different? Her nerves were frayed and shot; she felt trembly and nauseated. All she wanted to do was sit down and have a hot cup of strong tea.

Then she saw it. The cellar door. It had been opened—there was a new scrape in the dirt where it had swung out, and the spiderweb had been recently broken. Cautiously Morgan turned the handle of the door. With everything that had been going on lately, she had no idea what to expect. Inside, Morgan tugged the light string, but nothing happened.

"One second, Keady," Morgan said, starting to descend the cellar steps. *Thank the Goddess for magesight,* Morgan thought. Even without the light she could see perfectly well. She pulled the downstairs light cord, but it didn't work either. Morgan didn't pick up on any vibrations . . . but there, in the corner, some old crates had been disturbed. In a second her conversation with Moira came back to her—Moira asking for Morgan's old Books of Shadows, Morgan being vague. *Oh, no.*

The crate was open, and all her Books of Shadows were gone. Moira must have gotten them this morning before class. Her first Books of Shadows, with their entries about Cal, about Hunter. Moira might be reading them right now. She might be discovering the magnitude of what her mother had kept from her. Why did this have to happen now, when so much else was going wrong?

Morgan rubbed her forehead with one hand, trying to ease her tension headache. It had been good having Keady here for a while. Morgan had spilled about everything: the ruined carrots, the face in the window, the significance of the morganite, Moira being late, Moira apparently taking all of Morgan's early Books of Shadows. The poisonous smoke.

"It all seems to be building up to something," Morgan had told Keady.

Keady had frowned. "I agree, but what? It's no secret that Lilith isn't a fan of yours, but would she really go this far? This kind of coven infighting just doesn't happen that often. And simple disagreements and bickering wouldn't lead to out-and-out attacks, would they? Maybe we should contact the New Charter."

"Yeah, maybe so." Morgan couldn't help feeling a familiar twinge at the mention of the New Charter. Even after all these years she couldn't hear the words without thinking of Hunter.

Keady had stayed until she was sure Morgan felt better. Since she had left, Morgan had been lying on the couch down-stairs, Bixby on her lap and Finnegan draped across her feet like a very heavy hot water bottle. She'd been thinking hard, trying to see some kind of pattern. Okay, assuming this was Ealltuinn, going after Belwicket and more specifically Morgan, why were they doing it now? Was this autumn significant in some way? Besides being the first autumn since Colm had died? *Oh, Colm.* Her heart ached for him, and she could almost see the appeal of creating a bith dearc, a window to the netherworld, in order to contact a loved one who had passed on. Almost, but not quite. After seeing the damage it had done to Daniel Niall, Morgan had no desire to mess with dark magick like that.

"Bixby, you're such a good boy," Morgan murmured, rubbing him behind his ears. He purred deeply, his orange eyes at half-mast.

*Think, think.* That piece of morganite. The face in the window. The hex pouch. The smoke. Even Moira and Ian—maybe Ian's very presence in Moira's life was itself a clue.

Cal, Morgan couldn't help thinking.

Morgan and Finnegan both sensed Moira at the same time. Thank the Goddess she wasn't late, hadn't gone anywhere after class. Finnegan cocked one ear, opened one eye, then lay back down. Morgan braced herself to confront Moira.

Her daughter came in just as the sunlight faded and the wind started kicking up. She looked surprised to see Morgan lying on the couch during the day.

"Hi. What's wrong? Are you sick?"

"Not really," said Morgan. In an instant she remembered the awful fights she'd had with her own parents when she'd first discovered Wicca. They'd been not only offended, but truly afraid for her soul. They were still unhappy about it after all these years. Morgan remembered how she'd wished that they could try to be more understanding and thought now that their fears had made everything seem worse. She could try to do it differently.

"I saw that you found some of my old Books of Shadows in the cellar," she said, striving for a casual tone. "Have you been reading them?"

Moira looked at her, seeming to weigh her answer. "I went and got them this morning," she finally admitted. "I know you wanted me to wait till you got them, but . . . after the smoke and then everything Keady said Saturday—I'm just curious. I need to see how it all started." She shook her head. "I just feel like I need to know everything."

Morgan groaned inwardly at the idea of her daughter knowing everything about her life.

"I've only just started the first one," Moira said. She came to stand by the couch, looking down at Morgan. Moira's hazel eyes were full of secrets, worries, and concerns, but her face was closed, private.

"Do you have any questions?" Morgan's stomach was tight and her jaw ached from trying to keep her face relatively calm.

"I've not read much, like I said," Moira answered, sitting down in the rocking chair. "Just the beginning of the first one—it was where you had met Cal Blaire. I got as far as you discovering you were a blood witch, and then you thought you loved Cal. I've never heard you mention Cal, have I? Was he just a high school crush kind of thing?"

A startled laugh escaped Morgan. Jagged memories of Cal and what he had been to her flashed across her mind. In some ways the beginning of her involvement with Wicca had been so painful, so dangerous and huge, that Morgan had tried hard to live it down ever since. Maybe the truth was that she hadn't just kept those stories from Moira for Moira's sake—she hadn't wanted to relive that time herself.

At Moira's confused expression, Morgan coughed and said, "No, not exactly." She got up and took a Diet Coke from the fridge, then sat back down on the couch and pulled Bixby into her lap for comfort.

"It's stuff I never told you," she said. "I wanted to protect you, in a way." Moira's eyebrows raised. "Your dad knew some of it, but not all. The thing is, when I first found out about being a witch, being adopted, and being from the Belwicket clan—it was exciting and good because it answered a lot of questions and explained things about myself and my family. But it also introduced me to a world I didn't know existed. That world was not always good or kind or safe. And because of who I was—Maeve Riordan's daughter—people, other witches, were interested in me and whatever powers I might have. And on top of all that, Nana and Poppy were so horrified and unhappy and were so afraid I was going to burn in hell forever because I wasn't a good Catholic anymore. It wasn't like your experience here, the daughter of two witches, always knowing you were a witch, growing up in a community that accepts witches, our religion and powers. Just finding out I was a blood witch caused all sorts of pain and unhappiness, mostly for my family and some of my friends, but also sometimes for me."

Morgan was very conscious that she hadn't mentioned Ciaran MacEwan yet. She figured she could only handle telling Moira one difficult thing at a time.

"What do you mean?" Moira asked, pulling one knee up onto the seat of the chair.

"Well. Let me see." Even after nearly twenty years Morgan still felt a pang of embarrassment, of betrayal. "In high school I felt kind of like an ugly duckling. And Aunt Bree was my best friend. You remember Aunt Bree, from New York?"

"The one with the big house and three daughters?" Moira asked.

"Yes. Bree is still gorgeous, but she looked like that in high school. Imagine being best friends with her."

"Ugh. Tess and Vita are bad enough, in their own ways."

"Right. So no guy ever noticed me—I had guy friends but didn't go on dates or anything. And I was almost seventeen. Then a new guy came to school, and he was drop-dead gorgeous." Morgan swallowed hard.

"Yeah?" Moira said with interest.

"Yeah," Morgan said, sighing. "That was Cal Blaire. He was really good-looking, and all the girls fell in love with him, including me and Bree. His mom was a witch, a dark Woodbane, but I didn't know about any of that at the time. She'd come to my town, Widow's Vale, to start a new coven and uncover any bent witches who would join in her dark magick or to flush out any strong witches so she could take their powers. She was a member of Amyranth."

Moira's eyes widened. Amyranth had been a coven dedicated to working dark magick and accumulating power, by any means neccessary. It had been disbanded for almost ten years, but they would be notorious for generations to come. "Amyranth," she breathed. "The real Amyranth?"

"Yes. But I didn't know about Woodbanes or Amyranth or any of that. I met Cal, and he wanted to start a coven, just kids, where we would celebrate the Sabbats and stuff. And he was also supposed to find out if any of us had any real powers. He was surprised when I turned out to be a blood witch without even knowing it."

"I can't believe you were sixteen before you knew that." Moira shook her head. "Were you knocked over?"

"That's an understatement," Morgan said dryly. "But even then, untaught and uninitiated . . . well, I could do stuff. Not well, and not safely, but things just came to me. Spells. Scrying. It was a little scary sometimes but also really fun. Mostly it was like—here was something special about me that none of my friends had. I was good in math, but so were lots of kids. I wasn't ugly but not really pretty. My family was fine but not rich or important. But learning Wicca and having a blood witch's powers—that was all me and only me. It was incredibly thrilling and satisfying for me to be very, very good at something so unexpectedly."

Moira looked thoughtful. "I can see how it would be—and then you fell for Cal. Did he like you back?"

"Yes," Morgan said, letting out a breath. "Amazingly. Despite every other girl who wanted him, he wanted to be with me. That freaked Bree out, and she and I had a terrible fight. A bunch of terrible fights. And became enemies."

"You and Aunt Bree? Goddess. How awful."

"It *was* awful, losing my best friend. But it felt like Cal was the only person in the world who understood me or accepted me the way I was. And he seemed to really love me."

"What do you mean, seemed?"

Morgan made a face. "I guess, looking back on it, he did love me, in his own way." She looked down at her knees and absently played with a frayed thread. Bixby stretched, arching his back and yawning wide to show his fangs. "The thing is, Moira," she went on slowly, "Cal was the son of a powerful, dark witch. Once his mother realized who I was, she compelled Cal to get close to me so that she could convince me to join her or, if I didn't want to join willingly, so that she could take hold of me, take my powers and use them for her own."

Moira frowned slightly, obviously starting to see the parallels with Lilith and Ian.

"Cal was very convincing," Morgan said. "I absolutely believed he loved me. But at the same time, some things about him made me uneasy—I didn't know why. Then a Seeker from the council showed up to investigate Cal and his mother, Selene Belltower. I thought the Seeker was wrong about Cal and Selene—I thought he just wanted to destroy Cal out of jealousy or vengeance. You see, he was also Cal's half brother." Morgan paused to let out another long, slow breath, easing pain out of her chest. "One night he tried to put a braigh on Cal, to capture him, and they fought. I threw my athame at the Seeker and hit him in the neck. He went over a cliff into the Hudson River."

Moira was staring at her as if she had just revealed that their cottage was an elaborate hologram.

Morgan sighed and looked at her daughter. She forced herself to continue. "I thought I had killed him. Killed someone to save Cal. Everything started unraveling. It was a horrible, desperate time—I can't even describe how tortured I felt. Then, thank the Goddess, the Seeker didn't die. But he started trying hard to convince me that Cal and Selene were evil. I didn't know what to believe. All the while Selene was putting more and more pressure on Cal, insisting that he get me to join them. So Cal was putting more and more pressure on me, telling me we were mùirn beatha dàns, trying to get me to go to bed with him, telling me that everyone else was lying to me."

"I can't believe it," Moira said, wide-eyed. She shook her head, glancing away, then looked back at Morgan. "I mean, I can't imagine this—any of it. What happened? What did you do?"

"Finally Selene decided to just get me herself and take my powers from me so she could combine them with her powers and be that much stronger. Cal found out about it, and the only thing he could think of to do to save me . . . was to kill me before she got to me."

Moira's jaw dropped open.

"So he locked me in his seòmar—his special, secret room—and set it on fire." Nearly twenty years of distance made the words a bit easier to say, the memory almost bearable. "But I managed to send a witch message to Bree, of all people, and in the end she and our friend Robbie drove my car into the wall of the room and got me out. They saved my life. Bree and I were friends again. But Cal and his mother disappeared."

Several emotions crossed Moira's face—concern, sympathy, fear. "What do you mean, disappeared? He tried to *kill* you! And nothing even happened to them?" Her cheeks were turning red with obvious shock and outrage.

"Not even the Seeker could find them. Cal and Selene resurfaced, of course." Morgan's voice cracked a little, but she went on. These were things she had naively hoped her daughter would never have to know. Secrets she'd planned on sharing later, when Moira was older. "Cal turned against his mother and came to find me. Selene came back also to find me. Selene kidnapped Aunt Mary K., who was only fourteen. I had to find her and ended up in Selene and Cal's old house. The Seeker and I went there to save Mary K., and we got into a terrible magickal battle with Selene. I had no idea what would happen—she was so strong, and I wasn't even initiated. It was—there just aren't words to describe how it was. At one point Selene aimed a bolt of power at me that would have struck me dead. But Cal jumped in front of me at the last minute, and it hit him instead. He did it to save me, and it killed him. That's what makes me think he did love me, in his own way. Then it was just me and Selene, and a spell came to me—I think it was from my mother, Maeve. It trapped Selene, and she died. I caused her to die."

"Mum, I can't believe you never told me any of this," Moira said, strain evident in her voice. She looked distressed, and Morgan hated the fact that even after so many years, Cal and Selene still had the power to hurt someone she loved. "Did Dad know?"

Morgan nodded. "Yes—I told him about it."

"Then Selene was dead forever? You won?"

Morgan sighed again. "No, not exactly. A witch that power-ful—her body had died, but her spirit had escaped and moved into another physical form. She took over the body of a hawk and continued to live that way. And later she came back again, to try to kill me once and for all."

"Goddess, Mum. She came back *again*?"

Thoughtfully, Morgan said, "I think . . . I think I reminded her of herself, of her own potential. I was powerful because I'd been born that way. She was powerful because she had used dark magick to increase her powers. She had fed off others. She saw me as a threat because I wouldn't join her. And if I grew up, increased my strength, became initiated—I could only be her enemy. In the end she knew that if I went against her as a grown-up, I would defeat her. So she went against me as a teenager, but I defeated her anyway. And of course after her only son died trying to save me, she hated me more than ever. She killed Cal, and she knew it. But she blamed me."

"She's not still around, is she?" Moira looked worried, pinching her bottom lip between two fingers, the way she had when she was young.

"No," Morgan said, looking out through the small living-room window. Outside, it had clouded over and the first drops of rain began to hit the ancient, wavy panes of glass. "No, she's dead. She came after me for the third time, and that time she was finished."

"Finished how?" Moira's voice squeaked.

"I killed her," Morgan said sadly, watching the heavy gray clouds outside.

"When she was a hawk?"

"Yes."

Silence. Morgan still had very faint, thin white lines on one shoulder where Selene the hawk had ripped her skin with razor-sharp talons. She would always have those scars, but compared to the scars inside, which no one could see, they were nothing.

"How?" Her daughter's voice sounded fearful, as if she needed to know for sure that Morgan's old enemy was truly no longer a threat.

Morgan wondered if she had already said far too much and knew there was so much more her daughter didn't know. "I shape-shifted," she said. "I became a hawk, and I caught her, and I . . . trapped her spirit inside the hawk so that it couldn't escape again. And then she was really dead forever."

Moira was staring at her as if seeing her for the first time, and Morgan knew that it wasn't only because of her terrible story. It was also about knowing the depth and extent of Morgan's own powers. Morgan cast out her senses—Moira was both horrified by and afraid of her own mother. It felt like an athame piercing her heart to know she'd inspired her only child to feel this way. But there was something else. Awe.

Moira was quiet for a moment; then, unexpectedly, she rose and came over to hug Morgan. "I'm so sorry, Mum," she whispered, tears in her voice. "I'm so sorry you had to go through all that. I had no idea." Feeling a warm rush of love, Morgan hugged her tightly back.

"I can't believe you shape-shifted," Moira said, pulling back and looking into Morgan's eyes. "I thought shape-shifting was just in folktales. I didn't think anyone could do that."

"It isn't that common," Morgan acknowledged. "Moira, listen: I would do anything to make sure that you never had to go through anything like that. Do you understand?"

"You mean Ian. And Lilith Delaney."

"Yes," Morgan said pleadingly, wishing she could get through. "It's like watching my life flash before my eyes—only it's worse because it's you and I need to protect you. Just knowing you're seeing him makes me feel panicky, sick."

"But Mum, Lilith isn't Selene, and Ian definitely isn't Cal," Moira said earnestly, and Morgan's heart sank. "I see the parallels. I see why they would make you feel scared. But I still feel that I need to give Ian a chance. I need to give *me* a chance with him. If it's a mistake, I'll find out. But *I* need to find out—I can't just take your word for it, even though you lived through that nightmare when you were young, with another son and another witch. Ian and Lilith aren't Cal and Selene. And I'm not you." Her face looked open, concerned, eager for Morgan to understand.

Morgan sighed, mentally draping a cloak of protection over Moira. Everyone had to make her own mistakes. But did that mean Morgan had to let Moira walk into disaster?

"I'll be more on my guard, Mum," Moira promised. "I understand now why you're so worried, and I don't want you to be afraid for me. Can I see Ian if I always tell you where and when I'm meeting him?"

It wasn't a bad compromise. "Yes," Morgan said reluctantly, and Moira's face lit up. "But I can't promise I won't scry to find you if I feel you're in danger. And if I find out definitely that Ian is involved in dark magick, you have to promise me you won't see him."

"All right," Moira said, somewhat unenthusiastically. She glanced at the clock. "I was hoping to see him this afternoon. I was going to send him a witch message to meet at Margath's Faire. All right?"

Morgan nodded, not trusting herself to speak. She wanted to ground Moira, to keep her home. She wanted to follow her, to make sure she was safe. In the end she could do neither: if she tried to protect her daughter in those ways, she would only ensure losing her forever. She watched as Moira put on a jacket.

"I won't be too late, all right?"

Morgan nodded again and cleared her throat. "All right."

Then her daughter was gone, and Morgan was left with her memories.

# 5.
# Moira

Moira realized she had shredded her paper napkin into unrecognizable strips. She swept them into a little pile and walked up to the counter to throw them away. As she was turning back to her table, her senses prickled, and she saw Ian at the top of the stairs. He was smiling at her, and she gave him a wide smile in return. She pointed to her table, and he met her there.

"I'm so glad you suggested meeting," he said, sitting down. "It was a bit of a wiggle to get away—Mum wants me to gather some moss for her. What's that, an iced coffee?"

"Yes," Moira said. She felt just the faintest bit of unease when he mentioned his mum. Looking into his blue eyes, full of light, she wondered if there was some way of testing him or if she simply had to trust her instincts and wait. She'd meant it when she'd assured her mother that she was convinced of his innocence, but at the same time . . . maybe those stories about Selene and Cal had gotten to her more than she'd realized. She *had* promised she'd be careful, and she intended to be just that. "Do you want to order something?"

"Well . . ." Ian looked at the board. "Not really, actually. I was wondering if you wanted to get out of here. Do you want to come help me collect plants by the copper beeches, down by Elise's Brook?"

Moira knew Elise's Brook—it was one of dozens of tiny waterways that feathered through the southeastern part of Ireland. This particular one was just outside of town and bordered on both sides by woodlands. Since it was halfway between Cobh and Wicklow, Moira and her parents had often gone there for picnics or herb gathering. Besides the copper beeches, there were willows, sloes, furze, and hazel. She'd had to learn their Gaelic names for herbology class: faibhille rua, sáileach, áirne, aitheann, and coll.

"All right," Moira said slowly. "Is it raining yet?"

"Not yet," Ian told her as they got up. "I'm hoping it'll hold off. We should have almost an hour if we're lucky."

It took almost twenty-five minutes to walk to the brook. The late afternoon sun was hidden behind thick gray clouds, and Moira wished the fleeting sunshine had lasted longer. As they walked, Moira took a moment to send a witch message to her mum, telling her where they were going, as she had promised.

As soon as they were out of eyesight of the town, Ian took her hand and held it as they walked. His hand was warm and strong and gave Moira a pleasant tingle. Their eyes were level with each other since they were the same height, and it was both comfortable and exciting walking along as if they were officially boyfriend and girlfriend.

"Does your coven have circles on Saturdays, then?" Ian

asked. Instantly Moira was overtaken by memories of what had happened just last night. Why was he asking? Did he know something? She glanced at him quickly, but his face seemed open, with no hidden meanings.

"Yes," she said.

"Us too," said Ian. "Mum has what I call power circles, where she and a bunch of the older members try to work a kind of intense magick. Twelve of us younger ones often meet by ourselves and do our own thing."

"What do you mean, intense magick?" Moira asked, feeling her pulse quicken.

He didn't answer at first, and for a moment Moira wondered if he regretted bringing it up. "Oh, lots of chants and rants, I call it. You know. Superstars of Wicca." He laughed self-consciously. "I'm not so much into that—me and my mates mostly do tree-hugging stuff, you know, working with the moon, that kind of thing."

Okay, that didn't sound so bad. Tree hugging certainly wasn't dark magick.

They were approaching the small woodland grove, and Moira almost didn't want to step into the dimly lit thicket of trees, remembering her mother's terrifying stories about Selene and Cal. She glanced over at Ian, thinking, Do I trust him or not? Yes, she did.

Inside the woods it was still, and the air seemed warmer because they were out of the wind. It felt hushed inside, as if even the birds and animals were trying to be extra quiet. Moira cast her senses and picked up vague impressions of squirrels and birds and some small things she couldn't identify. If her mum were here, she'd have been able to identify every kind of bird and animal and even most of the insects. *I want to be as strong as that one day.*

"Let's see," Ian murmured, pulling a slip of paper from his pocket. "I've got a shopping list." He read the paper, then pulled a handful of little plastic bags from his jeans pocket. "Dog's mercury, for one," he said. "And it's going to be bloody hard to find it this time of year." He looked over at Moira and frowned slightly. "Are you sure you're on for this? I know it's boring. It's just, I really should do it, and I wanted to spend time with you."

"It's all right," Moira said. "I can help you look."

He grinned at her, and her heart did a little flip. She loved his smile, the light in his eyes.

"No," he said. "You sit down there. I have to start collecting some of this stuff, but you can keep me company. Tell me what you've been doing."

"Studying for classes. I submitted my ladybug spell to my spellcraft teacher."

"Really?" Ian laughed. "How'd it go over?"

"She thought the construction was elegant and clean but that the spell was frivolous and self-centered," Moira admitted. The comments had stung a bit, but she'd half expected them. "She said to read back in my parents' Books of Shadows, so I dug my mum's up and started reading them."

Ian stilled, crouched on the ground, and looked up at her. "Really? You hadn't read them before now? What were they like?"

"I'd read some, but not early ones," Moira said carefully. Why was he so interested in her parents' Books of Shadows? Maybe he's just trying to be nice, she chided herself.

"I haven't got far in these," she said, sitting down on a

thick fallen log. "But I'm reading about how my mum didn't even know she was a blood witch till she was sixteen years old. She'd been adopted, and no one had told her."

Ian shook his head. "I can't imagine not growing up with Wicca. That would be too strange. How did she find out?"

Moira hesitated. How much could she trust Ian? What if he *was* like Mum thought? No, she had to stop—this was Ian. "A blood witch moved to town and realized it and told her. It caused big problems, because my grandparents are Catholic and they didn't want anything to do with Wicca."

"These are your mum's adopted parents?"

"Yeah. Even now—I know they love her, and they love me and loved my dad, but our being Wiccan and practicing the craft still upsets them. They're worried about our souls."

Ian clawed at some dirt at the base of a tree. Gently he unearthed a small plant that already looked dormant for autumn. He sealed it inside a plastic bag and set it on the ground. "Well, they're trying to show they love you," he said, looking off into the distance. "Sometimes people can do amazingly hurtful things, trying to show they love you." It sounded as if he were talking more to himself than her, but then he shook his head and gave her a little smile.

"Anyway, it sounds like your mum's Books of Shadows are wicked interesting. You should keep reading them."

"Yeah, I'm going to." She wished she could just trust what he said, but she still couldn't help wondering—did he have another reason to want her to read the Books of Shadows? Was his mum using him to get to her like Selene had done with Cal and her mum?

The sun had almost set, and now Moira realized it was

almost dark. "Are you finding what you need?" she asked, doing her best to push away her doubts.

"I can't find a couple of things, but at least I got some of the most important ones," he said, collecting his bags. "I've done my good-son deed for the day. It feels like it's getting colder. Are you chilly?"

"I'm all right," Moira said, but her hands were rubbing her arms. Ian came to sit next to her and put his arm around her. They were alone in a deserted wood, and his warmth felt so good next to her. When he held her like this and looked into her eyes, she couldn't believe that he could ever deceive her. It was as if she could see his whole soul in his eyes and saw only good. Not angelic good, but regular good.

"I've got an idea," he said. "Let's go down and look in the water—scry."

"Scry? What for?"

"Just for fun." Ian shrugged. "For practice."

Moira bit her lip. She could almost hear her mother, warning her that Ian only wanted her to scry with him so he could test just how strong her powers were. Goddess, she wished she could stop questioning every little thing Ian said and did and just *trust* him. "Okay," she said. "Let's go."

Holding hands, they stepped carefully down the rocky banks to where the brook, barely six feet wide at this point, trickled past. There was a flattish boulder half in the water, and they knelt on it, then lay on their stomachs, their faces close to the water. At this spot a natural sinkhole created a barely shimmering circle of water maybe eighteen inches across. It was as smooth and flat as a mirror.

"Do you scry much?" Ian asked, looking down at his reflection.

"No—I'm not that good at it. I practice it, of course."

"In water?"

"Yeah—it's the easiest. My mum uses fire."

Ian looked up, interested. "Really? Fire's very difficult—harder than stone or crystal. But it's reliable. Is she good at it?"

"Very good." Moira stopped, uncomfortable talking about her mother with Ian. She leaned closer to the water. On a bright day she'd have been able to see snips and bits of sky through the treetops overhead. Today, at this hour, she could see only darkness around the reflection of her face.

"Let's try," Ian said softly. He edged closer to her so that they were lying next to each other, their chins on their hands, heads hanging over the water.

When her mother or anyone else from Belwicket scried, they used a short, simple rhyme in English, tailoring the words to fit the medium or the occasion. Moira was trying to recall one when Ian started chanting very softly in Gaelic. She met his eyes in the water, their two reflections overlapping slightly at this angle. Gaelic wasn't Moira's strong point, though she'd studied it and knew enough to have simple conversations. And of course many of the more traditional chants and songs were in old Gaelic. In Ian's chant she recognized the modern words *an t'sùil,* "the eye," and *tha sinn,* "we are." There were many more that she couldn't get.

Her gaze focused on her reflection in the water, but her ears strained to understand Ian's chant. So far she hadn't heard any of the basic words or phrases that she knew could be used as frames to surround a spell and turn its intention dark.

Was she being paranoid? Was she just trying to be safe?

Had her mother ruined her ability to just be with Ian, relaxed and happy? Silently Moira groaned to herself, but as she did, their reflections in the water began changing. Automatically Moira slowed her breathing and focused her entire energy on seeing what the water wanted her to see. Water was notoriously unreliable—not that it was never right, but it was so fickle in whether it would show the truth or not.

As they watched, their bodies pressed close, the chill of the boulder seeping through Moira's clothes, their two reflected faces seemed to split apart, like atoms dividing. Their images had overlapped, but now they separated. Then Ian's reflection seemed to split apart again, dividing into two other images. From Moira's angle she thought one of the images was a man, with dark hair and blue eyes. He was older and looked sad but vaguely familiar. But the other half of the image made her breath catch in her throat—it was a shadow, the shadow of a person, with blurred features. Its mouth opened and it laughed, with water showing through where the mouth was. It was just a shadow, not in the shape of a monster, yet the sight filled Moira with dread. She felt clammy and cold, and a chilly trickle of sweat eased down the nape of her neck. It was just a shadow—why did it seem so terrible?

Gulping, Moira looked away, down at her own reflection. It too had separated into two images. One image was a fire—in the shape of a face. The fire was smoldering, red-hot coals but seemed to offer warmth and comfort rather than destruction. Tiny flames licked at the edges, like strands of hair being blown in the wind. The other image was a person, just as Ian's had been. At first Moira thought it was her, but then she realized the person was a man. She frowned, trying to see closer.

Splash! Moira jumped back as a small stone dropped into the water, destroying the reflections. Startled, she looked up at Ian and wiped a few drops of water off her face. "What did you do? There was something . . . something else there."

Ian got to his knees, looking unhappy. "I thought I'd seen enough."

Moira also scrambled up, her limbs feeling stiff and chilled through. "Are you all right?" She took his arm and looked into his face, but his expression was blank and he wouldn't meet her gaze.

"Yeah. It was just cold there on the rock." Edging past her gently, Ian picked up his collected bags, then brushed off his clothes.

*He's lying. Did he see what I saw?*

"Come on, then," Ian said, trying to sound natural. He forced a smile and held out his hand to help her down from the rock. She took it, jumping down, and followed Ian as he picked their way back out of the woods. The closer they got to the edge, the cooler and fresher it seemed, and Moira could smell rain and hear it pelting the tops of the trees.

"Brilliant," Ian said, looking out at the rain and the darkness. He turned to her. "I'm sorry, Moira. We're going to get soaked."

*Moira? Where are you?* Moira heard her mother's voice inside her head.

She sent back, *I'm here, with Ian, at the brook. I'm on my way home.*

"It's all right," she said to Ian. "I've gotten soaked before. But are you all right? Why did you break up the reflection?"

He paused, not looking at her, absentmindedly flapping

the bags against his leg. "I don't know," he said finally. "It just—I wanted to get out of there."

Moira waited, holding his arm and looking at his face, his skin flecked with raindrops. "You can tell me," she said gently. "You can trust me."

His startled gaze met hers, his dark blue eyes seeming to search her face. A sad-looking smile crossed his face, followed by a look of despair that lasted only an instant. Moira wasn't sure if she'd really seen it. Stepping closer, Ian put a hand under Moira's chin. His skin was damp and cool. "Thank you," he said quietly, and then he kissed her, there at the edge of the woods in the rain.

Moira closed her eyes and stepped closer, slanting her head to deepen the kiss. It was so good and felt so right. Her worries and suspicions fell away as they put their arms around each other and held on tightly. But she knew there was something beneath Ian's skin, something he was worried about or afraid of. Her instincts still told her that he himself wasn't bad, or evil, as her mother would say. I can help him, she thought dizzily as they broke away from their kiss and stared at each other. Whatever it is that's upsetting him, it'll be all right.

# 6.
# Morgan

Morgan finished writing the recipe for the liver strengthener in her best handwriting. Unfortunately, her handwriting hadn't really improved over the years.

Right after Moira had left to meet Ian, Fillipa Gregg had dropped by for a quick consultation. Morgan had been glad of the distraction and, after doing some hands-on healing work, had concocted the liver cleanser for her. Tonight she needed to write up a strengthening spell and prepare a vial of flower essences for Fillipa to put in her tea for a month.

The sun was going down, but Morgan didn't need to think about dinner for an hour. It was taking all her self-control not to scry for Moira to make sure she was all right. Elise's Brook! In the middle of nowhere with Ian Delaney. Two weeks ago Morgan's life had been sad, unbalanced, but not threatening. Now danger threatened; it was almost as if she and the coven were under siege. Morgan knew she had to keep her guard up, watch her back, the way she had back in Widow's Vale so many years ago. She was keeping the animals inside more and locking all the doors and windows. Not that physical barriers would do any good if serious magick was being worked against her.

*Do something. Idle hands are the devil's workshop.*

Morgan smiled as she remembered her adoptive mother's words. Of course, Wiccans didn't believe in the devil, or Satan, in any form. But it wouldn't hurt to keep busy. Keeping busy helped her think. And maybe she could gather some ingredients for more, stronger ward-evil spells.

On one wall of Morgan's workroom were floor-to-ceiling shelves. All of her magickal supplies were there, from an assortment of crystals and gems to oil essences, dried flowers, powdered barks, spelled candles and runes, and incense. Maeve's four silver cups were there, polished and shiny from use. The Riordan athame rested in the velvet-lined box that Morgan had bought for it years ago. Maeve's green silk robe was folded carefully and wrapped in tissue paper.

It had been hard talking to Moira this afternoon about Cal. Maybe not as hard as she'd feared, but still difficult to talk about. And as bad as her past with Cal was, it was going to be much, much harder to tell Moira about Ciaran or Hunter. Colm had known about Ciaran and some of her history with Hunter. Telling Moira about her past—her story—was much more daunting, more painful. Morgan had thought it would get easier with time. That at some point she would know when Moira was ready to hear about her past. But waiting hadn't made facing the truth any easier. Morgan remembered what it had felt like, learning that she was the illegitimate daughter of Ciaran MacEwan. It had shaken her to the core, made her question herself like nothing else ever had. If she was the daughter of an incredibly evil witch, did that make her own darkness inevitable? She had known even then that it was going to be a constant struggle to stay on the side of goodness.

It had been, but not only because she was Ciaran's daughter. Every single person, every day, had to choose goodness over and over again. Every person, every day, could take one of two paths. It was up to that person to choose well. Choosing to work with bright magick wasn't a choice one made at the beginning of her career and then just forgot about. The temptation was constant. It was a choice that must be made continuously, despite need or anger or desire. There had been times when Morgan had known she could truly help someone, truly make a difference in someone's life, but it would have meant working the wrong kind of magick. And there had been times when Morgan could see how her own power would be increased substantially if she worked a certain spell or created certain rituals. If she were that much stronger, she could do that much more good. She always used her powers for good. She could protect her family that much more. She herself could be that much safer. But to get that power, she would have to pay the price of working dark magick, even if it were only for a short amount of time. And that price was too high. The memory of Daniel Niall, collapsed and broken after working with a bith dearc—a portal to the dead—flashed through Morgan's mind.

She had been tempted by dark magick. She couldn't hold her head high and say that she had never even considered it, that following the Wiccan Rede and minding the threefold law had come easily. Morgan was only too aware of the humbling effect of temptation, of the realization that she had such a desire in her, to be brought to the point of having to fight it.

Was that because she was human or because she was Ciaran's daughter? How easily had Ciaran slipped into darkness all those years ago?

There was more of Ciaran in Morgan than she ever wanted anyone to know. The only way to overcome that side of her was to look hard at it and face it head-on. The moment she pretended she was better than Ciaran, more immune to temptation than he was, that was when she would fall.

Morgan had to stop for a moment. Ciaran. She rested her head in one hand and rubbed her forehead. She took a sip of juice.

He had died four years after Morgan had put a binding spell on him and called Hunter to strip him of his powers. Thinking back on that grotesque scene still made Morgan's stomach turn. It was never clean or easy to strip a witch of his or her powers. Fifteen years ago it had been more common—now the New Charter stressed rehabilitation, reteaching, limited bindings. But to strip a witch of Ciaran's strength of his powers against his will—it was like watching a human being be turned inside out. Ciaran had never recovered from the trauma—not many witches did. For a blood witch to live without powers, without the blessing of that extra connection to the world, to oneself—most witches preferred death. Some members of the New Charter were only now trying to develop rituals and spells that could possibly restore at least some limited magick to a witch who had been stripped.

As for Ciaran—to say that he had never recovered was a gross understatement. After he had been tried and sentenced and sent to Borach Mean, a sort of rest home in southern Ireland for witches without powers, he had simply ceased to be.

Morgan had gone to visit Ciaran only once, about eight months after he'd arrived at Borach Mean. The memory made her cringe, and she almost dropped the small bottle of rose water she was holding. She'd had so many torn and confused feelings about what she'd done, about Ciaran himself. She recognized herself in him; she was undeniably drawn to him, her handsome, powerful father. He'd been charming and complimentary—when he'd wanted something. He'd loved her and been proud of her, had seen more potential in her than in any of his other children. But to truly earn his total love, Morgan would have had to step out of light and into darkness forever.

At Borach Mean the witch in charge had led Morgan to Ciaran, in an enclosed courtyard. The pale peach–colored stucco walls had sheltered plants of all kinds, each chosen for its scent or beauty. Herbs and roses all grew lushly, basking in the sun, releasing their scents to the warm air. They had all been spelled to be without power, of no use in any kind of spell. Just in case.

Her feet quiet on the dusty paving stones, Morgan had walked up to him, and he'd jumped: one sad effect of a witch losing powers was that they could no longer sense people approaching them, and they ended up being startled frequently. It had taken him several moments to recognize her. She'd been shocked and sickened by his appearance. He'd lost an incredible amount of weight and looked sunken and hollow, even frail. His hair was almost completely white, where before it had been a rich, dark brown with just a few silver threads. But it was his eyes that had changed the most.

Their hazel color, once so like Morgan's, had faded to a pale, mottled shade that seemed strangely lit from within.

"You." Morgan had felt rather than heard the word, his uncomprehending stare, the odd glitter of his almost color-less eyes.

"I'm sorry," Morgan had managed to choke out. Those pathetically inadequate words were supposed to cover so much—sorry you were so evil. Sorry you were my dad. Sorry you killed my mother. Sorry I helped bring you to this. Sorry that someone who could have been beautiful and strong and wise instead chose to be corrupt and destructive. And despite everything, sorry we couldn't have been the father and daughter that each of us would have wanted.

In the next moment Ciaran had lunged off his bench, fingers clenched like talons, and Morgan, startled, had taken a big step back. He had started spitting hateful words at her, words of revenge, accusation: "Traitor! Betrayer! Dog-witch! Nemesis! Foul, faithless daughter!" He had tried to throw spells at her, spells that, had he had his powers, would have flayed the flesh from her bones. As it was, his attempt to create magick only made him crumple in pain, retching, his fingers clawing at the light red dust on the ground.

"Ciaran, stop," Morgan had cried, raw pain squeezing her heart. And still he had spewed awful words at her. She had burst into tears, shaken by the horror of it all, and then, unbearably, Ciaran had started crying, too, as an attendant ran up. One witch had led Morgan inside, while two others had picked Ciaran up and taken him back to his room. The last thing Morgan had heard was his voice, a shattered, hollow croak, choking out her name.

Morgan could still smell the heated dust of Borach Mean, still feel the warm wind in her hair. Not long after that, she had moved to Ireland for good. Four years later, when she heard that Ciaran had died, she had gone to his funeral.

Moving the step stool, she continued to search for the ingredients she needed.

Ciaran's funeral had been in Scotland, where his wife, Grania, had lived with their three children: Kyle, Iona, and Killian. Her half siblings. Grania had finally divorced Ciaran after he'd been stripped. Morgan had heard about it from Killian, the only one of her half siblings she had any relationship with. He hadn't asked her to come, had advised against it, in fact, but she'd told him that she needed to and that he didn't have to let on who she was when she was there.

So she'd shown up at the small and ancient burial ground that the MacEwan Woodbanes had used for centuries. She'd worn a scarf and dark glasses to hide her hair and eyes. Almost two hundred people had been there: dark witches, come to mourn their betrayed and fallen leader, and others, his enemies, come to make sure he was dead at last. It had been very odd. Killian had spotted her but made no sign of recognition. Morgan hadn't known anyone else there except for a few council members, like Eoife MacNabb. Eoife also gave no sign of recognition.

Yet Grania, Ciaran's ex-wife, the one he had betrayed to become Morgan's mother's lover, had suddenly spotted her across the crowd and let loose a spine-cracking banshee howl.

"You!" she had cried. "How dare you show your face here? You, his bastard daughter!" Her face had contorted in resentment. "You and he deserved each other! How I wish you could join him in his grave right now!"

Everyone had turned to look. Morgan had stared at Grania, not saying a word, just knowing what she could have said. Grania had once perhaps been pretty, but thirty years of frustration and anger had twisted her face, made it seem lumpy and asymmetrical. Her hair was a harsh blond that ill suited her red, windburned face and pale, gooseberry eyes. She and Ciaran had had a rocky relationship. But clearly, even after all Ciaran had done to her, she still felt something for him, something that made it impossible to bear the reminder Morgan provided of his affair with Maeve.

Next to Grania, Killian had worn a pained expression—he hadn't joined in his mother's accusations, but neither would he defend Morgan against her. Killian mostly just took care of Killian. But Iona and Kyle—Ciaran's other children—had been another matter. Iona resembled Grania in looks—she was pale, dumpy, and had none of Ciaran's handsomeness, charisma, or grace. She'd stared at Morgan with plain hatred, but then her expression had turned to something else, something sly and knowing, almost like satisfaction: a smug, triumphant look that Morgan didn't understand. Could Iona have been glad that Ciaran was dead? He hadn't made her life easy, but she had professed to love him.

Then Kyle had surged toward her, hissing a spell. He looked more like Ciaran, but where Ciaran's features had been classical and chiseled, Kyle's were softer, more doughy. He had Ciaran's coloring, as Morgan did, and Killian.

His attack had been useless. Morgan had been initiated—she was far from an untrained teenager, unaware of her powers. Not only that, but she had already lost Hunter. Life had honed her, made her harder. Morgan, sitting there at her father's funeral, had been as hard and sharp and deadly as an athame. Kyle's power was undisciplined, unfocused, and Morgan had flicked his spells aside with a wave of her hand as if they were gnats.

This wasn't what she had come for. It gave her no pleasure to antagonize or hurt her father's other family. Sighing, Morgan had gathered her things and threaded her way through the crowd. She'd walked back toward the village and caught the next train out. Since then she'd heard about Kyle or Iona only seldom, usually from Killian, whom she continued to see maybe once a year or so, whenever she was in his area on business. Killian had changed little, despite a surprisingly early marriage and, at last count, three children. He was still happy-go-lucky, held no grudges, and managed to skip through life like an autumn leaf, tossed here and there by the wind.

Killian had told her of the political marriages of both Kyle and Iona, who had each chosen to ally themselves with powerful Woodbane families. Iona had taken her father's legacy seriously and had been studying intensively—though whether she could ever come close to filling Ciaran's shoes was unknown. Kyle had continued to soften, like an overripe cheese, and now it sounded as if he mostly played the role of country gentleman, managing extensive estates in western Scotland, supported by his wealthy wife.

Morgan sighed to herself. Okay, well, now she had managed to thoroughly depress herself. But at least she'd gathered everything she needed for the spell.

Back in the living room she lay down on the couch. It was dark outside now, and the rain had just started. Moira still wasn't back. Morgan was tempted to scry for her daughter but instead sent a witch message to Moira, asking her where she was. Thankfully, Moira sent back that she was on her way home.

Rubbing her forehead again, Morgan lay in the shadowed room, trying to keep a lid on her anxiety. Moira was safe. She was coming home. And tomorrow Morgan and Keady would ask Christa, Katrina, and Will Fereston to join them in performing a spell to trace the black smoke from last night. Morgan was also considering taking the hex pouch and confronting Lilith with it, possibly making some ambiguous counterthreats. Maybe she could scare Lilith into leaving her alone.

Yawning, Morgan stretched, then went "oof!" as Bixby jumped up on her. Absently she stroked his orange fur, watching his eyes drift lazily shut. With Bixby purring comfortably on her stomach, Morgan gradually let herself be taken by sleep.

*She and Hunter were making love. It felt oddly unfamiliar and at the same time as easy and regular as breathing. She could smell his skin, his hair, feel his short, white-blond bangs brush her forehead. It was as if he had been on a long trip and had just gotten home. Maybe this was one of their infrequent meetings: they were coming together in some city, somewhere, whenever they could.*

*"I thought you were going to settle down, come live with me," Morgan murmured against his shoulder, holding him tight. The sheer delicious joy of being with him, the feeling of connection, of rightness. This was where home was: wherever they could be together, for however long.*

*"I am," he whispered back, kissing her neck. "Just not as soon as I thought."*

*Morgan smiled against him, closing her eyes, relishing the moment, feeling gratitude for how much she loved him, that one person was able to love another person so completely.* "Make it soon," she told him. "I need you with me."

"Soon," he promised. "I'm sorry it's taken me so long."

"I forgive you." Morgan sighed, kissing his shoulder.

He grinned at her, the edges of his eyes crinkling. His eyes were so green, so pure and full of light. "Ta," he said. "And I forgive you."

"For what?" Morgan demanded, and the light faded from his eyes.

"For believing I've been dead all this while."

Morgan woke up crying.

Finnegan came over to the couch and gave her hand a tentative lick. Still sobbing, Morgan patted his head and tried to sit up, dislodging Bixby. *Oh, Goddess, oh, Goddess.* With a rough movement she pushed her hair out of her eyes. She coughed, tried to hold back a sob, and wiped her eyes with the back of her sleeve.

What time was it? Only five-twenty. She'd been asleep twenty minutes. Morgan quickly cast out her senses. Moira wasn't home yet but surely would be soon. Standing shakily, Morgan went to the hearth and threw some small logs sloppily onto the andirons. Her nerves were jangled by the dream, but kindling fire with magick was almost second nature by now. She huddled by the fire for several minutes, and she could feel the first tongues of flame trying to break through her intense coldness, the coldness that seemed to crack her bones.

What had that dream meant? she wondered miserably. She'd just had a startling, realistic dream about Hunter the same day someone had left a piece of spelled morganite on her garden path. There were no coincidences.

In the days, weeks, months, years after his death, night-marish Hunter dreams had haunted Morgan so that she'd often been afraid to sleep. How many times had she dreamed he was alive, only missing, not dead? How many times had she dreamed he had simply left her for another woman—then woken up with tears of happiness on her face because even his leaving her to be with someone else was infinitely preferable to his being dead?

But it had been ages since she'd dreamed of him so vividly, dreamed that he was still alive. This, the morganite, the face in the window, the black smoke—it was all adding up to something. Someone was haunting her with her past—someone who knew her well enough to know about Hunter. She needed to find out who, and how, and most importantly, *why*.

Morgan looked down at her shaking hands almost with detachment, as if she were in the middle of a science experiment and this was a side effect. She swallowed. Her mouth was dry. She hadn't felt this way in twenty years. *My world is no longer safe.*

*I need help.*

Standing, Morgan walked over to the phone. She flipped through her address book and found Sky Eventide's latest number. Sky was Hunter's cousin and, after Morgan, had probably known him better than anyone. All these years she and Sky had kept in touch, some years more than others. They'd never had a close or comfortable relationship, but they'd been united in their mutual love of and grief over Hunter and made an effort to keep track of each other. Sky had never married, though she and Raven Meltzer had gotten back together for a stretch and shared an apartment in London for several years before Raven moved to New York when her career as a fashion designer took off. These days it seemed like Sky usually had some cute guy or girl hanging around adoring her, until they annoyed the crap out of her and she cut them loose.

Sky answered at once, her clipped tone suggesting that Morgan had just disturbed something important.

"Sky? It's Morgan. I'm sorry—are you in the middle of something?"

"Just trying to get my bloody toaster to turn out one decent slice, the bugger. Have you noticed how hard it is to spell appliances?"

Just hearing Sky's voice stopped Morgan's nerves from dumping adrenaline into her system. It was so familiar, from so long ago, when Morgan had just been discovering magick and love and sadness all at once.

"Uh, isn't that *a-p-p-l-i—*"

"Oh, very funny," Sky growled, and Morgan actually smiled. "Smart ass. You know what I mean. They're impossible. Hell, even rocks are easier to control."

"I know what you mean," Morgan agreed. "I'm pretty low-tech."

On Sky's end Morgan heard the scrape of metal and a slight thud, as if Sky had given her toaster a blow.

"Anyway, what's going on?" Sky asked.

Morgan hesitated. Sky had gone through almost the same pain that she had so many years ago, when Hunter had died. She hated raking it all up for her. But she needed help.

"I'm—afraid," she admitted. She could almost feel Sky sit

up, her interest sharpen.

"Tell me what's going on."

"Weird things. I was looking out the window at night, and I had a vision. A face appeared next to mine in the window. I couldn't tell who it was, but it was someone fair. Then just this morning I found a big chunk of morganite right in my yard, on the path. *Morganite*. And it had been spelled to hold a person's image. Again, I couldn't make out who it was. It was blurry and the stone was full of flaws, cloudy."

"That *is* odd," Sky said slowly. "Is someone working against you? Or your coven?"

"That's not all." Morgan quickly described the black smoke at the circle and filled Sky in on her history with Lilith and Ealltuinn. "But those things don't explain who the person is that I keep seeing. Why send me images? What would that do?"

"Maybe just unnerve you?"

"Well, yes, but the images themselves aren't scary. It's the idea that someone's doing this on purpose, you know? And there's more—just now I fell asleep, and I had a dream. It was . . . it was about Hunter, about me and Hunter." She paused, swallowing. "And I said I forgave him for something, and he said he forgave me, too. I asked what for, and he said, I forgive you for believing I've been dead all this while."

After almost a minute Sky said, *"Really."* Her voice was concerned, thoughtful—and held a twinge of sadness as well.

"Yes," Morgan said, hearing a slight crack in her voice.

"Who around there knows about Hunter?"

Morgan thought. "My mother-in-law knows. You know I was a mess afterward, and she took me in. Colm knew about him. Some members of my coven."

"Do you think it could be one of them, trying to work on you?" Sky asked. "Maybe they've been resenting Hunter all these years? Either Colm doing this from the other side or maybe his mum, now that he's gone and can't protect you?"

Morgan took a minute to work through those ideas. Her automatic response was, *Of course not*, but she had to think through all possibilities.

"I don't think it's Colm," she said. "Colm knew about Hunter but never seemed that jealous of him. Hunter was gone, and Colm had me, and we had Moira."

"Did he wonder if you loved him as much as Hunter?"

Morgan sighed. Sky had a knack for asking the tough questions.

"He probably did," Morgan answered with unflinching honesty. "I mean, no one could replace Hunter—he was my mùirn beatha dàn, and Colm knew that. But once I was married to Colm, I did my best not to let him down or make him think he was second best. And I did truly love him."

"And Katrina?"

"No, Katrina is more the in-your-face type," Morgan said. "She wouldn't bother resorting to anything this subtle."

"Which leaves who?"

"Well, the leader of Ealltuinn, as I mentioned. But how could she know about Hunter? I mean, the morganite. Who could possibly know about that? Only Bree and Robbie. And they're not blood witches. And of course wouldn't want to do this to me."

Robbie was living in Boston, a partner in a law firm, married to a woman he'd met in law school. He and Bree had dated through high school and broken up in college, but both of them and Morgan were still good friends and kept in touch regularly.

"Who else?" Sky said. "Someone who would *want* to hurt you?"

Morgan thought. "Well, there's Grania," she said. "But it's been so many years since I last saw her, at the funeral . . . it doesn't make sense that she'd be doing all of this now. And I don't think she's all that powerful, frankly. Neither is her son Kyle. I'm not sure about Iona—but I do think Killian would have warned me if he knew I was in danger from any of his family."

"Right." Sky said. "Then we're still stuck."

"Sky," Morgan said hesitantly, "you don't think—there's no way—I mean—" She heard Sky draw in a deep breath, then let it out.

"I think we'd be able to feel it somehow if he were still alive, don't you?" Sky's voice was rough-edged but gentle. "We've both tried, with small means and powerful ones, to track him through the years. But since the day that ferry went down, I haven't felt his presence. I haven't felt him anywhere in this world. And I really think that I would. Not because I'm so powerful or even because he was, but because of our connection."

"You're right. I haven't felt him either. And I'm sure I would have as well," Morgan said. At that moment she realized that deep down she'd somehow been hoping Sky would say, Maybe he's still alive! Let's find him! *How sad, after all these years, to have that hope.*

"You're much, much more powerful than I am," Sky went on. "More powerful than Hunter. And your connection to him was stronger than mine—I'm only his cousin. I think you would have felt something if he were still alive."

"I would have," Morgan said, feeling deflated. "It was all just so horrible. Because I didn't see it happen—that seems to make it less real. They never found him. I never had that final proof. When it happened, I felt nothing. I didn't feel his living presence, and I didn't feel his definite death. I just felt nothing."

"Maybe that's what death feels like."

"I guess it feels different every time," Morgan said hollowly, thinking back to Cal, Hunter, Ciaran . . . Colm.

"I'm sorry, Morgan." Very few people saw this softer side of Sky, and Morgan was deeply grateful. She and Sky had practically hated each other when they'd met, and it had taken years for them to achieve this understated friendship. "I could come down," Sky said casually. "I'm between jobs." Sky traveled around and had most recently worked as a translator for the medieval studies department at the University of Dublin.

Yes! Morgan cried inside, but she forced herself to say, "Thanks, Sky. I should probably figure things out here first. I've got some good people around me. We'll scry. Maybe we can uncover more information. How about I'll call if things get worse or I need your help?"

"Are you sure?"

*No.* "Yeah—I'll definitely call you if things get worse."

"Well, keep your eyes open. If someone's really doing this, it sounds a bit scary. Be careful—protect yourself, all right?"

"All right. Thanks. I'll talk to you soon."

# 7.
# Moira

I have to write this down before I forget. I want to forget, but I know it's important to remember. Who said, "If man doesn't learn from history, he's doomed to repeat it?" Or something like that. That's what this is like.

I don't know how to explain it, how to talk about it, even to my Book of Shadows. Oh, Goddess, I walked the fine edge between light and darkness tonight, and even now I don't know if I chose right.

Selene is dead at last. I saw the life fade from the eyes of her hawk, and I know her spirit couldn't escape. I didn't kill a person in a human body, but I crushed the spirit of someone who was once human, someone who was incredibly evil, who had tried to kill me, had hurt my sister.

Does that count?

Does it matter if I myself wasn't human when I did it? If I shape-shifted into a hawk, then was it one hawk killing another, and does that make it less bad?

Goddess, I don't know. Maybe I am on the dark side

*now. I don't want to be. I want to work for goodness. Do I get to try again? Goddess, I need answers. I'm only seventeen.*

"Free!" Tess cried, throwing her arms in the air. Moira, sitting on the school steps, closed her mother's Book of Shadows and smiled.

"Mondays are always so long," she said as students from their school streamed past them. She kept a watch out for Ian—they'd had barely any time to talk today between classes.

"Is your mom still freaked about Saturday?" Vita asked in a low voice. "My folks were uptight all yesterday. It was the worst thing I've ever seen."

"Me too," Moira said. "Yeah, Mum seems really rattled. She hates to let me out of her sight. Yesterday I met Ian in town, but I'd told Mum where I was and all."

"Iiiiaaaannn," Tess sang under her breath. "Did you tell him about the black smoke?"

"No." Moira shrugged. She still couldn't shake the uneasiness she'd felt since scrying with him.

"How are things going with him, then?" Tess asked.

"Good," Moira said, nodding. She saw Tess and Vita look at each other. "What?"

"What's wrong?" Vita asked. "You're all distracted. Like you're not really here."

That got Moira's attention. "I'm sorry." She leaned closer so only they could hear her. "Actually, I'm totally weirded out about my mum."

Tess and Vita looked at her questioningly.

Moira hesitated. But if she couldn't tell her two best

friends, who could she tell? "My mum shape-shifted," she breathed. "Into a hawk." Her friends' eyes went wide.

"No," Tess whispered. Vita's mouth was open in shock.

Moira nodded solemnly. "Mum told me yesterday, and then I found it in her second Book of Shadows. These books have been something else," she said softly. "It's a whole different picture of my mum. Like she had a completely different life that I didn't know anything about. It's kind of mad."

"Do you know what happened?" Vita asked.

"Not completely," said Moira. "I mean, she told me about it, and I was like, oh, Goddess. But then I read that bit in her second Book of Shadows this morning and again just now. And for some reason, reading about it got to me in a way her telling me about it didn't. Like it was more real. But I've been freaked out about it all day."

"Don't blame you," said Tess, looking worried. "I don't know what I'd do if I found out something like that. I mean, shape-shifted! That's some wicked magick."

Moira nodded, her tension feeling like a knot in her chest.

"Did you mention it to your mum?" Vita asked.

"No. Not yet. But we've been having big talks." Moira sighed. "About her. Her past. I mean, it's good and all, but . . ."

"Come on over and get it off your chest," Vita offered. "My folks are at work still, and Seanie won't bother us." Seanie was Vita's twelve-year-old brother.

"Moira?"

*Ian.* Moira turned and there he was, standing on the step above her. He gave her a slight smile, as if unsure how she would be today. Last night he'd insisted on walking with her all the way to her house in the rain because he hadn't wanted her to have to walk by herself. They'd held hands, and he'd kissed her again, in the road, right before the light from Moira's house had hit them. All day they'd been exchanging glances between classes and during maths, the one class they shared.

"Hi," she said, feeling shy in front of her friends.

"I'll come, then, Vi," Tess said, straightening up and acting normal. "Moira, you want to come or maybe another time?"

Tess was giving her an easy out. Moira glanced at Ian, at the expression in his eyes, and she nodded gratefully at her friends.

"Another time?"

"Sure." Tess and Vita waved good-bye. For a moment Moira wanted to change her mind and run after them. It had been such a relief to confide in them, and she wanted to talk about it more. On the other hand, this was *Ian*.

"Are you all right?" he asked after the two girls had left.

"Yes. You?" Could he see all the emotion in her eyes?

"All right. I'm amazed we didn't catch our death of cold," he said, trying for a light tone.

"Must be all that echinacea and goldenseal Mum pumps into me," Moira said, and Ian grinned. There. Now he looked like himself.

"Want to go sit in the park for a while?" he asked, and she nodded happily. The doubts were still there, but somehow being with Ian made everything else feel all right.

"What does that look like?" Ian asked.

Moira tilted her head and squinted at the pile of leaves on the ground. "Nothing. A fat mouse?"

Ian grinned at her. They were sitting side by side on a bench in the tiny park two blocks from school. The wind was picking up, and it was getting chillier as the sun started to think about going down. But Moira wasn't going to be the first to move—not when Ian had his arm around her and they were alone. Not even her mum's worrying could budge her. Moira sent her a quick witch message letting her know where she was.

"Cair a bèth na mill náth ra," Ian sang very softly under his breath. He chanted more words so quietly that Moira couldn't hear them.

The leaves on the ground shifted and overlapped and rearranged, separating and drawing together. Soon they had formed the initials *MB*, there on the brick walk.

Moira grinned with delight. "Next thing you know, you'll be doing it with ladybugs," she said, and Ian laughed.

The wind scattered her initials, and she leaned closer to him, feeling cozy.

"No, not ladybugs," he said, still smiling. "But maybe something a little bigger." He began to murmur some words, and Moira thought she recognized their form as being a weather-working spell. She raised her eyebrows. Weather working was considered taboo unless you had a very good reason. Of course, so was turning pages in people's books without their permission and writing one's initials in ladybugs . . . but it wasn't as if any of it actually *hurt* anyone.

"Oh my gosh . . . ," Moira breathed, staring at the sky. Almost imperceptibly, Ian was sculpting the clouds above and had gently morphed them into a huge, puffy *M* and a huge, puffy *B*. She laughed, but he wasn't finished, and soon a large plus sign floated next to her *B*, followed by a capital *I* and a *D. MB + ID.*

Laughing, Moira gently smacked his knee with her hand.

"Lovely—the world's largest graffiti." They smiled at each other, and then Moira said, "That's amazing—thank you. But maybe you shouldn't risk working weather magick."

"There's no risk in playing with clouds," Ian said reasonably. "I've always done it. It can be so cool." In the sky the letters were already wisping away. It *had* seemed harmless, Moira thought.

"You try it," Ian urged her. "You know how."

Moira hesitated for a second. Members of Belwicket— especially uninitiated ones—were not allowed to work weather charms. *Belwicket has such a narrow view of things sometimes.* Anyway, she probably wouldn't be able to do it—she wasn't initiated and had no practice.

"Right, then. Here goes," she said, closing her eyes and thinking about what she wanted to do. She thought about the clouds, their heavy grayness and the letters Ian had formed. Then she began to chant her coven's basic form of weather-working spells, adding in a ribbon of allowing the clouds to be whatever they wanted to be. She was proud of herself for remembering to weave in a time limitation and a place limitation. Instead of forcing the clouds into a picture she wanted, she would let them create one of their own, using their own essences. Frankly, she thought her idea was really cool.

*Crack!* Moira's eyes flew open as lightning bleached the world. Moments later a huge rumble of thunder shook their bench.

Her startled eyes met Ian's. "What did you do?" he asked with a mixture of amusement and concern.

"I let them be what they wanted?" Moira said uncertainly.

Another huge crack of lightning split the air not far away. Moira smelled the sizzle of ozone and felt her hair fill with static electricity. The enormous clap of thunder that followed the lightning sounded like a cannon going off right beside her ear.

"I think it wants to be a mother of a storm," Ian said, standing up and taking her hand. "Please tell me it won't last long."

"Four minutes," Moira said, then gasped as the sky opened and sheets of chilly rain dumped onto the streets. All around them people scurried for shelter. Dogs whined and barked, shoppers ducked back into stores they'd just come out of, and the whole world looked as if someone had turned off the light.

"Teatime," Ian said as another wave of thunder crashed down around them. He pulled Moira quickly up the block, then turned and ran down another street. By now they were soaked and Moira's teeth were chattering. Two more blocks seemed to take hours, with the frigid rain pelting their faces and clothes, their wet backpacks becoming heavier by the second. Finally they could see the sign for Margath's Faire, and Moira leapt through the door after Ian.

Oh, warmth, blessed warmth, she thought, shivering. Light. The smells of cinnamon and tea and something baking and candle wax.

For a minute Ian and Moira stood inside the door, silently dripping. Then they headed upstairs to the café, where Ian spotted an empty table. They grabbed it, shrugging out of their sodden jackets and dropping into seats still warm from the last customers. Ian shook his head, and fine droplets of water hit the table. Moira held up her hand. "Hey! I'm wet enough."

He grinned and took a paper napkin from the dispenser. Leaning over, he gently patted her face dry, which made Moira practically glow. "I can see why you were concerned about playing with clouds," he said low, so no one could hear.

Moira made an embarrassed face. "Sorry," she said. "I thought the clouds would just make themselves into a nice picture."

"Your clouds seem to have had delusions of grandeur," Ian told her, and she giggled.

Privately, Moira was unnerved that she had worked such powerful magick. She just prayed her mum or gran never found out. They would have her hide.

Ian fetched them both hot tea and a plates of scones with cream and jam. You are wonderful, Moira thought, suddenly ravenous. She checked her watch—an hour before dinner.

"I better let my mum know where I am again," she said apologetically, feeling like a baby. But she had promised. Moira looked off into the distance, concentrating but not closing her eyes. She formed her thoughts and sent them out into the world, aimed at her mother.

*I'm at Margath's Faire with Ian. I'll be home when the rain stops.*

*All right. See you soon. Be careful.*

Blinking, Moira came back to the moment and smiled ruefully at Ian. He was looking at her curiously.

"Did you send a witch message to your mum?"

"Uh-huh. She likes to know where I am. She worries."

"You can send witch messages, and you're not initiated yet?"

Moira looked up in surprise from where she was spreading jam on her scone. "Well, mostly just to Mum. Tess and Vita and I practice, but it's not so reliable."

"That's amazing," said Ian, warming Moira inside. She shrugged self-consciously and took a bite of scone. "And you always let your mum know where you are? Like yesterday, at Elise's Brook?"

Now she was embarrassed. He must think she was a total git.

"Yeah," she mumbled, looking at her plate.

"No, no, don't get me wrong," he said, leaning over and putting his hand on her knee. "I'm not trying to tease you. I just think it's amazing you can do that. All right?"

Moira looked at him, at his earnest face, his eyes, the lips that had kissed her so many times yesterday. He meant it.

"All right," she said, but she still felt self-conscious.

"Anyway—everything okay?" Ian asked lightly. "Did Morgan of Belwicket suspect you had anything to do with the storm?"

"I don't think so," Moira said, just as a man from the next table turned toward them.

Moira glanced over and found him looking at her. She frowned slightly and met Ian's eyes, then looked back at her scone. The man seemed familiar—did she know him from somewhere?

"Excuse me," he said, in a strong Scottish brogue. "Did you say Morgan of Belwicket?"

"Why do you ask?" Ian said, a touch of coolness entering his voice.

The man shrugged. "I'm on my way to see her. Passing through town. On my way to Dublin. Thought I'd drop in." He took a sip of his tea, and Moira looked at him more closely. He looked very familiar. He was maybe a little older than her mum, with dark auburn hair and dark eyes. Moira didn't think she'd ever met him—she would have remembered. His face was very alive, very knowing, with laugh lines etched around his eyes and a half smile lingering on his lips.

"What do you want with her?" Moira asked. Things had

been tense lately, with the attack on the coven and all. But she didn't want to sound overly rude in case he really was a friend of Mum's.

"Dropping in, like I told you. Usually she comes to see me—she travels a lot. This time I thought I'd save her a trip."

Moira's eyes narrowed. So he knew her mum traveled a lot. "Really? Who are you?"

The man smiled charmingly, and if Moira hadn't been on guard, her defenses would have melted. He was very attractive, she realized, startled to think that way about someone so many years older. But at that moment he radiated good will, humor, benevolence. Ian took her hand under the table and squeezed her fingers.

"I'm her brother, dear heart," the man said. "And who are you?"

Moira's eyes widened for a second before a look of suspicion came over her face. "She doesn't have a brother. She only has a sister."

"Actually, no," said the man with a friendly smile. "She has her American sister, the delightful Mary K., and then she also has me and two other siblings. Or half siblings, I should say."

"No," said Moira.

"How do you know?" the man asked playfully.

Ian squeezed Moira's fingers again, but not before she said, "I'm her daughter."

"Her daughter?" said the man, his eyes lighting up. "You're Moira, then. But I thought you were barely twelve or so. How time flies. Say hello to your Uncle Killian. Killian MacEwan."

Moira frowned. Why did that name sound familiar? Ian's hand had tightened on hers almost painfully, and she shook her fingers free before he cut off the circulation. Had her mum ever mentioned that name? Had she ever mentioned a half brother? No. But then, Mum hadn't mentioned Cal Blaire or Selene Belltower or shape-shifting into a bloody *hawk*, either.

"How could you be her half brother?"

"We had the same da, sweetheart, though your mum didn't know it till she was practically full grown."

Moira thought back. "Angus Bramson? Maeve Riordan's husband?"

"Angus wasn't her da. It was Ciaran MacEwan, my father."

He spoke softly, so probably no one else in the tea shop heard them. Still, to Moira it seemed as though the world stopped for a moment, all conversation ceased, every movement stilled.

She knew the name Ciaran MacEwan. Everyone knew it. It was right up there with other historical mass murderers.

"I don't understand," Moira said. "Ciaran MacEwan was your father? My *mother's* father?" A chill of fear went down her still-damp back, as if she expected him to whip out a wand and put curses on everyone in the room. Especially her.

Killian gave a long-suffering sigh that managed to convey his own personal regret that he hadn't chosen his parents better. "Aye, that he was, I'm afraid. And Morgan's, too. But if you're her daughter, why don't you know that?" He cocked his head and looked at her.

Across the table, Ian looked frozen. Moira immediately felt horrified that he was here, listening to this stuff. It couldn't possibly be true. If it were true . . .

"Because it isn't true," Moira said firmly. "You're making it up. Why in the world would you think Ciaran MacEwan could be my mum's father? This is nonsense. I'm going." She stood up abruptly and grabbed her book bag. Ian got up also, moving his chair so she could get out.

"Come on," he said. "I'll see you home." He glanced at the stranger, but it wasn't a glance of revulsion or distrust. More like awe, Moira thought, and that upset her even more. *How could Ian be so stupid? Ciaran MacEwan was evil personified. That's his son!* She was so overwhelmed right now, she couldn't handle worrying about Ian and his motives. She had to be able to trust him, at least.

She pushed out of Margath's Faire into the street, to see that the rain had stopped and the sun had gone down and she had a long bicycle ride in the dark. Dammit. She'd just leave her bike at school and take the bus home.

"Hi, Morgan's daughter," came a voice from behind them: Killian's. "Can I offer you a lift? I'm going to your mother's now."

He had to be kidding. Like she hadn't heard enough horror stories about strangers in general and the MacEwans in particular. This guy's dad had helped develop the dark wave that had killed hundreds and hundreds of innocent witches and nonwitches.

"No," she said firmly, glancing back. "I can get home myself, thank you."

# 8.
# Morgan

Morgan answered Katrina's gentle tap on the door. Rain and wind gusted in with her mother-in-law.

"Hi," Morgan said. "Where did this storm come from? Moira's caught in it in Cobh."

"It's not a natural storm," said Katrina, sitting stiffly in a chair at the dining table. "You didn't work it, did you?"

"Me?" Morgan looked at her in surprise as she put the teakettle on the stove. "No, of course not. Why?"

Katrina shrugged. "Someone did. No one I recognize. But it is magickal."

Uneasy, Morgan filled the teapot and fetched two mugs. She'd been so deep in her thoughts she hadn't even sensed the magick behind the storm. Now someone was working weather magick. Was it Ealltuinn? Were they behind all of the things that had been happening? "I didn't sense it," she murmered

"You could, if you were outside for a minute," said Katrina.

Something in the older woman's voice made Morgan look

up. "What is it, Katrina?" She slid into a chair and started to pour the tea.

"Morgan—have you been working magick I don't know about?" Katrina looked uncomfortable and concerned. "I don't mean herb spells and practice rites. I mean big magick, dangerous magick, that none of us know about."

"Goddess, no, Katrina! How can you ask that?"

Katrina's blue eyes met Morgan's over the table. She hesitated, circling her hand widdershins over her mug to cool the tea. "I don't know," she said finally. "I just feel . . . off. I feel like something is off somewhere. Out of balance. And then that black smoke."

Nodding, Morgan said, "Keady Dove and I are trying to trace it. We need more people, though. Perhaps tomorrow you, Christa, and Will can help us."

"Yes, of course," said Katrina. "That's a good idea." She fidgeted in her chair, looking around. "I just feel—off balance." She seemed frustrated about not being able to explain it better.

"It isn't because of anything I've been doing," Morgan said. "But there's been some odd stuff happening, that's a fact."

She told Katrina about the face in the window, the chunk of morganite, and even her dream. "Plus there was the hex pouch and the black smoke. Now a worked storm." She listened and realized that the storm had already blown over.

"Odd, odd." Katrina shook her head. "Let's try to scry now. Maybe if we join our powers, we can begin to figure out what's going on. It doesn't seem like we can afford to wait until tomorrow."

Morgan glanced at the clock. It was almost six, but when

Moira was with Ian, time seemed to have no meaning. She nodded.

Morgan generally scryed with fire, which spoke the truth and could be very powerful, but often showed only what it wanted you to see. Colm had only rarely scried—it didn't work well for him. Some people used water or stone. Hunter had used stone. It was difficult and gave up its knowledge only reluctantly, but what it told you could be relied upon.

Morgan fetched a short pillar candle from her workroom. It was a deep cream color, and Morgan had carved runes into it and laid spells upon it to help clarify its visions.

Morgan set the candle in the center of the table, dimmed the room's lights, and sat down across from Katrina. They linked hands across the table.

"Goddess, we call on thee to help us see what we should know," Morgan said. "We open ourselves to the knowledge of the universe. Please help us receive your messages. Someone is working against us—please show us their face and their reasoning."

"We ask it in the name of goodness," Katrina murmured.

Morgan looked at the candle's blackened, curled wick. *Fire,* she thought, and pictured the first spark igniting. With a tiny crackle the wick burst into flame, coiling more tightly in the fire's heat. A thin spire of joy rose steadily in Morgan's chest: magick. It was the life force inside her.

*Breathe in, breathe out. Relax each muscle. Relax your eyelids, your hands, your calves, your spine. Release everything. Release tension, release emotion of all kinds. Release your tenacious grip on this world, this time, to free yourself to receive information from all worlds, from all times.*

Scrying was a journey taken within. The fire called to her, beckoned. The candle released a slow, steady scent of beeswax and heat. *Show me,* Morgan whispered silently. *Show me.*

A tannish blotch formed before her, blotting out some of the candle's light. Morgan squinted, and the splotch widened and narrowed. It looked like a . . . beach. The image pulled back a bit, and Morgan could see a thin rim of blue-green water, cloudy and cold looking, pelted by rain, crashing against the narrow spit of sand that flowed horizontally across her vision. The coastline was dotted with gray-blue rocks, pebbles, boulders, thick, sharp shards of shale pushing upward through the beach, thrust there by some prehistoric earthquake, now clawing the sky like clumsy fingers of stone.

A beach. A beach with cold gray water and stones. Where was it? It was impossible to say. But there was no southern sunshine, no pure white sand, no clear water showing rays and corals. It was a northern beach, maybe at the top of Ireland or off the coast of Scotland?

A dim, slight figure started wandering toward the water. Morgan knew better than to look directly at it: like many optical illusions, if you stared straight at a vision, it often disappeared. She kept her gaze focused on the center, feeling the slight warmth of the candle on her face. The figure became clearer. It, too, was the color of bleached sand, tan and cream, and it had splotches of crimson on its chest, the top of its head. It was tall, thin, and it was staggering. A man.

*Breathe in, breathe out. Expect nothing: accept what comes. Show me.*

The man approached the water, then dropped to his hands and knees, his head hanging low. *Who?* Morgan didn't ask the question, just let the word float gently out of her consciousness. Soon the figure seemed larger, closer. Morgan tried not to look, tried only to see without looking.

The man raised his head and looked into Morgan's eyes, and her heart stopped with one last, icy beat.

*Hunter.*

A much older, ragged Hunter. His hair was long and wispy and so was his darker beard. His eyes were dark, haunted, like an animal's, full of pain. His rag of a shirt was tannish, the color of the beach, except for a rust-colored stain sprayed across the chest—blood. His head, too, was marked with blood, old blood, from an old wound, and in that instant Morgan saw in her mind a jagged chunk of shale clipping Hunter across the head, leaving that blood, that wound. Scents rushed toward her: the bitter saltiness of the waves, the coldness of the wind, the metallic tang of blood, the heat of Hunter's skin. Seaweed, wet stone. Illness.

I can't breathe, Morgan thought, shock actually making her feel faint. As she stared, jaw clenched, the image of Hunter faded slowly. She gulped convulsively, trying to get air to her lungs. It was all she could do not to scream, *Bring him back!* But another image slid forward: a woman. She was dark, the light was behind her, and though Morgan peered desperately, she could make out no details. It was a woman, standing before a huge fire that was spitting and smoking into the air. The woman raised her hand, and in it was an athame. In her other hand she held a writhing black snake, its triangular head whipping back and forth as it tried to bite her. Morgan winced as the woman brought athame and snake together, and then she threw the serpent into the fire.

A huge, stinking cloud of smoke rose up, billowed over, and filled the cave. Cave? The smoke roiled poisonously and blotted out the woman's image. Morgan recoiled.

Suddenly the front door burst open and Moira rushed in. "Mum!" she cried. "Mum!"

Startled, Morgan dropped Katrina's hands and pulled back. A gust of cold, wet air swirled in and doused the scrying candle. Morgan blinked, trying to make sense of reality. She'd just seen *Hunter*. Had Katrina seen him, too?

Moira was there, followed by Ian Delaney, followed by . . . Killian?

"Mum!" Moira cried again.

Morgan's brain wasn't functioning properly. Katrina was blinking, too, obviously shaken by what they had seen. Morgan felt her heart slowly begin to thud.

"Honey, what is it?" she managed, her voice a croak.

Moira motioned back over her shoulder to Killian. "Mum, who was your dad? Your real father. Wasn't it Angus?"

*Oh, no. Not this, not yet.* She'd known this was coming— Moira was reading her Books of Shadows. And perhaps it should have come a long time ago. But right now, on top of everything else, it just felt like too much. Morgan's shoulders tensed as she looked at Killian. He shrugged again, an unrepentant look on his face. *If you can't tell your own daughter the truth . . .* , he seemed to say.

"It's—it's complicated," Morgan said lamely.

Moira's eyes widened, and she gestured to Killian. "So you *know* him?" Obviously she hoped that Morgan would deny all knowledge of him, but it was too late for that.

"Yes," Morgan said, wishing with all she had that this

wasn't how Moira was finding out. "He's my half brother. Killian, come in."

Killian stood a moment, glancing back and forth between Morgan and Moira. "Cute cottage you've got here," he finally said, a bit awkwardly, and then came over and sat at the table. "Is that tea?"

"Yes," Morgan said. "Moira, why don't you sit down, too." She looked over at where Ian was standing, just inside the door. "Ian, I'm sorry—this is kind of a bad time for us."

"I understand," he said, and he went up a notch in Morgan's opinion. He looked like a nice kid. Unfortunately, so had Cal. Ian squeezed Moira's hand, and she let him out the front door. Once he was gone, Morgan pulled out a chair for Moira, who sat down reluctantly.

"I'm so sorry, Moira," Morgan said.

Moira looked from Killian to her mother, her face pale. "I met him in the village," she said. "He says he's your half brother. He says Ciaran MacEwan was your father. Your father! What is he talking about?"

Morgan took a deep breath. Colm, be with me, she thought.

"You know that I was sixteen when I first found out I was adopted," she began. "I've told you about how shocking it was, how weird it made things in my family. And over the next several months I found out more about my birth mother, Maeve Riordan, and Angus Bramson."

"You've told me all this," Moira said. She picked up a paper napkin and twisted it in her hands.

"Later that same fall I discovered that Angus wasn't actually my real father," Morgan went on. She looked at Katrina, who shook her head sadly. "I found out that in fact another witch, Ciaran MacEwan, had had an affair with Maeve, and that was when she got pregnant with me. They were mùirn beatha dàns, but Ciaran was already married—they couldn't be together. I know Maeve loved him very much." Morgan refused to look at Killian, who was sitting quietly.

"And I think in his own way, he loved Maeve," Morgan went on. "But as I said, he was married, and he already had three children. Killian was his youngest child. I met Killian a long time ago, in New York, and we realized we were half siblings. Since then he and I have kept in touch."

Moira looked stunned and angry. "Ciaran MacEwan! One of the most evil witches in history was your father!" She looked at Killian. "You don't care?"

Killian shook his head slowly. "I wish many things had been different, lass," he said seriously. "I wish Ciaran had not been evil. I wish my parents had loved each other, I wish my dad had been different, I wish my mother could have done better for herself. But it's not Morgan's fault for having been born, and it's not my place to judge anyone. None of us are without stains. I'm happy to have Morgan for a half sister, no matter how we happened to get here."

It was times like these that made up for all the times Killian drove Morgan crazy. As close as she had always been to her sister, Mary K., she was still happy to have a sibling with whom she shared a blood bond. She smiled at him sadly, her half brother.

"But Ciaran MacEwan." The horror in Moira's voice was an eerie echo of Morgan's own reaction, so many years ago, to the revelation about her relation to Ciaran. Moira's napkin was in shreds and she started tapping her fingers nervously on a fork. "Did you ever meet him?"

"Yes," Morgan said. "I did. He was . . . already dark by then. He knew I was his daughter. He wanted me to join him, but I wouldn't. So he tried to kill me and take my powers. But all the same, in his own way, I know he loved me. He was proud of me. He saw something of himself in me."

"Goddess, I hope not!" Moira said.

"It's true," Killian said. "Not that your mum is evil, not at all. But of all of his children, Morgan inherited Da's greatness, his strength, and his ruthlessness. Your mum can be very ruthless." He smiled as he said it, and Morgan knew he didn't consider it an insult.

"Did Ciaran know about you before Maeve died?" Moira asked.

Morgan shook her head. "No. She had me and gave me up for adoption because she didn't want Ciaran to know. But he still came for her, and when she refused to be with him, because he was married and she was with Angus, he locked her and Angus in a barn and set it on fire." How bizarre to state the facts so calmly, Morgan thought.

Moira's eyes were huge and round. "Goddess," she whispered. "He killed them?"

"Yes." Morgan felt a familiar sadness. "He loved her so much, and he killed her. And he loved me and tried to kill me. And I loved him, and in the end I trapped him and bound him so his powers could be stripped. And he died because of it."

"You trapped him and bound his powers?" Moira whispered. "You bound Ciaran MacEwan?"

Morgan nodded, looking down at the table. "And he had

his powers stripped. And he was never the same after that, and he hated me for it. And then he died." She swallowed hard and felt that Killian was feeling the same ache.

"And Ciaran is part of you, and you're part of me. . . ." Moira trailed off, her eyes full of anguish and confusion. Morgan felt herself being torn apart all over again, watching her daughter suffer the same shock and betrayal she had once experienced. Only it was even worse this time, because Morgan would have taken on a world of pain to spare her daughter an ounce.

"I'm so sorry," Morgan said again, her voice cracking. "I should have told you earlier. It's just—I remember how horrified I was when I realized who my father had been. I would have given anything for it not to be true. And—for you not to have to live with that knowledge as well."

"So Ciaran loved your mum and then killed her, and Ciaran loved you and tried to kill you, and then you bound him and had his powers stripped." Moira shook her head. "And this is my family," she murmured. "This is who you are—who I am."

Morgan jumped up and went to Moira, gripping her shoulders firmly and looking deep into her eyes. "There's more to your family than that," she said. "Maeve was a good, strong witch. She didn't know Ciaran was married when she got involved with him. She loved me so much, she gave me away rather than see harm come to me. You have your gran and Poppy and Nana. You had your dad. I loved your dad, and he loved me, and it was good. Good and safe and true."

"Gran—did you know all this, all about Mum's past?" Moira's voice trembled.

Katrina nodded evenly. "As Killian said, it isn't Morgan's

fault who her parents were and what they did. Morgan is a good witch and a good person. The best daughter-in-law one could hope for. One's heritage is important, but one's own choices are more so. Morgan's got nothing to be ashamed of, and neither have you."

Moira just sat and stared at Morgan. "If you've got nothing to be ashamed of," she said, "why haven't you told me any of this? Why am I finding out about it from strangers in tea shops? How could you have lied to me all this time? What's next?" She looked away. "I don't know who you are anymore," she told Morgan, and Morgan felt tears come to her eyes. "I—I need some air." She strode to the front door and pulled it open, pushing through it into the night outside.

"Moira, wait!" Morgan cried, immediately heading after her.

Katrina stopped her, holding her by the shoulders, as Morgan had just held Moira. Morgan started crying, hanging her head. "I'll go after her," Katrina said. "You're both too upset. You stay here. We'll be back soon." She moved toward the door, her arthritis making her limp slightly.

"No, she's my daughter. I need to go," Morgan insisted.

Katrina fixed Morgan with a calm, steady gaze. "If you want what's best for her, you'll let me go," she said. "Moira needs a bit of space right now if she's going to come back to you. Do you understand?"

It went against her every instinct not to go after Moira herself, but Katrina was right—Moira didn't want to see her right now, and if Morgan chased her, Moira would keep running. There was too much danger out there now, danger Morgan didn't yet understand. Moira trusted her grandmother, and Morgan would have to do the same.

"Just—keep her safe," Morgan told Katrina.

Katrina nodded and headed out.

When the door closed behind her, Morgan sat down weakly. She wiped a napkin across her eyes, then dropped her head into her hands. "How many stupid mistakes can I make with her?"

"Quite a few, I should imagine," Killian said, not unkindly. "You'll see—things will be all right in the end."

If only things were that easy, Morgan thought dully.

# 9.
# Moira

Once outside, Moira stared around blankly, realizing there wasn't really anywhere to go. She had no car, and Vita and Tess both lived a good distance away.

The front door opened, and Gran came out. She walked over to Moira, limping slightly, and Moira realized that her grandmother was getting older. In fact, she'd seemed a lot older since Dad had died.

"Come sit here with me," Katrina said, patting the small iron bench that stood next to the front gate. Moira paused, then sat. Everything was wet out here from the rain, but neither of them said anything about their pants getting soaked.

"Did Dad know?" Moira asked. "About—about Mum's family?"

Gran smiled at her kindly. "Yes, your dad knew," she said. "He loved Morgan for who she is, not for who her people were. Tell me—what would you think of someone who married a man just because his family was rich and powerful and she was poor? She didn't love him, she just loved who his people were, what he had."

"I'd think she was awful," Moira said, frowning.

"What about the opposite, to *not* marry someone just because their people weren't who you wanted them to be? To think that someone's family is beneath them, not good enough?"

Moira sighed. "That's not good either, I guess."

"Morgan is Morgan," her gran said. "We searched her out years ago because she was Maeve's daughter, a Riordan, and we hoped she'd have the Riordan powers. But if she hadn't been a good person, we never would have invited her to help us rebuild Belwicket, no matter how powerful she was."

"But she's been lying to me all these years," Moira said, her feelings still raw and hurt. "Or at least not bothering to tell me the truth."

"You don't have to know every detail of your mother's past," Gran said reasonably. "No child does. It's your mother's job to love you and try to do the best she can to bring you up well. She isn't obligated to tell you every secret and make sure it's fine with you. All she can do is her best. If she makes mistakes, well, everyone does."

"But not everyone has *Ciaran MacEwan* for a father," Moira cried. "He's my grandfather! How am I supposed to live with that? What will people think about me when they find out?" A terrible thought occurred to her. "Oh, Goddess—tell me no one else knows about this. Does anyone in the village know?"

"Some of the coven. I'm sure others as well," Katrina said gently.

Moira moaned and put her face in her hands. "I'm Ciaran's granddaughter. I have his blood. What does that mean?"

"It means you face choices every day, like everyone else," Katrina said. "You will have to choose goodness over and over again your whole life. And you'd have to do that even if all your relatives were saints who had led blameless lives."

"When you first met Mum, did you know who she was?"

"Yes, of course. I sought her out, remember? When I found out a child of Maeve's existed, I learned all I could about her. I knew about Ciaran and everything else. When I met Morgan, I knew she was for Belwicket."

"You didn't mind her marrying Dad?"

"Heavens, no." Katrina paused for a moment, thinking. "I was thankful when she agreed to marry Colm, grateful that she would stay among us and help bring Belwicket back up to speed. I was grateful I was able to help her."

"Help her?" Moira looked at her gran. "How did you help her?"

"Your mum went through a bad time," Gran said, weighing her words carefully. "A friend of hers had died in an accident, and she was very, very upset. She'd already done so much to invigorate Belwicket. I knew that with her strength and positive energy, our coven could be strong once again. We could triumph over those who'd tried to destroy us. We needed Morgan, and she helped us." Gran paused and looked down. "So when I could help her, I was happy to smooth her troubles away," she said softly. "To help her adjust to her new life."

*Something feels off. Gran's uncomfortable.* Moira'd had no idea that her mum had ever gone through a "bad time" and that she'd had troubles. "What kind of troubles?" she asked, intrigued. "How could you smooth them away?"

Katrina frowned, as though she regretted saying anything.

"Sadness. Troubles from her life before. We all loved her so much and wanted her to be able to heal. Our love did a lot to smooth the way for her here." She stood up, slowly straightening. "The important thing is not to judge your mother, love. Try not to judge anyone. You can never know what causes another person to act, can never tell how true their motivations are. Now, I'm going in to help your mum get dinner together. Looks like Killian will be staying for it. You come in when you're ready, but don't stay out too long—your mother is quite worried about you. All right?"

"All right." Moira sat on the wet bench for a minute after her grandmother had gone inside. She couldn't shake the feeling that Gran had been keeping something back, something major. Had Mum had a nervous breakdown? Had she been in trouble with the police? Moira couldn't believe that. Had it had something to do with Ciaran? Who was the friend who'd died? She had so many questions and no answers.

Moira sighed, smelling the dampness from her storm still on the grass, her mother's herbs, the stones. She'd felt so happy with Ian today. He made her feel as though she could do anything. He thought she was amazing. If only she could see him now—feel his arms around her, hear his soothing voice. It would be so comforting, so wonderful. It would help soothe this awful pain she had inside.

She knew where he lived—across the headland, around the curve of the coast, maybe three miles away. Moira glanced at the living-room window. Killian was sitting at the table. Her mum was getting out plates. Gran was slicing bread. When they realized she was missing, Mum would scry to find her. But she might still have enough time to see him. Just for two minutes. Two minutes with him would feel so perfect.

After another quick glance through the window, Moira got her bike from around the back and silently wheeled it through the garden gate.

Moira had never been to Ian's house before, but she knew which one it was. He lived in the next village over, Hewick, and once Mum had taken some herbs to a friend who lived not far from Ian. She'd pointed out Lilith Delaney's cottage.

It was dark, going across the headland. There was no road here, only a rough, rutted trail that farmers used to move their sheep. The headlamp on her bicycle made a pale beam that bobbed every time she hit a pebble. Of course, Moira had magesight. Not as much as she would have after she was initiated, but she could see enough so that she could just manage to avoid killing herself by hitting big rocks or running off the road into a ditch.

Though Ian's house wasn't far, it took Moira much longer to get there than she had expected. Once she had pulled up outside the cottage's fence, she had a wave of second thoughts. This was stupid, to show up uninvited. Mum couldn't stand Lilith Delaney—Lilith couldn't stand her mum, either. And there was still the question of the black smoke from Saturday night. What if her mother was right about Lilith having been behind that? Even if Moira was right about Ian, that didn't mean his mum was good as well. And no one knew she was here. She thought for a second about sending her mum a witch message, then thought better of it. She'd just ride home.

Quickly Moira swung her leg back over the seat of her bicycle and was about to set off when the door of the cottage opened. A rectangle of light splashed onto the lawn, and then Ian's voice called, "Moira?"

Moira winced. The first thing she would do after she had been initiated would be to learn a complete disappearing spell. What was the point of being a witch if you couldn't get yourself out of stupid, possibly even scary situations like this?

"Hi," she said lamely, getting back off her bike. "I was just out, and—"

"You're upset," Ian said. "What happened after I left? Can you come in and tell me about it?"

Moira paused, torn. Something was pulling her toward Ian—she'd come here even knowing deep down that it could be dangerous. *Witches are supposed to trust their instincts, right?* Anyway, if Ian or his mom *were* going to hurt her, they could do it now whether she came into the house or not. With a sigh Moira opened their garden gate and met Ian on the walk. "It was pretty horrible," she admitted. "I needed to get out of there for a while."

Ian smiled at her. "I'm glad you're here. I'm so glad you thought I could help." He put his arms around her and held her tightly, stroking her hair and resting his head against hers.

Moira's heart melted. Her hair and jacket were frosted with mist, but now that he was holding her, warming her, giving her all the support and comfort she had desperately needed, she barely felt the chill. It had been right for her to come here.

He released her and looked into her eyes to see how she was doing. She managed a tremulous smile, and they started toward the house. As soon as Moira crossed the threshold, she smelled slightly bitter and burned herbs. Several things caught her eye at once: the glass-fronted bookcase filled with ancient-looking leather-bound books, used candles, crumpled silk shawls, and incense bowls; a ragged, red velvet couch, pushed beneath the set of windows, their panes clouded and in need of washing; and then, to her left, an open archway leading into what had once been the dining room.

Most witches Moira knew kept their houses soothing and restful, with things put away and kept clean. This much disorder was unusual, and Moira felt the back of her neck prickle. Through the archway she finally noticed that Lilith was working at the table in there, looking into a large chunk of crystal propped up against an old book. *She's scrying.* Automatically Moira looked at the crystal. In its mottled, flawed surface Moira saw an image of a man. It was quite clear: he was middle-aged, with long, light hair and a scraggly beard. He was wearing rags, like a homeless person, and his skin was sunburned and deeply etched with wrinkles.

In the next second Lilith looked up, saw Moira, and passed her hand over the crystal. The image winked out. Moira remembered her mum talking about Lilith using dark magick and wondered what she'd been doing. It had looked like ordinary scrying, but she couldn't be sure.

Then, aware that she was meeting Ian's mother for the first time, Moira managed a shy smile. "I'm sorry," she said. "I didn't mean to disturb you."

Ian's mother came over, wiping her hands on an age-worn housekeeping apron.

"Mum, this is Moira," said Ian, coming over to stand beside her. "I told you about her. From school."

"Oh, yes," said his mother. "It's Moira Byrne, isn't it?"

"Yes," said Moira. So Ian had told his mum about her.

That was either a really good sign—meaning he liked her—or a bad sign, if her mother was right that this was all part of some kind of plan.

"Welcome," said Lilith. "I'm so glad to meet you. Ian's mentioned you to me, so you must be special." She smiled, and Moira smiled back, feeling an odd sensation and not recognizing what it was. It felt as if she were in the woods and had suddenly come across an animal or an insect she didn't know: a slight twinge of fear, but also curiosity.

"What brings you out at night like this?" Lilith asked. She moved through the living room and went into the kitchen, which was through another set of doors. Their house was a good bit bigger than Moira's, but not as neat or cozy. Just big, neglected, and cluttered. Moira wondered what Ian thought about it.

"Oh, just wanted some fresh air," Moira said as Lilith put the kettle on the stove. She was surprised by how uncomfortable she was. This kitchen was a disaster, and Moira blinked at Lilith's obvious flouting of witchy habits. Her mum's kitchen was tiny but usually scrubbed clean, things put away, fresh fruit and vegetables in bowls. This kitchen was the opposite. It could have been such a nice room, large, with big windows. But there were unwashed dishes stacked everywhere, cooking pots with remains of meals from who knew how long ago, bunches of wilted herbs or vegetables lying around. Moira half expected to see a mouse sitting boldly on a counter, eating a piece of dried cheese.

Ian, too, seemed to be becoming less comfortable. "Mum, I'll do that," he said, taking some tea mugs from the cupboard. "We don't want to interrupt you."

Lilith stopped and gave her son an appraising glance. Moira couldn't tell if she was angry or hurt, but she again wished she hadn't come here uninvited.

Ian looked back at his mother steadily, and finally, with a somewhat brittle smile, she nodded good-bye to Moira and walked out of the kitchen. Ian stood silently for a moment; then the kettle hissed and he turned off the gas beneath it.

"I'm sorry, Ian," Moira said in a near whisper. "I didn't mean to barge in like this. I was so upset and just wanted to see you. I didn't mean to cause any trouble." At that moment Moira got a sudden, odd feeling, as if someone had just taken her picture. She looked around, but she and Ian were alone. Then she realized her mum was scrying for her and knew she was at Ian's. Trouble was coming. Well, as long as she was already caught, there was no use in rushing home now.

Ian got out a couple of tea bags and plopped one in each mug. "I'm *glad* you came to see me. You haven't caused any trouble," he said in a normal tone. "That's just my mom. There's just the two of us, and we don't see eye to eye about a lot of stuff." He filled the mugs with hot water and handed one to Moira. "Like this kitchen, for example. All I want to do is turn seventeen so I can get my own flat and have a decent place. All this mess makes me insane. Every once in a while I lose it and clean everything up, and then we have a big row. Mum doesn't see what the big deal is. I don't care who cleans up as long as one of us does. But she won't, and she hates it when I do, so I'm stuck."

"What about your dad?"

Ian's expression darkened. "They broke up a long time ago."

"Do you ever see him?"

Ian shook his head slowly. "Nah. Not in a couple of years. We moved here, and he didn't seem too interested in keeping in touch. I think he has a new family now."

Moira blinked. Odd—that sounded a lot like what she'd read about Cal in her mum's Book of Shadows. But still, plenty of people had divorced parents and didn't see their dads much. It didn't mean anything.

"I'm sorry," Moira said. "It's different, I know, but I do know what it's like to lose your da." Moira sipped her tea, wondering if she should just say what had driven her here in the first place. After all, according to Katrina, people knew the truth anyway, so it wasn't like she was revealing some big secret. No, the only person it had been a secret from was *her*, the one person who deserved to know. She looked up and saw Ian looking at her, concerned.

"Are you all right?" he asked.

"Ciaran MacEwan really was my grandfather," she blurted. "Mum told me everything after you left. It was all true. I feel like I'm, well, *destined* to be bad."

Ian made a sympathetic face. "Even if Ciaran was your grandfather," he said, "that doesn't change anything about you—you never even knew him, and he's gone now."

"But my mum let me believe someone else was my grandfather my whole life," Moira went on. "I feel like I don't even know her anymore. Like I hardly even know myself. Yesterday I was Moira Byrne. Today I'm Moira Byrne, granddaughter of Ciaran MacEwan. How am I going to face anyone?"

"Look—I know, and I don't care," Ian said seriously, taking her hand. Moira felt her breath quicken and a tingle of awareness start at the bottom of her spine. "Anyone who thinks it's a big deal, just ignore them. And that's whether they think it's good *or* bad."

"What do you mean, *good*? How could anyone possibly think it's *good*?"

Ian looked at her.

"Oh."

Dark witches. They'd be happy to find the granddaughter of Ciaran MacEwan. Without thinking, Moira glanced at the doorway, wondering if Lilith was out there. Had Ian known all along about Ciaran? Had Lilith?

Moira sighed and rubbed her forehead. "I'd better go. They were starting dinner when I left." *And my mum might be barreling down the road right now in her rusty old banger.*

She put her mug down and left the kitchen. She looked over into the dining room as she passed by, where Lilith Delaney was still working, small, half-moon glasses perched on her nose.

"Good night, Moira," Lilith said evenly.

Had she heard what Moira had been saying to Ian? There was no way to know. "Good night, Ms. Delaney," said Moira, trying to smile normally.

Ian walked her outside. The mist had let up; some of the clouds had cleared away and the stars were beginning to assert themselves again. Most of the moon was visible, and it laid a cream-colored wash of light over the landscape. Going home would be much easier than coming.

"Thanks, Ian," Moira said. "Sorry again to barge in on you."

"Please stop apologizing," he said. "I always want you to come to me if you need help. About anything." He looked awkward for a moment, then said, "I wish I had a better place for you to come to."

Her heart went out to him. "Nobody's perfect," she said, putting her hand on his arm. "There's always something wrong with everyone's parents or house or whatever."

"Yeah. I just can't wait to be on my own."

Moira looked into his blue eyes, lighter than the night sky, and saw his impatience. He wasn't like Cal. It was so clear. *I wish he would kiss me.* And then suddenly he was, leaning over and blotting out the moon. His lips on hers were soft but exploring, as if he was trying to memorize everything about her. She put her arms around his shoulders, excitement coiling in her chest, and wished ludicrously that her stupid bike wasn't between them.

Ian slanted his head slightly and put his hands on her waist. The pedal of her bike was digging into her shin, but she ignored it. Could she just break the kiss, step around the bike, and grab him again?

Then he was drawing back, his eyes glittering. "Move your bike," he said intently, and quickly she stepped around the bike, letting it fall to the soft, muddy grass. Then they were pressed together tightly, and Ian's hand was holding the back of her neck so he could kiss her. They seemed perfectly matched, their hips pressed together, their mouths slanting against each other, their arms wrapped around each other as if they were trying to meld.

She thought she might love him.

# 10.
# Morgan

Morgan thought she was going to explode. First she and Katrina had seen Hunter when they scried. Since Killian was there, they hadn't had a chance to talk about it alone. And when she hadn't been able to sense Moira outside, she'd scried for her and found her at Ian Delaney's house. Morgan had to find her, talk to her, tell her how sorry she was. She sent her a quick witch message. *Moira, please come home. Please—or I will have to come and get you.*

*I'm on my way,* Moira sent back, and Morgan almost sobbed in relief.

"Moira's coming back," she told Killian and Katrina.

"Oh, good. She'll be all right, you'll see," said Killian. "You'll make up."

Morgan smiled gratefully at her half brother, who'd grown up virtually without a father himself. Now Killian had three children of his own. He seemed more thoughtful, less self-centered. He stood, clearing the table, while Morgan just sat, her stomach knotting with tension.

Just then she felt Moira coming up the front path. Leaping from the table, she ran to the front door just as Moira reached it. As soon as she saw her daughter, she burst into tears and gathered her close. *Please don't push me away.* At first Moira stood stiffly in her embrace, but she slowly loosened up and gradually put her arms around Morgan.

"I'm sorry, honey," Morgan said. "I'm so sorry. I never meant to hurt you."

"I wish—I wish you had just told me the truth," Moira said.

"I know. I wish I had, too." Morgan pulled back and looked at Moira, brushing some damp hair out of her face. "But you're my family, and I'm yours. And that's all that matters."

Looking a little teary-eyed herself, Moira nodded.

Morgan started to draw her into the warmth and light of the house, but Moira paused, looking at the walk.

"I stepped on something," she said.

"A stone?"

"No." Moira looked, then leaned over and picked up something shiny from the brick path. "Here," she said, handing it to Morgan. "Did you drop this?"

Squinting, Morgan turned sideways in the door so the inside light would fall on her palm. Small, silver, a bit crusty but still glinting. She brushed some of the dirt away as Moira eased past her into the house.

It was a ring—who could have dropped it? She brushed more of the dirt away. Keady, maybe? Katrina? *Oh, Goddess.*

Morgan's heart clenched, and she wondered if she were dreaming again. It was a silver claddagh ring. They weren't uncommon in Ireland—many people wore them. But no one had one with the rune Beorc, for new beginnings, engraved on the inside. This was Morgan's ring, the one Hunter had given her a lifetime ago. This was the ring that had flown off her finger that day in Wales, when the ferry went down. And now here it was, appearing on her doorstep an hour after she'd seen Hunter.

Her eyes huge, Morgan stared at Moira. There were no words to describe what she was feeling, the emotions she was being assaulted with. She was losing her mind—she felt like she was about to collapse right there, in front of all of them. Who was doing this to her? Making her heart break all over again, when it had broken so many times already?

"Is it yours?" Moira asked. "Do you recognize it?"

Morgan managed a nod. The room swam around her; her breath came shallowly.

"Mum? You don't—feel right." Moira sounded worried. "Maybe you should sit down."

Morgan couldn't move until Moira took her elbow and led her to a dining chair. Her ring. It had fallen into the sea, with Hunter, her love. It had been torn away from her, wrenched away just as Hunter had been. How had the ring come back here? Only Sky, Bree, and Mary K. knew how she had lost it. Goddess, why was Hunter suddenly everywhere in her life, when he'd been taken from her so many years ago? The pain was too much, too much to bear.

Someone had deliberately put the ring there for her to find. Like the morganite. And it didn't make sense that it was Lilith—this had to be someone close to Morgan. Someone who knew her well. And the ring and the morganite, the vision and the dream, the scrying—they were all pieces of a puzzle, a horrible maze closing around her, scaring her, trying to drive her mad. *I'm under siege. Goddess, I'm in danger. And Hunter—my Hunter—is the weapon.*

"Mum, what's wrong?" Moira looked frightened. "What is it? The ring? Mum, you're scaring me!"

Morgan had no idea where to begin. Goddess, she didn't know if she could handle this. How many secrets had she kept from her daughter? Cal and Selene. Ciaran. Now Hunter? How many huge confidences could Moira handle in one week? How many more could Morgan handle? It was as if the whole tapestry of her life with Moira was becoming unraveled and not slowly, thread by thread—it was being torn, rent into pieces, and the ripping was painful and unexpected, leaving Morgan bare and vulnerable.

Her ring. She slid it onto the ring finger of her right hand. It fit perfectly, the silver warming instantly to the temperature of her blood. Her ring.

"Morgan . . ." Killian looked at her with concern. "Are you all right?"

"Thank you," Morgan said, speaking as if from a great distance. "I think so."

"Perhaps we should give Morgan some time," Katrina suggested gently. "Maybe you want to return to your lodgings, Killian?"

"If you're quite sure," he said, looking at Morgan.

She nodded. "Yes, I think—that might be best," she said, her voice strained.

"Well, then, I'll bid you all good night," he said, standing up. "I'm staying at Armistead's if you need me. Don't hesitate to call."

"Thank you." Morgan spoke automatically.

He leaned over and pecked Moira on the cheek. "I'm

glad I met you," he said. Then he and Morgan kissed each other's cheeks, and he let himself out.

"Mum, you look like you've seen a ghost," Moira said. "Are you going to tell me what is going on?"

Morgan was reluctant to speak in front of Katrina. Katrina knew all about Hunter, of course. But this was a moment that needed to happen between just mother and daughter, in private. She glanced at her mother-in-law.

As if divining her thoughts, Katrina stood. "I'd best be off," she said. "Didn't mean to stay so late."

"Let me give you a ride home—it's late," Morgan said, walking Katrina to the door.

"No, lass." Katrina shook her head. "The walk is good for me. You are needed here."

At the door Katrina paused, looking into Morgan's face. "It was Hunter we saw, wasn't it?" she said, glancing back to see if Moira could hear their conversation. "What do you make of it?"

"Yes, it was. I don't know what to make of anything anymore," Morgan said, feeling lost in a way that she hadn't felt since Colm had died.

"Call me if you want to talk," Katrina said, and Morgan nodded. They hugged quickly and Katrina began to walk down the path, her stiff leg making her gait awkward.

"Be safe, be quick, be home in a tick," Morgan murmured automatically. When she turned around, Moira was still sitting at the table, her head in her hands—someone waiting for bad news. She raised her head and glared at Morgan.

"Tell me what's going on," Moira said through clenched teeth.

Morgan sighed. Goddess give her strength. "This ring . . . was given to me by someone I knew before your dad."

Moira sat up straighter, interested. "Someone? Who? Mum, just tell me."

Morgan sat at the table beside Moira. "How far have you gotten in my old Books of Shadows?" she asked.

Moira shrugged. "I've been jumping around," she said.

Morgan nodded. "Well, then, maybe you haven't read much about him yet, or at least about what he ended up meaning to me. Moira, there was someone special to me before your father." She looked into Moira's eyes, unsure of how to go on. "He—he was my mùirn beatha dàn."

Moira flinched, pain flashing across her face. "Da wasn't?"

Morgan shook her head regretfully. "Your dad and I loved each other very much, but we weren't each other's mùirn beatha dàns. His name was Hunter. Hunter Niall. He was the Seeker who was sent after Cal and Selene." She stared at the worn tabletop, lost in the pain of remembering. "How I felt about him was unlike anything I had known. It was how love should be. We were made to be together, two halves of a whole."

Moira looked down at the table, shifting uncomfortably. "I always thought—I mean, that's what you and da seemed like to me."

Morgan's heart squeezed. "Moira, I'm sorry, I know this is hard. . . ."

Moira let out a harsh laugh. "What isn't, lately," she said. She stared out the window, and when she spoke again, her voice was softer. "So what happened?" she asked. "With you and this guy, Hunter?"

Morgan plunged on, just wanting to get everything out in

the open. "Well, for a while it didn't seem like we could be together—I was here in Cobh, with Belwicket, and I felt like I needed to stay here. Hunter was one of the witches who created the New Charter, and he was traveling everywhere. We hardly saw each other. I had decided we had to break up and go our separate ways—"

"Break up with your mùirn beatha dàn?" Moira cut in. "That's crazy."

"Yes, well," Morgan said ruefully. "That was his response, too. Instead he asked me to marry him, to have a handfasting." After so many years, those words still made her lip tremble, and a lump formed in her throat.

Moira turned to her. "What did you say?" she asked breathlessly.

"I said yes, of course." Morgan swallowed. "He was my soul mate. My other half. It was the happiest time of my entire life. All my wishes, all my dreams, my hopes—they were all coming true because Hunter and I would be together. Then the next day he had to go to a meeting of the New Charter. It was going to be his last one—he was going to tell them he had to quit traveling so much. Then he was going to come back and be with me and move to Cobh and we were going to start our lives together."

"Your lives . . . together," Moira echoed, looking slightly ill. "Here in Cobh."

Morgan couldn't imagine what Moira had to be feeling, hearing how different Morgan's vision of her future had once been from how it turned out—how another man had been the one she saw herself living this life with, not Moira's father.

Moira swallowed. "So, what happened?" she asked.

"He got on the early morning ferry," Morgan said slowly, tracing a rune for strength on the tabletop. The lump in her throat got bigger, and she blinked back tears. She hadn't spoken about that day in many years.

"A storm blew up out of nowhere," she finally got out. "The ferry went down, and nearly twenty people died. Including Hunter."

"Oh, Goddess," Moira breathed.

Morgan nodded sadly, feeling the familiar, heavy weight of grief in her chest. "Some people they managed to save, some bodies they managed to recover. But Hunter and twelve other people were sucked into the sea and never found. Drowned."

"Oh, Mum." Moira's eyes were full of sympathy, along with the pain and confusion. "This ring—" Morgan frowned at it, twisting it on her finger. "Hunter had given me this ring years before we got engaged. Like a promise ring. The day the ferry went down, I waited on the dock all day in the rain. When they finally said there could be no more survivors, I threw my hands out, like this"—she demonstrated, realizing that her hands were trembling—"and all of a sudden this ring flew off my finger and landed in the water. And it *sank*."

Moira frowned. "How can you be sure this is the same ring? Maybe it just looks like yours."

Morgan took it off and showed her the rune. "Beorc. For new beginnings," she explained sadly.

"But there's no way someone could have gotten your ring out of the sea, even if they had jumped right in after it. Much less after all this time. Mum, this doesn't make sense."

"You're right." Morgan met her gaze evenly.

"So where did it come from?"

"I don't know. It has to be part of something bigger. You

know things have been off lately. There's—there's more that's happened that I haven't told you." Trying to keep her emotions under control, Morgan filled her in on everything: the hex pouch, the morganite, the visions, the dream, seeing Hunter while scrying. "Now I just need to figure out what's going on and why." *Easier said than done.*

For a minute Moira was quiet, her eyes moving back and forth as she worked things out in her head. "Did you—did you ever love Dad as much as Hunter?" Her face was pained, and Morgan answered carefully.

"It was different, Moira," she said. "I loved your dad so much. He was the only man I ever lived with. We married, we had you. Those experiences build up to a much richer experience of love. I trusted your dad. I was so grateful for the fact that he loved me, and he was such a good person. I was so grateful he gave you to me. I appreciated so many things about him, and I tried to make sure he knew that. Yes, I loved him. Not the same as I loved Hunter, but I truly loved your father."

Moira thought for a moment. "It—it *seemed* real," she said. "Your love for each other, I mean." Her voice had a note of desperation. "I remember how you used to look at him—with love in your eyes. Like when you both teased me." She lifted one of her green strands and let it fall.

Morgan's throat threatened to close. "He was my best friend, sweetie."

"He was my best dad," Moira said, her voice suddenly cracking. Then she and Morgan were hugging, tears running down their faces.

"I'm so glad I still have you," Morgan said. "You're my most precious gift. I hope you know that."

Tearfully Moira nodded.

They held each other for a few minutes, and Morgan never wanted to let go. But eventually Moira pulled back. Morgan looked at her daughter, brushing the hair from her face.

"You should get some sleep," Morgan told her. "It's been a very difficult day—and I don't know what we're up against, but it seems more and more to be something—or someone—major. We'll need our strength."

Moira got up and headed for the stairs. "Thanks for telling me about Hunter," she said, looking back. "But I don't see how anyone found the ring and put it on our walk. I don't understand why someone would do it."

Morgan sighed. "I don't understand either. But I know it doesn't bode well. It feels—threatening. But I just don't know what the threat *is*, exactly—or where it's coming from."

"Well, don't worry, Mum," Moira said. "We'll find out."

Morgan smiled at Moira's teenage confidence and watched her daughter climb the narrow stairs.

Holding out her hand, she looked again at the ring, and fresh tears welled up in her eyes. Who was doing this? She needed some answers.

Her workroom was small, maybe nine feet by nine. Colm had built it for her soon after their handfasting. It had two small windows, high up on the walls, and a tiny fireplace all its own. Morgan kindled a fire there, rubbing her arms impatiently as she waited for the chill to lessen. Through one of the high windows Morgan could see the half-moon, partially covered by thick, heavy clouds.

Morgan put on her green silk robe, the one embroidered with runes and sigils, that had been Maeve's, decades ago. She drew three circles of protection on the floor, each one inside the other. Twelve stones of protection marked the twelve points of the compass. Next to the stones she lit twelve red candles for power and protection. Then she sat inside the smallest circle, closed it around her, and lit a red pillar candle in the center.

"I call on the Goddess of knowledge," Morgan said. "I call on my own strength. I call on the universe to aid me in my quest for the truth. I am here, safe within the Goddess's arms. I call on the ancient power leys of Ui Liathain, the power deep within the earth beneath me." She stretched out her arms, symbolically opening herself to knowledge. "Who is focusing on me? Who is sending these objects, these images, these thoughts? What do I need to find? What lesson is here for me, waiting to be revealed? Goddess, I ask you, please help me." Then she sat cross-legged in front of the candle, rested her hands on her knees, palms up, and breathed deeply, in and out. She focused on the small, single flame, the red wax melting, the scent of beeswax and fire and the wood smoke from the fireplace. Concentrating on the flame, she chanted her personal power chant, drawing energy toward her, opening herself to receive it. And she felt it, a bud opening within her, a flower beginning to bloom. Magick was rising and swelling in her chest, accompanied by a fierce joy that Morgan clung to, seized to herself. *Oh, magick.* Sometimes it seemed as if it was the only thing that made life worthwhile. It was a blessing.

Morgan kept her gaze fastened on the candle's flame. In that one flame she could see her whole life and all of life around her. Every memory was there on the surface, every emotion. But it was also like looking down on something from above—there was sometimes a distance that allowed her to see something more clearly, see the bigger picture, put the pieces together.

Now all she asked was, What do I need to know?

And suddenly Hunter was there before her. Morgan gasped, her breath catching in her throat, her skin turning to ice. Hunter was hunched over on a beach. The air was gray and still around him. The clothing he wore was in tatters, barely more than rags, offering grossly inadequate protection from the weather. His arms were burned brown from the sun, the skin freckled and leathery. His hair was much too long, wispy and tangled, with visible knots snarling the once-fine strands.

Morgan trembled. Holding her breath, she forced herself to release tension, but she could already feel the needle-fine threads of adrenaline snaking through her veins. His cheekbones, always prominent, now looked skeletal. The skin on his face had once been beautifully smooth, fine textured and pale. Now it was ridged, sunburned, peeling in places. There was an unhealed wound on one cheekbone below his eye. Grains of sand stuck to blood that had only recently dried.

Hunter was writing something in the sand, gibberish, childish doodlings. Morgan expected to see the beginnings of a spell, forms, patterns, something that she could understand, that would give her clues. Instead she saw formless meanderings, a stick drawn without purpose through the sand.

He looked up and saw her. *Hunter.* Pain clawed at Morgan's consciousness. It was so real, so vivid. If she could only reach out and touch him! His green eyes, once as dark and rich as a forest, now looked bleached by the sun and were surrounded by deep wrinkles. Slowly they widened in astonishment. His mouth opened in shock, then silently formed the word *Morgan*. He shook his head in disbelief. Morgan cried soundlessly at how tight his skin was on his bones. He was starving.

"Hunter." The word was a mere breath from Morgan, a slight release. *Oh, Hunter, where are you? What's happening?* Was it actually possible—could he have somehow survived the accident? What beach was this? The ferry had gone down in a small, populated cove. There was no way he wouldn't have been found.

He shook his head, his odd, pale eyes seeming to drink her in ravenously. *Don't help me.* Morgan heard the words silently in her mind. *Listen to me. You're in danger. Don't find me.*

*Are you alive?* She sent the words, as if she were sending a simple witch message across time, across death, across worlds. *Are you alive?*

His chapped and peeling lips crinkled in a grotesque mockery of a smile, and he shrugged.

*If you are alive, I will find you,* Morgan sent, and her power and determination were frightening and inescapable.

*No,* he sent back. *No. I'm lost, I'm gone forever.*

Hunter's image faded, his eyes too large for his bony face, his mouth forming words Morgan could no longer hear. Then she was alone again in her small workroom, breathing fast and shallowly, her hands trembling, clenching and unclenching. The fire in the hearth had dwindled to embers. The red pillar candle had burned down several inches. When Morgan glanced at the window, the moon was nowhere to be seen.

Had those images been real? Twice she had scried and seen Hunter—first with Katrina and again just now. Had she scried reality or simply what her innermost heart wished most to see—Hunter alive, even under such horrible circumstances? It had *felt* real. Oh, Goddess, what if it were real? What if Hunter were actually alive somewhere?

Slowly she stood and took off her robe, her hands shaking so badly, she could barely put her regular clothes back on.

She couldn't do this—she couldn't let herself believe Hunter was really out there if he wasn't, couldn't go through the pain of learning he was dead all over again. But how could she ignore these messages, coming to her one after the other? She had to know the truth. She would do whatever was in her power—which, if she pushed herself to the limit, would be intense—to find out if Hunter was alive.

Morgan moved numbly upstairs, checking to make sure everything was locked. Finnegan raised his head and growled. Automatically she glanced around: no evil spirits coming down the fireplace, nothing was on fire—then a flash outside caught her eye. In a moment she had cast her senses and picked up on a person outside, walking around the house. The living room was dark; no one could see in. But she could see out, and a tall, thin person with white-blond hair was outside her house.

Her heart stopped. *Hunter.*

Without thinking, Morgan ran to the door and flung it open, Finnegan on her heels. He growled and then barked several times sharply. Morgan stood in her doorway, and at the same moment her inner senses and her eyes informed her of the intruder: Sky Eventide came around the corner of the house just as Morgan identified her energy pattern.

"Sky!"

Sky looked up and gave a slight smile. "Sorry I didn't call first,"

Morgan began to breathe again, a rush of emotions overcoming her. It wasn't Hunter. Of course it wasn't Hunter.

She hurried over to Sky, grabbing her arm. "What are you doing here? Why didn't you let me know you were coming?"

Sky shrugged as they headed back to the house. She had left her pack by the front door and scooped it up as they went inside. "I was concerned after our phone call the other night, and decided to come check things out."

"Oh, Sky, I saw Hunter," Morgan blurted. "Twice today. I saw him!"

Sky's night-dark eyes widened. "What do you mean, you *saw* him?"

"I was scrying," Morgan quickly explained. "He was—much older, as old as he would be today. He was on a beach, wearing rags, and he was a mess. He was all windburned and battered looking—" Morgan broke off, unable to bear the memory of how haunted Hunter had appeared, how brutalized. "His bones were showing. He was starving," she went on, struggling not to break down. "He seemed to see me, and I said, *Are you alive*, and *I will find you*. And he said, *No, I'm lost, I'm gone forever. You're in danger, don't find me*."

Morgan took a ragged breath. "It seemed so real. It didn't seem like a vision, or a dream, or just a subconscious message. I mean—I scried, and I saw Hunter, and he talked to me. And I can't help thinking, Oh, Goddess, what if he is alive somewhere?" It was the first time she'd said it out loud, and a shiver passed through her as the words came out.

"How could he be?" Sky's voice was higher pitched than usual—she was clearly spooked, and Morgan knew that didn't happen easily. "He was on the ferry—people saw him get on it. People saw him in the water. People saw him disappear under the water."

"They never found his body," Morgan reminded her.

"Because he sank, along with the others!" Sky sounded angry, but it seemed as if she was just afraid to hope, like Morgan.

"There's more," Morgan rushed on. She held up her hand and showed Sky the ring Moira had found.

Sky looked at the claddagh ring, not understanding.

"Sky, this is the ring. My ring," Morgan said, her voice shaking slightly. "The ring I lost that day. It went into the sea. Moira found it on my front walk this evening. See the rune?"

"Goddess," Sky breathed. "Moira found this just outside?"

"Sky—it means something. All the pieces. The morganite. My visions. My dream. What if he's *alive?*" This time the words came out more forcefully, and Sky met her gaze, no longer arguing.

"The one thing I can't figure out," Morgan said, "is the attack on the coven. The black smoke. And it doesn't feel right here—others have noticed as well. How could there be a connection between Belwicket and Hunter? It doesn't make sense."

"No," Sky said slowly. "Not yet. But what you said, how it doesn't feel right here—I noticed it, too, as soon as I arrived. And listen, Morgan, when's the last time you checked your house for an enemy's marks?"

Morgan sat back, surprised. "Every day since Katrina and I found the hex pouch in the garden. Why?"

"Someone around here is out to harm you."

Morgan swallowed. She'd suspected that much already, but how could Sky seem so certain?

"There are sigils on every windowsill, both door frames, and on top of your garden shed. I found three different pouches, two somewhat serious. I put them in the far corner of your yard—we'll deal with them tomorrow. There's evidence of other things buried in your yard in three different places." She shook her head, her fine, light hair flying.

Morgan's whole body went cold. She and Moira were in danger—more serious danger than she'd even realized. How could she have let things get this far? "How could I have missed the sigils, the pouches?"

"I don't know," Sky said. "I can't believe you and Moira aren't in bed with the flu or broken bones."

"I've been working protection spells regularly since the strange things started happening," Morgan said. "I had no idea those things were out there." She rubbed her forehead. Who could be working against her? *And Hunter, Hunter.* The name was running through her mind in a constant rhythm, a background for anything else she said or thought. *Hunter might be alive. After all these years Hunter could be out there somewhere. Hunter, Hunter.* "How—how does this all fit together?" Morgan said, frustrated that she couldn't figure it out.

"I don't know," said Sky. "But if there's even a chance that Hunter's . . ."

"We have to know for sure," Morgan agreed. "We have to find out who is trying to harm me and my family—and we have to find Hunter."

# 11.
# Moira

What had Gran been talking about tonight? Moira wondered sleepily as she lay in bed that night. What kind of troubles could she have "smoothed over"? Gran had said a friend of Mum's had died—that must have been Hunter—and Mum had been upset. Gran had smoothed her troubles over. How? Why?

Moira's mind was reeling from so much new information about herself, her mother, her family. Suddenly everything she'd believed about herself, her mum—it was all wrong. She was the granddaughter of one of the most evil witches in generations! His blood ran through her veins, Moira thought, staring down at her wrist. Her stomach contracted as she was overcome by a wave of nausea. How could her mother have kept all of this from her? She didn't even know who her mum *was* anymore. And the one thing that had still been true—the love Mum and Dad had shared, that Moira had seen for herself—even that had been a lie. Colm and Morgan hadn't been each other's mùirn beatha dàns.

Moira blinked back tears. How could her dad have borne

knowing he wasn't Morgan's mùirn beatha dàn? Moira couldn't imagine being with someone who wasn't hers.

Moira ran over all the stories she'd heard about how her parents had gotten together. Mum had fallen apart after Hunter died. And when she'd fallen apart, Gran had taken care of her, and then Mum had married Dad and they'd had her.

Still trying to sort through it all, Moira drifted off to sleep.

*Moira's mother was in labor. Her brown hair, very short, was damp in tendrils around her flushed face. Mum looked very young and wide-eyed. Next to her stood Peggoty MacAdams, the village midwife, and with her June Hightown, another midwife. Peggoty was holding Mum's hand, and June was wiping her forehead with a cloth.*

*Morgan was breathing hard. Her eyes looked a question at Peggoty.*

*"It won't be long now, my dear," Peggoty said soothingly. She placed her hand on Morgan's forehead and murmured some gentle spells. Morgan's breathing slowed, and she looked less panicky. June poured some tea, pale green and fragrant, and Morgan gulped it down, wincing at the taste.*

*Finally Morgan was pushing, her face damp, the muscles in her neck taut and ribboned with effort.*

*Moira was startled to realize that this was her, being born.*

*Peggoty said, "Just a bit more, dear, there you go, that's right, and here's her head. . . ."*

*"Oh, what a lovely baby," Peggoty crooned, scooping up the infant and swathing her in a clean white blanket. "She's a big, fine baby, Morgan. She's beautiful."*

*"Is she okay?" Morgan asked.*

*"She looks perfect, just perfect," Peggoty said with approval. "Goodness—she's nine pounds even. A lovely, plump baby."*

*"Oh, good,"* Morgan said weakly, her head falling back against the pillows.

Peggoty beamed. *"And now I bet the proud papa would like to hold his little girl?"*

A man stepped forward hesitantly and held out his arms.

Moira's stomach tightened—it wasn't Colm.

It was a stranger. He was severe looking, tall and fit, with light hair, the palest blond. He appeared nervous but held out his hands, glancing over at Morgan. She opened her eyes and smiled at him.

With a kind of wonder, the man held baby Moira gingerly, as if she might disappear in a puff of smoke. He looked down into her face, and her eyes opened. The two of them stared at each other solemnly, as if to say, *Hello. I belong to you. I will belong to you forever.*

With a gasp Moira awoke. Her room was still dark; there was a faint streak of pink coming in at the bottom of her window shade. She was breathing hard and looked around her room to make sure nothing was out of place. Quickly she cast out her senses. Everything was normal. Or about as normal as it could be, given the past few days. Goddess, what a dream. She had seen herself being born. Everything about it had seemed so real, except for her father. Who was that? Why hadn't she dreamed about her dad?

Abruptly Moira sat back in bed, thoughts swirling in her head like leaves in the wind. *Goddess, think, think.*

Colm was her father. Everyone knew that. But Moira knew her dream meant something. She'd taken a dream interpretation class for her initiation. So what had this dream meant? That Colm hadn't been her father?

Moira sat up again, panicked. No, of course he had been. She would have known. Mum would have known. Surely her mother couldn't have lied about *that*. No. But then what did it mean?

Moira was wide awake. She raised her window shade so the palest light of the new dawn illuminated her room. Then she fetched her parents' Books of Shadows, Colm's and Morgan's, from the year she was born. She had read other Books of Shadows, but not these. Not yet. In Colm's she read about his growing feelings for Morgan, his admiration for her, his combined awe and respect for her "significant" powers. He thought she was beautiful and friendly but not openly interested.

Then she flipped through Morgan's, skimming the pages. She had moved to Cobh. She was growing to love Katrina and Pawel and Susan and all the others. She thought she might want to stay there forever. Except she missed Hunter so much, all the time. Her heart cried out for him. She ached to be with him—nothing was as good, as right, as when they were together.

Moira couldn't help feeling a pang as she read about just how deeply her mother had loved Hunter. Hunter, who wasn't Colm. Some protective instinct made Moira turn back to Colm's Book of Shadows. His job in Cobh was going fine. He was thinking it was time to settle down. He had dated several girls but couldn't get Morgan out of his mind. He knew she was seeing someone else. His feelings for her grew, and he decided he was falling in love with her. Not that it would do him any good. But he thought she was a one-in-a-million woman. Then it happened: he heard from his mother that Morgan had lost someone she loved. She was so upset that she couldn't think straight. She'd been hospitalized in Wales.

Colm traveled there and met Morgan's American parents

and sister. Morgan had had a breakdown, and his heart bled for her. In her grief she'd hacked off all her hair, the thick, shiny chestnut hair that had almost reached her waist. Now it was as short as a boy's, but it made her no less beautiful. He loved her so much; if only he could take care of her. It was all he wanted: the chance to take care of her.

On the next page Colm was elated: the unthinkable had happened. Morgan had agreed to become his wife. He knew she was heartbroken, though she wouldn't talk about it. She still seemed very ill, but he was sure she would be fine in time. She just needed warmth and love and care and good food. He knew he could make her happy.

Moira kept skimming the pages. Outside, the sun was just starting to creep over the horizon, mostly covered by clouds. Great. Just what they needed—more rain.

Shortly after their wedding Morgan was pregnant. They hadn't realized it at first because of her illness. Colm was ecstatic. He loved his wife: she seemed healthier and more beautiful every day. Slowly her grief was going under-ground—she had almost smiled the other day.

Moira swallowed hard. It was so sad to read about it—how much her dad had loved Mum, how long it had taken Mum to be able to truly return his affection.

Going back to Morgan's Book of Shadows, Moira read about how Morgan was waiting for Hunter at a tea shop in Wales. There was no entry from later that night, when they had committed to being together. And no more entries for two months. Then a short one, in a weak hand, that acknowledged Morgan's marriage to Colm. And then another, two months after that: Morgan was expecting a baby. She was happy about it—it was a ray of sunlight piercing her gray shadow world. A few words about Colm—how kind he was, how gentle, how Morgan appreciated his care. There was no mention of Hunter, only a sentence about being ill and deciding to stay in Ireland.

And no magick. Before, her entries had been numerous and lengthy—a combination of daily diary, larger, philosophical thoughts, the directions her studies were taking her, spells she had tried and their results, spells she had created, different tinctures and essences she had used and their outcomes, her plans for next year's garden, and so on. But these entries were sparse, bare.

Though Moira looked, she could find no mention of Gran helping Morgan, no mention of smoothing away her troubles. The entries that mentioned her only described her kindness and caring, her constancy, her support. Morgan didn't detail any healing rites, circles held for her benefit, nothing.

Moira flipped ahead, searching for a mention of magick. A week after her birth Morgan had put some protection spells and general good-wishes spells on her new baby.

Hmmm. Something was odd. Moira skipped back and forth, looking from Colm's book to Morgan's, at earlier entries and later ones. The dates in Morgan's were messed up for a while—she simply hadn't put dates in, and it was only by her telling of events, and comparing the entries to Colm's, that Moira was able to figure out when an entry had been made.

Colm had been much steadier—virtually every entry was dated. Moira continued to flip back and forth. Hunter died, Mum got ill, Mum and Dad got married a month later. One month. Pretty fast for someone who had been so in love, for someone not marrying their soul mate. But considering how ill Mum had been, how devastated, maybe she had just really needed someone to take care of her. And from the entries it seemed she really had grown to love Colm.

Then Morgan was expecting a baby, and Moira was born . . . in December, right before Yule. Hunter had died in March. Mum and Dad had gotten married in April. Moira had been born in December. Mum's Book of Shadows mentioned that she and Colm hadn't slept together before their marriage.

So Moira had been premature by one month. A nine-pound preemie. That didn't sound right. She couldn't have weighed nine pounds.

There were sounds from downstairs. Moira realized her mum was awake and getting breakfast, and now that she was paying attention, she realized there was someone else downstairs, too, a woman. Gran? Not Gran.

Quickly Moira threw on her hated school uniform, brushed her hair and her teeth, and headed downstairs, holding the two Books of Shadows.

She froze when she spotted the back of the strange woman's head—she had the same white-blond hair as the man in her dream. Then the woman turned around. "Good morning," she said evenly. "You must be Moira."

"Yes," Moira said. She clutched the books tightly in her hands, her heart pounding.

Morgan turned from the stove. "Morning, sweetie." She looked tired, and there were dark circles under her eyes. She gestured to the woman with a dishcloth. "Moira, this is Sky Eventide. We've been friends a long time. She was Hunter's cousin."

"You were Hunter's cousin?" Moira asked, a funny feeling in her stomach. The same hair as the man in her dream . . .

"Yes," said Sky, her expression guarded. She was unusual, not like Mum's other friends. Not smiling and remarking on how tall she was and asking about school.

"Oh," Moira said inadequately. She sat down at the table and poured some cereal into a bowl, then some milk, but couldn't bring herself to start eating. Her mind was whirling. Finally, keeping her tone as calm as possible, she asked, "Mum, was I born premature?"

Morgan looked surprised. "No—in fact you were late. The midwife said that nature decrees that a woman will be pregnant for exactly as long as she can absolutely bear it— and then another two weeks." She rolled her eyes. "Let's just say I was anxious for you to get here."

"And how much did I weigh?" Moira pressed.

"Nine pounds."

Moira's pulse raced. No, no, it couldn't be.

"What's all this about, anyway?" Morgan asked, coming to the table. She moved the teapot closer to Sky, and Sky topped up her mug.

Moira pushed the two Books of Shadows toward her mother. "I was reading these this morning, and there's something—odd. It says that you and Dad got married in April, but I was born in December."

Morgan blinked. "No, that isn't right," she said slowly. She sat back and looked at the ceiling, thinking. "We were married in—"

"April," Moira supplied.

Frowning, Morgan nodded. "And you were born December 15."

"Right."

Her mum looked at her, then shook her head. "No, there

has to be some mistake, something wrong with the entries. I know you weren't premature. Goddess, you were a whale."

Moira just looked at her mother.

"Why were you up this morning so early, anyway?" Morgan asked.

"I had a strange dream," Moira said. "It woke me, and once I was up, I—I wanted to read these."

"Studying for your initiation, are you?" asked Sky, and Moira nodded.

"What was your dream about?" Mum asked casually. Dreams were often discussed in Wiccan households, whether they were important, funny, meaningful, or frightening.

Don't let this dream mean anything, please, Moira pleaded inwardly.

"Me being born," Moira said carefully. "Peggoty MacAdams and June Hightown were there. And they said, doesn't the dad want to hold her?" She paused, giving her mother a hard look. "But the dad wasn't Dad. They handed me to someone else." She turned her gaze to Sky. "He—well, he looked . . . like you. His hair was very light, like yours."

Silence. Moira looked at her mom and felt her heart sink. Her mother was pale, stricken, her eyes large. Glancing over at Sky, she saw that the other woman also looked very solemn.

"So I was wondering," Moira went on. The words were so thick and her mouth so dry, it was a battle to speak. "When I was born and when you and Dad got married . . ." Her voice trailed off. "Whether I was premature," she finished softly.

Still no one said anything. Moira looked at her mother and saw that she and Sky were staring at each other as if the other one would have all the answers in the world.

Morgan swallowed. "Moira, I know that you are Colm's daughter, Colm's and mine. There's never been the slightest doubt about that. There was never a question." Her mum sounded absolute.

"Must be the dates are off," Sky suggested quietly.

"Yes," Morgan said firmly, standing up. "This is one thing you don't have to worry about, Moira, I promise you. You're definitely Colm's daughter." Her mother kissed her and smiled into her eyes. "I'm sorry. I know you've had a lot of shocks lately. But believe me, you were Colm's daughter and mine, and you made our lives complete. Your dad loved you more than anything. Okay?"

Moira forced a nod, but she felt as if her internal organs were collapsing in on themselves, as if, in moments, she would be a puddle on the floor. Her mother sounded so sure, so confident—but Moira had a terrible, horrifying feeling that she was wrong.

# 12.
# Morgan

After Moira left, Morgan sat at the table, her tea getting cold. It was as if someone had taken her life, put it in a kaleidoscope, and given it a quick shake. Everything was skewed, changed, *off*. There were so many questions piling up inside her that soon enough they would start to spill out. Was Hunter really alive? Was he sending her messages from the dead or was someone else? Hunter would never, ever hurt her—that black smoke couldn't have been from him. But it had happened at the same time as all the other signs, so there had to be a connection, didn't there?

And then there was everything Moira had just said. Goddess, was there any possibility that Moira was Hunter's . . .

No, she's Colm's daughter, Morgan told herself. Colm's and mine. Moira's dream—it had to mean something else. It had to be connected to all these other strange visions and dreams.

"I know what you're thinking," Sky finally said, breaking the silence that hung between them. "But Morgan, we can't just sit and wait for answers. We have to act. And I think the first thing we need to do is clean up your house. Having all those sigils and hexes around here can't be helping any of us think clearly. They were probably spelled so that *you*—or members of your coven, specifically—couldn't find them, because when *I* looked, they were popping out at me without too much trouble."

"That would make sense," Morgan said. She shook her head. "It's what I would do."

"If you were the type of person who went around spelling people to break their necks," Sky agreed. "Let's sort it all out right now."

"Yes," said Morgan, trying to shake off the weighty grayness that made her shoulders and neck ache. She needed to think clearly. "That would be a start."

Morgan fetched the Riordan athame, the ancient knife carved with generations of her family's initials. When she became high priestess, her initials would be added. She and Sky went outside, and one by one Sky showed her the hexes, spells, and sigils that she'd found sprinkled liberally everywhere. Working with Sky, Morgan passed the athame over the sigils and saw the sigils glow faintly silver or red. It was off alone that she saw nothing, but as she and Sky worked, Morgan began to sense the spells more easily.

"This is unbelievable," Morgan breathed as their number grew. "I just went over the house. I can't believe this is happening." A wave of nausea overcame her, and she had to sit down. So many years she'd lived peacefully, without the thought of dark magick. And now it was surrounding her and Moira, with someone out there waiting to use it to strangle them both.

"Like I said, they were spelled to keep you from finding them. Someone wishes you harm," Sky said with characteristic understatement. She held up a small glass bottle full of nails, pins, needles, and vinegar. "How's your stomach been lately? Any ulcers?"

"No," Morgan said, shaking her head in disbelief. "Goddess. I'm just so grateful that Moira hasn't been hurt."

"These people must be just astounded every day," Sky said, "when they read the paper and don't find an article about how your roof caved in or your brakes gave out or you slipped on your walk and broke your hip. You're stronger than they think. Or else their magick is pathetic." She looked at the pouch with distaste, then added it to the small pile in the corner of the yard.

"Katrina and I have been doing a lot of protection spells," said Morgan. "This house itself is built on an ancient power ley, and we tap into that."

"Oh, yes, the legend about the local power ley. Didn't know anyone knew where it was. Good. That's the only explanation I have for the fact that you're still standing. That and you're Morgan of Belwicket," Sky said. "Some of this stuff has been nasty."

All of a sudden Morgan felt as if she couldn't bear it. She collapsed to the ground. "Sky—," she began. "I thought I was done with all this."

"I know," Sky said. "And you should be. You've been through enough." Her black eyes became thoughtful. "But you're no ordinary witch. You're Morgan of Belwicket. Maeve's daughter. Ciaran's daughter. You are the sgiùrs dàn."

Morgan's eyes opened wider. *The sgiùrs dàn—the Destroyer.*

Ciaran had told her that years ago, as part of his explanation for wanting her dead. Every several generations within the Woodbane clan a Destroyer was born. A witch who would change the course of Woodbane history. "But didn't I already change Woodbane history, by helping to destroy Amyranth? By removing Ciaran from power? And now by leading Belwicket in a new direction?"

"I certainly thought so," Sky said wryly. "But maybe the wheel has something more for you to do."

The wheel of life. Fate. Karma. Morgan felt oddly inadequate for what the wheel kept dishing out. "Sky—I just don't know if I can fight anymore, not like I did back then."

Sky's gaze was calm and sure. "Morgan. You are stronger than you know. How strange that you still don't realize that."

Then she turned and began to set up what they would need to undo all the dark spells. It was harder to undo magick than to do it. They had to work backward, unraveling what had been wrought. It was easier working together, Morgan thought. If she'd had to do this alone, one step at a time, it would have taken so much longer. And unspoken between them was the same constant thought of where this could all lead, a reason to work as quickly and thoroughly as possible—*Hunter.*

By two o'clock that afternoon the house and yard had been cleared. The actual physical embodiments of the hexes and spells would be buried in the sand, down by the sea, where time and salt water would slowly purify them. Morgan and Sky began to relay new circles of protection. It was a shame there wouldn't be a full moon that night, but they had to work with what they had. They couldn't afford to wait even a moment.

They worked from the inside out. Starting in the northeast

corner, which was in the guest room, Morgan and Sky lit small brushes of dried sage. These they waved in every corner, in the closet, around the windows. Their smudgy, herbal smoke would help purify the energy and rid the house of evil intentions. They chanted protection spells in each room, sprinkled salt on every floor, and washed each window so that evil would be reflected and healing energy could flow through. Morgan drew sigils of protection on the walls above every door frame and window frame. In each corner of every room she put a small chunk of pure iron, surrounded by a circle of salt.

Outside, Morgan and Sky walked the perimeter of the property, carrying lit candles and burning sagebrush. They gathered handfuls of willow twigs and lightly slapped them all around the low stone walls that surrounded the house and yard. Again Morgan drew sigils of protection above every door and window, drawing them first with silver paint, then overlaying them with invisible lines, marked with her own witch's sign.

They traced Xs across each door and window with Morgan's athame and sprinkled salt in a solid line on the inside of the stone walls.

"You're going to look out your window and find your yard full of deer," Sky said dryly as they sprinkled salt.

"As long as they're not evil Ealltuinn deer, that's okay," Morgan said.

"So you still think this is coming from them?"

"I don't know anymore," Morgan answered. "I can't see how any of them would know about Hunter. . . ."

Sky met her gaze, and neither said anything. But Sky's eyes were filled with the same mixture of hope, desperation, and fear that Morgan felt. And Morgan even noticed Sky's hands trembling slightly. It was all either could do not to break down from the torture of needing to know if Hunter was really alive.

"We're almost finished," Sky said quietly, resuming her work.

In front of each of the garden gates they drew seven lines of protection so anyone entering with harmful intentions would find themselves slowed and perhaps even too confused to follow the path. Last but not least, the two women stood together and chanted the strongest power chants they knew, overlaying them with ribbons of protection, of ward evil, of warning, of reflection of harm. They went around the whole yard, all around the house and the back garden, singing and chanting, dispelling the last of the negative energy and replacing it with strong positive energy.

"Whew. That's done, and done well," Sky said, glancing at the sun's position when they were through. "Must be almost four."

"Moira will be home soon," Morgan agreed.

Inside the house, Morgan made a pot of strong tea. While they waited for Moira, she and Sky exchanged small talk, avoiding the one topic Morgan knew was all either could really think about.

"Alwyn's expecting a baby," Sky told her.

"So's Mary K.," Morgan said. "Twins, in fact. I'm going to be an aunt. I can't believe it's taken her so long. I thought she'd have nine kids by now."

Sky grinned, then seemed to listen for a moment. "Someone's coming."

"It's Katrina," said Morgan, casting her senses. She got up to let her mother-in-law in, then introduced her to Sky.

"Hello," said Katrina. "Morgan's mentioned you to me."

"Pleasure," Sky said with her natural reserve.

"Sit down," Morgan said. "I'll get you a cup."

Katrina took a chair, resting her walking stick against the side cupboard.

"Don't get old," she advised Morgan and Sky. "Christa Ryan tells me to walk two miles each day or become as stiff as an old board, so I do, but I'd rather be home working crosswords in front of the fire."

"Do you want me to try to help?" Morgan offered.

"Nae, lass. It's just these old bones. Don't trouble yourself," Katrina said, taking a sip of tea. Morgan had made the suggestion before that she try to heal Katrina's arthritis, but Katrina always shrugged her off.

Nodding, Morgan glanced at the clock. It was hard not to want Moira by her side every minute. She sent her daughter a witch message. *Don't be late. Not today.*

# 13.
# Moira

Moira was torn as she approached her house that afternoon. Sitting through classes had been torture, when all she could think about was all the questions she still had about Ciaran, her mum's past, and—Colm and Hunter. But she didn't want to face her mother yet, either. Still, she'd received the witch message from Morgan just as school had ended, warning her to come straight home—that it was important.

What now?

Moira took a deep breath, then opened the front door and saw her mum, Gran, and Sky sitting at the kitchen table.

"Hi, sweetie," Mum said.

"Hi." Moira dumped her book bag and sweater on the chair. "Hi, Gran. Sky."

"How was your day, love?" Katrina asked.

Moira frowned. She didn't want to talk about her day—she wanted to know why she'd had to come home so quickly. She tried to read her mother's face, but Morgan wouldn't meet her gaze. Then she sniffed the air. "Sage?"

"Yes," Sky said, when Morgan didn't answer. "We had to do some purification on the house."

"What do you mean?" Moira asked.

"Someone had put some bad-luck sigils around the yard," Sky said. "Your mum and I cleared them out."

Looking first at her mother, then at Sky, Moira said, "Bad-luck sigils . . . who would do that?"

"Perhaps someone from Ealltuinn," Katrina said. "But we're not sure. It's not safe for you. For any of us. We need you to stay here, where we can protect you."

Not Lilith, Moira thought in dismay as she sank into a chair at the table. Not Ian.

Finally Morgan looked into Moira's eyes. "Do you understand?" she said. "This is very serious, Moira. The coven is in danger. We are in danger."

"Okay," Moira said. She'd never seen her mum and Gran like this before. "I'll be careful." She glanced back and forth between Morgan and Gran. They looked scared but determined. Especially her mother. This morning's conversation had done little to erase her doubts. Now might not be the best time, but Moira had to know the truth about her father, about her birth, and she sensed somehow that the only way to get it was to ask her questions now, with Mum and Gran here.

Moira cleared her throat. "So, Mum, did you tell Gran about my dream? About this morning?" she asked.

Morgan blinked, surprised at Moira's question. "No, I— there's a lot going on right now, a lot—"

"I had this dream," Moira said slowly to Gran, cutting off her mum. "And in the dream my dad, he—he wasn't my dad. He was someone else."

"We've talked about this," Morgan said firmly. "Colm is your father, Moira."

Moira kept her gaze on Gran, focusing her powers on trying to feel Gran's response to her description of the dream. She's uncomfortable, Moira realized, feeling a growing dread. Just like she was the other day, when I kept asking her what she meant about helping my mother heal.

"Remember what you were saying to me?" Moira continued, surprised at how calm she sounded with the turmoil of emotions inside her. "About how you helped to soothe my mother's troubles after Hunter's accident?"

"Katrina, what's Moira talking about?" Morgan asked curiously.

Gran looked down at her teacup. "Yes, well . . ." Her voice trailed off.

"I just want to understand it," Moira said earnestly, leaning forward. "I've been reading Mum's and Dad's old Books of Shadows, so I have it from their view. But what do *you* remember about it?"

"It was a hard time," Gran said slowly. "We all do what we think is best."

Moira looked at Morgan, who seemed concerned.

"Katrina, are you all right?" Morgan asked.

"The weird thing is," Moira went on, wishing she could let this whole thing drop—wishing she weren't feeling more and more certain that this would lead to an answer she didn't want to hear. "The dates don't match up in the Books of Shadows. The dates when Mum and Da got married and when I was born."

Gran shook her head and gazed into her tea. "It's about time it all caught up with me," she said.

"What are you talking about? Are you sure you're all right?" Mum's face was pale, even paler than it had been when Moira had first walked in.

Gran looked up and met Morgan's eyes. "You don't remember much about that time, do you?"

Mum let out a breath, the way she did when she was tense. "Well," she said slowly, "not a lot. I was—so upset. Upset and sick. I hardly remember coming back to Ireland. I was in the hospital, in Wales. I had pneumonia."

It was almost as if Moira could see a wave of sadness settle on Morgan like a shawl.

"Yes, you had pneumonia, and you were beside yourself with grief," Gran told her. "Your love had died in that storm, and it was like most of you died with him."

Moira had never heard Gran talk like this—talking about Mum's past. No one ever had mentioned Hunter until this past week. It was as if a ghost had been living in their house all these years, silent and unacknowledged.

Gran looked directly at Moira. "Your mother was the descendant of our ancestral high priestesses," she said. "You know that. You know how Granda and I found out your mum was alive and went to find her to help us restore Belwicket."

Moira nodded.

"We grew to love Morgan," Gran went on. "We could see that with her power, we could perhaps one day re-create the coven that we had grown up in, that our parents had grown up in. Your mum was the key. Not just because of her power—it was her instincts, her curiosity, the experiences that had shaped her. I grew to care for her as for a daughter. And my Colm, I saw that he loved her as well, though he didn't say anything to me. But we knew her heart wasn't whole. I wondered what would happen between her and her young man. Every so often she would go off and meet him somewhere, France or Scotland or Wales. When she came back, she would be both happier and sadder, if you can understand that."

The only sound in the kitchen was Finnegan's light snoring and the beginning of a slow, steady rain outside. Moira felt as if time itself had slowed, as if she were in a dream again.

If only this were a dream, a dream she could wake up from and hear another explanation for from her gran. Why hadn't Gran been as quick as her mum was to assure her that Colm was indeed her father? Why hadn't she said that right off? Moira's stomach was locked in a million knots as she waited to hear more.

"I didn't ask about him, and she didn't volunteer anything," Gran went on, speaking as if Morgan weren't right there. "Then your mum didn't come back from a short trip, and a hospital in Wales finally called us. Morgan was incredibly ill with pneumonia. I contacted your grandparents in America, and they flew over. We all talked about what we should do, and in the end your mum said she wanted to come back to her little flat in Wicklow. So Pawel and Colm and I collected her, but she couldn't be on her own. I put her up in our guest room, and many of us took turns nursing her. The whole coven—there were ten of us back then—performed healing rites."

Gran paused, glancing around the room. "Anyway. Colm hardly left her side—I thought he'd become ill himself. In Wales we had learned of the tragedy, and the little bit that your mum managed to tell us confirmed the worst—she had lost her young man." Gran sighed, the lines on her face seeming to deepen with remembered pain.

Moira glanced at Morgan, who was listening with the same worry and dread in her eyes that Moira felt.

"Several weeks after the accident I was holding your hand," Gran said, once more directing the story to Morgan, "focusing on sending you healing energy, and I realized something felt different. I concentrated, and it came to me—you were going to have a baby."

Moira and Morgan drew in deep, sharp breaths in unison as the truth became real for both of them. As strong as her suspicions had been growing every moment, Moira still felt like she'd been punched in the stomach. She couldn't even respond, and neither could her mum.

"I felt so sorry for you, Morgan, but I was glad for you, too. You had a reason to keep going. I knew that you hadn't sensed the baby yet. Most witches would, if they were at all in tune with themselves, but in your state you barely knew if you were awake or asleep. I worried for you, Morgan. And I worried for your child. I worried that as ill as you were, as lost, you would never recover on your own. I talked to Pawel about it and to Susan, and we all talked to Colm. Today I don't know if I would have made the same decision. At the time it seemed like the best thing to do. Colm loved you, we loved you, and we wanted you to be whole again. You were the hereditary priestess of Belwicket. It was right that you stay here and regain the strength to use your powers for good, as you have."

"Katrina—what did you do?" Morgan asked in a voice that was nearly a whisper yet chilled Moira to the bone.

Gran sighed. "Susan and I created a spell that would heal

you, bring you back from the brink of despair. To keep you alive, to keep your *daughter* safe and alive . . . to protect you both," she finished, looking at Moira. "The spell . . . I took your pain onto myself in order to help you. It was only intended to bring you some peace, Morgan."

There was silence in the room as her words sank in. Moira started to shake her head, slowly. She reached out to hold the edge of the table, feeling dizzy. *No, no, this isn't happening.*

Gran continued. "We were waiting to tell you about the baby until you were healthier. But then . . . Colm came to me one afternoon, when you were beginning to recover, and told me that he had asked you to marry him—and that you had said yes. He knew about the baby, and he accepted it and wanted to be with you anyway. When he shared his news, I felt I understood. You wanted to die, Morgan, but knew that taking your own life was a direct violation of all Wiccan laws. And since you had to go on living anyway, you would make the best of it, with someone you cared for. My son."

"I loved Colm." Mum's voice sounded as if it were coming from far away.

"My dear." Gran reached out and took her hand. "I know you did. I'm not saying that. Believe me, if I hadn't thought that from the very beginning, we wouldn't all be sitting here today. I knew you. You never would have agreed to marry him if you hadn't had every intention of being a good and loving wife. And you were. You were the best thing that ever happened to him. I knew that, and he knew that."

Morgan looked stricken, deep in shock. Moira was beyond shock—beyond any identifiable emotion. It was all just too much.

"The spell was working, and you continued to heal. But

there was a side effect we hadn't realized—that the spell would blur your memories and cause your senses to be off for a time. Yes, you moved on. You married. But you believed the baby was Colm's. And we—we never told you otherwise. I don't know what to say, except that it just seemed right at the time for all of you. We believed the Goddess was having her way, that you were meant to have your daughter with Colm."

Morgan covered her mouth with her hand, gasping, and tears started flowing down her face. Sky's face was like stone, alabaster, unreadable.

Blinking, Moira tried to think—the room was going in and out of focus. She gripped her chair seat, wondering dimly if she were going to fall over.

"Gran," she said faintly, "Da wasn't really my father?"

"Your da was Colm Byrne," Gran said, her voice shaky. "And no father ever loved a daughter more. He was your real father in every way that counted, your whole life. He took joy in you, he joined his heart with yours. You belonged to him and he to you."

"Oh my God, Katrina," Mum finally said hoarsely, her hand to her mouth. "Oh, Goddess." Her eyes widened. "You said you *took* my pain. Your arthritis . . . that's how it began, isn't it?"

Gran stared down at the table, not answering.

"It's why you never wanted me to heal you," Morgan breathed. "Because it wouldn't have worked, not when your pain had been taken from me to begin with . . ."

"Because it's my burden to bear. I only wanted to help you live your life," Gran said. "And raise your daughter."

"I don't understand," Moira said helplessly. "Da knew, all this time? And Aunt Susan? Everyone knew?"

"Just me, Pawel, Susan, and Colm," Gran said. "It never made a difference to any of us."

"It makes a difference to *me*!" Moira cried, the knowledge overwhelming her, stripping her of reason. She jumped up so quickly that her chair tipped over onto the floor with a crash. Finnegan leapt up and barked. "Don't you get it? You've traded in my whole life! How could you do that? Who gave you permission? Now you're not even my grandmother!"

Gran looked as if she had been slapped, but Moira was too upset to care. Instead she grabbed her jacket off its hook and rushed out the front door. Finnegan leapt after her, bounding across the yard and just managing to squeak through the garden gate before it slammed against him. Moira didn't care where she ran—she just ran, even after her breaths were searing in her lungs, after her leg muscles felt numb. Still her feet pounded against the rain-soaked headland lining the coast of the sea, the cliffs to one side of her dropping thirty feet downward to the rocks below.

Oh, Goddess, oh, Goddess, she had no father. Colm was dead, but he wasn't her father, had never been her father. Yet she had loved him so much! He had been warm and loving and funny. He'd helped her build things, helped her learn to ride a bike, to skate, to ride a horse. It had always been him and Mum, him and Mum, at school things, at circles, at Sabbats. She needed him so much to have been her father! He was her dad! Her dad! Oh, Goddess, it all just hurt too much! Her whole life her dad had been living a lie, pretending. He hadn't been able to tell her the truth—or to tell Mum. How could he have not told Mum? How could Gran have done this? It felt so wrong!

At last Moira lost her footing, sliding and tumbling against the wet grass. Fresh dirt smeared her hands and face, but she lay where she had fallen, gasping in cold, painful breaths. Her hair soon felt wet. Overhead, the sky was darkening, the clouds blotting out any sunset there might have been. In this one afternoon her whole life, her whole past, had been ripped away, to be left just a blank.

Finnegan flopped next to her, whining, pressing his soft brown, white, and black side against her, licking her face. Moira burst into sobs, putting her arms around him, holding him to her. He licked her face and lay next to her, and she cried and cried against him, the way she had when she was a little girl. She wished she were dead. She couldn't bear the fact that her dad had known all along she wasn't really his, yet he'd loved her *so much* anyway. That seemed so sad and pathetic and unselfish that she simply couldn't stand it.

"Oh, Finn, Finn," she sobbed against him. "It hurts too much."

Her school clothes were sodden and muddied, her hair was wet, her face was tearstained and mud streaked. But she lay against Finnegan and sobbed, trying to let out the emotional pain that threatened to dislodge her soul from her body.

She didn't know how long she lay there, but gradually exhaustion overcame her and her sobs slowed, then quieted. She felt completely spent, utterly drained of emotion. Blinking, she realized vaguely that it was quite dark outside. Finnegan was resting by her side, taking the occasional gentle lick of her face, as if promising to stay as long as she needed him. Her chest hurt, and the ground was hard, and she was cold, freezing, and soaked through. But she couldn't get up, couldn't move, had no idea where she was. She would just lie here forever, she decided, almost dreamily. She would never move again.

"There you are," said a gentle voice, and Moira jerked in surprise. Finnegan hadn't growled, but he sat up alertly, his eyes locked on—Ian.

Moira felt frozen, stiff. Ian dropped lightly to sit next to her, seeming to neither notice nor care that he was going to ruin his clothes. Moira's first insane thought was that she probably looked like the Bride of Frankenstein. Then she thought fiercely, So what? My whole life just got ripped away from me—I don't care what I look like!

Slowly Ian put out his hand and stroked the light hair away from her chilled, wet face. "I felt you get upset this afternoon while I was being tutored," he said. "It was strange, like you were sending waves of upsetness. Then later I was putting up shelves in my mom's pantry—it's a disaster in there—and I pictured you running over the grass, with the sea in the background. It's taken me a while to find you."

"Thanks," Moira said, her voice small and broken. She struggled to sit up and felt Ian's arm around her shoulders.

"Brought a tissue," Ian said with a grin, handing it to her. Moira wiped her eyes and nose, knowing it was just a drop in the bucket in terms of what she needed. She crumpled the tissue and put it in her jacket pocket, feeling cold and miserable and self-conscious. What time was it? She glanced at the sky, but there was no moon. What in the world was she supposed to say?

Gently Ian pulled her against him so that her face was on his shoulder, his arms around her back. He stroked her hair and let her cry, and she felt the warmth of his body and his arms surrounding her.

# 14.
# Morgan

The second Moira ran out the door, Morgan jumped up after her, but Sky grabbed her arm, hard.

"Let her go," she said. "She needs some space. Finnegan's with her—and we can keep an eye on her in other ways, without just chasing her farther away."

Morgan hated using her powers to spy on her daughter, but she realized Sky was right—it was the only way to keep Moira safe right now without upsetting her even more. Through the window Morgan watched in despair as her daughter raced through the garden gate and flew up the road, her long straight hair whipping in back of her.

She felt numb. No, that wasn't true. It was just that the huge, varied emotions she was feeling were working to cancel each other out. Anger, disbelief, despair, sadness, regret. And all the while the hope that Hunter was really alive was in there, too, mixed in with everything else.

Katrina got heavily to her feet. "I'll be going, lass," she said, her voice subdued. "Now, looking back, I don't know how I could have thought this wouldn't rebound on us all like a hand grenade."

"How could you *not* have thought that?" Morgan exploded. "How could you have possibly thought this was a good thing for *anybody*? You wanted me for *Belwicket*? So you lied to me about my child for sixteen *years*? It's crazy! Not even about Moira— but about Colm, too. I believed he was her *father*. That had a huge impact on our marriage, our lives. Every time I looked at Moira, I saw Colm's daughter. Now you tell me all those thoughts were a *lie*. What were you *thinking*?"

The older woman's shoulders bowed, and she sighed. "We didn't know the side effects. I thought it was for the best. You were dying. I'm sorry." She sounded beaten and sad, and Morgan couldn't help feeling an instinctive sympathy for the woman she'd loved like a second mother for years now. But nothing gave Katrina the right to do what she'd done.

"You did this to my life, Colm's life, Moira's life so your *coven* would be strong," Morgan said. "How dare you? How *dare* you?" Morgan was shaking—she couldn't remember the last time she had been so angry.

"Belwicket is more than that, Morgan," Katrina said, pleading with her to understand. "It's our lives, the lives of our ancestors. It's our power. It's our heritage, yours and mine. And please understand, I didn't do it just for the coven. I did it out of love, too—for you and for your unborn child. You have to know that."

"Just leave, please," Morgan said quietly. She had no way to make sense of any of this at the moment, but she couldn't have even if she'd wanted to—she had something far more important to deal with.

"If that's what you want," Katrina said. "But please remember how much I love you." There were tears on her face as she closed the door behind her.

After Katrina left, Morgan paced the room nervously, emotions threatening to explode out of her like fireworks. She couldn't believe it—it was just too big, too huge, too amazing. On top of everything else, today she'd found out that her only child was Hunter's daughter.

"Oh, Goddess," she cried, turning to Sky. "Hunter's daughter!" She threw herself into Sky's arms and finally allowed herself to cry.

"Moira is Hunter's daughter," Sky said, repeating the words as if they were a miracle.

"I had Hunter's daughter," Morgan said, pulling back to look at Sky. "Hunter and I had a child." And then she thought of her marriage, of Colm, who had been so good, so accepting, and she felt terrible and furious all over again.

"They lied to me!" she said, letting go of Sky and starting to pace again. "More than that! They spelled me! *Spelled me!* All this time I've been living a lie! Every day of my life Colm knew our life was a lie, and he said nothing! He and Katrina and Pawel—I thought they were my family. They were deceiving me! For almost sixteen years—I can't believe it."

Sky nodded soberly.

"I still don't understand how it's even possible," Morgan said. "Hunter and I . . . we did all the appropriate spells. It's why I never even considered Moira could be his."

Sky gave a helpless shrug. "I don't know," she said.

"Well, right now I just need to be with my daughter. Maybe I should send her a witch message," Morgan said, sniffling and wiping her nose on her sleeve. Hunter's daughter. Moira was Hunter's daughter. She glanced outside, hoping to see Moira running back to the house. Now that she knew, she was dying to look at Moira carefully, to see where she left off and Hunter began. *Oh, Colm. Goddess, Colm, what were you thinking? How could you do this to me? I trusted you.*

"I think she needs time alone," Sky said, always straight-forward. "I don't feel her in the area. If she's not back in ten more minutes, we'll scry and go find her."

"She probably went to Ian's house," Morgan said, frowning with this fresh worry. "Like last night."

"Maybe not. She might just want to be alone."

"They did us such an injustice," said Morgan, and Sky nodded. "It's incredibly sad that Colm died, leaving no children."

"Moira was his daughter," Sky said gently. "She mourns him like a daughter. You know from your own experience about the bonds between parents and adoptive children."

"Yes, I do." Morgan thought of the parents who'd raised her, whom she loved so much. "But I also know there can be a special bond between blood relatives. In a way, it's like Moira has lost two fathers."

She sat down in Colm's leather chair. What would Hunter have been like as a father? Her heart constricted painfully, imagining how it might have been. His face, surprised at Moira's strong, tiny grip. Hunter changing a diaper with the same intense concentration with which he did everything else. Baby Moira sleeping between her and Hunter in bed. More tears rolled down her cheeks. How precious those moments would have been.

Sky crossed the room and sank down on the couch, leaning

back. "He would have loved to have had a daughter," she said, echoing Morgan's thoughts.

Morgan nodded, crying silently. After a few minutes she got up and washed her face and drank some water. "I'm going to scry for her," she told Sky. "I just need to know she's okay."

Then she lit the candle on the table and sat down, losing herself instantly to the peace of meditation. Scrying, she saw Moira, in the dark, sitting on wet grass. Ian was with her. He had his arm around her, and her head was resting on his shoulder. Finnegan lay nearby, panting and relaxed. She saw Moira nod, then both she and Ian straightened up slightly, awareness coming over them. They'd felt her scrying. Morgan sent a quick witch message to Moira, and Moira replied—curtly—that she was fine. Morgan warned that if she didn't return soon, she would have to come find her, then pulled out of the image and blew out the candle.

"Moira's okay," she said. "She and Ian are in a field some-where—maybe up on the headland, by the sea. But she'll be on her way home now, I believe."

"Good," said Sky.

"I just wish—," Morgan began hesitantly, then decided to go on. "I just wish I could see now who Ian is underneath. Maybe he's Cal all over again. Maybe he's not. I can't let him hurt my daughter."

"We could pin him down and do a tàth meànma."

"And have the New Charter all over us? No thanks. But it is tempting."

"Well, then, listen—there is something else we could do while we're waiting for Moira."

Morgan looked at her, knowing exactly what Sky meant.

"You said you scried and you saw Hunter. Tell me about that again."

Morgan did, describing what he'd looked like, how he hadn't appeared youthful, as he had in all her previous dreams over the years, but instead had aged. Not only aged, but had gone through some shocking physical changes. When she finished, Sky was silent, and Morgan asked, "What are you thinking? What can we do to know the truth?"

"I have Hunter's athame," Sky said thoughtfully. "It's out in the car. Daniel once told me about a spell where you focus intently on someone's energy, using one of their tools to help focus on them. It finds them whether they're alive or dead. I've been thinking all day—it's risky, but it's what we need to try. The thing is, you need three witches for it."

Morgan was quiet for a moment. Daniel Niall, Hunter's father, had almost killed himself trying to contact his wife in the netherworld. Contacting the dead was dark magick, ill-advised, and often ended tragically.

*But this is Hunter.*

She didn't have to think twice. "Let's do it," Morgan said. Sky went to the car. The only question was who to enlist to help. Hartwell? Keady? In other times, when she had a difficult question about magick, she would have turned to Katrina. Not now. She wished she could call up Alyce Fernbrake, who had worked at Practical Magick back in Widow's Vale so long ago. Alyce was almost eighty now and living quietly over the store she still owned but no longer managed. Morgan hadn't seen her in eight years. It would be presumptuous to call her for advice now.

The front door opened, startling Morgan. "Look what

the cat dragged in," Sky said, coming back in.

Moira looked like she had been hauled through a hedge backward. Several times.

Morgan stood up and ran to her. It was clear that she'd been crying hard, and it looked as if she had fallen. Finnegan was right behind her, panting, wet, and muddy. Sky grabbed his collar and a dish towel and started rubbing him down.

For a minute Morgan just looked at Moira. She saw her height and slenderness. And her hair, that fine, straight, light hair—it was more Hunter than Morgan. But the pain in Moira's eyes was a reflection of Morgan's pain.

Morgan drew her daughter to her. Selfishly, Morgan was grateful that Moira couldn't be angry with her about this the way she had been about Ciaran. This hadn't been Morgan's decision, Morgan's fault.

"I was worried about you," Morgan said.

"I just ran and ran and ended up on the headland, above the cliffs. Ian came and found me there."

"Oh." How had he managed to find her? "Did he . . . help you feel better?"

A nod. "I told him everything," Moira said, sounding both defiant and tired.

"Oh, Moira," said Morgan sympathetically. "I wish you hadn't. It's family business, our business."

Moira sniffled and shrugged helplessly. "I'm sorry—it all just came out. I had told him about Ciaran, too, and then afterward wished I hadn't. But I was so upset—I'm sorry. I know you're not sure about him and his mother, but he's been so good to me."

Morgan knew the last thing Moira needed right now was

to be pushed on the subject of Ian—and his family. "Well, why don't you go take a hot shower," she suggested. "Then we'll talk."

Moira nodded and headed upstairs.

"Morgan," Sky said when Moira was out of earshot, "I think I know who our third witch should be."

Morgan met Sky's gaze uncertainly. "Moira," she said simply.

An hour later the three of them went into Morgan's workroom. It was impossible for Morgan to keep her eyes off Moira—she kept examining every aspect of her daughter in order to find traces of Hunter, which now seemed so evident. And even her personality—she too kept much inside, like Hunter. They shared a similar dry humor. And Moira was tenacious, like Hunter—she couldn't let go of things.

"You don't have to do this," Morgan told Moira as she got out her own tools. "Usually it would be for three initiated witches. It's almost certain that Hunter is in fact dead—has been dead all these years. If he's dead and we contact him, we could all be in danger."

"I want to do it," Moira said.

"Right, then," said Sky. "Everyone take off every bit of metal. No jeans, Moira—they have rivets and a zipper."

Morgan hadn't taken off her wedding ring in sixteen years. It was hard to set it aside. Once Sky and Moira had changed into loose cotton pants and sweatshirts and Morgan was in her silk robe, Morgan and Sky drew seven circles of protection. Then Morgan drew three more circles of power. She gestured to the others to enter the circles, and she closed each circle.

Seated on the floor, they made a natural triangle, their knees touching. Sky took out Hunter's athame and Morgan's heart ached, seeing it after all this time.

A trident-shaped candleholder stood in the center between them; its black iron cups held three candles. Sky braced the knife across the middle bar of the candleholder so that the athame's blade was licked by one flame.

Sky had shown Morgan the written form of the spell, and together they had read it through in the kitchen. Now Morgan closed her eyes, and each of the three slowed her breathing, her heartbeat, and pooled their power so that it could be used.

Sky began the spell. Like every spell, it was a combination of basic forms overlain with instance-specific designations: the quest-for-knowledge form was in virtually every spell ever crafted. Sky wrought other delicate patterns around the basic structure, tailoring the spell with elegance and precision to search for a person, to promise to cause the person living or dead no harm, and to ward any harm from coming to them by cause of this. As a Wyndenkell, Sky was a natural spellcrafter, and she adapted this one gracefully and elegantly.

Then Morgan took up the chant, chanting first in her head, then softly aloud. She repeated Sky's basic form but wove her knowledge of Hunter into it, irretrievably chaining his image, his patterns, his essence to the spell. Using ancient words learned during years of study, she called on Hunter's energy as she knew it. If she had known his true name, this would have been a thousand times easier. Every thing—plants, rocks, crystals, animals, people—had a true name that was a song, a color, a rune, an emotion all at once. In the craft many witches went through a Great Trial, during which they learned their true name. Morgan still didn't know hers, and she'd never known Hunter's. As far as Morgan knew, no one had known his true name except for him. Instead she recalled all her memories of him and then sent those memories out into the universe, riding along the lines of inquiry Sky had formed.

"Moira?" Morgan whispered, and then they took each other's hands and held them, combining their energies, their knowledge.

Together they sent their energies out along the lines of the spell that radiated from them like spokes from a wheel. Moira was chanting her call-power spell and continuously sending her power to Sky and Morgan. Sky was repeating her quest spell, and Morgan continued to send out images of Hunter.

It was unclear how long they worked. They wove their words, their thoughts, their energies together until it felt as if they had created a tight, complex basket of silver. In her mind's eye Morgan could see it shimmering before her, becoming more and more complete, spinning and glowing. She focused on breathing in and out, smoothly, constantly, like waves, like the sea, her life force waxing and waning without effort.

Then she saw him. Hunter's face appeared in the silver ball in front of her, life-size, close enough for her to count every wrinkle, every scratch, every bruise. Her heart clenched with the mingled joy of seeing him and the torment of seeing him hurt. But what a gift, to be able to see him at all. He was sitting on a rough, sea-wet rock, his head in his hands. He looked up and seemed to see her.

His mouth made the shape "Morgan."

A shudder passed through Morgan at the sight of him, but she had to stay strong, had to find out the truth.

*Giomanach. Hunter. Are you alive or are you dead? Are you of this world or are you gone from this world?* Her words felt desperate, screamed, though she made no sound.

His face seemed to crumple then, his scraped, bony hand passing over his mouth as if to help him swallow pain.

*I am alive but not living. I am in neither your world nor another. I am nowhere.*

*Who took you from me?*

*I can never return.*

*That's not good enough! You are somewhere because we found you! Tell me where and I will come to you! Please—you have to tell me where you are.*

Morgan's breath was snatched away as Hunter bent over, shielding his face from her. His too-thin shoulders shook, his matted hair fell forward on his face. It was more torturous than anything she had witnessed in uncounted years. In her chest she felt a searing pain, then a damp warmth made her glance down. Her eyes widened as a ragged splotch of blood spread slowly across her robe, right over her heart. The shock of it broke her concentration, and when she raised her head, her eyes wide, the silver ball was gone, Hunter's image was gone, and all she could see were Sky's and Moira's stunned and afraid faces.

"Mum!" Moira gasped. "What's happening to you?"

Like a snake striking, Sky knocked Hunter's athame off the candleholder. It lay on the wooden floor, showing no glowing signs of heat but searing a charred pattern into the floor. Sky kicked it over onto the stone hearth, then moved the candleholder and took hold of Morgan's robe.

"Morgan!"

It sounded as if her voice were coming from far away, and

Morgan stared at her stupidly, then looked down at her robe again. The splotch of blood was the size of her palm now. Moving slowly, as if in a dream, Morgan pulled her silk robe away from her skin.

"My heart is bleeding," she whispered. "My heart is bleeding." A thin thread of panic threatened to coil through her veins, but Sky took her arm firmly.

"Moira, dismantle the circles, quickly." Sky's voice was commanding. Morgan watched with an odd, distant confusion as her daughter dismantled and erased circle after circle as fast as she could. When the last one was opened, Sky got to her feet and pulled Morgan up. "Let's go," she said briskly, and Morgan floated dreamily after her as Sky took her upstairs into the small bathroom. There Sky pulled off Morgan's silk robe and grabbed a faded tartan one, wrapping it around her. It was infinitely soft and cozy, and Morgan wanted to lie down in it and sleep forever.

Then Sky took a wet washcloth and began to dab gently at the dark red blood pulsing at the center of Morgan's chest. Moira stood in the doorway, her face pale.

"What is it, Sky?" she said softly.

"Her heart is bleeding," Sky said somewhat brusquely. "Get me some adder's tongue and some amaranth. Morgan should have some dried in her herb store."

As Moira ran down the steps, Sky helped Morgan into her bedroom. Soon Moira came back with two small neatly labeled glass vials. Sky soaked the adder's tongue and the dried amaranth leaves in cold water, then pressed them into a flat poultice and placed it on Morgan's chest. She covered it with a clean white cloth folded into a square.

"Moira," Sky said, "go outside and pick the last of the rose geranium petals. Mix them with a pinch of dried jasmine flowers and some fresh grated ginger. Make a tea and bring it up. Can you do that?"

Moira nodded quickly but lingered.

"Now, Moira," Sky said firmly. "Your mum will be all right," she added, more gently. "It was an unexpected reaction to the spell."

"My chest is throbbing less," Morgan said in a muted voice.

Moira left but soon came back holding a tray with a mug on it. Sky propped Morgan up with pillows so she could drink. Moira sat gingerly on the edge of the bed, careful not to disturb Morgan. Morgan looked at her and smiled, starting to feel more normal.

"Okay, note to self," she said. "When I do that spell, my heart bleeds. Have help available."

Her daughter smiled weakly, and Sky cracked a smile.

"A *most* unusual side effect," Sky said. "What do you think about it?"

Morgan met her eyes, black as jet, as onyx. "I think he's still alive."

Unblinking, Sky said, "I think so, too."

"But I don't know where. Sky, we have to find him." Morgan propped herself up on her elbows. "He's on a beach, which narrows it down to tens of thousands of miles of shorelines around the world."

Sky was silent, thinking. Morgan racked her brain, still muddled from the shock. What could they do?

Then Moira took a deep breath and said, "I have an idea."

It was as if Finnegan had started talking. Morgan and Sky just stared at her.

"What?" Morgan asked.

# 15.
# Moira

With Sky driving and Moira navigating, the three reached Lilith Delaney's cottage in fifteen minutes.

"What exactly did you see?" Morgan asked for the third time.

"It was him," said Moira, from the backseat. "Turn left up here, at the second lane. I didn't recognize him before because the Hunter in my dream was young and looked really different. But the one I saw in Lilith's crystal was the same person I saw in the silver ball."

"Are you quite sure?" Sky asked, her long, bony fingers tight on the steering wheel.

Moira nodded to herself and said, "Yes. If that was Hunter we saw tonight, then I saw him in Lilith's crystal last night. Do you—do you really think he's alive?" Hunter had looked horrible. Moira thought about Colm, how neat and cheerful and ordinary he had looked. So comforting, reassuring. Like a dad.

"If it's the same person from the silver ball, then yes," Moira's mum said, her voice constrained.

Moira had been trying to suppress her fear this whole

time, but now it was threatening to break through. She had no idea what to expect from Lilith Delaney now that it seemed like her mum had been right about her all along. "Here!" she said, peering into the darkness, recognizing the huge oak trees that lined the small road where Ian's cottage was.

Just six hours ago he had been so comforting on the headland, when she'd felt like she was losing her mind. Had all of that really been an act? Was he using her, trying to gain her trust the way Cal had used her mum? It seemed hard to believe he wasn't now.

But something in her was still praying that *somehow* Ian had nothing to do with his mother. She just couldn't reconcile her image of him, so kind, so caring, with another image of him actively working with his mother to harm them. *Please let it not be true. Not Ian. Please, please, just not Ian.*

The house wasn't dark, despite the late hour. A light was on in one upstairs room, and several rooms were lit downstairs. The three witches got out of the car, and Moira noticed that Sky was watching Morgan intently. A wave of light fell on her mother's face as they approached the house, and Moira almost gasped aloud. Her mum looked older, harder—stronger, and almost nothing like her mother the softhearted healer. Was this what she had looked like long ago, when she'd had to fight Ciaran and the dark wave?

They strode toward the house, and about ten feet from the front door Moira suddenly felt like she was trying to walk through gelatin. The air itself felt thick: it had weight and a heavy texture.

"What is this?" she asked in a low tone.

"Spells to keep unfriendly people out," Morgan said grimly,

pushing through it as if it were wet tissue paper. Next to her
Sky was murmuring under her breath, and Moira saw that her
mum was tracing sigils in the air in front of her.

The door opened before they got to it. Ian stood there,
still in his muddy clothes from before. "Moira?" he asked,
astonished. "Are you all right? What's going on?" He sounded
sincere. Moira would have given anything for him to really
care, but she couldn't risk him fooling her for another
minute. She turned away, not meeting his gaze.

"Where's your mother, Ian?" Morgan asked in a voice like
a brick.

"What's wrong?" he answered, his voice sounding formal,
less friendly. Just hearing the change of his tone made Moira's
heart sink. What had she been thinking? Lilith was his mother.
*Moira, Moira, how stupid are you?*

"What's this about?" Ian crossed his arms and stood in the
doorway. They were on opposite sides, had been all along, but
she had refused to see it. Her heart felt crushed, bruised.
"Moira?" Ian asked, looking over their heads at her, standing
behind them in the dark. "Are you okay?"

"Yes," she said shortly, more confused than ever.

Then a thickset figure appeared behind him, outlined by the
light spilling out onto the lawn. "Morgan Byrne," Lilith Delaney
said. "I confess to surprise. What could possibly make you
think you have the right to show up here and harass my son?"

"For your sake, I hope Ian isn't involved," Morgan replied
sharply. A shiver crept up Moira's spine at her mother's tone.
Morgan's voice conjured up images of glaciers, scraping their
way inexorably across a landscape of rock. "Let me see," her
mum continued. "I could have come to return a boxful of

pathetic, amateurish hexes, ill-luck charms, and injury fetishes that you've littered about my house and yard."

Lilith Delaney blinked and pushed ahead of Ian. "I don't know what you're talking about," she said, sounding bored.

Morgan laughed thinly, and Moira winced. "Please," her mum said. "Bottles full of nails, needles, and vinegar? Let's see—I think most children learn that in about the third form. Not very impressive—for a high priestess."

Moira knew that the hexes and spells put on the house and yard had been much more serious than that, with dangerously dark intentions and a great deal of thought and power put into them. Mum was obviously trying to goad Lilith by making it sound like a slow-witted child had created them. Moira could feel the coil of anger starting in Lilith's stomach.

"Are you done?" Lilith asked. "It's late, and the children have school tomorrow. Moira's already interrupted Ian's studies enough for one day."

Ian frowned and glanced at his mother.

"But then I guess she was upset, finding out she was a bastard daughter, just like her mother," Lilith continued.

*Oh, Goddess.* Ian had told Lilith about Ciaran and Hunter and everything. Moira took in a breath, then let it out, trying to release the raw sting of betrayal. She deliberately refused to look at Ian.

"You are so mistaken, Morgan," Lilith sneered. "You're ashamed of your father, who was one of the greatest witches to ever live. But you ought to be ashamed of yourself. You are weak, uncommitted, unfocused—you belong to a coven of dog-witches who have milquetoast circles where you all celebrate someone having a good day. Ciaran MacEwan! His blood should be celebrated, his memory revered, his lessons learned by every witch! But no—you think him evil. Your vision, your knowledge, is so small, so pedestrian, that you can't begin to encompass what a leader he was! You shouldn't be allowed to live, much less work your pointless and juvenile magick."

"We have different views," Morgan said, her face like stone. "But we have some things in common. Hunter Niall. I want to know what you know."

"Never heard of him," Lilith said, shrugging. "Now quit wasting my time." She stepped back into the doorway.

"You do know him!" Moira cried, rushing forward. "You were looking at him in your crystal the first day I came by!"

Lilith's eyebrows raised slightly, then she rolled her eyes and started to shut the door, refusing to even acknowledge Moira's words. In the next second she froze almost comically, as if suddenly pretending to be a statue. Her hand was on the door, but her back stiffened and the only thing she moved were her eyes, which widened and focused on Morgan.

Moira saw that her mother's right hand was stretched out, palm facing Lilith, and as Moira watched, Morgan slowly began to close the fingers of that hand.

Lilith Delaney whimpered, and Moira stepped back and brought her hand up to her mouth. She'd never seen anything like this. Never seen her *mother* do anything like this. Morgan kept her hand outstretched, but the more she closed her fingers, the more Lilith seemed to crumple against the door. It was clear that Lilith was striving to not look afraid, but Moira could feel the prickles of fear emanating from her, the way she had felt her anger a minute ago.

"You will tell me," Morgan said, her voice low and terrible to hear, hardly human. *Mum?* It was hard to keep from panicking—things were spinning out of control so fast that nothing made sense anymore. How could her mum be so cruel, so deadly? Moira's legs felt weak, and she struggled not to fall to the ground.

Lilith's eyes were still wide, but they shot a momentary glance at Ian, who was standing to her side. He reached out to touch her. "Mother?" he asked, concern in his voice. He turned to Morgan, angry. "Stop it! What are you doing?"

"It's a binding spell, Ian," Sky said, her voice as dry and calm as a desert rock. "Morgan's always been particularly good at them. Must be Ciaran's blood."

There was a spike in the fear that Moira felt coming from Lilith, fear and disbelief.

Lilith hadn't thought Mum was so strong, Moira realized. She'd had no idea who she was up against. Even after everything Moira had heard about her mum, even after the stories about the dark wave, it was hard for Moira herself to believe.

"Hunter Niall," Morgan said again. "Tell me everything you know." Her voice was like thunder, felt but unheard, deep tremors rolling through the five of them.

"I know nothing," Lilith spit through stiff lips. Morgan made an almost imperceptible movement, and Lilith whimpered again.

"Stop it!" Ian cried, trying to step between his mother and Morgan. "Moira! Make her stop!"

Moira ignored him, feeling her heart rip apart. She hated to hear the pain in his voice, but she couldn't give in. He had lied to her, betrayed her. She was so ashamed of how stupid, how naive she had been. Even after her mum had warned her about Cal, had tried to make her see the parallels, Moira had refused to believe it. She'd thought Ian was different. She'd been wrong.

"Where is Hunter Niall?" Morgan pressed, and when Lilith didn't answer, she closed her fingers a bit more. Lilith seemed to shrink against the door, her knuckles white, as if someone were wrapping her in a cloth of pain and twisting it. Her knees bent slightly, and Moira could see tiny beads of sweat appear on her upper lip.

"The thing about binding spells," Sky added conversationally, "is that they can do quite a bit of damage without leaving a mark." She let these words sink in, and then she looked at Lilith and said, an edge of steel in her voice, "The other interesting thing is that you're not the only one at stake here." She glanced first at Ian, then looked back to Lilith, making her intentions clear.

Moira bit her lips, tension making her muscles feel like knotted wood. *Tell Morgan what she wants to know. Do not force her to harm your son.*

Feeling ill, Moira started to sink to her knees in the wet grass, giving in, but instantly stood when Sky's eyes flicked to her. She could not show weakness. She could not become a liability in this desperate situation. She was Moira of Belwicket, Morgan's daughter, and she would show that she had her mother's strength. Locking her knees, she clenched her hands at her sides and pressed her lips firmly together. Only now was she beginning to understand what it must have been like for her mother when she'd found out she was a blood witch, when she'd realized that Cal was using her, when she'd had to fight the darkest forces Wicca had seen in generations. She'd never be able to look at her mum in the same way again.

"Moira saw you looking at an image of Hunter Niall in a crystal," said Morgan. "Tell me what you know. Don't make this worse than it has to be."

"You don't know who you're dealing with," Lilith snarled.

"Neither do you. You would be hard-pressed to come up with someone who could scare me," Morgan said coldly. "Not after my father. I've felt the foul wind of a dark wave against my face. I've gone face-to-face against Ciaran and defeated him. I've been hard to impress since then. Now, for the *last* time, you will tell me what you know, or after tonight *you* will know what it's like to be hard to impress."

With that she clenched her hand into a fist, then twisted it sideways, and Lilith crumpled like a puppet with cut strings. She slumped to the ground, curled around the door, her face contorted into a mask of pain and rage. Ian dropped to his knees next to her and put his hand on her shoulder, then shot Morgan a look of anger.

"Stop it! Stop it!" he said harshly, and Moira closed her eyes for a moment and stepped back, still unable to bear seeing Ian frightened, angry, hurt.

Flecks of blood appeared at Lilith's lips, but she could not speak. Morgan made the tiniest gesture with her closed hand, and a high keening escaped from Lilith and split the night air, a howl of agony.

Morgan leaned closer, not looking at Ian. "I can do this all night," she said slowly. "Can you?"

Lilith's face deformed one last time, then suddenly she spit out, "It was Iona! Iona MacEwan!"

Moira saw her mother step back, visibly shocked. "Iona. What about her?" she demanded.

Iona? Moira thought. Ciaran's other daughter?

"She'll know the answers you want," Lilith said.

"And where's Iona?" Sky said, her voice sounding like a dry knife on leather. "Where is she now?"

Lilith seemed to wrestle with this answer. Her short, heavy body was still frozen on the ground, and Moira thought that if she could move, she would be writhing and screaming. Then she burst out, "Arsdeth."

"Where is Arsdeth?" Sky snapped.

With an effort Lilith gasped, "North. North, by the sea."

Morgan looked at Ian. "Get a map."

He clearly wanted to refuse: his face was red with anger and overlain with worry for his mother. But Morgan's voice was a force field, and Ian stood and disappeared into the house. A few moments later he returned, a much-used and faded map of Ireland in his hand. He threw it on the ground between Morgan and Sky, and Sky picked it up.

"Arsdeth," she said. "In the north."

Moira swallowed hard as she saw a dark red drop of blood slide from Lilith's nose to sink onto the worn stone step under her head. Goddess, this was a bloody night. She understood now what Keady had meant when she'd told Moira it would be better to never truly understand what Morgan was capable of. So much pain and terror already. Did she have enough of her mother's strength in her to bear it?

"Arsdeth," Sky murmured again, tracing the map with her finger. "Oh, Goddess, here it is. Arsdeth, way the hell up north in County Donegal, by the ocean."

Morgan looked at her, and Sky nodded. Then Morgan said to Lilith, "What will happen to you if we go there and find you've been lying to us?" Morgan let Lilith have a minute to think about it. "What will happen to your son? Your house? Your coven? You do know you'd never escape me." Her tone was conversational, mildly curious.

There was no response, and Morgan rocked her fist from side to side slightly. A crumpled sound of agony came from Lilith, and once again Moira had to look away. "You know that I'll track you to the ends of the earth if you flee, if you've lied to us?"

Lilith nodded. Ian looked as though he was trying not to cry. Goddess, how could she turn off her feelings for him? How could he have betrayed her to his mother? Nothing would ever seem normal again. In one short week, one long night, her life had changed dramatically forever.

"Lilith," Morgan said, her voice sounding horribly gentle, "think about this. Do you believe I'm my father's daughter?"

A flash of fury sparked from Lilith's eyes. Her lips, stained with blood flecks, pressed even more tightly together. Her nod was unwilling, but it was there.

"You are right," Morgan whispered, and straightened. She nodded to Sky, who was looking at her curiously. Sky folded the map and put it on the ground next to Ian. Ian angrily scraped his sweater sleeve across his eyes. Moira couldn't resist meeting his gaze one last time. To her surprise, the look he gave her was anguished, but not full of hatred.

Morgan had already left Lilith and was walking to the car when Sky said softly, "Morgan?"

Morgan turned to look at her, and Sky met her gaze, then flicked her glance over to Lilith, still on the ground. Quickly Morgan turned and strode back to the high priestess of Ealltuinn. "I release you," she said, her voice low and steady. Her hand sprang open, and with an audible gasp Lilith seemed to melt onto her doorstep.

"Mother?" Ian said, his hand on her shoulder. He gave the three of them a last glance, then went inside to return moments later with a blanket, which he pulled over his mother. Her face was waxen, and the blood from her nose shone dark and red against her skin.

Morgan turned again and walked to the car, her back stiff, hands hanging like claws from her sides.

Moira followed her quickly, sliding into the backseat as Sky started the car. She still couldn't believe what she'd just seen— her own mother had hurt someone on purpose. Had frightened and threatened someone. *Bound* someone. Miserably Moira leaned her head against the window, wishing she could just shut down and stop thinking, stop feeling.

In the front seat she saw Sky glance quickly at Morgan, saw her mother's shoulders bend and her head droop—and then she heard her mother start to cry. Not just smothered sniffles, but huge, heaving sobs.

Then Moira remembered one of the most basic Wiccan teachings, the threefold rule—*What you send out comes back to you—times three*. Morgan had just sent horrible pain to Lilith—what would be returned to her or to Moira and Sky for participating?

Sky shifted the car into a higher gear, and Moira saw that they were going back toward town, where Sky could get on the highway going north. "Morgan, it's all right," Sky said. "You need to be strong now. You had to do it. For Hunter."

"Oh, Goddess," Morgan sobbed. "What have I become? Who am I?" And she cried harder. Those were the only words Moira heard her mother say the rest of the night.

# 16.
# Morgan

In the end it took almost seven hours of driving to get to County Donegal. There was little traffic, but the roads were small and often curvy or hilly. Dawn was starting to break when Sky stopped the car not far from Arsdeth.

Morgan looked back at her daughter, sleeping in the backseat. What had she been thinking, dragging Moira into this? Moira ought to be at home, just waking up to go to school. Some mother she was. *Oh, Colm, help.* Colm had been her rock, her anchor, all those years. It was his steady presence that had allowed her to put her painful past behind her. His gentle insistence that she live in the present, that she continue to find joy and meaning in her life was what had enabled her to fulfill her dream of becoming a healer.

Nearly twenty years ago she'd thought she'd seen the last of truly dark magick. For all these years in Ireland with Colm, it had been a triumph to live a quiet, satisfying life, filled with healing rites, study, school, and Saturday night circles. Now *this*, plunging back into strong, hurtful magick, dealing with people who reveled in darkness and pain—it was so deeply wrong. That outside forces were causing her to sink back into darkness and fear, rage and revenge, filled her with fury. She was the Destroyer. She would end this, here and now.

Next to her Sky was looking fatigued. She had worked a couple of keep-awake spells during the night but hadn't let Morgan share the driving. Morgan had cried for an hour, and by then they had been on the highway and Moira had fallen asleep. They had thrown a blanket over her when Sky had stopped for gas, and when they got back in the car, Sky had glanced over at Morgan and said, "Bloody hell."

There had been blood on the front of Morgan's sweatshirt.

When the bleeding had abated, Sky had convinced Morgan to rest for a while.

Now, with dawn approaching, Morgan was feeling better. At least she wasn't crying anymore or oozing blood.

"We don't have a plan," said Morgan, and Sky made a noise like a bitter chuckle.

"Let's turn around and go back home, then," she said.

"You know—we could be walking into a trap here," Morgan said. If Hunter *was* alive, why was Iona just now letting Morgan glimpse the truth? Could they even trust Lilith's information? These signs that had been coming to her . . . they had a purpose behind them. Had Lilith set Moira up to "catch" her scrying for Hunter? She certainly hadn't been very careful about hiding the image from Moira, and if she was behind those hexes and spells at Morgan's house, then she was capable of more secretive magick. Then there was Hunter's warning, too, not to come. It all pointed to the fact that this was a trap. Iona *wanted* Morgan to search for Hunter—but why?

Trap or no, Morgan couldn't stop now. She had to find Hunter.

"I know," Sky said. "But what choice do we have?"

"I should have left Moira at home," Morgan said.

Sky shrugged. "This is her life, her father. She would never have allowed us to leave her behind."

"Maybe so."

"And Morgan—you need her right now. Hunter needs her."

Morgan swallowed hard, thinking about this.

Behind them Moira stirred, then sat up, yawning. "Where are we?" she asked, and then Morgan watched the memories of the night before cross her face.

"Almost to Iona's," Sky answered her. Turning, she said, "I have a friend who lives not far from here. Maybe I should call her and you could stay there, just for today. Your mum and I don't know what's going to happen."

Morgan was grateful the suggestion came from Sky, but not unexpectedly, Moira's reaction was an instant furrowing of the brow, a determined expression on her face. "No, thank you."

Morgan turned to face her daughter. "Moira, last night was terrible. But it was nothing compared to what we might be facing. I can't guarantee that Iona won't be expecting us, that we're not heading into a trap. In fact, I'm sure we are." Morgan shook her head, thinking with dread of what might lie before them. "All my instincts are telling me to run a thousand miles from this situation, but I can't—not if Hunter's still alive. That's my choice, but it doesn't have to be yours." She looked deeply into Moira's hazel eyes, like her own, but with slightly less brown, slightly more green. "We lost your dad six months ago. I can't risk anything happening to you. I can't let it. Iona could be much worse than Lilith ever was. Please, go to Sky's friend's house."

"No."

"I wonder where she gets that from?" Sky murmured.

Sky had the foresight to begin casting pathfinding spells while they were still almost twenty kilometers—a good half hour or forty-five minutes—away. Even with the spells, they took wrong turns and got lost twice. Without them, they never would have found their way at all.

Arsdeth itself was a small, unremarkable village, not as quaint as some more southern towns, but with an older feel to it. It was rougher, less civilized in a way, with bits and pieces of ancient castles visible in the distance.

On a side street in Arsdeth they stopped the car and Morgan scried. She closed her eyes, lit a candle she placed carefully on the dashboard, and called images of fire to her, building her own power and strength. She pictured Iona as she remembered her from Ciaran's funeral, then asked the Goddess to show her the way to her. In her mind she wandered down roads, turning, heading north, then east, then north again. Eventually she saw the house, an ugly redbrick saltbox, with white-painted window frames and doorway.

"Okay, head north." She consulted their map. "We'll hit it up at this intersection. Then I'll tell you where to turn."

"Right, then," Sky said, shifting into a higher gear. "Let's go wring some information out of this woman."

Morgan knew that what was ahead of them was going to be very dangerous. There was no way to turn back now. Not when Hunter might be at the end of the trail. Not while there was still the slightest shred of hope. She still couldn't believe all of this was really coming from Iona. Iona wasn't strong enough—but then, Killian had told her that since their father's funeral, Iona had vowed to become stronger.

Ciaran's funeral. Morgan sat up. "Sky. Ciaran's funeral! At Ciaran's funeral Grania, Kyle, and Iona were furious I had come. Kyle tried to put a spell on me. But then Iona—Iona smiled. As though she had a secret." Morgan shook her head, remembering. "She knew she had taken Hunter from me."

They finally found Iona's house. Sky carefully turned the car and parked it facing outward, back toward the road, in case they had to leave in a hurry. Morgan pulled a windbreaker over her sweatshirt to conceal the bloodstain in front. As calmly as they could, Morgan and Sky took several minutes to lay new and stronger ward-evil spells on the car.

Looking behind her, Morgan made sure Moira was beside her. She paused for a moment, casting out her senses. Frowning, she walked to the edge of the driveway and looked past the house.

"She's up there," she said, pointing. There was a low hill behind Iona's house, and on the hill were the battered remains of what had once been a Celtic stronghold.

"Up in the castle ruins?" Moira asked.

"Yes." She looked at the two of them. "Are we ready?"

Moira nodded, though she was unsuccessful in keeping the fear out of her eyes. Sky's face was grim, resolute. They pushed through the hedge bordering the driveway and headed toward the hill.

There was no path, and the turf was spongy with rain. Soon their shoes and pants bottoms were soaked through and flecked with grass. They'd reached the first gentle slope of the hill when an unearthly baying sent chills down their spines. The next thing Morgan saw was four large Rottweilers, tearing down the hill at them, barking ferociously. Their jaws gaped, showing large white fangs that seemed ready to snap a tree limb in half. Suddenly the dogs were almost upon them, and Morgan felt Moira freeze with fear.

"Stop there," Morgan said softly when the dogs were ten feet away. Holding her hand out flat, she sent out a sensation of running up against a wall and a calm, quiet, happy feeling, where life was good, bellies were full, and there was a raw steak waiting back at the house.

*Gentle things,* Morgan crooned in her mind. *Sweet and calm. We're friends, friends to you, we mean no harm.*

The four dogs stopped with almost comical suddenness, their front paws backpedaling and screeching to a halt on the wet grass. From snarling, vicious, out-to-kill man-eaters, they became almost bashful giants, bobbing their heads and pulling their lips back in apologetic grins. Muscular tails began wagging as they stood in a confused group, wondering what to do next.

Morgan walked up to them, held out her hand for them all to smell. Sky did the same, and Morgan made sure Moira did also.

"We're your friends," Morgan said gently. "Remember us. Remember us." She traced the rune Wynn on each silky black forehead, writing happiness and harmony on them.

The huge black-and-tan dogs stood aside, cheerful puppies wishing they had a tennis ball. They watched the three witches walk past them up the hill, unconcerned.

Every muscle in Morgan's body was coiled and ready for anything. Her blood was singing with tension, adrenaline flowing through her veins like wine. Each breath took in more oxygen than she needed, each sense was hyperaware: the clouded blue of the sky, the scent of the wet grass. No birds sang here; there was no other life than the four dogs they'd just left.

They were maybe thirty feet away from the ancient stones when Morgan became more aware of Iona's presence. In a gaping window hole, where she had looked only a moment before, stood Iona.

Iona looked nothing like Morgan remembered. At Ciaran's funeral Iona had been plump, doughy, with a heavily made-up face. This Iona was thin to the point of being skeletal, with burning, overlarge eyes. Her skin was chalk white, as if she spent too much time indoors, and her hair was stringy, wispy, and prematurely gray. This was her half sister, but as unlike her as if they shared not one chromosome, not even the ones that made them inherently human.

With no warning Iona's hand snapped forward and a crackling, spitting blue ball of witch fire shot toward Morgan. Instinctively she raised her own hand to deflect it, but the fire grazed her skin, causing a stinging burn.

Iona laughed, showing a gaping mouth, the skin of her jaw stretching grotesquely. "That was a welcome, sister," she said. "I've been expecting you, of course. Ever since that idiot Lilith told me you'd be coming. Pity about Lilith—she was a blubbering mess after you finished with her. She hasn't held up quite as well as I'd hoped. But she played her part well: you are here. I can only imagine what you had to do to get her to admit where I was."

Morgan kept her face expressionless. "I started crushing her capillaries, from the outside in. They're very, very small and very delicate. If you damage enough of them, you bleed to death."

Morgan's senses prickled as everyone's tension level ratcheted up a notch.

For an instant a wary, speculative look crossed Iona's face but disappeared at once. "Sounds nasty," she said dismissively.

Morgan narrowed her eyes, wondering if Iona had ever believed the rumors about Morgan's power all these years. Whatever it took, Morgan had to convince Iona that she was no match for her. If she could frighten Iona, Morgan might not be forced to do things that would diminish her own soul.

"It was," Morgan was surprised to hear Moira say.

Iona looked at Moira, and Morgan forced herself not to panic. *Moira, stay back, be invisible,* she sent.

"It was very ugly," Morgan said evenly. "I was sorry to do it. But it's only a fraction of what I will do to you." This wasn't her true self, who she was inside. It was a warrior Morgan—one who only came out in times of need.

"Ooh, stop, you're scaring me," Iona said in a bored tone, leaning against the crumbling stone window. "By the way, where are my dogs?" Her tone was casual, but Morgan picked up on her true emotion—fear.

"They were in my way," she said, and Iona's eyes darted around, searching. Her jaw, with its tissue-thin skin, tightened.

Slowly Morgan realized that she felt no fear and surprisingly little anger. She was icy and unstoppable. She was Morgan of Belwicket. This pathetic excuse for a witch was just someone in her way. The feeling simultaneously thrilled and terrified her.

"Where is Hunter Niall?" Morgan asked. "Lilith told me everything she knew. I'm sure she would have preferred to be loyal to you, whatever your hold on her is. But in the end she crumbled. She had no choice. But you do. I recommend you choose wisely."

"Why, I heard Hunter Niall drowned in a ferry accident almost sixteen years ago," Iona said lightly.

"Iona," Morgan said, her voice glacial, "tell me where he is." She was becoming more and more tightly wound, a rubber band about to snap. She didn't want to cause harm here. She didn't want to. But she would.

"Tell me!" she shouted, flinging out her hand. An ancient stone burst apart next to Iona's head, shooting ragged shards of rock in a star burst. Iona flinched and turned away, but Morgan saw scrapes on Iona's cheek and flakes of stone in her thin hair.

Morgan could feel Iona's fear growing—but she could also sense fear coming from next to her. From Moira. She cast a quick glance at her daughter, sending her as much warmth and reassurance as she could. Moira's face was a mask—she was fighting hard not to show her true emotions, Morgan knew. But she was terrified inside, and Morgan wished with all her heart she wasn't here to witness what Morgan was doing.

"How dare you!" Iona shouted. Morgan whipped back around to face her. Iona brushed at herself—she was covered with dust and rock flakes. She looked at Morgan, her eyes burning. "This place is sacred!"

Wordlessly Morgan snapped out her other hand, her fingers stiff and tight. Another rock exploded, on Iona's other side. This time Iona cried out and covered her eyes with her hands. Gingerly she brushed at her face, leaving pale streaks of blood where her fingers had been.

"My eye!" Iona snarled, then looked up in concern as they heard a rumbling, scraping sound. The explosion had weakened part of the wall, and a large boulder was teetering on the edge above her. Quickly Iona jumped down onto the grass in front of Morgan just as the boulder fell and crashed into the window frame, right where she had been standing.

Morgan now had Iona's full attention. Clearly her half sister was angry. Her lips were tight with annoyance, her face streaked with blood, her eye was swelling, and she was glaring at Morgan.

"You don't know who you're dealing with," Iona said in a deadly voice. "You have no idea the things I've done or who or what I've become"

"Really. Just who are you, *Iona?*" Morgan said, filling her voice with unheard waves of power like tiny seismic shocks, intended to cause discomfort and anxiety. Next to her Moira shifted on her feet. Sky stood quietly, tense and at the ready.

Iona's eyes flared slightly and again she lost her composure for a split second. "I've become my father's daughter," she said in a voice full of rage and triumph.

With a calculated force Morgan thought, *Push,* and Iona was slammed against the back of the stone wall behind her. Her breath left her lungs with an audible "oof!" and she struggled to hold on to her balance.

"Hunter Niall," Morgan reminded her in a steely voice. "Where is he? Or should I start trying to persuade you?" She latched onto the image of Iona before her, pictured her ear, and whispered some of the words she had learned from her tàth meànma—or Wiccan mind meld—with Ciaran all those years ago. Iona shrieked, grabbing her ear, her face screwed up with pain. Morgan imagined it felt as though a railroad spike were being driven into her brain.

Iona writhed against the wall, screaming curses at Morgan that had no weight.

Morgan took a deep breath and released her. "You see, Iona," she said, "I've *always* been my father's daughter. Now stop wasting my time. Where is Hunter?" The urgency for an answer was so great inside her, she was no longer even forcing this cold, hard anger to terrify Iona—it was real. It was everything she was right now—a great, pulsing need to find Hunter.

Iona, trying not to weep, managed to stand up and lean against the wall. With no warning she stood ramrod straight and shouted a spell. Morgan felt her knees buckle and her muscles become lax. She dropped to the ground, knowing instantly that Iona had managed to put a binding spell on her.

"You twit!" Iona screamed, standing over Morgan. "All these years you've had no idea—no idea about what I did to you—to your precious Hunter!"

Morgan saw Sky move forward, but Iona stopped her with a flex of her hand.

*Stay put, Moira, don't move,* Morgan sent, knowing her daughter had to be terrified. Her mind was reacting quickly, feeling her way through the invisible bond that Iona had put on her.

"You're nothing," Iona shouted at her. "You're Ciaran's bastard, his mistake, his embarrassment!"

At the same moment Sky and Moira began chanting together, softly—they must have exchanged witch messages. They were working a spell to interfere with Iona's.

Morgan concentrated and felt the binding spell weaken. Iona was powerful but not nearly as strong as Morgan. Moira and Sky had weakened Iona's spell, and now Morgan could take care of the rest. With a burst of energy Morgan pushed her way through the spell, not bothering to dismantle it piece by piece but simply breaking it altogether. She broke free just as Iona was turning her focus to Moira and Sky, realizing the meaning of their chant.

Instantly Morgan again sent the pain to Iona's ear with Ciaran's dark words. Iona shrieked even louder, curling up as if to get away from the agony. Sky moved closer to Morgan— Iona couldn't hold her back any longer. Iona was on her knees on the grass, both hands pressed to her ear.

Morgan counted to twenty slowly, then she released her. "You are a joke," she said with unnatural calmness. "Do not make me ask again. Hunter Niall."

Iona sat up again, holding and rubbing her head, her bony face marred by hatred. "Haven't you figured it out yet, Morgan of Belwicket? *I* made the ferry go down. *I* did it, made that wave. *I* took the ferry." Her eyes were glittering with an unnatural brightness, and Morgan began to believe that twenty years of fury and resentment had made Iona insane. "And I created a bith dearc that opened above the water. *I* took Hunter. Poor thing, he was actually trying to swim to shore when I sucked him through it."

Morgan shook, rocked to the core at the idea of what Hunter had gone through. "You? How could *you* possibly do that?" she got out.

Iona smiled coyly, still looking like a wreck but starting to enjoy her own story. "With his true name. I have Hunter's true name."

*No! No, no, no.* Morgan tried to hold back her panic, knowing Iona would sense it, but she could feel the ragged edges of fear reaching for her. To know something's true name was to have ultimate power over it. Total control, in every way. Morgan had learned Ciaran's true name and had used it to stop him for good. How could Iona have learned Hunter's?

"Years ago I met a witch named Justine Courceau," Iona went on, as if reading Morgan's question on her face.

*Justine*—the woman who had collected names—the woman who Hunter had once kissed. Hunter had told Morgan that Justine had been bitter when he had made it clear nothing would never happen between them, but . . . that couldn't have been enough of a reason to go along with Iona's scheme. And besides, Justine hadn't known Hunter's true name.

"She hated Hunter and had spent years searching for his true name," Iona went on. "She finally found it using a bith dearc to speak to the dead. I offered to buy it from her. The silly woman wouldn't sell it." Iona's mouth crooked upward in a horrible mockery of a smile. "So I killed her. And took her soul—her power—for myself. With her power joined to mine, I was unstoppable. I was my father's daughter. And I wanted you to suffer. I wanted to cause you pain—so I created the bith dearc and stole Hunter from you with his true name." Iona stopped, wiping the disgusting glee from her face and attempting to look more in control. She laughed. "How does that make you feel?"

Oh, Goddess, Morgan thought in horror. Now she understood why Iona was oddly strong. She had taken someone's soul, absorbed her power. Who knew if she had even stopped at Justine? Iona was power mad, but the corruption of souls—of the power—was eating away at her, Morgan realized. Iona had gained power, but the power was killing her and destroying her. An icy hand clenched around Morgan's heart as she realized that Iona might have taken Hunter's soul, too. Morgan's knees started trembling, and she prayed it didn't show. A thin, cold line of sweat had started at the back of her neck and was snaking slowly down her spine. She felt surrounded by death and horror and hatred, and all she could think of was Hunter. *Hunter, Hunter. Please don't let that have happened to him.* She swallowed carefully and kept an iron grip on her self-control.

"Iona, where is Hunter?" she repeated flatly—staring at the shaking, weak witch huddled at her feet.

"Oh, no, he isn't dead. No, no, that would have been too quick, too easy. Hunter's been alive all this time." Iona imparted this information as if sharing a delicious secret. "Can you imagine? You grieved like a widow for all these years. And he's alive! If you call his existence living."

*Oh, Goddess, she's insane. Goddess, Please help me. Please get me through this. Hunter's alive.*

Sky stepped forward next to Morgan. She grasped Morgan's elbow. "Where is he?" Sky demanded. Morgan was grateful—it gave her a minute to pull herself together. Finally she knew for sure. Hunter was *alive.* A dull throb started in her chest, and she felt the warm, heavy stickiness of blood flowing.

Iona cackled. "On an island," she said triumphantly. "An

island cloaked in fog and rain, where no one goes. An island where nothing grows, nothing lives, and every day is exactly the same as the day before it. Hunter has been there, suffering, all this time, since I pulled him there through the bith dearc. Because of you and what you did to my family."

"Alone on an island?" Morgan asked, clearing her throat and strengthening her voice. Alone for sixteen years on an island. Surely he was mad by now. The thought of her beloved Hunter, her mùirn beatha dàn, going through such unimaginable torment for sixteen years almost knocked her to the ground.

"No," Iona said, surprising her. "There are a few other witches there, those who had angered the MacEwans through the years. I don't keep track of them. Why bother? They are nothing."

"Tell us how to get there," Sky said, her voice like stone. "Or I will gouge your eyes out and feed them to what's left of your dogs." Her tall, slender frame was rigid with tension, her hands clenched at her sides. Her face was inscrutable, still, her black eyes piercing.

Iona blinked. Morgan felt Moira step back.

Iona seemed to think for a few moments. "North," she said, then smirked. "In the ocean."

Morgan let every ounce of menace rise up in her. She gave full rein to every hateful thought, every desire she'd ever had for retribution. Malignancy welled up inside her, and she let it flow outward toward Iona. It was grotesque, the antithesis of everything she had worked toward in her life. It was darkness, it was against the Wiccan Rede, it was power and threat and bleakness and a complete absence of love or life or hope.

When it reached Iona, an invisible miasma of the worst of

human expression, she recoiled and started to gag, grabbing her throat with one hand, bracing herself against the stone wall. Her burning eyes seemed to start from her head; her tongue looked swollen.

Morgan watched her writhe in pain. *How far am I willing to go?* She would go as far as it took.

Sky took Morgan's arm and shook her gently, and Morgan swallowed hard and with effort squashed the feelings rushing deep inside her and crumpled them into a tight, dark ball, scratchy and painful, that she pushed to the bottom of her consciousness. Looking into Sky's troubled eyes, she nodded. Iona coughed and sank to the ground, gasping. She was shaking, her eyes wide and frightened.

"Where is the island?" Sky repeated with quiet menace.

"Between North Ulst," Iona said, her voice sounding strangled and thin. Her white hands were shaking, fluttering around her uncontrollably. "And the Isle of Lewis." She choked on a sob and turned her face away, one hand clutching at the grass.

"Are we just leaving her here?" Sky asked Morgan as they turned away.

Morgan paused. They didn't have a braigh—a chain used to bind witches. There was no time to deal with bringing Iona with them, constantly having to watch over her. "We'll send a witch message to the New Charter," she decided. "Have them send someone to come get her right away." Morgan glanced back at Iona, who was bent over, moaning. "She's in no shape to do much anytime soon," she said.

They walked to the car, and Moira was silent and sad next to Morgan. Morgan knew she had changed her daughter's image of her forever. What would that mean in the

coming years? What would it do to Moira's ideas about magick and about love? As they headed down the hill, Morgan
heard Iona moaning. But she kept walking forward, always
forward, toward the car. To turn back would be to set in
motion something beyond reconciliation.

They passed the four Rottweilers on their way to the
car. Morgan walked past them and got into the car, pressing
her hand over her still-bleeding chest. She leaned her head
against the window as Sky and Moira got in. Casting her
senses, she realized that they were both on the edge of
breaking down: frightened, sad, upset, anxious.

After they flew through Arsdeth, some color returned to
Sky's pale face. "Hunter's alive," she said, looking at Morgan.
"We're going to find him. That's what matters."

# 17.
# Moira

By the end of that day they had reached the Isle of Lewis. The drive had been tense, with no one speaking much until now. Moira's hands were still trembling, and no matter how many deep breaths she took, she couldn't seem to get her heart rate to slow down. She'd thought what she'd seen with Lilith had been incredible, but that fight between her mum and Iona . . . she'd never felt such sheer terror in her life.

And worse, she'd felt helpless. She knew she and Sky had helped a little, when they'd worked together to weaken Iona's binding spell on her mum. But that had probably been Sky mostly. What if Moira was just holding them back? Her power was nothing next to that of Morgan of Belwicket.

*Morgan of Belwicket.* Moira finally understood the awe she'd always heard in people's voices when they said those words. Her mum was a stronger witch than she'd even believed existed in the world. She'd thought the stories had to be exaggerated, but now . . . it was all so unbelievable. Had that really been her mum, whirling spells at Iona that had reduced her to a whimpering mess on the ground?

"Let's just go now," Morgan said.

"No." Sky's voice was final. "It's dark. No one will rent us a boat at this time of night. And we're all exhausted—we need to be prepared for what's ahead."

Curled up in the backseat, Moira listened to them argue, torn between a strong desire to find Hunter as soon as possible so she could come face-to-face with the man she'd just learned was her father—and a terrible fear of it at the same time. There had been so many shocks, so many terrors in the past twenty-four hours alone. She was still consumed with the grief of learning that she wasn't really Colm's daughter, the horror of knowing that her mother was *Ciaran's* daughter, the intense disbelief of seeing for real what Morgan of Belwicket was capable of. And underneath it all—a fresh, piercing pain over Ian's betrayal. How could she deal with meeting Hunter now, in the middle of all of this? But how could she *not* yearn to see him, to know him? To save him from whatever that terrifying woman, Iona, was doing to him?

*Iona.* Just thinking the name brought a bitter taste to Moira's mouth. She'd always known evil existed, but today she had seen it close up, alive. She shivered, pulling her jacket more tightly around herself.

"He's *alive*," Morgan was saying sharply. "We have to go *now*! Hunter's out there and he's alive, and we're going, right now!"

"Morgan," Sky said, her voice just as sharp. "We *don't* know what's waiting for us out in the middle of the bloody ocean. We *don't* know what kind of power or magick we're going to need to use out there. But I *do* know that I couldn't light a damn candle right now! And neither could you!"

"But—," Morgan began.

"You're Morgan of Belwicket! You may be one of the most powerful witches to walk the earth, but you're not a goddess!" Sky said, raising her voice. "You're not totally invincible, even if you think you are!"

Moira's eyes got larger. She propped herself on one elbow to see better. Her mother was looking at Sky with a shocked expression on her face.

"Is that how you think I see myself?" Morgan asked in a small voice.

Impatiently Sky shook her head and ran a hand through her fine, light hair. "No. I'm sorry. I didn't mean that. I'm saying that we all have limits. Look, Morgan, Hunter was—is—my cousin. I grew up with him. He's like my brother. We were best friends. Don't you think I want to find him? Don't you think I'm desperate to see if he's truly alive? Don't you think I'm desperate to get to him as soon as possible?"

Morgan didn't say anything, just looked at Sky. Her face was scraped and her hands still had dirt on them. She looked pale and wrung out and like she was about to cry.

"Iona's waited sixteen years to do this," Sky went on patiently. "She knows we're going to the island. She gave us just enough information to possibly find it. Lilith was a plant of hers. Don't you see? All of this is her *plan*."

Morgan looked away, then looked back and nodded.

"If Iona has been consuming souls and increasing her power through dark methods, we're going to need to be in better shape to fight her," Sky said. "Everything in me is telling me to jump into the ocean right now and *swim* out there to get Hunter. But I know that if we are going to try to save him, if we're going to go up against Iona on *her* terms, on *her* ground, we need to be able to pull out all the stops. Do you follow me?"

Morgan sighed.

"A few hours," Sky said, sounding weary and beaten. "That's all I'm asking for."

Morgan nodded again. "You're right," she said quietly. "I hate it, but you're right."

Moira sat up, brushed the hair out of her eyes, and wiped away the tears that had slipped out. She looked down at her hands, which were still shaking. *Be still,* she thought, focusing her energy and shutting out all of her fear and confusion. As she watched, the trembling began to stop. Moira felt a small jolt of triumph.

"Right. Good," said Sky. She started the car again and drove off. Two minutes later she said, "Look, there's a bed-and-breakfast. Tomorrow morning we'll rent a boat. All right?"

"Yes," Morgan said, sounding exhausted.

Moira gathered her coat and put it on. Dread welled up in her, and she swallowed back her nausea. She could do this. She could be strong, too. Her mum needed her. And her—Hunter—needed her, too.

The sky was barely streaked with pink and orange when Moira, her mother, and Sky got up the next morning.

Moira had slept like the dead, closing her eyes as soon as her head hit the pillow. She'd had many dreams, but the only one she remembered was of Hunter. In it he had said, "Don't find me, I am lost forever," and Moira had responded, "I must find you. I'm your daughter." Tears on her cheeks, she'd sat bolt upright in her narrow bed. She'd lost one father six months ago. Today would show whether she would gain another one or lose him as well. But how could she see a stranger, Hunter, as her father?

Down at the harbor Sky was negotiating to rent a twenty-foot fishing boat for the day. It was big and clunky, with an outboard engine and a canvas tarp on aluminum poles as the only cover. To Moira it looked ancient and only vaguely seaworthy. Its name was *Carrachan:* "Rockfish."

Moira's mum turned to look at her. "You're staying here," she said in a no-nonsense tone. Moira's mouth dropped open in shock. After all this—after facing Iona without flinching and seeing her mum become another person, she was being asked to stop *now*? Her mother went on: "You're fifteen, you're not initiated, and you're my only child. I cannot lose you. You're going to stay in the bed-and-breakfast until we get back. Don't wander around. Stay in the room and don't open the door."

"What?" Moira cried, staring at her mother. "You can't be serious! After all this?" She waved her arms in a completely inadequate description of the last three days. "You need me!"

"No discussion," her mum said firmly. "You're staying here. Sky and I will do what we have to out there, but I won't be able to think if you're not safe."

"I am not staying here," Moira said, setting her jaw and looking down at her mother. "I want to be with you. I want to be there if—when you find Hunter."

Her mother's face softened. "Moira—I've lost so many people I've loved. If I lost you, too, I couldn't go on. Do you understand? I couldn't go on." Her brown eyes looked searchingly into Moira's. For a moment Moira felt a twinge of guilt. Her mum *had* lost a lost of people: Cal, then Hunter, then Dad. Her birth parents.

But none of that changed the fact that Moira had to do this. "I'm going," she said firmly.

In the small boat Sky had pulled on an ill-fitting life vest. Her pale hair was already being tossed by the wind.

Wordlessly Morgan pointed back to the bed-and-breakfast.

Moira felt a spark of anger. "I'm part of this!" she cried. "He's my bloody real father!" It didn't sound right, coming out of her mouth—Colm was her father. But she knew it was still the truth, and stranger or not, if Hunter needed help, she wasn't going to sit by and do nothing.

Morgan shook her head, her eyes full of pain. "No." Then she turned from Moira and climbed down to where the boat was tied. She stepped into the boat and pulled on a life vest. At Sky's word she pulled up on the rope tying the boat to the pier, and Sky pulled back on the throttle. The small engine roared to life. Without a backward look Sky sat back and took the old-fashioned tiller under her arm. There was no steering wheel, no console—only battered vinyl seats, ripped and smelling of fish.

Moira stared unbelievingly. Were they really going to leave her here, on an island a thousand kilometers from home, with strangers? Were they really going to make her sit out this final stage when they were looking for her birth father?

She didn't think so.

The boat was slowly pulling away from the pier, its engine already sounding asthmatic. Without allowing herself time to think about whether it was a good idea or not—she knew it wasn't, but she was way past caring—she sprinted forward and threw herself off the pier as hard as she could.

Whoosh! She hit the surface of the water hard, going

under before swimming back up. The plan had been to actually land *in* the boat, even if it was headfirst. Morgan and Sky both turned at the splash, and in an instant Morgan was grabbing her arm and hauling her upward.

"What were you thinking, Moira!" Morgan shouted.

*Air, breathe, air.* "You're not leaving me!" Moira shouted back when she'd finally gotten her wind.

Sky had slowed the engine and was looking at Morgan inquisitively. Moira looked at Sky, then at her mum. Total exasperation crossed Morgan's face, but finally she shook her head. They wouldn't turn back—they'd wasted too much time as it was.

Her mother took off her life vest and handed it to Moira.

"What will you wear?" Moira asked.

"There are only two," her mother said shortly.

Moira looked around. They'd left the harbor behind and were passing slower-moving fishing boats. It had been sunny, with just a few puffy, cotton-ball clouds in the sky when they'd set off. The sea had looked a rich blue-green, full of life.

Now, only minutes later, Moira could scarcely see any blue in the sky at all. An endless, heavy-looking mass of gray clouds was sweeping across the sky as if pushed there by a huge, invisible hand. Moira moved forward to sit on one of the vinyl side benches up front. The sea was the color of lead. Instead of perky little white-capped waves, it was churning, uncomfortable, roiling with some deep disturbance. There were no birds overhead, Moira noticed. Seagulls had been thick by the harbor, bright white and gray, raucous cries filling the air. Now it was as if they had been erased from the picture.

She looked up to see her mum looking solemnly at Sky.

"Come into my parlor," Sky said dryly.

*Said the spider to the fly.* Iona had sent this weather. There would be more, Moira knew. They were going forward, even if this was a trap.

Moira sat shivering. Her shirt, jacket, jeans, socks, and sneakers were soaked, and she was freezing. The temperature had dropped about fifteen degrees and the wind had gotten brisker. Salty spray occasionally flew up into her face, feeling like needles hitting her skin.

Sky turned the boat slightly, aiming for a gap between two big islands. The ride became much rougher as the boat cut across the current. Moira sneaked a glance at her mum, who was staring straight ahead, white-faced and determined. Morgan looked over at her, and her eyes were so sad and solemn that Moira felt a touch of panic.

Crunch, crunch, crunch. Her hands were white-knuckled from gripping the handhold on the side of the boat. Her face stung from salt spray and wind.

*Oh, no.* A familiar sensation began in the pit of her stomach. She swallowed convulsively. Then her mouth flooded with saliva, and with her last few working brain cells she realized she needed to hang over the edge of the boat *now*, because she was going to vomit.

More salt spray hit her face—she was closer to the water. She started to cry, her body suddenly racked by sobs. She'd never felt so lost in her whole life.

Then her mother was there, scooping her long hair back, her hand on Moira's neck. When Moira's stomach finally seemed not only empty but inside out, Morgan pulled Moira back up. She'd taken a bandanna out of her back pocket, and she wiped Moira's stinging face. Moira was sobbing now, knowing she had to stop right away, knowing she looked like a baby, knowing her mother had been only too right about wanting her to stay.

"I'm sorry," she sobbed. "I'm sorry."

"Shhh, shhh," said her mother. "It's hard. That's why I didn't want you to come."

"I'm sorry," Moira repeated, shivering again.

Morgan studied her for a second, then closed her eyes. She spread out the fingers of her right hand and placed them over Moira's face, touching her temple, her forehead, a vein in her neck. Then she started to murmur words in Gaelic, a few of which Moira recognized from class, but most unknown. Within moments Moira breathed a sigh of relief. Her pounding head, racking nausea, fatigue, and fear were easing.

Within a minute Moira tentatively let out her breath. Oh, Goddess, she could breathe without pain. She took in slow, deep breaths, feeling pain and tension leave her with every exhale. She opened her eyes just as her mum opened hers.

"Thanks," Moira said, feeling a new sense of awe. Her mum had healed her before, but now Moira truly understood where the ability came from—a source of power deeper than she'd ever imagined. "That's so much better."

"We need you in good shape," Morgan said, and hugged her.

It was right then, at that moment, that Moira realized that her mother's powers as a healer were probably exactly equal to her power to destroy. It was almost blinding, this huge example of how everything in life was both black and white, good and bad, healing and destructive. Mum always called it the thorn on the rose, and Moira marveled at how complete everything felt, how reassuring it was, in some way, that the wheel always turned unbroken.

Morgan took her hands away and shook off any magickal energy that was left over. There were pale violet circles under her eyes; she looked sad and weary and oddly expectant, as though she were waiting for bad news.

Within Moira's next breath, the whole world went gray.

Blinking wildly, Moira could still see her mother, less than three feet away, and could still see Sky, three feet in back of her. Everything else was gone.

"What is this?" she cried as Sky slowed the engine to a crawl.

"Fog," Sky called back. She cut the engine and swung the tiller all the way to one side and fastened it there; now they would go in slow, tight circles for a while. She stood and came to the midsection of the boat, where Morgan and Moira were. The three of them peered uselessly out, but it was as if they were surrounded by a thick, gray wool blanket.

"Well, I can't see a bloody thing," Sky remarked. "Goddess only knows if we're about to beach up on some rocks—I thought we were still pretty far away, but who knows? We're in the middle of bloody *nowhere*. Goddess, Iona's much more than a pain in the arse."

"So we need to get rid of the fog," Moira said, trying to think.

"Well, yes," said her mum, running her hand through her hair and getting stuck almost immediately in a tangle. "It's just that we have no way of knowing how much is there, how wide it is, where to move it to."

*Fog.* Fog was made of water vapor. "Can we make all the tiny water drops in the fog sort of stick together, be attracted to each other?" Moira asked. "Then they would turn into rain and fall. Rain would be miserable, but you can see through it."

Her mother looked at her, blinked, then looked over at

Sky. A slow smile split Sky's usually solemn, thin face, and she nodded.

Moira felt a spark of pride—maybe she *could* hold her own with these two strong witches. She was Morgan's daughter after all, and she had to remember that.

Moira, Morgan, and Sky held hands and concentrated. Sky worked the main part of the spell. They concentrated on feeling each infinitely small atom of moisture floating in air, boundless numbers of them. One tiny particle joined another and was joined by a third. Slowly a chain reaction started where each water molecule joined with others and still others. They became heavy, too heavy to float in the air, and began to drift downward, pulling others down with them as they went. Within minutes a frigid rain pelted down, soaking them instantly. The small canvas roof didn't cover where Sky sat by the tiller and offered little in the way of protection for the other two. Rain slanted at them sideways, stinging their faces, drenching their salt-sticky hair.

It was miserable. But they could see.

Sky cranked up the engine and took hold of the tiller. They were through the two islands of North Ulst and Lewis, headed out to open sea. The rain followed them. The waves were still spine-jolting. Time ceased to register as they made their way across the leaden sea. It seemed as if they would be crossing this water forever. They passed a smaller island on the left. Ahead of it, slightly east, was another, even smaller island.

"We should be able to spot another one soon," Sky said, raising her voice over the waves.

The whole world lit up with the biggest bolt of lightning Moira had ever seen. Her hair stood on end with the electricity, and every detail of the horizon was blotted out. *Boom!* It was followed immediately by an enormous, rolling peal of thunder that shook Moira right through her body into her bones.

"We must be getting close," Sky said, grim determination on her face. Her eyes were dark, like obsidian, her skin pale and leached of color. Her wet clothes stuck to her tall, graceful figure, and she gripped the tiller hard with both hands.

Morgan turned to Moira. "Don't touch anything metal," she instructed, then lifted her arms to the sky.

"Morgan! Don't!" Sky shouted. Startled, Morgan turned to look at her.

"Save your strength," said Sky. "Don't waste it here. I can see the island ahead. We'll need you more later."

Morgan nodded and sat down. Sometimes Moira thought she could see the island, but mostly she could see nothing but rain, highlighted by huge, spiky lightning bolts. The booms of thunder rolled through them incessantly, one merging with another.

The wind picked up. Waves doubled in size and crashed against the boat like wrecking balls, jarring Moira, making her teeth rattle, almost pulling her hands from where they clenched the torn seat cover. When she looked in one direction, she saw a wall of sullen gray water. When she turned her head to look over the other side of the boat, she saw another wall of water. The sea itself seemed to have come alive, awakened by the uneven chortlings of their motor, angry at their presence. It seemed to well up around them, eager to drag them to the bottom of the sea.

*No sinking,* Moira told the universe. *We are not going to sink. This is not the ferry. We are in control. We are protected.*

"I see it!" Morgan shouted, pointing off to the right. They had almost passed it—if they'd kept going, they'd have headed out into open sea.

Sky tried to turn the tiller but strained—it was stuck. Morgan joined her, and the two women pulled the long wooden bar with all their strength. The boat creaked ominously—it didn't want to turn—and Moira refused to think about their fate if the tiller should break and they had no way to steer. Iona isn't going to win this, she thought fiercely. She will not win. Just as she was about to go help, the tiller finally budged, working against the waves, the wind, the rain.

The island itself looked like a row of giant, black, moss-grown teeth, sticking up out of the water like some huge, decayed jaw. Lightning flashed every other second, and the thunder was so constant it was impossible to tell where one clap ended and another began. Every jagged streak of lightning highlighted this rocky wasteland, and the closer they got, the more uninhabitable the island seemed.

*What if this has all been a wild-goose chase? What if Iona was lying? What if we came all this way for nothing? What if Hunter's really been dead for years?*

Moira felt a blanket of despair settle over her and knew it was futile to battle it. She looked at her mother and Sky and saw the same gray feeling of helplessness cover their faces like a shade.

Her mother frowned and rubbed a hand over her wet forehead. Then light dawned in her eyes. "It's a spell!"

Why was Mum bothering? It was pointless to struggle, to hope, Moira thought with weak despair. They were all going to die.

Morgan drew runes in the air: Eolh, for protection, Thorn,

for overcoming adversity, Tyr, victory in battle, Ur, strength, and Peorth, hidden things revealed.

Slowly Moira realized what was happening. Her head began to clear, and she stood up and joined Morgan. Together they repeated them. At the tiller Sky joined them, and as the three drew Peorth in the air, there was a tremendous bolt of lightning, and suddenly the island was upon them, rearing up like a dragon from the sea, so close they were about to be dashed on the rocks. The sea, the despair, and even the distance had been an illusion.

Frantically Sky grabbed the tiller. Moira sat next to her and pulled also. Morgan scanned the shore magickally and then with one hand shielding her eyes from the rain.

There was no place to land a boat. The shore was rocky and jagged, sharp, broken boulders protecting the island at every turn. They kept on, and finally, just as Moira was afraid that she had no strength left in her arms, her mother spotted a tiny inlet, just a small stretch of sand barely big enough for their boat. Sky and Moira steered the boat into it, wincing as they bashed against rocks with an unholy scraping sound. They beached, the V-shaped hull of their fishing boat completely unsuited to being pulled up onshore. Morgan jumped off the boat, looking wobbly on land, and managed to secure a rope to a twisted and deformed tree that grew out of a crack in one rock.

Then Moira jumped down into the sand. Sky leapt down after her, and they looked at the boat, tilting dangerously sideways on the beach. The propeller was halfway out of the water, long, slimy strands of seaweed twisted around it. It was amazing that it had worked at all.

As far as they could see, there were only rain-slicked

black rocks, sodden sand, stunted and gnarled trees, and storm. There was no sign of any human existence. Moira kept blinking against the onslaught of rain, trying to peer into the distance. She cast out her senses. There was nothing.

Her mother reached out and took her wet hand. Sky took her other hand. The three of them walked forward, their feet leaving squishy footprints in the slippery sand. Moira tried casting her senses again and felt a dull ache in her head, but nothing else.

The sand weighed her feet down. Her chest felt odd, tight, and the pain in her ribs was sliding slowly back. The idea that they had to get back in that boat and somehow get off the island filled her with a gray, hopeless fog—and this, she was sure, was no spell.

They walked literally across the island, a distance of maybe half a kilometer. It tapered to an arrowhead shape, rounded at the tip, maybe sixty meters across. The wall of rock ended, too, cutting off the beach at its other side. Moira searched the land, looking for anything that would indicate that any other human had been here. There was nothing. Only a dead feeling, a numbing of her senses, a dulling of her emotions. This place was spelled, created to be a mindless prison. Hunter's not here, Moira thought frantically. This had all been a trap; Iona had lured them here to capture them. She had to get out of here— she had to get her mum and Sky out of here.

But before she could speak, Morgan squeezed her hand and strained forward. Moira followed her mother's gaze, and her mouth dropped open. In the face of the tall rocks was a cave opening, barely visible. But they could see the outline of a person, a human, shuffling toward them from the entrance.

# 18.
# Morgan

He had to be here—he had to, Morgan thought in despair. But she could feel nothing, pick up on nothing. She had risked her daughter's life to try to save her mùirn beatha dàn's. But there seemed to be nothing here—only grotesque, deformed trees and sharp bits of rock that stabbed at her feet through her shoes. She gripped Moira's hand more tightly. *Hunter is here somewhere. He simply has to be.*

Then she saw it—an opening in the wet, black rock face. A cave. Visible only because of a faint, flickering light deep inside the rock. The light was blocked, and slowly an outline appeared, a person. A human being was walking toward them.

Morgan's heart constricted painfully, her eyes straining to see into the cave's darkness. Holding hands, she, Moira, and Sky hurried toward the cave. There was no need for words. Their hearts and minds were too full to speak.

They were almost upon the cave when the figure shuffled awkwardly out into the storm, into the palest, most fractured bit of light available. It was not Hunter.

"Oh, Goddess!" Morgan whispered, staring in dismay at the wizened old woman. The woman had wild, tangled gray hair, large, vacant eyes, and sunburned skin crinkled in folds over a face that scarcely looked human. A woman. A leftover witch, put here by some MacEwan, possibly Ciaran, for all Morgan knew. Put here and forgotten for who knew how long.

The woman's faded gray eyes fastened on them blankly. "You're not real," she muttered indistinctly, shaking her head and looking away. "You're not real. They never are." She turned around and began to head back into the cave.

"We're real," Morgan called strongly, starting to follow her. "We're real. We're looking for—"

Her words wisped away into the wind. A second figure was blocking the cave entrance. This one was tall, thin, gaunt. He had long, pale blond hair and a darker blond beard. His eyes were deep set and an odd, light green, as if bleached by the sun and sea.

Morgan could do nothing but stare silently, desperately praying that this wasn't an apparition, that what she was seeing was real. She was shaky, unsteady on her feet as the figure stepped slowly closer.

*Oh, Goddess, it's Hunter!* Hunter, after all these years! He stared at them, first Morgan, then Moira, then Sky, as if recognition was taking a long time to seep into his brain.

"Do you see him?" Morgan asked Sky, not taking her eyes off him.

"Yes," Sky croaked, her voice broken. "Yes, I see him."

"Hunter. Hunter," Morgan said inadequately, tears springing to her eyes.

"Morgan," he whispered in disbelief. Frowning, he shook

his head, not seeming to make sense of what he was seeing.

A few quick steps brought Morgan right up to him, where she had to tilt back her head to meet his eyes. He looked so different—it had been so long. Goddess only knew what atrocities he'd lived through these past sixteen years. But deep within his oddly light eyes, Morgan saw the Hunter she loved.

He raised one shaky, bony hand, the knuckles bruised and scraped, and ever so gently brushed a strand of wet hair off her cheek. Bursting into tears, Morgan threw her arms around his waist, clasping her hands in back of him as if she'd never let go.

"Hunter, Hunter!" she cried, her tears mingling with the rain. Sixteen years fell away as she closed her eyes and pressed her face hard against his ribs. Then his arms came around her, pulling her even closer as he rested his head on hers. Here was Hunter, her love, back from the dead. It was a miracle, a blessing. "I thought I'd never hold you again," she sobbed. "I thought I'd never, ever see you."

"Morgan," he said, his voice a raspy croak, ruined, but definitely Hunter's voice. "Morgan, my love. You're life itself, you're my life."

"And you are mine. Always." Morgan's heart had stopped when she saw him; now it seemed to thump slowly once, twice, and more. A damp warmth seeped through her sweatshirt: her heart was bleeding again. This was Hunter, and he was speaking to her. He was alive, and she had found him. As she held him, she felt him start to tremble and realized that he, too, was crying. Pulling back, she looked up at him, at his tears, at his dear, beloved face, now broken and battered and much too thin. She blinked, then glanced at the sky to see if the sun had come out. It hadn't—the clouds still hung heavy and low, deep gray and sullen. Quickly she looked from Hunter to the rocks to the sea to Sky, who was weeping silently, a smile on her face, to Moira, who stared solemnly at this stranger who had fathered her.

Everything was brighter, the colors deeper, richer, as if a filter had been taken off her eyes. Every sound seemed clear and precise and exact—she could hear each small wave breaking, each twisted tree branch creaking in the wind. Moira and Sky looked so bright and alive. All those years ago, on the dock in Wales, when she'd felt nothing of Hunter's spirit, everything had dimmed. Everything had become dull, every sight and sound had seemed as if a fine, thin wall of cotton separated it from Morgan. Now the wall was gone, torn away by the indescribable joy of seeing Hunter again.

"She told me you had died," Hunter said hoarsely. "She told me you had died, trying to save me when the ferry went down. Then I saw you, days ago, saw you scrying for me."

"I don't know why I couldn't find you before," Morgan said. "I tried, so many times."

Hunter looked down at her sadly. "You found me now because Iona wanted you to find me," he said. "I told you not to come. Iona wanted you to come here, to get you here."

A dull dread sank over the joy in her heart. She and Sky had feared this, and they'd been right. Now they were here, as Iona had planned, and would have to face whatever she had in store for them—whatever she'd set up.

In the next second Morgan's breath left her in a harsh gasp, and she froze, unable to move. *Iona.* Morgan recognized it as the same binding spell that Iona had used—was it only yesterday?—at the ruined castle. The New Charter had promised to send someone right away—and no one had warned Morgan that they hadn't successfully taken Iona into custody. Iona's powers must be much stronger than Morgan had realized. Who knew what she had done to the people who had come for her? Morgan felt a pang of guilt that she hadn't done something more to Iona when she'd had the chance. She focused her energy, trying to break through the binding spell . . . but nothing. Stunned, her mind clouded by emotion, Morgan looked to Hunter.

"Morgan!" Hunter said next to her as Sky and Moira ran over.

"Mum, Mum, are you okay?" Moira asked, her eyes wide with horror. Sky took a moment to reach out and grab Hunter's arm, as if to reassure herself that he was real, then turned her attention to Morgan.

"Don't touch her!" Iona said, appearing between two tall black rocks. "What I have is for her alone." Slowly Morgan edged her eyes over to see her half sister standing above them, holding a dark stick in one hand.

"Hello, all," Iona said, giving them her disturbing, skeletal smile that seemed to unhinge her jaws. Her thin, graying hair was plastered to her skull with rain, and Morgan wondered again why Iona seemed so old, so ill, yet burning with such an odd energy.

"Sixteen years of hard work have finally paid off," Iona said, her voice sly and satisfied. "Poor Morgan. Haven't you figured it out yet? Lilith Delaney's been keeping tabs on you for years, but I didn't decide to move on you till this year."

That was important, Morgan thought dimly, trying to think, trying to fight her way through the spell as she had before. Why now? With her mind she examined the edges of the binding spell, testing its strength. It was stronger than yesterday's. She had to focus and concentrate on getting free, on fighting Iona. If she thought about anything else—Hunter, Moira, Sky—all would be lost.

"Me. The visions, the dreams. I sent the morganite—I even sent the ring," Iona gloated. "That was a brilliant touch, I must say. The actual ring! And now you finally find your heart's true love, only to watch him die! You get to suffer twice!" She threw back her head and laughed.

"I can't help you," Hunter whispered to Morgan. He sounded like he was near tears. "I have no powers. Over time this island binds powers."

"It's all right," Sky told her cousin kindly. "It's all right."

"Mum?" Moira said. She had edged closer and was standing very still, trembling.

*Stay back and be invisible,* Morgan sent.

*You need me,* Moira sent back.

Think, think, Morgan told herself fiercely. Unravel the spell. Figure out why now? Iona had mentioned the ring, the morganite, the visions, the dreams . . . but not the hexes and spells around Morgan's home. Had those been an extra touch from Lilith—her own personal vendetta?

*Focus.* It didn't matter right now. What mattered was learning Iona's intentions and uncovering the best way to defeat her. She had gotten her power from taking the souls of other, more powerful witches. Would that make her vulnerable somehow? She looked up at Sky, whose dark eyes watched her, worried. Taking in very slow, shallow breaths, Morgan visualized herself to be strong, whole, powerful. I can break out of this binding spell, she told herself. I'm Ciaran's daughter. But more important, I'm Maeve's daughter, Maeve of Belwicket. I have her blood, her power in me. I am the sgiùrs dàn—the Destroyer.

Morgan raised her hand.

A look of fleeting surprise crossed Iona's face and she frowned. She raised her stick, and Morgan felt the force of Iona's rage crash against her mind, pushing into her consciousness. Buckling over onto the sand, Morgan frantically slammed up every mind block she could think of, remembering the last time she'd had to fight this hard, two decades ago. But she was no longer an uninitiated teenager. She was stronger, with a wealth of power and knowledge. Wincing, she felt Iona pressing harder. If Iona managed to get inside, Morgan would have no chance.

"Let her go!" Morgan heard Hunter's splintered voice dimly, from far away. "You have me! Isn't that enough?"

"No," Iona said, her voice tight. "I want you both."

*Think, Morgan!* How integrated were Iona's souls? How hard was it for Iona to keep them focused? To control their power? What kind of power would it take just to use them?

A throaty chuckle of triumph reached Morgan's ears. Iona was enjoying watching Morgan bent to her will. Morgan knew that given the opportunity, Iona would kill them all. Kill Moira. Her daughter. The very thought filled Morgan's blood with anger.

Then suddenly, with no warning, Iona was gone, no longer pushing against Morgan's mind. Morgan keeled over, her face hitting the wet sand. Immediately she pulled her shaking arms under her, rising to her hands and knees. She spit wet sand out of her mouth and stood up.

"I want you to have the chance to fight," Iona said. "And *lose.* I want Moira to watch you die, as I watched my father die," she went on, stepping carefully down the rocks. "And then I'm going to take your souls. Well, yours and your daughter's and Sky's. Hunter's isn't worth much at this point."

Watch Ciaran die? Morgan thought hazily. They said he died alone at Borach Mean.

"Can you imagine what I can do with your power?" Iona asked, already looking awed by the thought. "I'll have your power inside me." She shook her head, pleasure showing on her sunken face.

"Why now?" Morgan asked. "Why wait sixteen years?" Her mind raced as she tried to think clearly, desperate to protect her daughter. The beginning of an idea started to form. But to try it could cost her her life.

"I wanted you to have a child," Iona answered, as if it were obvious. "I wanted her to be old enough to suffer, losing you, the way I suffered. I wanted your loss to be greater. See?" She flicked her stick over at Moira, and Morgan's stomach clenched as her daughter cried out in pain, wrapping her arms around her chest. Morgan lunged to protect her, but Iona flung out her hand. Gasping, Morgan dropped to the sand, feeling as if knives were cutting into her lungs with each breath; she was being flayed slowly from the inside out. She prayed it was only an illusion. Struggling, she tried to put up a wall between her and the pain.

Moira was whimpering now, curling up.

"It makes it so much worse," Iona observed calmly. In that moment Sky suddenly took out her athame, which she'd been concealing in her pocket. She held it out toward Iona, focusing on the tool as her lips moved silently to form a spell. Rocks flew up from around them and launched at Iona.

Astonished, Iona whirled and at the last second managed to deflect most of them, with a few only grazing her neck. A thin band of blood appeared, dark red against her white skin.

"How dare you?" Iona cried angrily, raising her stick again. The athame fell from Sky's grasp and thunked into the wet sand, buried up to the hilt. Sky dodged as Iona fired crackling, spitting balls of furious blue witch fire at her. One careened off a boulder and slid past Morgan, singeing her face and making her flinch. Sky reached for her athame, but Iona held out her hand and drew the athame to her. She gave Sky a malicious smile, then tossed the athame into the air, away from Sky. It whizzed above her to bury itself in a twisted tree, right over Moira.

Quickly Morgan gathered her strength and choked out a laugh. "A child? That's pathetic, Iona, even for you. Was that really it? Or did it take that long to amass enough power to fight me? We all know that I'm so much stronger than you."

Anger flushed Iona's ghastly face and her eyes sparked. Yes, Morgan thought. She was getting to her—just a few more well chosen words and Iona would be pushing her way into Morgan's consciousness. Iona raised her stick again—but didn't use it. She seemed to sense something. Morgan watched, breathing shallowly, as Iona slowly looked around her.

Sky was crouching behind a dark, wet boulder. Moira had edged up against the tree. Her face was contorted with pain, and tears ran down her cheeks. The old woman Morgan had seen, plus two more forgotten witches, were milling around, watching this happen but with no comprehension on their blank, childish faces. Clearly they were also powerless to help and beyond caring what happened to them.

*Come on, Iona, try to get into my mind.* "You know it's true.

I am strong and you are weak," Morgan went on recklessly. "Father said so."

That did it. With a snarl of rage Iona threw both of her hands out, and instantly Morgan felt it, her furious, barbed consciousness, crashing against Morgan's mind like a burning battering ram. Once inside, she would wipe Morgan's mind clean, steal her power, drain her soul. It was a chance Morgan had to take. For an instant Morgan dropped her mind blocks, and Iona was inside her head, twisted with hatred, power starved, greedy, clutching at Morgan's powers. Morgan steeled herself, ignored her terror, and scanned what she could of Iona's mind.

The soul of the witch Justine Courceau, insane with rage and a frenzied desire to escape; another, lesser soul of a faded witch who had crossed Iona without even realizing it. *And Ciaran.* Morgan gasped as she recognized the soul of her father, the soul she had joined with once before in a tàth meànma. *Ciaran! Oh, God, no wonder Iona is so powerful now! No wonder she could hold me in a binding spell.* Somehow she had reached Ciaran's soul when she'd killed him and pulled out the knowledge and strength that had been crushed when he was stripped of his ability to use magick.

Gritting her teeth, Morgan drew on every bit of power she had within her and once again slammed up her mind block, forcing Iona out. Iona fought her viciously, but Morgan squeezed harder and harder, and then her mind was free again, and Iona was just pressing against her.

It had taken just a moment.

"Why do you even try to fight?" Iona snarled, coming closer. "We all know how this will end."

*We need to join our powers!* Morgan sent a witch message to Moira and Sky, wincing with each word. *Ciaran's soul is inside Iona! She must have killed him and taken it.*

*What should we do?* Moira sent, and Morgan was surprised at how steady her daughter felt. Anyone looking at Moira would have dismissed her as out of the fight, but she was strong—stronger than Morgan had realized. Stronger than she herself knew.

*Bind her.*

Iona was circling them now, keeping an eye on Sky but ignoring both Hunter and Moira.

Iona was still pressing against Morgan's mind, still holding the razorlike spell of pain on her. In Morgan's haze of agony, words floated toward her: "You have the power to devastate anything in your path—or to create unimaginable beauty." Ciaran had told her that, right before she had bound him. He'd said, "You're the sgiùrs dàn." The Destroyer. The one who would change the course of the Woodbane clan.

It had been so many years since she'd needed to call on the very depths of her power. Yet as a teenager, she had bound one of the most powerful witches of all time. She had helped stop a black wave, a thing that had regularly killed hundreds of people, whole villages.

It had been a blessing, all these years, to not have to work magick like that, magick that made one touch the edge of darkness. Now she was soaked through, cold, and shot through with an unholy pain. The man she loved was powerless, in desperate need of help. Her only daughter was in danger. And they needed her to save them.

Morgan sank back on the sand and closed her eyes. She called on the very depths of her power, every aspect of her history—of her ancestors. She was the Destroyer, and she would defeat her enemies. She let every muscle go limp, from her eyelids to her toes. Every single feeling flowed out of her and onto the sand. Caring, anger, pain, panic, joy, longing, all seeped out of her motionless body. She felt dead, numb, and with it came a kind of freedom. She imagined herself rising, dressed in white, a shining aura around her. She imagined her small silver athame to be a mighty sword. She pictured herself able to deflect any spell, crush any attack, triumph over any foe. Even her half sister. True, Ciaran's soul was in Iona, but without him Iona was weak. It was Morgan who had inherited Ciaran's strength, out of all his children. It was Morgan who had inherited Maeve's strength, her mother who had loved her so much, she had let strangers adopt her so she would be safe. Morgan was the sgiùrs dàn.

*Be ready,* she sent to Moira and Sky. *Gather your power—everything you have. I will tell you when to send it to me. It will be harder without touching. But it's our only chance.*

Her eyes opened. She got to her feet, pain held at bay for now.

Iona stopped and stared at her. She raised her stick, but with a harsh phrase Morgan deflected it. Iona's face twisted into an ugly mask of rage. She shouted out something, and Morgan instantly knew it was Hunter's true name. Iona sketched a rune in the air, called a color to her, and then turned to sneer at Morgan.

"He is mine," she snarled. "He's nothing but a walking puppet." She slashed one clawlike hand through the air, and Morgan watched in horror as identical slashes appeared across Hunter's face and chest, as though a tiger had raked him. In his state it was enough to make him stagger backward, lose his balance, and fall heavily against a low rock. He lay still where he fell.

*My love! My love!* Morgan's eyes blazed with the pain of seeing her soul mate attacked. And then the realization came to her. Iona was doing all of this to Hunter because she knew his true name.

*And I know Ciaran's true name.* All those years ago, she'd learned Cairan's true name the night she first shapeshifted. Stepping forward, her hands clenched into fists, Morgan faced Iona. Iona turned her sights to Moira, who was standing now, her young face resolute. *No!* Morgan thought, but Iona swept her hand again, and Moira crumpled to her knees, welts across her face.

It was time. Her face anguished, Morgan met Sky's eyes. *Yes,* Sky sent. *Do it, no matter what. It's why you're here.*

*Moira,* Morgan sent. *It's time. I need you—I need you to fight through the pain and send me your power.*

Morgan closed her eyes, took in a deep breath, and felt waves of power come to her from both Sky and Moira. She was amazed at the strength she could feel from her daughter, even injured.

"An nal nithrac," Morgan began. "Bis crag teragh. Bis nog, nal benteg."

"How pointless," Iona said, her voice angry. "Amusing, but pointless."

Morgan opened her arms wide. She was full of power, the power of generations of her ancestors. She was made of power, she was power itself.

"I am the sgiùrs dàn!" Morgan cried, and her voice, clear and strong, pierced the air, pierced the fog of Iona's power. Iona looked startled and took a step backward, then straightened her shoulders and strode forward.

"You're nobody!" Iona cried. "You're nothing! You're going to be the first to die!" She held out her stick, about to begin a new spell.

Morgan felt Moira drawing some of her power back and whirled to see what her daughter was doing. In one move Moira was back on her feet and lunging for Sky's athame. She pulled it from the tree and whispered something, then threw it at Iona, hard, furious power showing in her eyes. Iona tried to deflect the athame, but Moira must have spelled it with a ward-evil spell, and it hit her shoulder, knocking her off balance. Iona clapped one hand to her shoulder, where dark blood was oozing sullenly through her robe. Morgan whirled to see Moira standing by her tree, angry red marks on her face, furious power showing in her eyes.

With one hand Morgan flashed the shape of a rune through the air, even as she began to sing the first notes of Ciaran's true name. Iona gaped at her, but Morgan continued as swiftly as she could, calling a color from the air, singing the tight, hard song that defined who her father was to the entire universe. In seconds she was finished.

"You are going to die!" Iona shrieked. She raised both arms and started to swing her stick in a huge arc over her head.

"I know your true name!" Morgan commanded. "Enough!"

Iona wavered, her arms jerking as she tried to keep her balance. The major part of her strength, Ciaran's soul, was now under Morgan's command. Iona fought against her, her bony jaw clenched until Morgan thought it would snap.

"I am the Destroyer, Iona," Morgan shouted. "Didn't your father ever tell you that?" She felt tall and terrible, and even as Iona struggled against her internal force, Morgan's power swelled and rose. She was the conduit for power that had been held deep within the earth for centuries. It was gathering now, rising, and pouring out from her. Sky grabbed one hand, sending her power to Morgan.

"Ciaran is powerless. You are powerless!" Morgan cried, pointing at Iona.

Iona stood there, shocked and with the first glint of fear on her face. But she wasn't beaten yet. Harsh, dark words were pouring from her lips, and her arms moved, writing sigils in the air. A slow rumbling shook the sand beneath their feet, and Morgan whirled to see its source. The cliff above the cave was spitting, the rocks being rent with the last bit of Iona's stolen power. Even with Ciaran bound, she had enough power to craft a spell that was rending thousands of tons of black basalt, fracturing a hill of stone. Rocks and pebbles, boulders and shards, began to rain down on them.

Morgan hurried toward the sea, with Sky following close behind. Morgan grabbed Moira's hand and yanked her backward. Hunter was looking up at the wall of rock, then at Iona, and Morgan rushed forward to drag him into the water.

"It won't be enough!" Iona shouted, laughing.

Huge waves of stone tumbled down the side of the hill, thudding into the sand, bouncing off one another. In a split second Morgan had made her decision. *Scaoil,* she thought, and she sent her power out in a tightly coiled knot that knocked Iona squarely on the chest. Her back hit the rough wall by the cave, and in the next instant a huge boulder tumbled down, sweeping her thin body to the ground like a stick puppet.

Moira cried out and covered her face, looking away. Morgan gathered Moira to her, still urging everyone backward. They were up to theirs necks in the frigid, salty water, and still cannon-ball-sized rocks were striking the water all around them. Morgan treaded water, keeping Moira, Hunter, and Sky in sight. Her face crumpled as she saw two of the withered witches pinned beneath a house of rock. The cave had been crushed, no doubt killing any who had been inside.

Eventually the hill was nothing more than a crumbled rock pile, half as tall as it had once been. There was only a small area of sand still visible, and slowly, all holding hands, the four of them made their way through it, shivering uncontrollably as the cold air hit their wet bodies.

Teeth chattering, Morgan turned to look at her family, all of them.

"It's over," she said wonderingly. "It's over." Tears of joy washed the salt from her eyes, and then they were all hugging, crying, laughing.

"Thank the Goddess." Morgan felt completely and utterly drained but so thankful.

"Blessed be," Sky said, smiling and shaking her head.

*Morgan.*

Morgan froze, blood draining from her face. Hunter, Sky, and Moira all looked at her quizzically, and she held up one finger.

Iona's voice was surprisingly strong in Morgan's thoughts. How had she survived the rock slide in her weakened state?

*Morgan. This isn't over,* Iona said. *At this moment Lilith and Ealltuinn are making their final move—on Belwicket. You're not home to protect it. By the time you get back, everything you knew and loved will be a black, smoking plain. You see, I am my father's daughter.*

A dark wave. As soon as Morgan thought the words, her whole body shook, as though a shock of ice water moved through her veins. She felt dizzy. *No. It can't be.* Not Belwicket. Not her coven, her home!

"You're lying!" Morgan shouted desperately, looking back at the stunned faces of her family. "You haven't the power! You haven't the skill!"

"Perhaps not," Iona's voice replied from behind Morgan. Stunned, Morgan spotted Iona crawling weakly from a small space beneath several fallen rocks. She was battered—a huge cut bled fiercely on her arm, and she limped, scarcely able to stand—but she was alive. Iona reached the sand and cackled, enjoying Morgan's stunned expression. "You bound Ciaran," she said. "But you didn't bind me. And what you don't realize is that I am not relying only on my own power"—her voice was weakened now, no better than a desperate hiss—"but also that of my ally, Lilith Delaney. It's *Lilith* who cast the dark wave spell. That was what she truly wanted all along—to rid her country of the so-called good Woodbanes, like Belwicket. It was just a fortunate coincidence that I wanted their future high priestess dead."

As Morgan opened her mouth to reply, Iona suddenly extended her hand and spat out a chain of ugly words. *"Feic thar spionnadh! Thèid seòltachd thar spionnadh!"*

Morgan barely had time to react as a sharp spear of energy, glinting silvery blue in the sunlight, sped toward her. Automatically she threw up a blocking spell. She was shocked that Iona would try to hurt her in her weakened state—what possible good could it do her? But then her thoughts turned darker. Iona was clearly beyond reason. She was crawling blindly toward a single purpose—hurting Morgan.

As Iona's attack reached Morgan, something unexpected happened. Morgan had long known that her element was fire, and so she called on the power of fire to add strength to even her most basic spells. But as Iona's sharp spear of light reached Morgan, it bounced off the shield she'd created and turned to roaring orange flame. Before Morgan could take in a breath, the flame turned upon Iona and consumed her.

"No!" Iona wailed as the flame overcame her body. The fire grew, and soon an oily, roiling black smoke—eerily like the smoke that had invaded Belwicket's circle—emerged from the fire. Morgan gasped. In a matter of seconds the flame burned to nothing and winked out. No evidence of Iona's body remained on the beach. No smoke, no charred earth, nothing. Morgan stared, disbelieving, at the spot where Iona had stood. She's dead, she thought finally. Evil serves no purpose. It consumes you. But before she could react further, she remembered Iona's final promise.

"We have to get home as soon as possible," she cried, turning back to her family and running for the crude boat they had rented only hours before. "There's a dark wave coming for Belwicket!"

# 19.
# Moira

They had to swim back to the beach where they had left their boat, since rock slides had destroyed most of the original path. Sky, Morgan, and Moira held on to Hunter, helping him along. They climbed on board with difficulty, and Morgan and Sky pushed the boat off the sandbar. Sky started the motor, and then the island was in back of them and they were headed out to sea. Moira shivered, not only because she was freezing and wet and her face burned where Iona had raked it: what had happened on the island had been far worse than anything she could have expected. All those poor people—dead. That horrible witch, Mum's half sister—dead. Not just dead, Moira thought. Burned to death by her mum's own deflection spell. She'd thought she couldn't be any more horrified by what her mum was capable of, but she'd been wrong. There wasn't even time to react, though. Because the four of them were heading back home, where another, even bigger disaster awaited them

Moira had heard about dark waves, of course, but during

her lifetime nobody had seen one. When she'd asked her mum about it, she'd explained as best she could—it was a huge, sweeping cloud of evil, made up of tortured souls who were hungry for new energy. A dark wave could kill any number of people, it could level houses, it could leave a village as nothing more than a black, greasy field. Moira was torn between her terror of what they'd find when they reached Cobh and the many other emotions battling inside her at the sight of Hunter, real and alive in front of her.

Hunter shook his head, the slashes on his face covered with dried blood. "I still can't believe it," he said hoarsely. His eyes looked so large in contrast with his gaunt face. "I'm so afraid I'll wake up and find this was a dream."

Morgan laid her hand on his arm. "No," she said. "This is real. We're alive, and you'll never be back there again. Of course, it will be a long road back after—after everything you've been through. And unfortunately, there's no time to start healing just yet. We still have something else to face."

Nodding, Hunter wiped the sleeve of his shirt against his eyes. Then Morgan looked at Hunter's shirt and frowned. In the center of his chest were dark stains, one on top of the other, that had happened in the same place again and again. She looked down at her own dark sweatshirt, then again at Hunter's. Hunter's heart had been bleeding, just as Morgan's had.

Moira couldn't keep her eyes off Hunter. This was her biological father. Colm, gentle, warm, loving Colm, was her da, but this man . . . he was half of who she was. And while Colm was gone, Hunter was here. But she was still as lost as ever about what that actually meant. Could she ever know this man as her father? Was it a betrayal to Colm, who had loved her with everything he had?

The sea had calmed, and it wasn't difficult to speak over the sound of the overtaxed engine. The four of them were solemn, beaten physically and emotionally and facing a dark wave.

"So this is your daughter," Hunter said, nodding at Moira. Moira shot her mum a meaningful glance and saw Sky do the same. Hunter's eyes took it all in.

"Yes, this is Moira," her mum said, then cleared her throat. "Moira Byrne."

"Byrne." Hunter looked at Moira again, speculatively, and she blushed.

"I'm a widow," Morgan said awkwardly. "Colm, my husband, died six months ago."

"I'm sorry, Morgan," Hunter said, and he seemed sincere. He loves her, Moira thought. She could sense the emotion coming from him in waves despite his obvious weakness. Raising her eyebrows slightly, Moira looked again at her mum.

"What?" Hunter asked, noticing Moira's look, a slight frown on his face. "What are you not saying?"

Morgan started picking at a loose thread on her soggy jeans. Moira knew she did that when she was nervous. Actually, Moira did it, too. "I have something to tell you," her mum said, not looking up. "At first I thought it should wait. This must all be so much for you to take after . . ." She stopped and took a deep breath. "But you need to know. Perhaps it will even help somehow. The truth is, I found out only—oh, Goddess, only a couple of days ago—that Moira is . . . I was pregnant with Moira already, before I got married. Before I was with Colm."

Confusion crossed Hunter's battered, exhausted face. It was clear he was struggling even to speak at all and to understand the meaning of words he hadn't needed to use in so long.

"I'm your daughter," Moira burst out, surprising even herself. "From when you and Mum were in Wales. Before you died. I mean, I'm sorry, you didn't . . ."

Hunter's green eyes grew even wider, taking over his too-thin face. His mouth opened slightly, almost hidden beneath his scruffy beard. Looking from Morgan to Moira and then to Sky, he didn't seem to know what to say.

"We didn't know," Moira went on more strongly. "Mum had been spelled—by my grandmother. She hadn't meant to make her forget the truth, but it happened, and then she and Dad just—" Moira stopped, seeing the growing confusion on Hunter's face. "It's a long story. But it just came out—the same time we learned you were alive."

Hunter stared at Moira blankly, as if his mind was working too slowly for him to comprehend what she was saying. He looked over at his cousin for confirmation, and Sky nodded gently.

"Oh my God, Morgan," Hunter said in his scratchy voice. "We have a daughter." He looked at Morgan again, and Moira could see his love for her shining on his face.

"Yes," Morgan said, her eyes bright with tears. "We do. But—but I still can't figure out how."

"What?" Moira asked. "What do you mean?"

"I shouldn't have been able to get pregnant." Her mum looked a little embarrassed. "We took precautions." She turned to Moira. "That was another reason I had no idea you were Hunter's."

Moira knew about pregnancy prevention spells and how a blood witch would only be pregnant if she consciously skipped them. Somehow in all the chaos of learning Hunter was her father, she hadn't stopped to think how that didn't make sense. "But you got pregnant anyway," Moira said.

"I think I might know why," Sky said slowly, and the others turned to look at her. "Remember what I already said, Morgan, about the Goddess having her way? Well, you are the sgiùrs dàn, fated to change the course of the Woodbanes. Maybe you were fated to have Moira. Maybe your precautions didn't mean anything in the face of fate."

Morgan blinked. "But—that means that fate has something important in store for Moira."

"Like what?" Moira asked nervously, a chill going down her spine.

"I don't know," said Morgan. "But I do know that after what I saw you do on the island, you'll be up to handling whatever comes your way." She gave Moira a proud smile, and it warmed Moira deep inside.

"My daughter," Hunter said wonderingly. "I have a daughter." He gazed at Moira, drinking her in with wonder until she looked away, feeling suddenly shy. Yes, she was his daughter—but she'd been raised by another man. And she wasn't ready to make sense of all of it yet.

What if Sky was right—what if her birth had been fated? Her own mother had played such a huge role in the Wiccan world. If she was meant for something similar, then she couldn't let anyone down. Moira pictured Tess, Vita, and her gran—all back in Cobh, unprepared for the danger coming at them. A week ago it wouldn't have occurred to her that she would help fight a dark wave. Now it was unthinkable not to. She tried to sit up straighter, ignoring her aches and pains and cuts and bruises. "We need a plan," she said firmly. "To beat the dark wave."

\*　　　\*　　　\*

Back on land, Morgan and Sky rented a small charter plane to take them directly back to Cobh. It would take only three hours, compared to two days of driving. The flight had cost pretty much everything Morgan and Sky had in their combined accounts, but that didn't matter.

Now that they were on the plane, headed for home, any lingering joy at finding Hunter had been put on hold. As horrific as the island had been, Moira knew she was facing something far worse. Part of her wanted to run and keep running. But there was no way she could leave her coven, her house, her town to face a dark wave without her.

"Da made a—a simpler spell before I . . . left," Hunter said. He spoke slowly and not very smoothly after not having had to talk in years. Sometimes he had to pause to think of a word. "I knew it well once, but it's . . . gone." He frowned in frustration, his sunburned face wrinkling. "I haven't been able to work magick for sixteen years . . . ," he said; then he looked out the window, his voice trailing off, as if even admitting that was too painful to bear.

"How long did the long version take?" Sky asked Morgan.

"A little more than an hour, I think," Morgan said. "I have it all written in my Book of Shadows, but I remember that we coached Alisa for days before and even then had to help her during it." She shook her head. "I don't see how we could do it. And anyway, Alisa was able to survive performing the spell because she was only half blood witch. The spell would destroy a full blood witch. I don't see how any of us . . ."

Hunter started to speak, then coughed. It took him a moment, and finally he was able to get the words out. "The spell Da worked, it could be performed by full blood witches," he said. "If only I could remember it, or—"

"I'm just not sure where Uncle Daniel is," Sky said. "I haven't spoken to him in a couple of months. He still travels a lot."

"Da's all right, then?" Hunter said cautiously.

"Yes," Sky said, a slight smile on her face. "He's doing well. Seeing you again will give him another fifteen years at least. But I don't know where he is, and we don't have time to track him down."

"As soon as we get home, we'll go to Katrina's," said Morgan, her face set. "Most likely the coven will be there. Maybe they'll have come up with something."

It would be hard seeing Gran again, Moira thought, for both her and Mum. But again, it was a small consideration compared to the dark wave. Right now they all had to focus on that.

By the time they landed at the small commuter airport in Cork, the weather had turned nasty. To Moira, it felt as if she hadn't seen sunshine for years. The minute she stepped off the plane, she frowned. When she touched the ground, she felt a jolt of nausea that made her swallow quickly.

Morgan narrowed her eyes. "Do you feel bad?"

"I'm going to throw up," said Moira, looking for a trash can.

"It's the dark wave," her mother explained. "It makes blood witches feel awful, hours before it arrives."

They were all tired and hungry and ill. Moira's face was killing her. Now her mum stopped, looked at the sky.

"How much time?" she asked Sky.

"Three hours? Four?" Sky said, and Hunter nodded.

"At best."

Home! Moira thought with relief when they reached the cottage. She would never take it for granted again—there had been more than one time in the last twenty-four hours when she'd believed she'd never see it again. Now she was going to do her utmost to protect it.

"This is where we live," Moira heard her mum explain to Hunter. He still seemed dazed, half there. He kept touching things, running the tips of his long, thin fingers over objects, textures, as if he had to reidentify everything.

Inside, Bixby was hiding under the couch, his pupils wide and his tail fluffed. Finnegan barely greeted them, sniffing Hunter before he slouched under the dining-room table, an occasional low growl coming from his throat. Hartwell Moss had been taking care of them, but she wasn't here now.

"They know," said Moira's mum, referring to the animals. She sounded ill.

Ten minutes later Morgan and Sky were poring over Morgan's old Books of Shadows. "See, it took the combination of the four of us," Mum was explaining in a low voice. "Daniel, me, Hunter, and most importantly—Alisa. And it took hours. I don't see how we can possibly . . ." She shook her head.

"What if we each take a part?" Moira suggested, resting her head in her hands. Her skin felt clammy and cold, her head felt as if it would soon explode, and she never wanted to see food again.

"With this version of the spell, we'd all be in great danger," Morgan said in distress.

"And I won't be of any use," Hunter said, sounding at the end of his rope. Morgan had immediately fixed them all an herbal concoction to help give them energy and take away the nausea, but so far it hadn't been doing very much. Hunter took a sip of his and grimaced.

"I feel like death," Morgan said. "Hunter has no power. Let's just get to the coven and see if they know anything."

The short walk to Katrina's seemed to test their limits. Moira was dizzy and bone tired, and everything seemed to smell awful. Hunter especially looked bad, dragging his feet, swaying sometimes. His face was an unhealthy white beneath the sunburn, and his eyes kept closing as if he could barely go on. Morgan put her arm around his waist, supporting him. As soon as they were within sight of the old store, its door opened and Katrina hurried out.

"Morgan!" she cried. "Thank the Goddess you're here. You know about the dark wave?"

"Yes," Morgan said, letting Katrina usher her into the coven's meeting room. By unspoken agreement, they would deal first with the dark wave—later with their personal matters, if they had the chance. Inside, Moira saw most of the initiated members of the coven. They were obviously suffering the dark wave's effects. Pale and hollow eyed, they came forward to greet Morgan, hugging her, and Tess and Vita ran forward to greet Moira.

"Where were you?" Tess asked, looking frightened.

"I'll have to tell you later," Moira said. "But it's good to see you." She pushed her way through the crowd of people surrounding her mother and saw that the coven was looking at Hunter with undisguised interest.

"This is Hunter Niall," Morgan said shortly. "He created the New Charter." That seemed to be all the explanation she was going to offer for his presence, his extraordinary appearance.

"I haven't asked this yet because it seems too easy," Moira said. "But why can't we all just leave here now? Let the dark wave have the buildings but save the people?"

Morgan shook her head wearily. "That doesn't do any good. It's too close. The wave would follow us."

A sudden pounding on the door startled them—no one had felt anyone approach. Katrina answered it, and Ian stood there, breathing hard. Moira's heart slammed against her chest as all the horrible events of two nights ago—three?— came back to her, and she looked away.

"I'm not sure," he began, trying to catch his breath. Through the doorway Moira could see his mud-spattered bicycle dropped on the ground behind him. "But I think we're all in danger."

Morgan put her hand on his shoulder. Moira saw her look at Sky, as if to ask, Is he being honest?

Sky looked over his head and nodded at Morgan, and she nodded back. Moira guessed they weren't picking up on any hidden agenda or falseness from him. She wasn't either. The night they had visited Lilith, she'd thought he'd betrayed her—he'd participated in Lilith's work. But was he here now, going against his mother? Moira was so afraid to let herself believe in him again.

"My mother's coven left this morning before dawn," Ian said, nervously looking around. "In her workroom I found— stuff to work dark magick with. Really dark magick. I hadn't really known it before." His voice was sad. Moira closed her eyes briefly and cast her senses, reaching for Ian's emotions. She blinked her eyes back open, her heartbeat quickening. It was genuine, Ian's pain—genuine and overwhelming. She was almost sure he was telling the truth, and doing so was ripping him up inside. "I didn't want to know what they were doing. But now there's something awful in the air."

"We're pretty sure Ealltuinn has created a dark wave," Morgan said, and Ian flinched in shock. "It will destroy everything around, all of us. Everything."

Ian looked nauseous. "A dark wave? I didn't think anyone could do those anymore."

"Ealltuinn has found a way," Morgan said. "Now we have to stop it." She turned to Hunter. "Do you remember *any* of your dad's simplified spell?"

Hunter looked at the ceiling, concentrating hard. Silent words came to his lips.

Outside, the wind kicked up, blowing a small branch against a window. The light coming in had a sickly greenish tinge to it, like the light before a tornado.

"No!" he said finally, his fists clenched in frustration.

Morgan's face fell.

Oh, Goddess, Moira thought. What now? We need a plan. There must be some way to fight this!

"It's still in there," Sky said to him, gripping the back of a chair. "She didn't wipe your mind, just bound your magick."

The other coven members stood around, listening. Some smaller groups were discussing ways to act, but no one seemed to be coming up with much.

"I don't know what she did," Hunter said, his cracked lips tight with tension. "I just know I can't remember . . . a lot. I don't have any power."

Moira could hear his frustration and could hardly imagine what he must be feeling. Would she ever get to know him, even close to as well as she'd known Colm? Would she ever see him healed and happy? Or would this, today, be her only memory of him? Her heart ached at the thought.

"Dammit!" Morgan said suddenly, smacking her hand on the table. "She can't win, not now! We have to stop this."

Katrina and some others nodded, but they all looked uncertain and afraid.

"Can we all just join together and use the strongest protection spells we know?" Christa Ryan asked, rubbing her temples.

"A dark wave isn't just fought," Morgan explained. "It has to be dismantled."

We have to stop it, Moira thought desperately. We're all going to die—none of the past two days will have meant anything. Iona's defeat will mean nothing. The four of us together defeated her—surely we can defeat this now. That was when it came to Moira: *The four of us together . . .*

"Mum?" said Moira, swallowing down her nausea. "I have an idea. I think Sky's right—that Hunter still has the spell locked up inside his brain. He just can't remember it. You could do a tàth meànma with Hunter, getting the spell from deep inside, where he doesn't remember."

"I thought about that," Morgan said. "But . . ." She paused, looking at Hunter. "I don't know how well he could stand it right now," she finished softly.

Hunter's eyes hardened. "I can stand it," he said, clearly using every ounce of strength left in him to make the words sound firm and believable.

Moira glanced down at the floor, overcome by the power of his feelings for Morgan, how much he would do for her. And . . . for Moira, too. She could feel concern for herself in him as well, even though he'd only just learned she was his daughter.

"Still, I'm not in great shape myself," Morgan said. "Iona drained so much power from me."

"I know," Moira said. "Get the simplified spell from Hunter, then send it to me. I'm not initiated yet, but I have power. You said it yourself—how strong I am. And Sky can help, joining her power with mine."

"No," Morgan said flatly.

"Mum, it's the only way," Moira said urgently, leaning forward. "None of us, no one in this room, has what it takes to do this alone. You and Hunter at least have some experience with a dark wave. You know both me and Sky, you know how to work with us. We have to do it. And what happens if we don't try anything? Are we all just going to sit here and die? *After everything?*" Moira met her mother's eyes, pleading with her.

"Moira may be right," Sky said reluctantly. "We have maybe an hour before the dark wave gets here. One person working the spell alone might not make it, even with the shortened version. If both of us are working simultaneously . . ." She looked up. "We just might pull it off."

"We've no other good plans anyway," said Hunter. "None of us are thinking clearly—we've all been through too much. We can either stay here and die, or we can go fight it."

"I hate all of these options," said Morgan, looking from face to face.

"We all do," said Sky. "But there is one problem. We need more than one witch to work the spell, and my powers are still quite weak. I don't know if I . . ."

"Please let me help," Ian said. His face was solemn and grim. "For years I've not asked questions about my mother's work—even though deep down I always felt something wasn't right. I've gone on and done my own thing and tried not to see what she was doing, she and the new members she recruited to Ealltuinn. But now I see what a coward I've been." His voice dropped so that they had to lean in to hear him. "I need to help make this right if I can. Please let me help. I'm initiated, and I have a fair amount of power."

Moira knew—in every fiber of her being—that he was telling the truth. She'd been right about him all along. Maybe Lilith *was* like Selene Belltower, but Ian was *not* Cal. And she hadn't been a fool for trusting him after all. Even with all the danger they still faced, knowing that helped.

Morgan looked at Sky, who looked at Hunter and Moira. Moira waited anxiously, thinking, *Please, please, please.*

It was only after her mother hesitantly said, "All right. We have no choice," that Moira allowed herself to realize she would be going up against a dark wave. But there was no time to be afraid or to panic. If the dark wave killed her, she would go down fighting, trying to save her family, her coven, her town. Her mum had made the same decision, when she was barely seventeen. Moira was an ancestral Riordan. She was Moira of Belwicket, with her mother's strength, her grand-mother's, her great-grandmother's. And Ciaran's strength also. He'd used his power for evil. Moira would use hers for good.

Nodding, she said, "Let's go."

They decided to meet the wave as it approached the vil-lage, on the high road by the headland and the cliffs. It was hard to walk fast, with how awful everyone felt, but they tried to hurry, going over the plan as they went. The twelve strongest members of the coven would station themselves in a circle of protection around Moira and Ian. They might not help, but they couldn't hurt, and everyone had agreed to stay together. The rest of the coven would be nearby, sending whatever power they could to Moira, Ian, Morgan, Sky, and Hunter.

"Moira," her mum said, easing closer to her. Her voice was low, confidential. "I have to tell you: dying by a dark wave is much worse than dying almost any other way. And by far the worst thing about it is that your soul then joins the collection, and you become one of the hungry, desperate for energy, for life. That's what we're facing today. I want you to understand just what you're going up against."

Moira tried to ignore the aching, hollow feeling in her chest. "I understand, Mum," she said, keeping her voice as strong as she could. "But as long as we're together, it will be all right. You and Hunter and me and you, all together."

Her mother's eyes grew bright with tears, but she just nodded and squeezed Moira's hand. "I love you," she said. "More than life itself."

"I know," Moira said. "Me too."

"Looks like here," Sky said, a few feet in front of them. They slowed, and Sky looked up at the clouds, then down the road. The air itself felt foul, a mixture of oily fumes, smoke, depression, illness. On the farthest horizon Moira could just barely make out an eggplant-colored line.

Her heart sank down into the pit of her stomach. "Is that it?" she asked faintly.

"Yes," Hunter said grimly.

Moira met Ian's eyes, which were solemn and wide. He gave her a quick nod.

"Yes, I think you're right," Morgan said, sounding tired down to her bones. Moira saw her watching Hunter, as if to make sure that he was miraculously still alive. Desperately Moira hoped they would have more time together. They deserved it. Moira was sad for Colm, sad that he hadn't been her mum's mùirn beatha dàn, and still devastated that he hadn't been her own biological father. But it didn't change the fact that Hunter *was* both of those things—and Morgan and Moira deserved the chance to be with him. To know him, even, in Moira's case.

"Right, then," said Sky. She sounded tired also, cranky, but she seemed in better shape than Morgan. "Looks like it's going to sweep right on through here. I think Moira and Ian should be in the middle of the road. We three should be over there, maybe. There's a copse of shale—it looks like there's a crevice in it. It won't save us, should it make it here, but it'll shelter us from the worst effects before it does." She looked up at the small crowd of anxious but grimly determined coven members.

"Twelve of you, take your posts," Sky said. Katrina, her sister, Susan Best, Keady Dove, Christa Ryan, and Sebastian Cleary broke away from the group and began positioning themselves. They were followed by Hartwell Moss, Fillipa Gregg, and Michelle Moore, and then Brant Tucker and Brett and Lacey Hawkstone moved to the other side. Lastly, Will Fereston took his place.

"Good," said Sky, looking tense and pale. "Now, are we clear on what's going to happen? Morgan's going to get the spell from Hunter."

"We hope," Morgan muttered.

"Yes, we hope," Sky said somberly. "Morgan will pass it on to me and to Moira. I will pass it on to Ian, then join my power with Moira's. Moira, you're going to work on the first and third parts of the spell. Ian will work on the second part, which is long. At the right moment Moira will ignite it. Got that?"

Moira cleared her throat. "Yes. Got it." Inside she was quaking with fear and a kind of bleak, private admission that this might all very well be for nothing. Her head was pounding, she felt queasy and shaky. But she wasn't going to show it.

Ian nodded, his jaw tight.

"We'd better move," Hunter said, his voice sounding like rocks scraping metal.

Moira forced a smile at her mum, who was slowly walking backward away from her with a desperate look on her face. Her mum looked stricken, as if she would give anything not to leave Moira right now. And every part of Moira longed to reach out and grab her, to hold on and never let go. She was terrified to face the dark wave without her mum at her side. Her mum, who she understood would do anything to protect her. But now it was her turn to protect her mum.

"Go on," Moira urged softly, working to keep her turbulent emotions cloaked. Her mum nodded stiffly. Then Morgan, Hunter, and Sky disappeared below the shallow copse. Now Moira had to wait till Morgan contacted her with the spell.

"I'm sorry," Ian muttered, looking down. He looked as bad as Moira felt.

"It isn't your fault," Moira said. "I'm sorry—about the other night."

Ian nodded. "That was awful. But it wasn't *your* fault." Then he reached out and took her hand. Both their hands were cold, trembling, but Moira seized his as if it were her lifeline. She wouldn't have to go through this alone.

The sky to the east was sickly green, tinged with purple. There was a foul stench in the air. Anxiously squawking birds of all types were flying past as fast as they could, escaping in the way that wild animals have of knowing.

It was very near.

*Moira.* Mum was ready. Moira quickly closed her eyes, trying to blank her mind for the tàth meànma with her mother. It would be extremely difficult, since they wouldn't be able to touch. She had to have absolute concentration. Then her mother's consciousness was there, pressing on her brain, and Moira immediately opened her mind to let her in. Surprisingly it hurt, and Moira winced and tensed up at the pain of it. *I forgot to warn you this would hurt. We didn't have time to prepare properly with fasting, meditating, and so on.*

*It's okay,* Moira sent back, gritting her teeth. Then, with Morgan guiding her, Moira opened her eyes and created a circle with purified salt around her and Ian. She put out Morgan's four silver cups, carved with ancient Celtic symbols and representing the four elements: earth, air, fire, and water.

*On this day, at this hour, I invoke the Goddess,* Morgan told her, and Moira repeated the words. "You who are pure in intent, aid me in this spell."

And on it went, the first part of the spell. It had been greatly simplified, but Moira still needed to define it, clarify her intentions, and identify all the players and parts.

Next to her Moira heard Ian start to speak as he received his part of the spell from Sky. He moved in a carefully crafted pattern that would define the spell's limitations: exactly where, when, why, and for how long the spell would ignite. The things it would affect, the things it wouldn't.

Looking tense and frightened, he knelt and drew sigils on the ground and in the air. Finally Moira finished the first part, and she waited anxiously for Ian to finish the second part before her mum would coach her through the third.

*Okay, now Ian's done,* Morgan sent, and Moira nodded. *This third part is the actual spell.*

Slowly and carefully her mum fed Moira the words to say, the words that defined for all time exactly what this spell would do. Moira needed to move at certain times, to trace runes in the air or on the ground, to rub salt on her hands, to spill water on the ground. She started feeling really terrible about halfway through, when the throbbing pain of the tàth meànma, her rising nausea, and the abhorrent stench in the air all combined to make her sway on her feet. *What next?* she thought, forcing herself to concentrate. Her mother repeated what she was supposed to do, and, almost in tears, Moira began it. Then her head started spinning and Moira seemed to lose all her peripheral vision. An acrid taste rose in the back of her throat and her stomach heaved. Clapping her hand to her mouth, she fought it down, then fell to her hands and knees in the mud of the road.

*Moira!* Mum sent urgently. *Moira, get up! You have to get up! Get up NOW!* Panting slightly, Moira raised her head and blinked. She was shaking, every muscle trembling uncontrollably. Oh, no, she thought in despair. *They're all going to die because of me.* It was too much, this responsibility. What had she been thinking, promising everyone that she could do this? She had been too bold, too arrogant—and everyone she loved would pay the price. She took in another shallow breath.

Around her the twelve coven members were watching her with desperate expressions. She met Katrina's eyes, saw the fear and horror in them, the love and regret. Her gran's lips were moving silently; all this time the coven members had been chanting protection spells, ward-evil spells, spells to try to limit the sickness Moira and Ian felt.

*Go on!* Morgan sent urgently. *You can do this, Moira— you're almost done!*

Moira stared down the road. The dark wave was almost upon them. Birds who hadn't escaped were dropping dead from the sky. She could see bits of shredded tree, pulverized rock, wisps of burned grass blowing ahead of the wave. Moira gagged with every breath, covering her mouth. Death was coming. Death was here.

"Now!" Sky yelled out loud, then coughed. "All of you twelve, send your powers to Moira and Ian! Chant your protection spells! All of us together!"

Then her mum shouted, *"Ignite it!"*

Her mum believed in her. She believed Moira could stop the dark wave. Now it was time for Moira to believe in herself. She reached into the very deepest reserve she had, summoned her last bit of strength, and slowly, slowly staggered to her feet. *I call on you,* she thought, imagining her strong and powerful ancestors—her mother, her grandmother, Maeve, and everyone before them. *I call on your power.* It was amazing, the rush of energy that suddenly flowed through her. She *could* do this. She was Moira of Belwicket, daughter of the sgiùrs dàn, *fated* to be born. Today, this moment, she would prove her birthright.

*Yes. I must. It's up to me.* With a huge effort Moira threw up her hands. With her last breath she shouted the ancient Gaelic words that would ignite the spell. Her hair was blowing backward, she was struggling to keep her balance, but again she shouted it, louder this time. Next to Moira, Ian also shouted, his arms out from his sides. A third time they shouted the words.

What's wrong? Moira wondered hysterically. It should have stopped! What's wrong? What did we do wrong? We missed something, we skipped something, Hunter misremembered. The spell was wrong.

She watched in horror as the people forming the line of protection scattered, running to the sides of the road and flinging themselves down face first. Then the cloud was upon them, barely licking the place where Moira and Ian stood.

I'm going to die, Moira thought with one last moment of clarity.

Then suddenly a rip appeared in the fabric of the universe, an odd, eye-shaped nether place. A bith dearc, Moira realized. In a split second the dark cloud was sucked into the rip with more force than one could imagine, like a plane suddenly becoming depressurized at thirty thousand feet. The wave, large enough to cover a field, was pulled through the bith dearc in a matter of seconds. Moira fell to the ground, her hands sinking into the soft mud. It seemed to root her to the earth, and she grabbed a tough clump of muddy grass and held on to it. She saw Ian fall. He'd been standing a fraction of an inch closer to the bith dearc, and he was being pulled inexorably toward the opening. In another second he would be through.

"Moira!" Morgan shouted, racing toward them. "Moira!"

Ian was on his stomach, clawing at the ground, his eyes wide. Without hesitation Moira reached out and grabbed his hands, the mud making them slick. There was a half-buried rock in the ground and she braced her trainers against it, leaning back and pulling with all her might. Feeling as if she were in slow motion, Moira gave a huge heave, her teeth gritted, eyes screwed shut, veins popping on her neck. Then all at once Ian was free and the bith dearc sealed seamlessly, leaving no trace of ever having been there.

Moira's mum dropped down next to her, grabbing her and holding on tightly, tightly. Sky skidded to a halt next to her, grabbing Ian's leg, anxiously making sure he was all right. Behind them Hunter knelt down awkwardly, breathing lightly and shallowly, a clammy sweat dewing his skeletal face.

Moira put her muddy arms around her mum and hugged her back. Then she pulled away and turned around. "Is Ian all right?" she asked shakily.

Ian nodded. He was sitting back in the dirt of the road, looking stunned, sweat only now breaking out on his forehead. "You saved my life," he whispered.

Morgan laughed, brushing Moira's hair off her face, "You saved us," she said, her eyes shining with obvious relief, joy, and pride.

Moira smiled. Then, with no warning, she covered her eyes with one hand and started to weep.

# 20.
# Morgan

"I see," Morgan murmured into the phone. "Yes, yes, I think that would be best. When? Tomorrow. I think we can do that. It will be late tomorrow, though."

Hanging up, she looked over at the table to see four pairs of eyes watching her inquisitively. Morgan sat down and put her hand on Ian's arm. "The New Charter has found your mother and eight of her followers at the border between England and Scotland. They wanted to know if I could come up to identify Lilith and file formal charges against her."

Ian looked down at his bowl, a slight flush rising to his cheeks. Sky, Hunter, and Moira waited sympathetically. They'd all been gingerly hunched over bowls of soup for lunch. It had been only two days since the dark wave, and everyone still felt awful. Morgan was drained but had been busy creating teas and herbal concoctions for everyone in the area. She'd also tried to work some magickal healing but found it strained her still-weak powers. Right now they had to let time do its work.

"What are you going to do?" Ian asked quietly.

"I'm going to go identify her," Morgan said gently. "And file formal charges against her."

He nodded, still looking at his bowl. "Can I go with you?"

"Of course."

Only Morgan and Ian went. Sky had wanted to be there to see for herself that Lilith was being punished, but they agreed it was better for her to stay home and watch Hunter while Moira was in school. He was still unsteady on his feet sometimes, weak, and also just absentminded and foggy. He looked slightly more normal, with short hair and no beard, and his bruises and face slashes were healing well. But he couldn't eat very much, and his nightmares would take a long time to work through. He had settled into the guest room at Morgan's house, and Sky had moved down to the couch.

There was no reason for Moira to go. She, too, was still healing both physically and mentally and wouldn't add much to Morgan's testimony. She and Hunter were getting to know each other, and one of the first times he'd smiled was when she had cracked a dry joke. Morgan and Sky had looked blank, and Hunter had been the only one to get it. Morgan smiled, remembering it.

Sky hadn't been in America twenty years ago when they'd battled the last dark wave, and this had been her first experience with one. It had left her as shaken and drained as the others. Morgan envied her these few days alone with Hunter, getting to know each other again, picking up where they had left off. But as soon as her obligation with Lilith was over, she would rush back. Despite having the rest of her life to spend with him, she felt a need to seize every minute.

She looked over at Ian, pretending to read in the train seat next to her. After the wave had gone, the coven had met back at Katrina's store to comfort and help each other. Katrina had come forward and offered to let Ian stay with her, and he had agreed, at least for a while. He knew his mother would probably never come back to share their house again.

"This is going to be hard," Morgan said sympathetically.

Ian nodded, then sighed. "She was all I had," he said. "I've no idea where my dad is. Don't really want to find him, anyway. Mum had been getting worse and worse, and I just didn't want to see it. Our house—" He shrugged. "Maybe in a while I can go back to it."

"Take your time," Morgan said.

For a moment Ian looked as if he wanted to say something, then thought better of it.

"What?" Morgan prompted him.

"You're Ciaran's MacEwan's daughter," Ian said hesitantly. "You—you know. Did you—did you love him?"

Morgan hesitated, understanding Ian's pain all too well. "I didn't really know Ciaran," Morgan said. "Actually I only saw him a handful of times before he died." *Before Iona killed him.* "But there's something between a parent and child—you want, or maybe need, to love a parent. I have the best adoptive parents anyone could hope for. Really good, caring people who did their best by me. I never knew Maeve. I knew Ciaran was evil, I knew he would betray me or use me or kill me if I didn't join him. Yet what I felt for him was very much like love, despite everything. Something deep inside me felt good that he was proud of me, proud of my powers, that he wanted me to join him when he didn't want his other children. I almost wanted his approval. It crushed me to have to bind him, to have his powers stripped. It was the worst thing, the worst decision I ever had to make. But he was my father. And he loved me, in his way." She paused. "Does that help?"

"Yes," Ian said softly, looking out the train window. "It does, a bit."

Lilith and her followers were being held at a New Charter building not far from Scotland's southern border. When Morgan and Ian arrived, they were led into the manager's office. Matilda Bracken was tall, gray-haired, and severe looking but smiled warmly when she saw them. Rising, she came to meet them.

"Morgan Byrne of Belwicket," she said. "How very good to meet you. Well done, down in Ireland."

"Thank you," Morgan said. "It took all of us, including Ian Delaney here."

"Yes, Ian." Matilda took both his hands in hers. "I'm sorry to meet you under these circumstances, my dear."

Ian nodded uncomfortably.

"Morgan, first I need you to identify Lilith Delaney and then to fill out a form about your charges. Then, Ian, you'll have a chance to see your mother."

Lilith was being held in a small room. The doorway was spelled so no one could enter or leave, but Morgan could see Lilith through the open door. She pressed her lips together as she saw that Lilith's face still bore signs of the bruising that Morgan's attack had caused. What a terrible night that had been.

"Yes, that's her," Morgan said.

Lilith rose from her narrow bed and literally spit at Morgan through the doorway. "It still isn't over," she said, her eyes glittering. "It will never be over."

The prime emotion Morgan felt was sadness. "No, Lilith," she said. "It *is* over. Iona is dead. You're here, and unless you're rehabilitated, you'll be in the care of the New Charter for the rest of your life. Your house and workroom are being cleared and purified."

Lilith actually looked surprised. "No."

"Yes." Morgan paused. Certain questions still gnawed at her. "Tell me, why did you agree to work with Iona? What was in it for you?"

"Power," Lilith said, as if this were obvious. "She helped me gain control of Ealltuinn. She sent strong people to work with me. We're going to find the power leys of Ui Laithain and use them to become the most powerful witches this world has ever seen. Once I get out of here, you're just going to be a memory." She smiled at the thought, her eyes taking on a crazed gleam.

Lilith's hold on reality was clearly slipping. She had no comprehension of her situation, what her future held.

"That's why you kept an eye on me and reported on me to Iona?"

"Yes. Little enough, for all she did for me."

"What about all the hexes this past month? Why bother? Iona never mentioned them—they weren't part of her plan, were they?"

"I can think for myself just fine," Lilith retorted, her voice rising. "Those were intended to harm you. To show you you're not welcome." She frowned. "They should have worked better.

You or your brat should have had accidents, hurt yourselves."

"I guess you underestimated us—both of us," Morgan said, feeling a spark of pride in her daughter. "You know that it was Moira in the end who defeated your dark wave?" Lilith's frown deepened. "How did you learn to create a dark wave, anyway? It's clearly beyond *your* strength."

Lilith's face grew tight with fury, and the answer was right there.

*Iona.* It had been in Ciaran's knowledge when Iona had killed him and taken his power.

"So why now?" Morgan pressed. "Iona made a point of telling me that now was the perfect time for all of this— before I defeated her, that is."

Lilith looked ready to explode. "She had to move now," she muttered, "before you became high priestess. Before Moira was initiated. And—she was growing desperate."

"She was dying," Morgan said. "The souls whose power she took were eating away at her. She wasn't strong enough to hold them in check for that long. She was losing control, and she had to act before they tore her apart forever."

Lilith looked contemptuous. "You can think that if you want. But Iona is strong; she'll recover from whatever you did to her. And I'm her partner. Together she and I will be able to crush the New Charter. And when we do, we're going to come after you."

There was nothing to say to that. But Morgan did have one last thing to discuss with Lilith. "Ian is here," she said.

"Ian? My boy?" Lilith looked eager, coming to the door.

"Yes. You can explain to him why you abandoned him," Morgan said. "Why your pursuit of power was stronger than your love."

The older woman's eyes narrowed and she stepped back. Morgan turned and headed down the way she had come.

The long train ride home was mostly quiet. When Ian had returned from seeing his mother, he'd obviously been crying, but his face was stoic.

"Time works wonders," Morgan said inadequately, even though she knew firsthand that some pain never seemed to ease.

"Yes, thank you," Ian said, then resumed looking out the window.

I'm going home, Morgan thought, joy blooming in her heart. Home to my daughter, to Hunter, to safety and calm.

Katrina was at the train station to meet Ian. It was thoughtful of her, and Morgan was glad she'd reached out to him. Despite the terrible injustice she'd done to Morgan and to Moira, Morgan believed that Katrina was a good person and would be of great help to Ian during this lost time.

Then she was home. The front door opened before she was halfway up the walk, and her family waited for her. Moira, her daughter, who had saved them all, and Hunter, her Hunter, who was home again at last.

"Welcome home," Moira said.

"Yes," Morgan sighed, reaching out to hug one after the other. "Yes."

# Epilogue

"So we've set it up for me to be initiated at Yule, only six months late," Moira said to Tess. She and her mum had made the decision together to wait a little longer, give themselves some time as a family to heal from everything and for Moira to begin to get to know her birth father. "You've not changed your mind, then?"

Tess rolled her eyes. "You only ask me that once a month. Hand me that garland."

Moira handed Tess a garland of woven grapevines and autumn branches. They, along with some others, were decorating their circle room for the Mabon celebration. This year would be especially joyous, commemorating the first anniversary of the defeat of the dark wave.

"Vita's going to be initiated at Imbolc and me at Yule, and that leaves just you," Moira pointed out.

"I'm proud and happy for you both," said Tess firmly. "But it's just not for me. I need the hammer."

Moira handed her the hammer. Tess pounded some

short tacks into the wall and placed the garland on them. Across the room Vita was helping to decorate the altar with gourds, fresh vegetables, fruit, and more autumn branches.

"This place is looking fantastic," Katrina said, coming over to hug Moira. Moira smiled. It had taken a while before she had been able to forgive her grandmother, but it had been such a relief when she had. Gran had made the wrong decision, but Moira believed that she had thought she was acting for the best.

A couple of months after she and Moira had sorted things out, Gran and Morgan had gone for an all-day walk, and by the time they'd come home for dinner, they'd also been on better terms. It was so much easier this way, especially since Ian still lived at Gran's.

*Hmmm, where is Ian?* Moira looked around, then spotted him carrying in a large wall hanging. It was black, with a silver zodiac sign painted on it: Libra, the balance. At Mabon the day and the night would be exactly balanced, the same length, and then the next day the dark would start to dominate until spring.

It was kind of funny, Moira thought, how she still got a fluttery feeling in her chest whenever she saw Ian. They had been seeing each other for a year now. The more she'd gotten to know him, the more amazing she thought he was. For the past three months he'd been helping her study for her initiation, and she was impressed again and again by how smart he was, how quick he was to understand. They were a good team. And his kisses . . . Moira gave a pleasant shiver.

With help from Brett Hawkstone, Ian hung the wall hanging behind the altar. Ian had worked so hard to fit into Belwicket. People in the coven had been suspicious at first, but he had steadily proved himself by taking part in circles. With Gran's continued support, Ian had become at home with Belwicket.

"What do you think?" Ian asked, coming over. He gestured at the wall hanging.

"It looks great," Morgan said. "Where did you get it?"

Ian looked surprised she didn't know. "Tess made it."

Mouth open, Moira looked up at Tess, who shrugged and smiled. "I was expressing myself artistically," she said.

"Well, it's terrific," said Moira. "I'm really impressed." Tess smiled again, seeming a bit self-conscious.

Moira glanced at her watch. "Time for me to get home, guys," she said.

"Thanks for all your hard work," Gran said, kissing her. "You must have been collecting branches for days."

"Ian helped," Moira said. Then, holding hands, they left the store and began walking to Moira's.

"Can you stay to dinner, then?" Moira asked him. As soon as they were alone on the road, their arms had gone around each other. Moira hooked her thumb in his belt loop as they matched strides.

"Not tonight," Ian said. "I think Katrina's got a shepherd's pie in the oven. Some night this week, though."

She smiled at him, then sobered as they reached the section of road where they had performed the dark wave spell a year before. Only recently had the grass started growing back on both sides—it had remained scorched and sparse for ten months afterward.

"Will we ever be able to get past this place without it feeling bad?" Moira wondered aloud.

"I don't know," Ian said.

So much had changed since then. Hunter had never left her and Mum's cottage, and the guest room had become his. In the past year there had been so much rebuilding: rebuilding Hunter's health, her mum rebuilding her relationship with Hunter. Moira and Hunter had slowly gotten to know each other, a bit shyly at first, and then more and more comfortably. She still called him Hunter, though. She couldn't bring himself to call him Da.

At Moira's garden gate Ian stopped. "I better get back," he said. He bent down and kissed her, and she smiled up into his eyes. "Can you meet me tomorrow?" he asked. "Before the circle? Take a walk or something? Or we could go to town, get tea."

"Yes," she said happily. "Come by around two, all right?"

He nodded and kissed her again. Then Moira stood and watched him walk down the road, back to Gran's.

Inside, the house smelled like baking bread and beef stew, and Moira sniffed appreciatively. Hunter was setting the dining table, and her mum was just coming in from the back garden with some fresh bay leaves.

"Hi, sweetie," she said, smiling. "How's the decorating going?"

"Good," said Moira, sitting down in the rocking chair. "It all looked really great."

"I've always liked Mabon," Hunter said. His voice had smoothed out quite a bit but would always be slightly hoarse, Moira thought. She watched him as he moved around the table. He looked very different than when she had first seen him. Over the past year he had gradually put on weight, and now she could no longer see his knobby spine through his shirts. All of his bruises were gone, but there were scars he'd always have.

His magick had come back, very slowly. It had been hard, watching his frustration as he couldn't perform the simplest

spells. Then one day he'd been able to snuff a candle by thinking about it. Just that had made him so happy, Moira had
almost cried. It had increased after that, and though Mum said
he wasn't as strong as he had been, she thought he would
continue to get better.

"Okay, supper's ready," Moira's mum said, starting to
serve up the bowls.

The three of them sat down around the table. The sun
had almost set, and inside the cottage it was cozy and lamplit.
Moira picked up her spoon and waited while Hunter cut slices
of bread.

"Thank you," said her mum as Hunter served her first.
The smile she gave was so deep, so perfectly happy, that it
made Moira feel warm inside.

Next he passed Moira her bread. "Thanks." Every once
in a while she was still surprised that this man, living in their
house, sharing every meal, was her actual father. And after a
while her guilt over the feeling that she was betraying Colm
by caring for Hunter had lessened. Gran had promised her
that Colm would have wanted her to be happy and to have a
relationship with her biological father.

And Hunter really *was* an amazing person—she could understand now why her mum loved him so much. He was funny in a
really dry way, but Moira could trust him to be serious when she
needed him to be. She loved talking with him about spellcraft—
his mother had been a Wyndenkell and a great spellcrafter. She'd
met his father, Daniel, her grandfather, who had been old and kind
of crotchety but pleasant enough. Aunt Alwyn had been really
nice. Sky came back every couple of months to visit.

Moira's whole life, whole family, had changed. But it was

good. It had been good before, with Dad and Mum and her, and it was good now. She was so lucky, so fortunate. Tess and Vita hadn't seen it that way, when she'd first told them about Lilith, and the island, and Iona. They'd felt so sorry for her, going through that. But Moira wasn't sorry for herself. Those horrible experiences had helped her so much in learning who she really was and what was truly meaningful to her. Since they'd gotten back, she and her mum had far fewer rows about unimportant things. They'd been reminded of what was truly important.

Now she sat at the table, warm and happy, already planning what she and Ian would do tomorrow before circle.

"I've been thinking," Hunter said into the silence.

Moira and Morgan both looked up.

"Oh, good, that's coming back," Moira's mum teased, and Hunter looked at her with a pained expression. She laughed— she laughed more often now.

"Despite your attempts at wit," Hunter went on, as both Moira and her mum laughed, "I've been thinking that this is good, what we have, the three of us."

"Yes, it is," Morgan said, her eyes shining.

"I'd like to make it permanent," Hunter went on, his voice softer. Morgan's eyes widened, and Moira stopped eating, her spoon in midair. His sculpted face caught the candlelight, and Moira saw the smile gently curving his lips.

"Morgan, for the second time, will you be handfasted to me? You're my heart's love, my heart's ease, my savior in every sense of the word. Will you be my wife?" Hunter reached across the table and took her hand.

Moira held her breath. She'd known this would be coming

and hadn't been sure how she'd feel. But now she knew—it was right. It was perfect.

Morgan looked at Moira, then back at Hunter. "Yes," she said, her voice clear and firm. "Yes." She looked again at Moira, love and hope showing plainly on her face.

Moira was speechless, looking from one to the other. She felt strange and happy and surprised and excited and a tiny bit sad as well.

"I think it's a very good idea," she said, nodding. "I really do."

Morgan tilted back her head and laughed, and Hunter laughed, too. Reaching out, he took hold of Moira's hand, and she reached for her mum's, and the three of them sat around the table, joined. They had gone through pain and horrors and tests of fate to get here. But they had made it. And they were a family.